TALES OF NYARLATHOTEP

FEATURING STORIES BY
DAVID HAMBLING ~ C. T. PHIPPS ~ MATTHEW DAVENPORT
ERIC MALIKYTE ~ ANDREA PEARSON
DAVID NIALL WILSON ~ DAVID J. WEST

Cover art and design by David Dodd

First Edition - 2023

"Milord, the followers of Re will be upon the capital within the hour," a slave spoke to Apophis Zul, kneeling with his head to the stone floor.

"I know," Apophis Zul replied, his voice deep and commanding.

It was almost dawn and the hated sun-worshipers had timed their attack for when their god would be in ascendance while his god would be at his weakest. For millennia, Stygia had stood at the center of the civilized world as a bulwark against the savages who had risen in the time since Atlantis sank and Acheron burned.

Great Stygia was the last of the old civilizations and had outlasted most of the new. Aquilonia, with its pagan Cimmerian lord, had drawn its last breath an age ago, and Zamora having been sacked by Hykarnians when Apophis Zul had been a boy.

It seemed inconceivable that, at last, the once-mighty empire of the river Styx should be brought low by barbarians, but it was undeniable. Their armies had abandoned them, the peasants were in revolt, and daggers had been stuck in the handful of acolytes who had not defected to the other side. Priests of Seth-Yig had joined the followers of Re'Kithnid,

Bastet, and Hathor-Niggurath to wield the magics of the Old and New Gods together against him. He, the high priest of the Black Pharaoh.

"Come with me, slave," Apophis Zul said, bidding the bald man behind him to rise with a near-imperceptible motion of his scaled fingers.

"Yes, milord," the slave said, confused.

Contents

Foreword

*"And where Nyarlathotep went, rest vanished, for the small hours were
rent with the screams of nightmare."*

-HP Lovecraft, Nyarlathotep

Nyarlathotep.
    The Crawling Chaos.
The God with a Thousand Forms.

When H.P. Lovecraft wrote "Nyarlathotep," it was a short story
that spoke of a mysterious man who resembled an Egyptian Pharoah
with a legion of followers. He led these followers to ruin less through
malice and more a kind of terrifying enlightenment that resulted in the
destruction of the world. A very similar depiction of how HPL spoke
of the Cult of Cthulhu being "free and wild and beyond good and evil,
with laws and morals thrown aside and all men shouting and killing
and reveling in joy."

Later, he would appear in *The Dream Quest of Unknown Kadath*
where he worked instead as a sort of anti-guru or Bodhisattva who
bestows unnatural knowledge upon Randolph Carter. Carter, obsessed
with discovering enlightenment, finds himself regretting his choice as
Nyarlathotep grants him what he came for and lots more besides. He
would also make appearances in "The Dreams in the Witch House"
and "The Haunter of the Dark."

Nyarlathotep is almost unique among HP Lovecraft's pantheon of
amoral, maltheistic, twisted, and alien deities. Not because he's any less
of a malevolent force—albeit not precisely evil—but because he is
distinctive among the cosmic horrors in that Nyarlathotep is chatty.

Few of Lovecraft's monsters would lower themselves to speak to something so insignificant as a human, any more than we would a flea. But, the Herald of the Outer Gods takes a child-like glee in revealing the things man was not meant to know to see what happens.

Just as Lovecraft loved satirizing Western religion with *The Call of Cthulhu* and *The Dunwich Horror*, Nyarlathotep works as a critique of the Eastern concepts of finding a greater truth to the universe. Ignorance is bliss within the confines of cosmic horror and Nyarlathotep repeatedly pulls the warm blanket of self-delusion from many individuals. Worse, he is a figure that otherwise smart individuals like Carter actually seek out for their secrets.

There's a reason Nyarlathotep has shown up in many other author's work as the primary antagonist or a herald for darker forces. Stephen King used it as a name of his central villain, Randall Flagg, and Brian Lumley had him as the collected gestalt of all the Great Old Ones assembled into a single being.

He is, of course, also the central antagonist in *The Call of Cthulhu* chronicle *Masks of Nyarlathotep*, which is widely considered the greatest adventure module of all time. Later, the HP Lovecraft Historical Society would do a radio play adaptation of the module that I recommend for its black humor and adventuring fun. It's because, of all the monsters Lovecraft created, Nyarlathotep has a *personality*.

Tales of Nyarlathotep is the fourth book of the Books of Cthulhu series: *Tales of the Al-Azif*, *Tales of Yog-Sothoth*, and the *Book of Yig* preceding us. Many of the authors for this volume have written in the previous ones and I heartily recommend them. The Books of Cthulhu books tend to be more pulpy action than pulpy horror but there are plenty of both in this volume. There is also some new material that I hope you enjoy.

We've got a wide variety and mix of stories this time, ranging from horror ("Cookies for the Gentleman"), pulp adventure ("Andrew Doran and Curse of Nephren Ka," "The Apophis Sarcophagus"), to dark fantasy ("Cinderella and her Outer Godfather") and even outright urban fantasy ("Dream Math," "Coolidge and the Enchanted Dagger"). I'm especially pleased to note Brian Lumley gave his good friend David Niall Wilson permission to use the character of Titus Crow, a legendary post-Lovecraft character, who is making his first appearance in decades.

So, without further ado, enjoy this collection of dark and spooky tales about the only Lovecraftian god who cares about humanity. Like a kid with a magnifying glass and a bunch of ants.

The Black Pharaoh's Test

By C.T. Phipps

"**M**ilord, the followers of Re will be upon the capital within the hour," a slave spoke to Apophis Zul, kneeling with his head to the stone floor.

"I know," Apophis Zul replied, his voice deep and commanding.

It was almost dawn and the hated sun-worshipers had timed their attack for when their god would be in ascendance while his god would be at his weakest. For millennia, Stygia had stood at the center of the civilized world as a bulwark against the savages who had risen in the time since Atlantis sank and Acheron burned.

Great Stygia was the last of the old civilizations and had outlasted most of the new. Aquilonia, with its pagan Cimmerian lord, had drawn its last breath an age ago, and Zamora having been sacked by Hykarnians when Apophis Zul had been a boy.

It seemed inconceivable that, at last, the once-mighty empire of the river Styx should be brought low by barbarians, but it was undeniable. Their armies had abandoned them, the peasants were in revolt, and daggers had been stuck in the handful of acolytes who had not defected to the other side. Priests of Seth-Yig had joined the followers of Re'Kithnid, Bastet, and Hathor-Niggurath to wield the magics of the Old and New Gods together against him. He, the high priest of the Black Pharaoh.

"Come with me, slave," Apophis Zul said, bidding the bald man behind him to rise with a near-imperceptible motion of his scaled fingers.

1

"Yes, milord," the slave said, confused.

"Follow," Apophis Zul said, gesturing to the entrance to the Forbidden Temple's inner sanctum. It had been constructed over the course of a century with a thousand slaves dying in the process. Their blood had added to the power of the place, consecrating it to the God with a Thousand Faces.

"It is forbidden," the slave said.

"This I command," Apophis Zul said, not having the desire to obliterate the slave with a wave of his hand or drown him with a mouth full of flesh-eating scarabs that he could make appear at will.

"Of course," the slave said, nodding vigorously.

The long stone hallway was illuminated by torches of blue fire which never went out but needed a monthly tithe of human fat. They illuminated blasphemous hieroglyphics that depicted the humiliation of the priests of Seth who had once ruled Stygia since the days of Kull.

The blood of the Serpent Men had been thick then, pure and undiluted, but lust for the monkey-like humans around them had weakened their power. Attempts to fix this by breeding brother to sister had backfired with the gods cursing the resulting children to be stunted, sickly, or fools.

Apophis Zul had thought himself clever then, casting down Thoth-Amon by stealing his ring and turning to older more powerful gods than Seth. The magic flowed through his body like a river, and he had changed himself into a purer, stronger vision of his kind. Rains of byakhee and hordes of tunnelers had answered his prayers, laying waste to all who dared call themselves his enemy.

Unfortunately, he had overreached. The Cult of the Many-Faced One had grown vast, but he had been too free with its secrets and drunk on the power at his fingertips. The Dagonite Deep Ones had poured forth to sack the coastal lands, the ghuls had dragged his soldiers underground to become food for their larders, and those simpletons with their lifeless human-like idols had reminded him that steel slit the throats of wizard just as well as man. Alliances between ancient enemies of the Stygian priest-kings that would have been unthinkable a century before had shown there was no force capable of uniting people quite like hatred. Man and monster alike had joined king, noble, priest, as well as slave in their quest to see the greatest city on Keb, the world, destroyed.

Apophis Zul could knock down a city's walls and drown them in lakes of fire or blood but making them obey was harder than it seemed. Most men preferred death than service to a monster, particularly if the monster required their sons and daughters as sacrifices. There were costs to the great magics as well, with the usual prices of blood and pain not enough, no matter how much they gave. The stars had turned against them and most of his peers had either sunk into torpid slumber as corpses in buried tombs, collapsed into dust from overexertion, or were carried off by things they could conjure but not put down. Fools.

"Tell me, slave, have you ever heard of Nyarlathotep?" Apophis Zul asked the slave.

"No, no, my lord," the slave lied, terrified. It was the sacred name they used to refer to the Many-Faced God and one that was blasphemous for anyone but the high priests to know. Yet, like all secrets these days, too many had been free with their tongues no matter how many Apophis Zul had ordered ripped out.

Apophis Zul smiled with his lipless face and let his long, forked tongue slither across the rictus of his mouth.

"It is the true name of the spirit we summoned into the Pharaoh's grandfather. The one that made him great."

The slave didn't respond, undoubtedly thinking about the fact said Pharaoh had been considered the greatest tyrant who had ever lived. A man who had ordered entire cities put to the sword, and built insane—but terrifying—structures that had required tearing down much of ancient Stygia to construct. Half of Stygia had burned to the ground in one night when he'd played his shepherd's pipe to drive all who listened irrevocably mad. Indeed, it was this Pharoah, Nephren-Ka, who had contributed most to the fall of Stygia's greatness.

"I see," the slave said, confused.

"We tried to summon him again and again because the secrets that spilled from his lips when we could coerce them forth were enough to strengthen our magic tenfold," Apophis Zul said, wistfully. "But when he ascended the Black Pyramid to the stars, we could not bring him forth again. His brothers and sisters became hideous things with a dozen mouths while his children exploded with human-headed rats from within their bellies. Their blood was too diluted, their minds too weak to carry the spirit of a god."

The current Pharaoh, a useless boy of twelve, carried none of the ancient blood at all. He had been a mouthpiece for Apophis Zul and his ilk in hopes of reassuring the people that the worst times were gone. That had been a mistake. The lion does not explain itself to the gazelle. In the end, it had only weakened their standing further.

The pair of them entered the antechamber of the Forbidden Temple where the priestly vestments woven from the chest hair of Leng's ape-men, incense of Kadath, and knives of Acheron steel were present. Apophis Zul took only one item, the jeweled *nemes* headdress of the Black Pharaoh. It would be needed, along with the *sekhem* scepter, to bring about the end of this nightmare.

"Accompany me to the main chamber," Apophis Zul said.

"Milord," the slave was terrified now.

"What is your name?" Apophis Zul asked.

Stunned by the request, the man took a deep breath.

"Narmer, lord."

"Obey," Apophis Zul said, annoyed he had to waste power to control the man's will. If he had to ask twice then truly his authority had diminished.

Narmer paused for a second then blinked.

"Yes, milord."

There was a slight hesitation, a second of defiance, a single moment of resistance that signaled to Apophis Zul that he had made the right choice. The Nameless Pharaoh had impregnated a hundred women and caused a dozen men's bellies to explode with offspring as a jest, but few products of these unions had lived.

Those that did had gone on to become powerful sorcerers or mad killers themselves, sometimes both at once. But a few had also spread their seed. None of them had been controllable and thus nonsuited to continue the official line of Pharaoh's. But they could be hosts—powerful hosts—and that had its own value. Narmer was the product of one demigod's rutting with another slave and now would serve a purpose far grander than any of his ilk deserved.

4

"Place the nemes upon your head," Apophis Zul said.

It was a sacrilege beyond imagination and any slave who committed such an act would have required hours of deliberation to devise a torture horrible enough to slay him with. However, these were unusual times and Apophis Zul intended further abominations.

Narmer obeyed and soon looked every inch the Pharaoh himself once he wore his raiment. Why not? They were both humans pretending to be gods. It's just Narmer had some divine blood in him. It was just diluted with the blood of human swine. Like fine wine mixed with offal.

"Sit upon the throne," Apophis Zul said. "You will understand soon."

"Yes, milord."

Narmer did not hesitate at this moment, for what was one more blasphemy after a series of them. Upon doing so, though, the man's body straightened as a look of unimaginable horror passed across his face. It was a look that Apophis Zul had seen many times upon the faces of sacrifices or those unprepared priests when he conjured something from the Outer Void. It was also followed by a scream that would have deafened Apophis Zul if he'd had human ears to listen. Narmer's dying cry was the sound of a man face-to-face with things that he had not been prepared to see.

That was another reason they were falling now to the barbarians at the gates: the slow death of magic. Apophis Zul had never thought it possible, but more and more priests of the Outer Gods and Great Old Ones had proven themselves to be charlatans. They recited the words, offered the sacrifices, and even sometimes believed, but could not connect themselves to the true masters of reality. There were no dreamers among them who could project their minds to the distant shores of Carcosa or the other places where the true magic flowed.

New Gods existed as well, conjured from humanity's ideas of more human-centric interpretations of the true masters of reality. It was difficult imagining for a being as old as Apophis Zul that anyone could want to worship something that was just a greater and more powerful version of a human, but he was not a peasant or slave. A fact he felt a twinge of hypocrisy over as Apophis Zul rubbed the black sun amulet under his robes while muttering.

"*G'rrllan'agaa'nahrasha*, Nyarlathotep! *G'rrllan'agaa'nahra-sha*, Nyarlathotep! *G'rrllan'agaa'nahrasha*, Nyarlathotep! Heed me, oh Messenger of the Outer Gods! Father of the Old Ones! Prophet of Yog-Sothoth! Son of Azathoth! Embody yourself in this body, Great Black Pharaoh, oh mine! Come forth! Come forth!"

Truth be told, he should be out there among his followers hoping to find more mundane ways of stemming the tide of Stygia's fall. Even if he was one of the last truly great wizards among his kind—the others' blood and magic more water than wine—they had armies. Some of his fellows were futilely attempting to assemble a defense with their untested slave soldiers and Hyksos mercenaries who were as likely to turn against the Great Lords as fight against the hated revolutionaries despite their shared gods.

Apophis Zul knew, in his quieter moments, that he had let the kingdom's management fall to the wayside in the wake of his quest for ever greater mystic power. Eunuchs and functionaries had plundered the gold meant to outfit their warriors while the sacred rites had become mere excuses for debauchery than actual placation of the spirits. They'd overcorrected as the doom that was coming to their land became increasingly clear and most of the palaces' servants had either ended up burning in last minute charnel pits or fled, regardless of whatever horrid punishments he'd promised to mete out on the deserters.

Apophis Zul had simply not believed that their patron god whose reality was unmistakable could allow them to fall. Had they not offered many first born of the Shemish during the Moloch feast days? Had they not carved his god's other names into every possible vessel to spread word of his power as well as prestige? Names that even slaves like Narmer would have recognized versus the one they had kept for themselves as his high priests like Bel'Moloch, Nergal, Tiamat-Ashuran, Typhon, and Lokas the Black Bull. Was not their betrayal of all other, lesser deities complete? What more did the many-faced one require?

Apophis Zul felt all too much like a peasant praying for relief from the lash or hunger, and it was not a pleasant sensation. He was of the old blood and should not be on his knees, huddled in the dark.

Narmer's scream ended as the room's angles seemed to twist and the air became a noxious mixture of smoke with the gases of another realm. Narmer's eyes, now as dead as the rest of him, looked up as the spirit of something infinitely older than the Earth itself animated his body like a child with a doll. The voice that escaped it was like a sickening echo of a dozen men speaking at once in a deep cavern. "Hello, Apophis Zul."

Apophis Zul was honestly surprised his master had answered his call and more than a bit relieved. Something he struggled not to show in his expression. He had sacrificed dozens of slaves, some with greater blood than Narmer, in hopes of conjuring his master. Sometimes *things* had answered but never his master, and most had been more interested in a good meal or rutting than heeding his wishes.

"Master," Apophis said, kneeling on the ground. "I have come to beseech your wisdom. It has been many long years since we have last spoke."

"Has it?" Nyarlathotep asked. "I haven't noticed."

Apophis could not help himself but spoke out of turn. "It has been almost a century, lord, since you wore the skin of the Black Pharaoh."

"Ah yes," Nyarlathotep said. "An evening's amusement."

Apophis Zul struggled to control his pride because displaying insolence rarely ended well when dealing with the gods. Certainly, he had punished enough of it when dealing with his fellow mortals.

"Blasphemers and heathens come to pillage Stygia, to burn it to the ground, and defile your sacred places. Their prophets and warrior-priests have promised to put all the old clergy to the sword, loot our treasuries, and destroy every engraving of every name so that we are forgotten."

"They will succeed," Nyarlathotep said, simply. "Or, rather, they have succeeded. In this world and in many others, I stand on the ruins of Stygia. I see it paved over to build new cities, I see the ashes of that city, and I see the world dead and lifeless far past that point. Mind you, I also see the city before it will be constructed and the precious sands of time you worship where it will thrive. A particularly grandiose colony of scurrying creatures offering prayers and blood to the sky while calling it empire."

Apophis Zul kept his temper in check. The conversation was not going the way he intended, but even the off-handed words of the gods could be deeply illuminating. He knew other worlds existed, but the Black Pharoah's words implied variations on this one were real as well as the gods existing simultaneously across multiple time periods. He would have very much desired a scribe, hopefully a hard-hearted or fanatical one, to transcribe the god's words exactly for later study. However, that was hardly the most pressing point right now.

"It is within your power to save your worshipers, my master," Apophis Zul said, careful not even to phrase it as a request let alone a demand. Nyarlathotep was a chaotic god who was as likely to reward defiance and punish the faithful as the reverse. If not for the vast power he'd seen it wield, he might have heeded Thoth-Amon's words that conjuring lesser gods were less likely to be Stygia's doom.

"Yes, it is," Nyarlathotep said, a bored expression on his already rotting face. Narmer's body would not be able to hold the Black One's essence long. Perhaps Apophis Zul had overestimated the slave's pedigree.

Apophis Zul released a breath he had been holding in. The god was playing coy, he knew, and there was no choice now but to ask directly. Throwing his hands up into the air, he prostrated himself with his face pressed against the stone floor at the foot of the throne.

"Please, Ahtu, the Crawling Chaos, the Black Wind, the Dweller in Darkness, and the Whisper in the Night, save my people from the horror that is about to befall them."

"No," Nyarlathotep replied.

"No," Apophis Zul said, not raising his head. "No?"

"That's what I said, yes."

Apophis had been prepared for many answers but the sheer bluntness of his god's response was too much. He'd sacrificed too much and put too much of himself in his worship of the dark god to back away now, but the loss of Stygia was something he could not imagine surviving. So, against all good sense, he looked up and spoke, "But *why*?"

"Would you remove a spider to protect a fly that has been cocooned?" Nyarlathotep said, his face now a skeletal, oozing mass.

This was all too much and a kind of suicidal foolishness that could pass for courage came over Apophis Zul. Rising to one knee, he gazed into his god's visage. "But we have been loyal to you! The sacrifices, prayers, and —"

"Why do you think prayers matter to me?" Nyarlathotep asked, dryly. "That the fawning and chorus of lesser beings serves any purpose? Do you think I feed from it? Grow stronger? Need your kind's mewling and requests for wealth or healthy babes? The smoke of burnt children and the hearts of slaves give me no pleasure. One soul in a billion of your kind ever shows the slightest bit of promise and it is not through religions that they achieve enlightenment. At least no more than any other path."

It was the most Apophis Zul had ever heard from his god and all of it left him feeling as empty as the River Styx in egress. Had he wasted his life? What even qualified as wasting one's life if the gods cared nothing for one's deeds, good or ill? Could a god who disdained worship even be called a god? Or was it simply a force far above man like a lion before a rodent?

"Ah, now you begin to understand," Nyarlathotep said, looking interested in their conversation for the first time. "Or at least begin to. Now ask the question you hold in your heart, and we will see if it provides you the secrets you desire."

Apophis Zul didn't know what he meant and was briefly terrified the god would smite him for standing there like a fool. Unwilling to let this happen, he blurted out the first question that occurred to him. "If you do not want prayers or sacrifices? What do you want?"

"Amusement."

Such a frivolous yet insightful answer. "Amusement."

The corpse of Narmer started changing from the rotted desiccated thing it had been to something wholly different, as if it were becoming the flesh of something else entirely, more shadow than man. "Indeed. Would you like a wish, Apophis?"

9

A wish? Such things were the subject of old wives' and children's tales. There was no magic that could grant anything one desired simply by willing it. If there was, Apophis would know of it. Yet, certainly, his god was perhaps one of the few beings capable of granting such a thing.

"Yes, master," Apophis Zul almost choked on his own reversal of fortune. "Please. I would love a wish."

"Then allow me to put you to the test," Nyarlathotep spoke. "Listen to me tell the tales of those touched by my presence. In the time it will take the hordes of the Sun worshipers to breach this temple, I will provide you with insight into my nature. If you can answer one question when these are done, you will receive whatever your shriveled little reptilian heart desires."

If there was a warning in the Black Pharoah's words, Apophis Zul did not hear it and focused instead on the god's promise. No matter how rarely divine tests worked out for mortals.

The Beginning

Cinderella and Her Outer Godfather

By C.T. Phipps

A long time ago in an accursed land far, far away, there lived a wealthy landowner named Marcus and his young daughter, Anna.

Marcus was the descendant of a powerful line of warlocks. Once his family commanded the spirits of the Dreamland, regularly conversed with Nyarlathotep himself, and were routinely invited to dine with the spirit of Abdul Alhazred in Azathoth's court. Unfortunately, Marcus was not the equal of his ancestors and quickly spent his vast fortune on frivolous entertainments. Anna, who possessed an uncommon intelligence, confronted her father one night after he came home from yet another drunken binge.

"Oh Father, what are you going to do?" Anna asked. "Our house is built upon the great underground cities of our ancestors where the intelligent rats gnaw and play! If you continue to waste our fortune, who will take care of them?"

Marcus cuffed her across the face before replying.

"Silly girl, I have already come up with a solution to my problems. The Deep Ones from distant R'lyeh offer gifts of gold and great caches of fish to whoever will marry into their accursed bloodline. I attempted to offer you to one of their men, but they said you were too young. More's the pity, but I suppose I shall simply have to lie down and think of the fortune."

Anna, of course, was horrified by his words because her ancestors had long ago promised their descendants to Yog-Sothoth. The Deep Ones, with their degenerate rites and unnatural appearance, were uniformly pledged to Great Cthulhu. It was a blasphemy of the highest order to switch their family's allegiance.

Unfortunately, Anna's pleas fell on deaf ears and her father married one of the Deep Ones a week later. This particular Deep One, a haggish woman named Salyssa, had more human blood than most and was able to pass herself off as a mortal woman with the right combination of veils. Her daughters, Eris and Carnyl, were even more human-looking but still possessed tell-tale signs of their inhuman parentage.

Perhaps Anna might have won them over had she been a respectful, obedient child who joined in the depraved rites of Father Dagon and Mother Hydra. However, Anna was the descendant of warlocks. Every night, she snuck out into the forest behind her home to carry out the fell rituals devoted to Yog-Sothoth's glory while praying to the Key and the Gate for deliverance. Even Anna's dog Muffin was sacrificed to the Outer God, showing the young daughter's piety.

Such disrespect did not go unpunished, however. At first, Marcus made a halfhearted attempt at defending his child but the stresses of his unnatural marriage got to him and he hung himself.

It was then Eris said, "We should sacrifice her to Great Cthulhu, Mother. Toss her in the ocean where she can join the ranks of all those who refuse to venerate He-Who-Is-Dead-But-Sleeping."

"No," Salyssa said, staring at her children. "As much as I would like to, Anna is a daughter of an ancient bloodline. Were we to kill her, we would bring the wrath of Yog-Sothoth down upon us for he is in all places at all times. No, instead, we shall punish her for her misbehavior. We shall inflict such indignities upon her that she will come to worship Great Cthulhu voluntarily and take a Deep Ones husband."

"She doesn't deserve such an honor," Carnyl said. "However, I like the plan of hurting her. What shall be the first thing we do to her?"

"We shall take away her name, because it is the first thing her father gave her," Salyssa replied. "From this day forth, we shall refer to her only as Cinderella. She shall sleep in the fireplace amongst the ashes and with the rats."

Both daughters thought this was an extremely good plan and had a hearty laugh over it. They took away all of Cinderella's dolls, burned her dresses, and forced her to work as a servant. In time, they came to deny she had ever been the daughter of their stepfather. The neighbors, fearing retaliation from the cult of Cthulhu, ignored the young daughter's plight and allowed the Deep Ones to treat her as a slave.

Cinderella, however, found the life less taxing than it could have been. Her stepmother and stepsisters could not have known the rats in the walls were her friends, frequently bringing her news of the outside world and whispering all manner of dreadful secrets. As the years went on, she heard of the prince who was leading their country in the place of his hopelessly mad father.

The prince, a handsome blond-haired warlock named Benedict, was a believer in the old ways and followed them fervently. Greedy arrogant nobles took the prince's faith as a sign of weakness, though. They believed in the Great Old Ones only so much as it brought them power. The resulting civil war had devastated the noble houses of the land, and Benedict had called forth an army of flying polyps to devour his enemies and their forces.

While his magnificent victory was a sign to the whole world of how the Outer Gods favored the prince, the gruesome destruction of the rebelling noble families had left the kingdom without an eligible bride for its heir. Rather than marry outside the kingdom to one of the families who worshiped the strange idol-less god from Arabia, it was said Benedict had begun searching the ranks of commoners for a potential spouse.

"Oh," Cinderella sighed, one day, sitting in her fireplace. "If only I could marry into the royal household. Then I could practice my ancestors' religion in peace and keep Yog-Sothoth's altar filled with the hearts of men as opposed to the animals I trap in the woods."

"You can," one of her rat friends replied. "You are the descendant of Eibon, greatest of all the ancient magicians, and inheritor of his sorcery. Were you properly trained, you could summon forth one of

13

Shub-Niggurath's young to make Prince Benedict your willing slave and breed with him many fresh offerings."

Cinderella smiled at her friend, stroking his furry human-shaped head. "You are sweet to say, friend rat, but I am not properly trained. My father cared more for drink than dread supplications. Why I do not think he ever waylaid a traveler so the hungry ones entombed below could have a meal!"

Cinderella was a child of good morals despite her faithless father. The fact the dead-but-sleeping remains of her ancestors were not fed by her stepfamily caused her no end of fitful nights.

"Feh!" the rat replied, surprising Cinderella. "I am surprised at you child, ignoring the power of the Outer Gods. They are there to be seized, not given. The secrets of ages past lay sleeping in the tomes of your forefathers. One merely has to seek these books out and possess the will necessary to perform the rituals within."

Cinderella blinked, considering the rat's words. "You mean to say that I should seek my grandfather's books and use them to summon a messenger of Yog-Sothoth?"

"Indeed I do," the rat replied. "The Deep Ones, craven fish-men that they are, have locked away your ancestors' libraries in the attic rather than destroy them. You must sneak the key from one of your stepsisters and study them in secret. In time, you will master the black arts and the world will be yours to command."

Cinderella felt embarrassed that a rat had been required to tell her such things. "I *will* do this. I will study the magic of my ancestors and wreak a mighty vengeance on my stepsiblings."

Stealing the key to the attic proved to be simplicity for the Deep Ones had long since abandoned active torment of Cinderella. She had become just another short-lived mortal, destined to be devoured or driven mad by the imminent rising of the Old Ones. Cinderella scoffed at such arrogance, knowing well that what was imminent to the Old Ones could last longer than the duration of humanity's reign on Earth.

Studying the *Book of Eibon*, *Pnakotic Manuscripts*, *De Vermis Mysteriis*, and other works, Cinderella became well-versed in all areas of the occult. Choosing a particularly auspicious moment in the solar calendar, Cinderella lured a hot-blooded traveler to the heart of the forest. There, she sacrificed him on Yog-Sothoth's altar before repeating mantras not meant for human mouths to perform.

Hours passed before a nightmarish black centaur stepped from a gateway to the primordial abyss. The creature had a body akin to a horse but covered in a thick alien exoskeleton. Its head was long and whip-like with only a yawning chasm in place of a face. Instantly, Cinderella fell to her knees and bowed before one of the many faces of Nyarlathotep, messenger of the Outer Gods.

"Milord," Cinderella cried, falling to her knees. "I am not worthy."

"Be at peace, daughter of Eibon, for I appear only to those who have caught my interest. Your ancestor long ago predicted your situation and ventured to distant Kadath where he passed by the puny gods of the Earth to speak with me. I am to grant you your fondest wish and see it is brought to fruition."

Cinderella clapped her hands with joy, never imagining such an august personage would be her patron. "Then, if the choice be mine, I would marry Prince Benedict and destroy my stepsisters as well as their hateful mother. I wish to be queen of all the realm and dwell with my beloved at the court of Azathoth for all time, listening to the otherworldly pipers who serenade the blind idiot god."

"Easily done," Nyarlathotep said, giving a courtly bow. "First we must replace the rags you wear with silks from the plateau of Leng. We shall give you jewelry made by the finest artisans of Ulthar. Your rats shall be made into coachmen, the skull of your father buried nearby turned into your coach. Your features will be changed as well for you are beautiful but only by human standards. I shall spare for you an entourage from the warlock courts of a place unpronounceable to your tongue. Finally, you shall wear a pair of glass slippers given to me as a present by a fallen priest of Hypnos."

"Glass slippers?" Cinderella asked, surprised such a thing existed.

"They carry upon them a dreadful curse of the Elder Gods to punish those who seek to pry too deeply into mysteries not meant for frail mortal minds," Nyarlathotep said, conjuring the slippers between his right hand's eight fingers. "You, Cinderella, are touched by the Outer Gods and shall suffer no ill-effects for wearing them. Lesser minds, however, will be driven mad from the glimpses of the

Dreamlands they provide. Even your stepsiblings are too human to endure such secrets."

"Oh my lord, this is a princely gift!" Cinderella said, stunned by the Outer God's generosity.

"As befits a princess," Nyarlathotep replied. "I must warn you, though, the stars were not quite right for my summoning. You must return before midnight or all of my gifts will be undone."

Coincidentally—or perhaps because of fate—the prince was presently hosting a ball in hopes of finding an eligible mate. The ball was not going well, the young women Prince Benedict encountered were either too frightened of his dreadful religion or too mired in local superstitions to change their ways to match his. There were cultists to the King in Yellow, Cthulhu, Ithaqua, and Tsathoggua, but not a single follower of the Outer Gods.

"Oh, why must I be surrounded by such churlish savages?" Prince Benedict lamented. "Am I to be forced to marry a ghoul bride in hopes of having someone who does not quake in terror of the proper way of living?"

As if answering the prince's audible plea, Cinderella arrived with all the pomp and ceremony befitting a daughter of the primordial warlock-kings. Tongue-less slaves from distant realms rolled out carpets of human hair while painted faceless dancers enthralled the prince until the arrival of their mistress. The prince's heart skipped a beat upon seeing Cinderella, enraptured by the asymmetrical beauty Nyarlathotep had given her features.

While later versions of this tale would have you believe they danced all night, in truth it was Cinderella's love of the arcane which won Prince Benedict over. From the cyclopean architecture of Elder Thing temples to the distant world of Yuggoth, the two discussed all manner of things not meant for human ears.

So enjoyable was the time had by the pair that Cinderella nearly missed the deadline given to her by Nyarlathotep. Hearing the chiming of the Yithian-made clock, however, she immediately rushed out the door to escape in her skull-carriage. Along the way, she dropped one of her glass slippers, playing along to destiny's plan.

The next days passed miserably for Cinderella and Prince Benedict. Cinderella's stepsisters were furious the prince had not chosen them, taking out their rage on their normally unnoticed sibling. Prince Benedict, by contrast, was enamored with the mysterious girl and brought all the soothsayers of the land to find her.

Each of them failed, often perishing in ways which could only be described as the wrath of the Outer Gods. Prince Benedict, desperate to find Cinderella, decided to test the slipper on the young women of his kingdom. The consequences of doing so mattered little to him because he could sense it was the will of the Outer Gods they marry. Despite the hundreds of young women driven mad in the process, the prince could tell he was getting closer to finding the mysterious girl who captured his heart.

Eventually, Prince Benedict reached Cinderella's house where she was locked away in the basement in hopes the family's pet shoggoth would devour her. Salyssa had grown tired of her continued defiance and possibly sensed the growing power within her. Fortunately, Cinderella had learned the spells for mastering a shoggoth to her will.

No sooner had Eris tried on the glass slipper and gone mad, stabbing Carnyl to death with a knife, did Cinderella burst from the basement with her newfound pet and ordered it to feast upon her stepmother. Salyssa's last words were a plea to Dread Cthulhu to rescue her but, of course, that god lies dead but sleeping.

"Who are you that commands the rebellious servants of the Elder Things?" Prince Benedict asked, impressed by her dramatic entrance.

"I am the woman you seek, blessed by Nyarlathotep and the Outer Gods, destined wife to you and mother of a great kingdom," Cinderella proclaimed, curtsying in her rags because she was addressing royalty.

Though she did not possess the non-Euclidean features which had so attracted him before, Prince Benedict tested the glass slipper upon her. Cinderella, having seen many more terrible things than the sights they showed her, remained completely sane. Well, as she and the prince measured sanity.

"At last!" Prince Benedict said. "My bride!"

"At last!" Cinderella said. "My husband!"

The two were married in an obscene ceremony soon after, ordering debased celebrations to all the Outer Gods and Old Ones throughout the land. That very year, twins were born possessing all the attributes associated with Yog-Sothoth's unnatural children. For, you see, both the prince and Cinderella had the Outer God's blood in their veins and Nyarlathotep had arranged for their bloodlines joining in aeon's past. The royal family summoned their godly ancestor on the twins' eighteenth birthday, destroying the kingdom utterly and flattening most of Europe in the process.

In reward for their actions, they were all raised up to dwell in Azathoth's court in wonder and glory forever.

The End

Where the River Ends

A *Cowboys and Cthulhu* adventure

By David J. West

Outside Fort Duchesne, Utah Territory, 1859

The posse rode their horses hard until the sweat gleamed on the animals' flanks and the froth at the corners of their mouths turned pink with hints of foaming blood. Exhaustion was upon all of them, close to faltering and yet they doggedly continued their pursuit of the dark-clad rider. The rider was only a few hundred yards ahead when he turned abruptly to the lefthand path and vanished inside a red-rimmed slot canyon almost invisible as it melted into the towering, boulder-strewn mesa. Grey mountains were looming beyond like sharp citadels and the willows beside the creek whipped back and forth in the breeze.

The foremost rider of the pursuers, a slim Ute brave called Bishop by the white men, brought his appaloosa horse to a sudden halt at the edge of the slot canyon's red-lined mouth. The echo of hoofbeats escaping down that narrow causeway taunted the posse. Ravens overhead cawed in a mocking tone.

Several of the other Utes immediately wheeled their tired horses around and cantered slowly back the way they had come, as if the escape into what must surely be a box canyon below the mesa was just as good as if the dark rider had escaped behind impenetrable castle walls and was utterly safe from these half dozen heavily-armed men.

"What are you doing?" Porter Rockwell, the long-haired gunman beside Bishop roared. "He went that way!"

Bishop shook his head. "I do not want to let him go, but we cannot follow there."

"Why not?" asked Porter. He tried to lead his palomino horse around, but Bishop moved his snorting appaloosa forward blocking him.

"No," answered Bishop, raising a hand as if he were about to lay a blessing upon the irate white man.

"What do you mean, no?" Porter blinked as if this were but a dream, a waking nightmare of insanity. They were so near; he could feel how close they were to capturing the dark rider. "Let's go! His horse must be as tired as ours. He's trapped! We got him!"

"You go down there," Bishop said as he pointed firmly, "and there is no coming back." He shook his head for emphasis.

Porter considered Bishop as trustworthy a Ute as he had ever known, but he was still dubious.

"What the hell is that supposed to mean?" he said with a good bit of venom, hoping to play upon the Ute's sense of bravery and honor. "You wanna just let him go? A desperado that molested and stole from your tribe, and murdered your people?"

"I am not saying that. He will be back someday, and we can try and bring him in then."

"Try? Why wait? What kind of sense does that make? If he can go down there and come back, so can I," Porter said, giving Bishop a frown dark enough he hoped to make the Ute crawl into a hole.

"You are not understanding me," Bishop said, as he pointed at the slot canyon. "This gulch devours men, it is an evil place. It lies upon the path of the Skinwalker. The veil between worlds is thin here and beyond the bounds of what we can say."

"Hogwash!"

"Sometimes it is just a pile of stones," Bishop nodded solemnly. "Sometimes it takes you somewhere else."

"Takes you? Through the mountain? Other side of the bluffs? What the blazes are you talking about? We're burning daylight, let's get him!" Porter's palomino stamped, as impatient as his rider.

"I am not going," Bishop said adamantly. "It's not the other side of the bluffs, it is another place."

"Talk sense! You're saying he has friends? We'll get ambushed?"

Bishop's face was as taciturn as ever, but he was clearly frustrated that the white man was not catching his meaning.

"That path," he pointed with great emphasis, "takes you to another world. If we go, we will not return. I am not ready to walk the path of spirits and leave my family. I will not go."

"So, I'm on my own?" Porter drawled. "I thought you had more sand than that."

Bishop shook his head.

"You are a determined man, Rockwell, but I do not know if even you could come back from that place."

"What's down there?" Porter asked, trying to get a little more from Bishop, to understand the Ute's apprehension. He had never seen the man so immoveable when it came to the hunt.

"Time is different there." Bishop gave a deep sigh. "When I was a boy, the dark rider came to my village, and robbed us. He murdered my grandfather for a stone idol found among the ancient ruins in the Book Cliffs. He escaped into this same canyon before the braves could catch him. Sometimes that canyon is not there, or at least it is not visible to our eyes. I have not seen the dark rider since I was a boy, but he looked much the same today as he did then, and I am near forty winters old."

"I've never heard any talk about the canyon that devours men before," Porter said.

"We never speak of such things to white men," Bishop answered. "I am telling you because I have much respect for you. But I will not speak of this again because it invites the old gods."

"What? No one ever spoke about old gods here," Porter protested. "Ain't no old gods here."

"They are like a dry river." Bishop came as close to a sardonic chuckle as he ever did. "Might be gone now, but when the rains come, a river flows there that you can see and touch. The river is always there, even when it is dry. The river is forever."

Porter held the reins of his impatient horse.

21

"That's a mighty fine sentiment, but every moment we hesitate that murderer is getting farther away. I'd think you'd want to deliver him some justice."

"Justice will come for him in the end whether we deliver it or not," Bishop said.

Porter tore off his hat. "You got an aphorism for everything today, don't you? But I ain't gonna let him get away with it again. I'm bringing him in. Let's go!"

"Then you do it alone. I cannot take that path," said Bishop firmly. "I ask you again, let this go."

"You know I can't." Porter spat.

"Then take this," Bishop said as he reached for something around his neck. "May my sacred bag bring you blessings of the Great Spirit."

Porter scowled but took the medicine pouch and slung it over his own neck as the Ute had previously worn it, then he hurriedly rode on down through the canyon.

The slick rock canyon was narrow enough that the posse would have been forced to ride single file. On his own now, Porter was hyper-aware of what could be an ambush in front of him, but he was on fire to catch this desperado. He would bring this outlaw to justice.

Moving like this was foolish. It was usually best to have one man tracking, watching the ground for any sign, while another was keeping an eye out for traps and anyone lying in ambush.

No such luck now, but then Porter had done it this way on his own many times before. He had also made a promise long ago to protect him.

In only a few moments the slot canyon opened to a hundred feet wide, surrounded by towers of red sandstone cliffs while grey walls of granite threatened in the distance. Scrubby brush grew in clumps along the bone-dry stream bed, which he followed for a hundred yards as it curved to the left.

In an eroded corner of the creek, the bleached skull of a bull elk lay half covered in sand and gravel. To his right, the rest of its bones were scattered about like the tossed sticks of a children's game.

Hoofprints stood out plain in the dry rusty sand. Porter scanned ahead looking for any hint of life. He saw nothing beyond the dying vegetation. No birds or small vermin. Not a lick of movement.

The prints followed the creek bed another twenty paces then mounted up the edge of the slope and into the sagebrush. Porter looked as far ahead as he could and there was no sign of a horse and rider, but Bishop's hesitancy had given the desperado time enough to gain ground.

Chewing at his mustache, Porter forged ahead. When no gunshot rang out, he decided he could watch for signs on the hard packed ground and be sure he was on the right trail.

Holding his six-gun at the ready, he rode on through the brush. The clumpy yellow grass was only a foot or two tall along the edge of the dry creek bed. As he rode farther on the slim trail, a strong wind slapped him in the face, and he closed his eyes against the stinging dust.

Porter was sure his eyes were only closed for a heartbeat against the harsh breeze, but as he opened them, he noticed that the grass was tall, green, and almost up to the horse's belly. Everything smelled moist. Looking around, there was no mistaking the difference in humidity and foliage. It was like he was back east along the southern Mississippi again. This was not the high desert he was used to.

The medicine pouch hanging across his sternum seemed to thrum. He might have looked to see if there were a bumble bee inside when he became aware of other changes surrounding him. Wondering if he was about to ride into a swamp, he paused his horse and scanned all about himself.

The hall of red cliffs were absolutely gone, replaced instead by a border of tall, emerald trees. He had not noticed them as he rode forward. True, he was hunting for signs, but he could not have missed such a lush forest in the dry wilderness. He had only been riding for a few paces since scanning the distance ahead.

The hoofprints that had kicked minuscule amounts of detritus on the ground told him that he was still on the trail of his quarry, but this was not the same world from which he had just come. Looking behind,

23

Porter could see a trail through the tall wavy grass like the wake of a ship.

Where was he?

He twisted about in the saddle looking in every direction. Anything familiar had vanished like a ghost, leaving only the strange, silent forest. The sky was a deeper blue than usual, if that were possible. Puzzled, he pondered in the moment if Bishop hadn't been right about this place and that he should follow his own trail back the way he had come. He may have done just that except…

A woman's piercing cry broke his awed reverie.

Alert, his pistol still in hand, Porter raced his palomino toward the sound of commotion, just a short distance into the thick trees. Breaking through the dense foliage, he saw a dark-haired Indian woman wearing only a scanty, torn, green dress. The woman's hair was tangled in the brambles of a vine covered tree. She was menaced by a cat beyond the size and scope of anything he had ever seen. The tawny cat was massive, a living nightmare with dagger-like teeth jutting from its open mouth. Rippling muscles on its shoulders were flexed and ready to spring. It looked as big and deadly as a grizzly bear, but much more agile.

The woman's teeth were clenched, as she whipped a short length of rope at the cat.

The monstrous cat cried out again, and Porter realized that the woman hadn't screamed. It was the tremendous beast making the bizarre caterwaul.

"Hang on," Porter said to the woman. "I got this."

The cat screamed again and turned its attention from prey to Porter.

Porter's horse panicked, sensing the deadly attack. It reared back, throwing off Porter's aim as he was tossed to the ground, losing both the air in his lungs and grip on the six-gun.

The gun's discharge was life-saving as the great cat balked at the thunderous sound, disturbed by the sharp echo.

The cat redirected its attention, as the woman pulled against the thorns and brambles that bound her to the tree.

Regaining his wind, Porter searched frantically for his gun. It was only a few feet away. Porter strained for the pistol as the cat swung its monstrous head back around and leapt for him just as his fingers gripped the hickory handle. Pulling the trigger as fast as possible was instinctual.

The heavy weight of the cat crushed any breath he had retrieved in the moment, and he was ready to vomit, as a sudden gush of hot blood covered him.

After he emptied the gun, Porter reached for his bowie knife, and he savaged the heavy body above him until he knew the huge beast was dead.

It took a supreme effort to get out from under the heavy cat. The big, dagger-like teeth were a marvel wholly unexpected by Porter and he considered taking one as a trophy of sorts. Then he remembered the woman that had been facing the beast.

"It's dead now," he said, lifting his hat up a bit so she might see his face better.

The woman tentatively moved beside the tree. He then saw that her incredibly long hair was caught and wrapped in a tangle of branches, trapping her fast against the foliage.

"I think I can get you out of that," Porter said.

She was beautiful and voluptuous, and chattered at Porter suddenly, but he couldn't understand a word.

"Slow down, what language are you speaking? You've not got enough clothes on to fly a kite, let me give you my coat," he said, taking off his worn coat and moving to put it over her shoulders in reverse despite it being drenched in the tiger's blood. He kept his eyes averted as best he could from her somewhat exposed body.

He finally saw something of their environment beside the trees. A wide, green river curved through the jungle not far away. It was as wide as the upper Missouri, perhaps a few hundred yards across, with slight eddies proving its powerful current.

The woman muttered something unintelligible once more and resisted his help, letting the coat fall from her shoulders, as he reached to break apart the green branches.

"Hang on, I'm trying to help." Porter realized he was literally drenched in the blood of the big cat.

She motioned toward the dead cat and said a few more quick lines that he could not possibly follow.

"That thing still scaring you? I'm fine. It's all the cat. You know what? I'll show you it's dead. I'm gonna take me one of them big teeth." He handed her the coat once again and she held it limply in her left hand. Porter then strode over and knocked one of the big, curved teeth out and put it in his vest pocket.

She seemed to have realized that she could not understand Porter either and went mute.

"Not sure what you were telling me," Porter said. He then pointed at his horse and made a gesture asking if the woman had seen another rider.

She nodded and pointed to the west. She took another step but yet another long strand of hair was still caught in the thorns and vines.

"Guess I'm hunting in that direction then, you wanting to come with me? Once I get you out of that tangle of course. I'm sure I can get you out, one way or the other." He looked at the stout green branches that held her like a demon's fingers and pondered if it wouldn't be easier to cut her hair off than deal with the thick, twisted cordage. Still, he got to work with his knife cutting the brambles that caught in her long hair.

He almost had her free when movement sounded from just beyond sight, coming straight at them. He cut the last few strands of her hair free with his knife, not caring any longer about being delicate.

The woman cowered and seemed to urge Porter to flee.

"I ain't leaving you to another one of them beasts," he said, reloading his pistol and holding it at the ready.

She pushed him, as if urging him to go. Then pointed to herself and the deep green river beyond.

Porter was flummoxed and kept a tight grip on her wrist, not allowing her to run from their perceived cover just yet.

"Whatever it is, I ain't leaving you to it alone."

It sounded like there were several somethings coming through the forest.

"You know how to use one of these?" he asked the woman, as he withdrew an extra pistol from his belt, but she stared blankly at it. "Fair enough, if you don't."

There was a murmur and the snapping of twigs underfoot.

Porter squatted to see beneath the canopy of trees in the direction of the ruckus, there was blurred movement darting between the tree trunks.

"I can't tell what it is," he whispered to the woman. "But I'm ready for anything these days." He held a pistol in each hand.

A trio of men came through the thick underbrush, two of them were dressed alike in grey overalls. They looked similar, like they could have been father and son.

The third man wore a dark suit, had neatly combed hair parted in the center and a trimmed mustache. As his eyes fell on Porter he smiled.

"Porter! I wondered if I would find you here."

Porter searched his memory but was quite sure that the man was a stranger.

"Do I know you?"

"No, I don't suppose you do yet," the man said as he smiled. "I was quite a bit younger, and you of course were much older."

"Say again?" Porter asked as he wondered if this wasn't a madman.

"I am Nikola Tesla, we went on a journey years ago, for me, but in the future yet for you I suppose, judging by your lack of grey hairs." He then turned his attention to the two men in overalls. "Porter Rockwell meet Grant and William Hastings, my assistants in this endeavor. They help me operate the *Horizon*." He then turned to the two men explaining, "I went on a journey with Porter, the infamous gunslinger, to the lost city of R'lyeh when we sealed the Gate of Dreams, keeping Cthulhu bound for yet another season. Perhaps that is why we have met now at the crossroads of time so that I could impart that information to Porter and he would know what to do in that future excursion for him and long-ago venture for me. I suppose it does get confusing."

The two men nodded to each other as if this all made perfect sense, but Porter was irritated at the insane explanation.

"I'm quite sure we have never met," Porter said. "I'd remember."

"Indeed, you would, but here we are in this crossroads, and thus, we should have some time to get reacquainted, deal with the present threat and then get back to our own temporal homes."

"You're using a whole lot of big words and yet you aren't saying a damn thing. You responsible for this woman being trapped and left as bait for that monster cat?" Porter growled.

"Her? Why that's no woman," Tesla answered. "The true native Americans refer to it as a water baby."

Porter frowned deeply.

"You can call the tribes whatever you want, and some of them are savage as hell, but they are still people," Porter said.

"She is not human," Tesla said, "but has only taken on our form as a means of illusion, for protection. Usually—well sometimes—they assume such a form to waylay and drown men. Stories of the fae doing such things are common enough upon both our continents."

Porter cocked a suspicious brow at that.

"You must have guessed from my accent that I am European?" Tesla remarked.

Porter spit, answering, "You don't say."

Tesla faced his two men and said, "I would like nothing more than to examine the creature and discover the source of its ability to transmute itself. There must be something with frequency that rearranges its molecules by sheer willpower. Capture it and I will examine it after our true endeavor is accomplished."

The woman cowed, surely understanding intention if not word and deed.

As the two men in grey overalls moved closer to the woman, she shook and backed away. Porter was on the verge of intervening violently on her behalf when she shrunk away slightly and changed in appearance. Her skin sagged as if melting and she grew hairier by the second until she was no longer a beautiful woman, but a hair-covered creature resembling a slight but very shaggy, moss-covered ape.

Porter was astounded and stepped back in horror and rubbed at his eyes.

"I must be dreaming. Why was she trapped here? What did she want?"

28

"She most likely wanted to gain your confidence and then drown you in the river there," Tesla said as he pointed to the nearby water. "She could have easily escaped the great cat, but was more than willing to let you think yourself the hero and thusly be fooled as a rescuer and then led to your doom."

"She was stuck in them brambles. She weren't ambushing me," Porter said. "I'd know."

"I understand they are malevolent creatures," Tesla continued. "Fae beings do not operate upon our human system of morals."

Porter shook his head at the hairy creature. "Now what?"

The water baby took a few furtive steps towards the river.

"Stop it," Tesla commanded his men.

The water baby bolted for the river with the Hastings in swift pursuit. They were almost upon it when Porter intervened.

"Let it go!" he shouted, and fired a shot at the Hastings' feet.

Earth exploded beside them, and the sound of gunfire echoed over the river.

The Hastings wheeled if only for a moment, but the creature was faster and easily escaped them and dove into the river. Once within the embrace of the dark waters, its head briefly rose several yards out, glancing back at the men, then it dipped and vanished from sight.

"That was unhelpful," Tesla lamented to Porter. "Think of all we could have learned from a thorough examination. But that is not why I am here."

"Oh," Porter asked sarcastically. "Then why are you here anyway? To get me to question my own sanity?"

"I told you we are at the crossroads of time and reality. I need your help, or at least someone you may remember said you would be willing to be of assistance."

"What?" Porter shrugged. "I don't think you really want my help in messing with a changeling. Bad luck I'll wager."

"Yes, well as I said, that was not the reason we came here either," Tesla conceded.

"Oh, and what was that for?" Porter asked as he searched his pockets for a cigar, finding none.

"The intersection of realms is open; someone is attempting a summoning. An invocation to allow passage to that which is banished. When I sensed your presence, I knew this must be the time to impart the knowledge of our future adventure."

"What? You sensed my presence? What are you, some kind of spiritualist?"

Tesla shook his head.

"Certainly not. I am a scientist."

"You talk like one." Porter furrowed his brow.

"Nevertheless, we are here now for the express purpose of stopping one of the agents of Nyarlathotep from opening a gate."

"That name sounds a little familiar." Porter rubbed at his jaw.

"It should," said a tall, grey-mustachioed man as he stepped out from behind the wall of foliage. "I'm sure I've mentioned my intent to thwart his plans whenever possible."

"Mr. Nodens," Porter said, recognizing the man. "I should have known you'd be involved with this nonsense."

"Ain't nonsense, Port," Nodens said as he tipped his hat. "Tesla here knows what he is talking about, I only filled in some of the more esoteric things that your kind doesn't usually cotton to. I told him how to adjust the frequency on his invention to bring us all here."

"Maybe you can tell me what the hell is going on?" Porter asked. "Where the hell are we? I'm hunting for a killer, I go through a narrow draw and suddenly I sure ain't in the state of Deseret no more."

"You surely aren't," Mr. Nodens affirmed. "We are at a crossroads, maybe partly of your so-called Deseret, but this land has been a place that lies thin between the veil since time immemorial. Gates seem to open of their own accord here and sometimes things go in and sometimes they go out. You came in for the same reason we did, to get that dark rider. To Tesla and his men, we came in a week ago, to you it was maybe a half hour. Time is a funny thing."

Porter snorted at that. He didn't bother to carry a pocket watch. His days and nights were ruled by the sun and moon. What use did he have for the timekeeping of other people's schedules?

"Don't get in a tussle now with the boys over that creature," Nodens continued. "They're just curious is all. 'Sides, who knows what your good will might have engendered with the hairy little gal."

Porter frowned at that and searched his pockets for his flask. Finding it, he kept an eye on his new companions as he downed the entire bottle in a single go. He closed his eyes, sighed heavily, and then looked at them.

"All right, what do you want from me?"

"That's what I like about you, Porter," Mr. Nodens said as he clapped him on the shoulder, "You're always willing to get your hands dirty. Follow me."

"Don't mention it," Porter grumbled in response as he followed the mysterious old man to the river's edge.

"We haven't much more time," Nodens said. "Look down there and you can see the Rift getting ready to open. Just up yonder we have Mr. Tesla's little steamship outfitted with his inventions to help deal with this possible incursion." Nodens gestured downriver to what looked like the bright orange glow of a sunset.

Porter shielded his eyes, gazing toward the glow. "See that, down where it looks like the river ends?"

"That sunset?" Porter casually asked. "Ain't it too early for that?"

"Not here," Nodens answered with a smirk. "That is the beginning of the biggest rift between worlds in your lifetime. *The* Rift, as far as your world is concerned."

Porter frowned and spun about realizing that the cloud-covered sun on the opposite side of the sky resembled nothing so much as a smoky god and the light streaming from where the river ended was indeed something else entirely.

"Think of it like a crack in a pane of glass, and you think that rain is leaking through. But it isn't just rain. It's more like a porthole on a ship that's well below the ocean's surface. It won't just leak water in, it will sink your world."

"We gotta seal the crack?" Porter asked.

"Exactly," Nodens said with a nod. "Get your horse, you'll need it to get home when this is through."

31

Porter retrieved his horse's reins and followed his new companions along a winding path through the trees. As they were walking beside the river, he noted several times the slight impression of a face watching them, hidden among the reeds. Surely it was the water baby. But he felt no threat from the being and focused on Tesla and Mr. Nodens as they explained more of this crossroads phenomena, not that most of what was said made a lick of sense to his ears.

Tesla began a conversation with Nodens, as if it were something discussed well before they had encountered Porter.

"Give me a lever long enough and a place to stand and I will move the Rift on an intercosmic scale. I think my Peace Ray can do it."

"That's good," Nodens replied, "Since the Da'aths exists outside all of space and time, you could insert a new creation from any point in time, whether it be past, present, or future."

Porter rolled his eyes trying to fathom what they were talking about, but each continued their journey down the path in the forest as if everything said was plain as day to one another.

"The Gateway of Da'aths is the opening of a pathway through the abyss itself," Nodens went on.

"I see," replied Tesla.

"Some of the most noted sorcerers have gone mad upon seeing its very edge. The abyss in the Qliphothic realm has no life of its own, as the very source of evil it is both intrinsically connected to and yet parasitic in relation to the Divine Light."

"And do you serve the Divine Light?" asked Tesla. "Whatever that is."

Porter rolled his eyes once more, so utterly incomprehensible was the conversation that he doubted his own sanity upon hearing it.

"As near as you can understand, I suppose so," Nodens replied. "Though I am an agent of myself rather than what you might call God."

"I'm not sure there is a god anymore," Tesla said.

"One? Ha," Nodens laughed. "There are more than I care to count, but in relation to the Rift, we are only concerned with a few. That I have mentioned to you already."

"Gamiszarra?" Tesla asked.

"Yes, the Living Island has already come through, but his hold here is tenuous at best. If Hudson can be dispatched, Gamiszarra will fade back through regardless of the talisman binding him here. Are you listening, Porter?"

"Huh? You talking to me?" Porter asked. "It all sounds Greek."

"I *am* speaking to you," Nodens replied. "You cannot possibly fight the Living Island, but you can slay the man that summoned and binds him to the realm. Hudson, or as you think of him, the dark rider."

"His name is Hudson?" Porter asked.

"It was when he began studying the art and ways of the Antiverse. He is now a pawn of Nyarlathotep and seeks to be an opener of the way."

Porter arched his back and stretched his hands out, ready to draw his pistols. "Trust me, if I see the dark rider, I'll shoot him."

"I knew you would," Nodens said, before continuing his discussion with Tesla. "Watch out. If the Rift is fully opened, you could see anything come through."

"I understand," Tesla said.

Porter looked at him and frowned.

Nodens went on, as he brushed a long vine out of the way. "Balance your Peace Ray between the Rift and the Gamiszarra if you can. I need you to be careful. No mystic—not even the most heretical of kabbalists—has ever explored more than a few dimensions in the Qliphothic realm. Seeking knowledge of the Qliphothic is both ethically and physically dangerous. Mystics who study the Tree of Death tend, unsurprisingly, to die in the most brutal fashions, or at the very least develop a disturbing fascination with annihilation and oblivion. Such madmen, like Hudson, have since established themselves in an attempt to usurp our universe, which is finely balanced on a razor's edge of divine symmetry. If certain natural forces varied in their values by the tiniest fractions, not even stars could exist."

Tesla nodded his head as if all of this made perfect sense to him, but Porter felt like he had been thrown into a cold lake.

"I don't know what you are talking about Nodens," Porter interjected. "You talk about gates and broken windowpanes letting the ship sink, but how can anything come through a gate that could destroy the earth?"

Nodens rubbed at his mustache as he answered. "Good question, Porter. Eons before humanity, beings of mind-shattering power roamed the planes of these lifeless universes. The most secret lore of the Qliphothic realm obliquely lists these entities as the Kings of Edom, these beings which came from unstable worlds some might say God created and destroyed before our terrestrial cosmos came into existence. Parables from ancient oracles and the ravings of mystics driven mad by studying these Kings suggest that these entities source from dimensions collapsed into oblivion eternities ago. Age after age, they moved from one plane to another, becoming ever more powerful. For billions of years no other power stood against them, for none was there to stand across the chasm between mysticism and desolation. Not one in a billion barren worlds might suffer a King of Edom's visit in a trillion years but where the Kings of Edom came, they and their servitor spawn wrought utter dissimilation of what matter was encountered. The horror of dissolution must have been inconceivable."

"Any of that got anything to do with that murdering desperado I was hunting when I came here?" Porter asked.

"It does indeed," Mr. Nodens said, "The desperado—as you so quaintly put it—is a mystic who is seeking communion with the antigods. He hopes to open a channel and allow their entry into our world and thusly begin a horrific end."

"What? Why?" Porter asked.

"I suspect he has deep-seated hatred and pain consuming his mind and heart," Nodens said. "Likely as not he is mad along with being incredibly intelligent. Whatever terrible deed he accomplished with your pursuit of him was a means to an end in his hopes of opening the passageway within the crossroads. I suspect he took a key from the Utes—one they didn't even know they had—which could open this gateway."

"You talk different to me than you do to Tesla," Porter observed, as they came around a thick tree and found a steamship waiting for them at the edge of the river.

"So, I do, just keeping everything in an understandable venue for each of you."

Porter sniffed at that as he looked upon the steamship. She wasn't very large, perhaps not more than thirty feet, but she looked heavily encumbered with a wide variety of scientific equipment that was far beyond his understanding. There were pulleys and weathervane-type contraptions as well as a large umbrella shaped device on the front but pointed backward and half upside down.

The two Hastings climbed aboard and one set to work in the wheelhouse, firing up the steam engine while the other seemed to be setting the bizarre contraptions up front to whatever their purposes.

Nodens took Porter's attention once more, saying, "It's nothing personal, you know what you know, and he knows what he knows and rarely do the two meet in twain."

"Twain!" Tesla said, "Where is he now?"

"Who?" Porter responded, assuming that the question had been for him.

"Never mind, you will meet him later and he will accompany us as well on our venture to R'lyeh, years from now," Tesla said, with more than a hint of satisfaction.

"Great," Porter sarcastically responded, "another person I don't know."

"Yet," Tesla corrected.

"Don't overwhelm the man," Nodens said. "Just let him do what he does."

"Overwhelm me? I don't understand even a half of what you all have been talking about with the void, rift, and crossroads and lever to balance the world. Why am I even here?"

"To do what you do best, my friend. You've killed more of these lesser trespassers than about anyone I can think, without going mad in the process. That's quite a feat. Your job is simple. Keep Tesla and his men alive, kill anything that tries to stop them, and you let them handle the technical otherworldly stuff."

Porter chewed at the edge of his mustache. "This would be a whole lot simpler if you stuck around and gave me a hand in that. I know you've got some kind of magical ace in the hole."

35

"You are that ace, Porter," Nodens said, giving him a warm slap on the shoulder.

Porter grimaced.

Nodens shrugged.

"Don't be glum," Nodens said. "I saw to it that they packed you a supply of ammunition and even a few extras that you would find handy."

"It helps to have another pair of eyes when I'm slinging lead," Porter replied.

Nodens smirked as he shook his head. "Like I said before, I can't be any more involved than I am in seeing to it that you humans intervene here. My setting this in motion is as far as I dare get involved without attracting any more attention from Nyarlathotep and his ilk. Last thing I want is the forces of Hastur or even Tsathoggua looking your way."

Porter glanced at Tesla for those names meant nothing to him. Tesla echoed Nodens shrug.

"You've got this, Port. Take care of Nikola and you'll be able to ride back through that draw in the canyon and be at the foot of the mesa in no time at all."

"What about this man I'm hunting?" Porter asked.

"If you are successful, you'll be dealing with him directly. He is down there where the river ends," Nodens said.

"This Hudson feller?" Porter asked.

Nodens chuckled lightly. "Ah, for him a name is just a suit of clothes. But he is flesh and blood for now, so you may be able to fill him full of lead and halt his transfiguration for a spell."

Porter grunted with irritation at that answer. "Don't suppose you packed any of my other articles for this venture, did you?"

"Go ahead," Nodens gestured to Tesla. "Show him the weapons I gave you requisition for. But Porter, I only had him bring one flask of whiskey for you, you gotta stay sharp on this one."

"I'm always sharp, just need something to whet my appetite," Porter said.

Nodens laughed aloud. "All right, have it your way. Until next time." He gestured to the gangplank for the steamship and then turned and walked away from them with a brief wave and tip of his hat. As lightning tore their attention toward the swirling warp of a vortex in the distance, in the mere fraction of second it took as they looked back to where Nodens should have been, he was gone like the darkness at dawn.

"I hate it when he does that," Porter muttered.

They clambered aboard the steamship. A variety of machines were placed all over the small ship in tight fashion, allowing only for one man at a time to pass each other upon the narrow deck. Bizarre machinery with wires and pipes went every which way, resembling a rat's nest to Porter's eyes. He recognized the steam machinery used to power the vessel, but the rest had little practical understanding for him. The most interesting thing to him was what might have resembled a cannon save that it had no barrel, instead it possessed a wide umbrella-like apparatus pointing forward from a central mass of gears, coils, and a clockwork apparatus.

"What is all of that?" Porter asked.

"In essence, it refracts waves of energy," Tesla explained. "Some of what you see ahead is a rip in the frequency that keeps our dimensions separate."

Porter squinted as he attempted to understand what was to him utterly unfathomable.

The younger Hastings stood by a mechanical winch at the back of the steamship as the elder undid a rope which had fastened the ship to a large fallen tree. It was how they had secured the craft when they came ashore and found Porter. When Porter saw the mechanized thing, he marveled at its expediate nature. It did the job faster than a trio of men could have.

"Trust me, friend," Tesla said. "It will make sense to you someday. But we must get under way. Mr. Hastings, kindly take us downstream."

"Aye, aye, sir," called the younger of the two, as he threw back a large iron wheel and cranked up the steam power of the little ship. He then sent a short burst of steam out a whistle and the ship puffed and lurched as it left the shoreline and proceeded downriver.

Tesla checked various dials and regulator switches, the likes of which Porter had never dreamt of.

Porter harrumphed at that and asked, "Where are my weapons?"

"There, in those steamer chests," Tesla said, gesturing toward two large trunks on the foredeck. "I believe they should be to your liking."

As the chests were opened, Porter's obvious amazement betrayed his taciturn exterior. His eyes widened fiercely upon the huge cache of ammunition. The first chest held boxes and boxes of cartridges, a year's supply for several firearms; shotgun slugs, a 45.70 buffalo gun, and long magazines that he picked up and wondered aloud at what they were.

"They are for the Gatling gun," Tesla said.

"What's that?" Porter asked.

Tesla sucked in his breath through clenched teeth then asked. "What year is it, Porter?"

"1859, you know that," Porter replied. "Why?"

Tesla shook his head. "Not from where I left. I'm afraid I brought you the best weaponry I could from 1890."

Porter threw back the second chest and saw a stack of what looked like brown paper wrapped candles with ridiculously thick wicks.

"You wouldn't know dynamite in 1859, either, would you?" Tesla asked.

Porter frowned. "What are they?"

"They are explosives. Much easier to use and more portable than black powder. It should be most handy for your use against any denizens of the dark that may attempt to accost us."

"Uh huh," Porter replied.

"William," Tesla called to his assistant, "please give him a demonstration. Better to alert our foe, which almost certainly knows we are already underway, than have our gunman unsure of how to utilize them."

The elder Hastings picked up one of the sticks of dynamite, showed Porter both ends and pointed to the blasting cap as he placed it. He struck a match and then lit the fuse which sparked and spat, giving off noxious fumes as it quickly raced toward the end. When only an inch of fuse was left, he tossed it overboard and as the light faded into the murky water, an uproarious belching explosion sounded from several feet under the surface, sending a great splash up at them.

"You've got to watch your timing, they're quick, and we thought it best to have waterproof fuses," William said. "You try it."

Porter took one of the sticks, placed a blasting cap as he had seen done, and lit the fuse with a struck match.

"Quick now, throw it away," William ordered.

Porter tossed his farther, with a greater arc than had William. It landed a good distance from the boat and exploded just as it touched the far bank. A concussive force slapped Porter in the face, almost dislodging his hat. A small amount of dirt and rock rained back toward them a moment after the explosion.

"I can see the value in that," Porter said with a wry grin. "And this Gatling gun?"

William held up a finger, then pulled a stocky contraption from the bottom of the first chest. It looked like six rifle barrels arranged in a circular tube with a single firing mechanism and handle at the rear. He mounted the gun on a forward platform and showed Porter how to load with the long devices that Hastings called "magazines."

"This crank loads it as you fire. It will send an awful lot of lead downrange quickly."

"How much do those things hold?" Porter asked.

"Thirty-six rounds apiece, and you can reload real fast like this." William racked the crank with his left hand as his right held the trigger on a handle and fired off the full magazine into the surrounding shrubbery and riverfront. He then rapidly reloaded and did it again.

"Now you try," Tesla said.

Porter followed suit, loading a magazine stick, and then leveling the gun and firing away. He swiveled quickly as if following the lead of imaginary foes. He raked the gun up and down, tearing down tree branches and splashing stones along the riverbank. When the gun was empty and the barrels spun once more, Porter stopped the crank.

"Now that was something!" Porter exclaimed. He was genuinely impressed with the strangers now.

Tesla noted, "You moved that like you know what to expect."

"When Nodens is involved, I've had to expect a whole lot of things I never imagined before."

"And they didn't strike you as maddening?" Tesla asked.

39

Porter shook his head. "I don't know what you mean."

Tesla gestured with his hands in the air. "Like the things are so horrible that your mind breaks and can't hold it all. I've tried to let the Hastings know what to expect, but its beyond words. I hope they are all right when they finally see one of these old ones."

"Monsters," Porter spit. "Just monsters, they ain't nothing I should do but shoot some lead at 'em."

Tesla rubbed at his nose. "Yes, well, I expect you to be as prepared as possible. We shall see your dark rider imminently. I suspect we'll have a good view as we round this bend in the river."

The younger of the Hastings took the ship into the center of the river and as they came around the wide bend, they got a full view of the Rift. It, too, seemed to be centered upon the wide watery expanse, and the entirety of the river appeared to be flowing right into it. Beyond the orange glow was a solid black iris, as if the nothingness lay just beyond their perception and Porter could see nothing farther.

Directly in front of the Rift, however, was a small island which had a single man standing upon it with his arms upraised as if beckoning into the void.

As the ship approached with its constant drumming chug, the dark man looked over his shoulder and signaled to dark shapes that crouched upon trees that overhung the river. Thin black wings unfurled, and the skinny bodies took to the air. With curling horns on their heads, and forked tails trailing behind, they looked like ebony devils coming to claim the souls of the dead.

But Porter wasn't dead yet. He recognized these winged things as nightgaunts. They swooped to and fro through the air before diving toward the boat.

"Keep your heads down!" called Porter as he readied the Gatling gun.

As the first of the nightgaunts came screaming forward, Porter opened up and sent a rain of hot lead into the chest of the batlike demon and flung it crashing into the river. The second and third dove sideways away from the steamship in an effort to avoid the flying rounds, but Porter was quick and led the gun swiftly, catching one through the wings and forcing it to crash into the drooping trees. The third had its tail shot off and it howled in pain before taking a wide arc to counterattack.

A fourth had swung the long way about and raked a clawed hand at Porter, shredding the shoulder of his jacket and just missing his flesh. The Gatling gun was empty, and Porter drew his pistols and emptied them into the retreating fiend with a barrage of curses.

Struck multiple times, it fell into the river with nary a gasp.

The tailless nightgaunt savaged the far side of the steamship as it attempted to attack the younger Hastings who was piloting. Hastings had not been unarmed, however, and emptied his shotgun into the featureless face of the monster.

"Are there anymore?" Porter asked, scanning the eerily glowing sky.

"Mr. Hastings," Tesla called out, "fire up the generator, we are close enough for the Peace Ray."

"It's ready, sir!" shouted the elder Hastings.

A powerful electrical hum sounded from within the bowels of the ship. Tesla put on a pair of protective goggles and sat in a chair fixed right behind the backward umbrella-looking contraption. A beam of white light shot from the centermost portion and moved along the darkest point of the Rift forcing it to shrink upon contact.

A pained howling sounded from somewhere out in the depths. Porter didn't know what that meant, but he guessed they were less than a quarter mile from the small island and less than a half mile from where the river met the Rift. He wondered if the current would force the ship into that dark pit before Tesla could close it.

Shambling monstrosities plowed through the trees on the banks and dove into the river before Porter could get a good look at them. The corner of his eye said they were big, but what were they? They must be swimming now, coming at the ship from both sides.

Tesla's Peace Ray wavered back and forth over the dark iris, forcing it to grow smaller and smaller.

Porter was sure now he could hear the dark rider—this sorcerer named Hudson—shouting in anger from the surface of the bare little island.

"Star spawn! Porter, I see them!" Tesla shouted from his observation chair.

Unsure what that was, Porter scanned the river and reloaded the Gatling gun. He could not see anything in the deep green waters, until he caught a hint of bubbles racing for the stern.

He cranked the gun and sent a shower of bullets into the bubbles' path. A squid-faced monstrosity rose from the river, bellowing like a butchered ox. But this thing was not butchered. It slapped a slimy green hand with six-fingers over the rail of the steamship and yanked, tearing off the topmost plank of the gunwale, then it disappeared back into the depths.

The ugly, multi-eyed face of another rose then dropped back on the opposite side of the river, and the steamship lurched as something struck it from beneath. Flabby, clawed hands scraped the underside and the timbers threatened to snap.

Porter grabbed two sticks of dynamite and lit the fuses simultaneously then tossed one over each side of the ship just as the fuse had nearly run out. Each exploded and instantly the banging upon the hull ceased.

Then all three star spawn gripped whatever they could reach, scuttling to climb aboard the already overloaded vessel.

Porter leveled the Gatling gun at the nearest of the three and cranked the lever as the gun belched fiery lead into the green mushroom-head of the tentacle-faced star spawn. Bullets split the head wide open, yet it would not die. The pulped sludge making up what was left of its head began to ooze back and reform as if the incident were happening in reverse.

Porter's eyes bulged in morbid fascination. He swapped out the magazine and unloaded at almost point-blank range once more, further ripping the bulbous mass in half, then as the gun emptied, he reached and took hold of a piece of dynamite and lit the fuse with a snap of his wrist. He tossed the crackling tube into the open gash of the wounded head and the slime of ages formed around the stick, covering it whole. The black eyes slid back up on the face of the beast and it stared at Porter blankly before the explosion sent pieces of the monster all over the side of the ship and river. Porter ducked his head just in time for his hat to take the brunt of the flabby monster's gore, which now painted the side of the ship the foulest green.

The ship rocked back the other direction as the next star spawn gripped the gunwale and attempted to capsize the steamship. Luckily, Tesla's machinery made for heavy ballast and kept the ship beyond what the monster could tip and sink her. It was only a matter of time. Two of them could tip the boat over if they worked together.

The next star spawn had been wounded by the earlier dynamite and was trailing further behind the steamship. It was not out of the fight but gave Porter a moment to deal with only one of the beasts.

Porter had an idea. He grabbed the tether line that had been used to attach the steamship to land. An expert at ropes around the ranch, he made a wide circle and lassoed the stout cordage around the squamous neck of the thing and slammed home the hoist, which suddenly cranked on the winch. The rope rapidly grew taut and pulled on the makeshift noose squeezing against the neck of the monster.

The star spawn fought and clawed at the rope, but it was already too tight, and its flabby fingers could not reach the line to cut it. The tentacles on its face stood out erect as the rope strangled the ferocious beast, growing ever tighter as it pushed against the side of the steamship to escape its fate. Well, until the rope squeezed too tight and its head was popped clean off. Putrid ichor erupted like a fountain as the horrible thing went limp. Both gory head and body sank into the waiting river.

The final star spawn dipped its head under the water and Porter couldn't see it.

Knowing the dynamite could do some damage, he grabbed two sticks and lit them. He threw each on either side of the rear of the steamship, hoping he could drive the monster to come directly behind, unless he was lucky enough to land one right on top of it with the first throw. But he didn't bet on luck.

There were two explosions, almost simultaneous, close behind. Almost as suddenly as they burst through the top of the river, the last star spawn rose from the depths and grabbed the rear of the ship.

Porter tossed a ready stick at the monster, but it batted the dynamite aside with one of the tentacles on its face. The stick flew behind, landed in the river, and exploded without having harmed the monster.

Attempting his rope trick once more, Porter tossed the loop at the beast, but it knocked this aside with its hand, too, and the line went taut and caught it on the wrist.

This is not what he wanted.

The star spawn used the leverage of the steamship itself to pull against the line and as the rope grew tighter, the winch smoked as the rope burned against the machine. Just as the monster's hand was about to pop off, the winch flew free from its mount and splashed into the river.

If the solid black eyes of the star spawn could be seen to dilate, they did as a malevolent twitch of its mouth curled beneath the writing tentacles and it pulled on the steamship forcing the ship to lurch back and river water to swamp the back side.

Porter blasted the buffalo gun into its face, smashing eyes and pulping tentacles, but the behemoth did not let go.

"If it gets water into the engine it will blow!" shouted the younger Hastings.

"It didn't need to hear that!" answered Porter as he was reloading.

The star spawn redoubled its efforts hefting more of its flabby bulk onto the rear of the ship causing more river water to pour over the smashed end.

The elder Hastings fired his guns at the swollen face of the creature as Porter grasped another stick of dynamite. With the barrage of bullets coming at it, the monster missed the stick which blew its head apart, raining gross material all over the rear of the steamship and its crew.

The blubbery carcass slid off the rear deck and sank into the river. The ship lurched forward when the strain was suddenly released, just as Tesla shouted a warning. "Get ready! The real challenge lies ahead!"

The dark rider stood on the bare and rocky island as he mystically conjured at the shrinking Rift, like a sculptor forcing the statue out of marble. With each gesticulation of his arms and even fingers, spidery cracks formed at the edge of the Rift, forcing it to open ever so slightly with each refrain, as if each stanza of some infernal verse, each note of the profane awoke a terrible song in the fight of their lives. It was a symphony of destruction.

Tesla fired up his machine and sent a bolt of almost invisible energy radiating into the center of the portal. Ripples went out from the center and some of those cracks and webs the rider had opened sealed back up.

The dark rider turned, his hair flying over his sweat-stained face, which contorted in a mask of rage. He cried aloud and further drew upon the arcane to bend reality to his will.

Those on the steamship watched as something crawled out from the widest section of the Rift, something akin to a centipede but its round head and clasping jaws were as large as a long-horn steer, its length was as much as a half dozen of them. It wormed its way around the Rift and then, finding gravity on this side of the veil, it fell into the river below with a riotous splash. In no time it was snaking its way through the green waters like a serpent.

The monster was not lost on Porter, who reloaded the Gatling gun and opened fire into the river. Bullets hit the carapace with an audible *thunk* and the centipede beast went deeper, avoiding the rain of bullets. There was a brief respite, where every eye was cast upon the waters, every eddy and slight rock of the waves was suspected as they searched for the multilegged monster.

"Maybe you hit it?" suggested the younger of the Hastings.

"I doubt it," Porter muttered, as he scanned everywhere. "Didn't see any bits fly off."

The ship lurched and rocked as the monstrosity scuttled aboard the aft deck with the speed and hideous grace of an insect. It seemed to understand where it could avoid the Gatling gun.

As the thing fully crawled up into the wheelhouse, the younger Hastings raised a rifle to fire but was caught in its champing jaws. His face betrayed a silent scream as the great pincers smashed his chest and lungs and he was severed in half.

"No!" cried the elder Hastings, as he fired with his own rifle, but the shots from the lesser rifle had no effect.

Porter tore the Gatling gun from its mount and leaning it near the forecastle, he cranked the arm until the cylinders ran dry, sending a dozen rounds of 45.70 into the terrible maw of the monster, pulverizing its face and half of its seemingly caustic gaze.

It was not dead yet.

Its tail, replete with a massive stinger, jammed into the gunwale, narrowly missing Porter. Tearing wood and rail apart with its backswing, it lashed out once more, knocking the Gatling gun to the deck.

Porter drew the shotgun from its scabbard and gave both barrels into what was left of the monster's head and cracked bulbous eyes. Effectively blind, the beast writhed and whipped uncontrollably, but only succeeded in pulping the dead Hastings corpse before losing its balance upon the ship and falling overboard in a great splash of water. As the ship moved forward the beast lost its ability to pursue the vessel.

Tesla continued his repair of the Rift with his Peace Ray. A second centipede monster crawled halfway through an opening lower on the central Rift. As Tesla swung the ray to confront that entry, it closed and cut the centipede in half. Leaking orange entrails, the monstrous centipede fell into the river with much less malevolent aplomb than its forebear.

Hudson turned to face them now that he had been unable to call for more denizens of the outer dark to serve him.

"I knew this might happen," Hudson proclaimed. "Did you think I wouldn't be prepared?"

"We faced your preparations," Tesla answered. "Now the bill is due. Surrender yourself or die."

"Ha! You have only faced the lowliest of what I conjured. I began with the strongest, but let you face the weakest first." With those words, he rose into the air, hovering above the small island. Only a few feet at first but he soared higher in the air with his arms bent at the elbows and held upward looking like a saint in the old pictures.

"I can hit him square," Porter said, as he leveled the rifle.

"Do it," Tesla answered. "There will be no reasoning with him. He has made his choice."

Just as Porter pulled the trigger, the small island Hudson had been standing on shimmied in the water and it, too, rose. In so doing, it caused a great wave which moved the ship and all aboard, causing

46

Porter's aim to be thrown wildly off. He could hardly keep his feet on the deck as the island rose higher forcing the river to swell and twist about, sending the ship back upstream.

A deep sonorous roar filled their ears and Porter assumed it was the Rift. But that looked much the same as before, though Hudson was now more than fifty feet in the air beside it.

"Shoot him if you can, I will try and hit that thing before it becomes fully aware of us."

"What thing?" Porter called back against the din.

"The thing making that noise," Tesla shouted.

Raising itself from the muck and slime of ages, a titanic behemoth stood now on four great squat legs. River mud coated the lower half. Porter could not tell what color it really was, but he saw the burning eyes as they looked back at him.

It was a chimera of sorts, resembling half a dozen different creatures that Porter knew and some things he did not. It was utterly alien and its size was beyond imagination. How could mere bullets harm this thing with a shell or scales like an armadillo or turtle, when its burning eyes were as large as a barn door? Teeth or tusks jutted from its mouth as big as trees. It was so vast that he could hardly see the Rift anymore.

This might have been as close to quitting as Porter had ever felt, the sheer monstrosity and size of the thing was beyond daunting, beyond fighting, beyond hope.

"Porter, hit Hudson. He controls the beast. Let me slow it down for you," Tesla said as he focused the Peace Ray on the juggernaut of nightmares and fired a blast.

Orange rays hit the outer shell of the giant thing and it grumbled in pain, before shuffling around and letting its massive scaled back protect it from the Peace Ray. It dropped into the river then and the waves sent the steamship spinning farther back upstream, tossed like a child's toy. There was no way Porter could manage a shot at Hudson, he was barely able to hang on to the ship as it heaved.

"When the river calms, I'll fire again, I really think I hurt it, but you must kill Hudson before he reopens the Rift and calls forth another Old One," Tesla said.

47

"Damn! That's an Old One?" Porter cursed to himself, if he could hardly stand, how could he shoot?

"A lesser one," Tesla answered. "It may be Gamiszarra, the Living Island. I'm not sure."

Porter's face contorted at the scientist's mundane explanation of the unfathomable.

They had been pushed back upriver almost a quarter mile, much too far for Porter to take an accurate shot at Hudson with his pistols or rifle.

"I need to get closer!" Porter called to Tesla, who had already gotten the ship pointed in the correct direction and was steaming back toward the Rift and the oncoming behemoth. The elder Hastings had taken up the wheelhouse in replacement of his lost son.

The ship's chaotic push upriver slowed as the river's current fought against the backwashing of Gamiszarra's approach. A series of new ripples struck the keel of the ship tipping it this way and that as the gigantic entity shambled toward them.

With the monstrous Old One approaching, Porter would not be able to get a shot at Hudson before the terrible behemoth overcame their steamship and smashed it to kindling.

"You got a backup plan?" Porter shouted over the din.

Tesla didn't answer. He focused the Peace Ray at the Rift. The black iris was sealed shut, leaving just a dull orange glow where once had been an open doorway to another realm.

Lightning arced from Hudson's position toward the steamship.

Porter couldn't see the sorcerer but guessed he was protected by the oncoming Old One.

River water swirled back with each step of the titanic thing and twisted the steamship about, drenching Porter. Tesla swiveled the Peace Ray and kept its continuous beam upon the Rift.

Gamiszarra was almost upon them, and Porter imagined its massive foreleg crushing the steamship. He dropped the rifle he had been hoping to use on Hudson and loaded another magazine into the Gatling gun. He cranked the full load into the face of Gamiszarra but beyond a mere twitching of its eyes, it was in no way hindered. A great clawed foreleg was lifted above the steamship like a hammer ready to fall.

Tesla switched the Peace Ray to the Old One's head and a renewed bolt of energy pulsated at the mighty being. Gamiszarra fell back a pace or two, attempting to avoid the radiation which blasted it in the face unceasingly.

Porter shouted, "Wish you would have told me you had that up your sleeve."

"You still need to get Hudson," Tesla answered. "I won't be able to hold off Gamiszarra for long."

"If I can hit Hudson, it will end this?" Porter asked.

"If you can, Gamiszarra will be recalled back to the other side of the Rift," Tesla explained.

"He's already here!"

"This is a two-birds-with-one-stone maneuver," Tesla responded. "But timing is everything. Hastings!"

Hastings who was still in the wheelhouse, suddenly pushed the steamship, taking it to its maximum speed which had been held in reserve until now. The little ship narrowly sped around Gamiszarra and was zipping downriver toward the Rift and Hudson who still hung in the sky like a marionette.

Porter grabbed the buffalo gun from where it had been wedged against the gunwale and took careful aim. He could hear the monstrosity Gamiszarra behind them as it wheeled about and plunged through the river, racing after them.

The great steps of the insanely huge monstrosity caused river water to swell and lift the ship, speeding it along to their destination. Luckily, Porter was able to maintain his sea legs enough to get a bead on Hudson. He prepared to take a shot.

Without the Peace Ray being fired on the Rift, cracks formed and spread over the orange glow. Light danced outward where pieces broke away and the black abyss opened again. The scope of what he was seeing was beyond Porter's ability for words. Thoughts raced through his mind on what was real, what was madness and his small part in this insane universe, but he remembered the feel of cold steel and knew what a bullet could do to a man.

49

He centered the rifles sights on Hudson, steadying himself as best he could. He pulled the trigger and sent a series of shots into Hudson's chest and legs. Dark blood splattered against the sorcerers' trousers and shirt. Red rain fell from the wounds. The dark figure hanging in the air jerked as if invisible strings were plucked one by one.

"We haven't much time!" Tesla shouted. "Porter, no matter what happens to me and the ship, when this is done, go find your horse and try to ride back the way you have come. I believe you shall make it through your own gate."

Porter didn't look at him, his gaze fixed upon the twitching Hudson, still suspended in the air, but he asked, "You think so?"

Tesla nodded. "I do, because you must make it back through. Otherwise, I would have no memory of you and our journey to R'lyeh which is in my past and your future."

Porter rolled his eyes at that explanation and cast a look back over his shoulder at Gamiszarra, the Living Island who was coming at them causing a surge in the river's water with every titanic step.

The Peace Ray was fixed upon the glow of the Rift and healing it like ice to a burn, the black fading away just as the twitching feelers of more of those hideous crawling things were about to pass through.

Hudson's head was slumped down as if in his death throes he was looking at his toes. It shot up and fixed his blazing mad gaze upon Porter and Tesla. His hands stretched forth and lightning danced outward, blasting across the steamship's prow, ripping planks from the forecastle and gunwale. Splinters and metal brackets rained upon Porter, and he shielded himself with his hands as best he could.

The roar of Gamiszarra behind was deafening and Porter could hear nothing but the tumult, though he saw Tesla shouting and pointing.

The river surged and sent the steamship tipping up at almost 70 degrees. For a moment that balance remained, and Porter took aim once again as the ship was carried aloft.

Closer now, they were separated by less than a hundred yards. Porter aimed for the center of Hudson's face and pulled the trigger. A buffalo gun does a lot of damage and Hudson's face was gone in a red haze with the bark of the rifle.

Then Porter flew through the air as he heard an ear-splitting, wood-splintering crunch behind as Gamiszarra trod upon the steamship.

Porter slapped the water hard and lost his breath. He lost the rifle, he lost his hat, and almost lost his life. He saw sunlight glimmering above as the impossibly huge foot of Gamiszarra came crashing down. And then vanished. Not like the giant monster had stepped away, but faded like smoke. Tesla had been right about his mad ramblings and the monster was recalled back beyond the Rift with Hudson's death. All these thoughts raced through Porter's mind as he sank deeper into the river. He had no strength left to fight the current, no strength to even fight to catch a breath. He was lost, done, too weak to do anything but drown.

He felt clawed hands grasp his coat and pull him ferociously near. One of those dark creatures must have been scouring the trail of the steamship waiting to pounce. This was the end. He would drown in the dark river and be eaten by scaly monsters. No one would ever know what became of him, and his name would be a curse. This was the end.

Darkness folded over him. A heartbeat drummed in the dark and he wondered if it was his own or that of a Deep One. The slime of ages caressed his back, and reeling within the long dark abyss, he wondered if this was Hell. No angels would come to light his way. Not here.

He felt the pouch thrum against his chest, as if it sensed a power all its own.

Then he was pushed and pulled upward, light from a smoky god of a sun above greeted him.

He burst through the surface of the river as strong rough hands tossed him unceremoniously upon the grass-covered bank. He coughed roughly and tried to get his bearings along with a breath, but his eyes played tricks on him, and he could not see. Shadows moved in front, and it took a long time to draw a comforting breath of warm air.

A rough hand moved over his cheek and beard. He knew then it was the water baby that had saved him. She chattered an unintelligible word, placed his soaking wet hat upon his head and then he heard a splash before she vanished back into the river.

Unknown to Porter, a short distance away two beings stood by, having watched the entirety of the conflict.

"I told you," Nodens spoke first.

The Crawling Chaos, in the guise of a dark pharaoh, grunted. "So be it, I would not have believed the Paohmaa would forgo the opportunity to slay a human that lay so completely within their power."

"Well, he did save the water baby from the saber-toothed cat."

The Crawling Chaos scoffed. "That was a ruse, and you know it."

"But then he also saved her from being captured by Tesla's men and getting experimented on."

Nyarlathotep stared. "They could not have captured her. That was a ruse as well."

Nodens grinned. "Ah, but she still knew that in his heart he would not allow them to do anything to harm her, so point of fact, he saved her. And she decided to repay that kindness despite the enmity between their species."

Nyarlathotep shrugged as much as a shadow of noble bearing could. "Very well, this test between the beings of the human world and that of the fae is done. Even I can be surprised once in a millennium."

When he was rested and felt well enough, Porter waved goodbye to the river, understanding that the water baby was watching him from her hiding place. He finally found his horse and rode on back to where he had slain the big monstrous cat. From there he could track himself to where he had come from. Finding signs of his passage wasn't difficult as no rain had washed away his trail through the tall grass. He glanced back once more and then rode down the trail.

Maybe he felt a slight tingle from the medicine pouch as he passed through that invisible gateway. The next thing he knew, he was in the red-rimmed slot canyon. Looking back, he could see nothing out of the ordinary. Nodding to himself, he rode on.

Porter came riding out of the slot canyon. To his astonishment, Bishop was waiting there, looking much the same as when they had parted.

"Guess I shouldn't be surprised you're here," Porter called out to him. "You must have had a change of conscience and decided to come on in after me. Only took you three hours to muster the sand." He wasn't usually so harsh with a good man like Bishop but after such an unbelievable adventure of horror, he had a bit of spite in him.

Bishop looked at him, then up toward the sun, then back to Porter and slowly shook his head.

"You only just rode into the canyon a few moments ago. I was waiting to hear gunshots or if you would change your mind."

"Few moments ago? I feel like I've been gone for at least three hours," Porter argued.

"More like three heartbeats."

Porter looked at the ground and read the terrain like a civilized man could read a book. Bishop had not ridden away from where he had left him. It had only been moments for the Ute.

Porter's own haggard appearance was also beyond what he might have been able to do to himself in that last few moments just out of sight. Each man took in the others version of events.

Porter just shook his head. "Maybe you're right, but I was still gone for hours."

"I believe you," Bishop said as he grinned. "With the legends I have heard about this canyon, you're lucky to have made it back at all."

Porter rubbed at his beard. "I suppose you're right." He tossed the saber-tooth to Bishop, who caught it handily, his eyes widening at the monstrous fang. "Maybe you're the only one that would believe my story anyhow.

The End

The Apophis Sarcophagus

A Captain Cross Adventure

By David Hambling

Chapter One

And I will show you something different from either
Your shadow at morning striding behind you
Or your shadow at evening rising to meet you;
I will show you fear in a handful of dust.

—T.S. Eliot, "The Waste Land"

Now I ride with the mocking and friendly ghouls on the night-wind, and
play by day amongst the catacombs of Nephren-Ka in the sealed and unknown
valley of Hadoth by the Nile.

—H.P. Lovecraft, "The Outsider"

London, 1928

The afternoon was golden, and the Crystal Palace Tea Gardens buzzed like a hive. Each round table had a parasol raised above it, all were occupied, and the air was alive with the tinkle of cake-forks on crockery and the murmur of polite conversation. As soon as a table was vacated busy waitresses descended to clear the crumb-strewn plates and empty teacups. The lengthening queue of waiting customers snaked back around the side of the gardens.

As he approached, Cross paused to lean on his stick and survey the scene. His worries about being lured into a trap had evaporated. This was no place for an ambush. He was more concerned whether his mysterious correspondent had the foresight to secure a table, or whether there might be an uncomfortable wait in line, or a wearisome tramp back up the hill to the less busy Sunnyview Café.

The handwriting looked female, and she signed herself "Seshat," after the Egyptian goddess of books and scribes. She promised an unmissable bargain of great rarity from the tomb of a pharaoh and gave the time and place for the proposed rendezvous. There was no return address. All Cross could do was turn up or ignore the offer. And the Captain was not a man to miss any opportunity.

He bypassed the queue and went in as though meeting someone. Three-quarters of those present were female, but only two tables were occupied by lone women. One was grey-haired, and intent on slipping morsels to the Pekinese on her lap. She did not give him a second glance, though the dog gave him a suspicious look. It was his gait; the step of a man with an artificial leg, walking with a stick , put them on their guard.

When the younger lone woman spied Cross her face lit up and she tentatively raised her hand, then lowered it. She looked away, then looked back to check that he had seen her. She would not, Cross thought, have made a good spy. She was young, which was not a good sign.

"Miss Seshat, I presume?" he said, speaking in a low voice and removing his hat.

"Yes, yes, sit down please—Captain Cross."

He sat awkwardly. Sometimes people assumed he was drunk; others, seeing the regimental tie, understood the reason for his clumsiness.

She was even younger than she looked from a distance, no more than twenty. Cross's daughter, who was a worldly-wise fourteen, would have said that Miss Seshat looked "fast." She applied this insult freely to any young woman who wore too much makeup and too little skirt, or who was too forward, too loud or laughed too much. Cross's daughter was quite the conservative, unlike Mrs. Cross who had been pretty fast herself once. The two regularly clashed over the issue of the New Woman; Cross stayed well away.

This particular New Woman wore a dress which, though not as long as it might be, was perfectly respectable. Her bobbed hair and the quantity of kohl eyeliner would have condemned her, though, and cigarette ends in the ashtray were the final damning proof of the woman's abandonment.

Cross thought she looked charming. He was very aware of the weight of the guns in his two coat pockets. Perhaps they had been an unnecessary precaution. You never knew.

A pot of tea and two cups stood on the table, signifiers of a modern woman who did not need to wait for a man to order for her.

"So pleased to meet you," Cross said. "When one receives a request to meet with an unknown correspondent, one never quite knows what to expect."

"I don't really know anything about you either," Seshat said. "I got your name out of a directory. After a sort of personal recommendation. Here, have some tea."

Her accent came straight from one of the better girls' boarding schools, flowing like a crystal stream. She might be a flapper, but not the sort who needed to work for a living. Now he noticed the turquoise and lapis lazuli bracelet around one wrist. An original, not a Woolworth's imitation.

She poured two cups, and dropped four sugar lumps into hers, one after another.

"Is there milk?" Cross asked.

"There's mint in it," Seshat said. "You don't need milk. Would you mind awfully telling me a little about yourself? How did you get into this business?"

Her smile, though awkward, was genuine. Self-consciousness made her endearing rather than intimidating.

"There is little to tell. I deal in rare old books, like so many others," Cross said. "Been in this game since the War, when a slight contretemps with some unfriendly Turks left me unfit for active service."

If he were talking to a man, at this point he would rap his false leg with his stick, a concise and effective explanation of his condition. But with a lady the gesture would have been gauche.

"But not just any rare books," Seshat said with slight hesitation. "A particular sort of book, I believe."

"My little niche is what one would broadly class as forbidden books," Cross said. "Matters such as heretical theology, deviant philosophies, demonology, the occult. And other banned subjects."

Many girls her age had never heard of pornography; others reveled in it. Some of the books that passed through Cross's hands were, or had been thought to be at one time, pornographic, and the collecting of expensive antique books of that type appealed to a particular sort of man.

"Good," Seshat said. "That's what I heard. Forbidden books. A rather.... specialized field. Whatever inspired that?"

"Well, now you're getting back into ancient history," Cross said. "When I was at school there was a regular trade in banned books of a certain type—what we used to call yellow literature."

"Naughty French novels," Seshat said, with a small laugh. "Smut for schoolboys."

She was evidently from that set which considered itself unshockable and heaped praise on books like *Ulysses* which appalled their elders.

"We all loathed Chaucer, Dickens, Shakespeare. But in the common rooms and dorms, there was literature which was read with avidity and exchanged like gold dust...."

He could picture them now, titles like *The Lustful Turk, Venus in Furs,* and *Mysteries of the Verbena House,* badly typeset on cheap paper but opening worlds of wonder and delight.

"It turned out that buying such books required no more than reckless self-confidence, which I happened to possess. I found that my best way to secure a supply was to become a dealer, allowing me to read everything that came out for no cost and even making a small profit—despite the attempt of the authorities to shut down the trade. One day in a certain bookshop, I came across something which had ended up on the wrong shelf, probably due to its yellow cover. It was my first encounter with the so-called occult, and was both disturbing and exciting. I sold it on at a handsome profit, though there were some complications." That was when Cross found that some books were dangerous. Not simply forbidden, or illegal, but dangerous in and of themselves, and that their contents had the power to shatter the health and sanity of those who were unprepared. "To cut a long story short, I became enmeshed in the world of forbidden books. When I parted company with His Majesty's Army, my interest became my occupation and my living. And so, you see me here now."

"I thought you might have become interested through being in some group, like the Golden Dawn," Seshat said. "I sort of assumed you'd be someone more involved."

"Involved?" Cross said, raising an eyebrow. "My dear, I could tell you stories about just how 'involved' I have been over the years that would make your hair stand on end. But anyone can tell stories, so I shan't spin unbelievable yarns."

"Well," Seshat said. "I don't suppose it really matters so long as you're reliable. I'm told you are, and I believe it."

"That's very reassuring."

Reaching into a bag under the table, Seshat produced a red leather cylinder embossed with a gilt glyph. A scroll case, the type used by museums and libraries, its wooden cap marked with the same glyph inlaid in gold and the numerals XXIII. Whatever it was, it came from a major collection, though Cross did not recognize the mark.

"This papyrus is what I want to sell," Seshat said, removing the cap and fumbling inside.

"Stop!" said Cross, overcome with horror. "You can't treat priceless antiquities like that."

"Don't be such a fusspot," Seshat chided, sliding the document out of the cylinder far enough for him to see. "My hands are perfectly clean. I've handled this lots of times. I suppose there isn't space on the table for it."

"Just put it away for the time being," Cross said, waiting for the hammering in his chest to subside. "Better if you just tell me about it first, we can move on to inspection later."

Cross was swiftly reappraising the woman. He had been expecting a widow wanting to sell off her husband's collection of "strange books," that was the usual pattern. Or someone else who had inherited something esoteric and did not know what to do with it. But this was a different kettle of fish.

"It's from the Third Dynasty," Seshat said. "The last king of that dynasty is usually called Huni, but correctly known as Neferkara or Nephren-Ka. You know him?"

That question, and more importantly the look that came with it, said she did not want to waste her time with an amateur who would not appreciate the value of what she was offering.

Cross permitted himself a slight smile.

"A much-misunderstood chap," Cross said, "but knowledgeable in his way."

Neferkara had been accused of necromancy and other abominations, but there was no good historical record of his reign. It might have been he was deliberately erased. He was supposed to have built a major funerary complex which had never been located, and his name was much bandied about in esoteric circles, usually by people who should know better.

"This papyrus is from his tomb," Seshat said. "It's one of a set containing ritual invocations formulated by Neferkara himself and dictated to his priests. The contents have only ever been seen by a handful of people."

"That would make it quite remarkable," Cross said. "If it happens to be true. But nobody is going to pay a penny without provenance."

"Provenance?" Seshat asked.

"A chain of ownership leading back to the source. I can't tell you how many fake papyri I've been offered over the years. You can't walk down a side-street in Cairo without some fellow trying to sell you a supposed find from a pharaoh's tomb, with some cock-and-bull story about how his grandfather found it one day in a cave. Forgeries, the lot of them. The good ones take original papyrus—a clerk's shopping list or a tax bill—and add some royal cartouches and a few ibises and pretend it's a great lost treatise "

"Oh," Seshat said, and this time seemed deflated. Surely, she had not expected him to make her an offer on the spot? Even the most optimistic confidence trickster would not attempt that when dealing with an actual dealer, rather than a naïve sun-struck tourist.

"So," Cross said, "why not tell me about its history, where you got it from?"

She colored and fumbled for words. If she was playing a part, she was making an excellent job of it.

"It's a family heirloom," Seshat said at last. "You see, my family was in Egypt during the Protectorate. In fact, my great-grandfather was quite an important person in the administration. And, because he had the opportunity, he collected antiquities. Without paying for them."

"Indeed?"

"Oh, he was as corrupt as they come," Seshat said cheerfully. "He'd send his police out to catch tomb robbers and bring back everything they found, let the robbers go and send them off to get more. He didn't care about all the murderers or rapists on the streets, but by golly he knew all about the tomb robbers. He built up quite a collection."

Cross wondered if that included her bracelet.

"They say most of the tombs were plundered long before Howard Carter and his fellows got there. Papyrus usually got used for wrapping paper. The robbers were after gold, so it's lucky it survived at all. And did your great-grandfather leave this souvenir of the Third Dynasty to you?"

"Well, no," Seshat said, laying her hands flat on the table and looking at them. "To be perfectly frank, I took it from my father's library."

"I don't know what you've heard," said Cross slowly, "but I'm afraid I can't very well deal in stolen property."

"Great-grandfather stole it in the first place!" Seshat said. "And this way it has a chance of getting back to the right people. I'll take a finder's fee, anything. Because, Mr. Cross, I really, really need money, because I really, really have to get away from my family."

"I'm sorry to hear that, but I'm not in a position—"

"Look," Seshat said. "What I was saying about the occult...they are practitioners, my family. Very active practitioners. But I don't want any part of it, or them."

He resisted an impulse to tell her to calm down. After all, she might have a great deal to be agitated about. But he knew better than to be drawn into family matters.

"Provenance is still the key," Cross said. "If you wish to remain incognito, clearly you will not be able to vouch for the origins of this papyrus."

"Clearly not," Seshat said, recovering herself.

"And there's no other way to validate it—" Cross said, and stopped mid-sentence. "Though there might be. The papyrus is one of a set—an incomplete set?"

"As a matter of fact it is," she said, her gaze sharpening. Miss Seshat was no fool.

"Well, well, well," Cross said.

Two years earlier Cross had been closeted with a London collector, a hermit whose whole house had been taken over by its library like a garden overrun by climbing roses. The ceilings were high, the windows were tall and narrow, and untidy towers of books grew everywhere, soon to be forgotten in the excitement of new acquisitions. He had wanted to show Cross the Liber Parva by Albertus Magnus, an unauthorized French edition of von Junzt, Paracelsus' Archidoxes and a litter of miscellaneous scrolls, including what appeared to be a papyrus from the Third Dynasty containing invocations addressed from Neferkara to Apophis.

"It will need a proper translation," the collector had told him. "The rough version I have suggests it may be evidence for a direct connection between Neferkara and the 'Black Man' of the European witch-cult."

That was the collector's obsession: finding a common source for all the different occult traditions. He believed that the central figure, represented as a goat-headed man of European witch-lore, was the same in every culture in the world. Cross, who knew how that chimerical figure wavered and shifted like a mirage the closer you came, suspected the quest was a will-o'-the-wisp that had led many scholars off on an endless road. And given him plenty of business.

"Will you sell it once you've had it translated?" asked Cross.

"I've no use for Egyptiana," said the collector offhandedly. "Could it be a useful swap?"

"Very much so," said Cross. The vogue for all things Egyptian, coupled with the upsurge in the occult, had created a booming market. "I'll just have a look and make a few notes if you don't mind."

He drew on cotton gloves to inspect the papyrus…

…And two years later Cross might have stumbled on more from the same set. It might be something else, but there was only one tomb of Nephren-Ka.

"What?" she asked, interrupting his thought.

Cross looked downward, at her ankle, at a tattoo depicting an eight-pointed star.

"Your ankle," Cross said. "The sign of Seshat, I believe."

"Oh *that*," Seshat said, raising her foot slightly. "*They* put that on me. *They* hate that I show it off, but tattoos are quite the thing right now, so why not?"

Cross unbuttoned his cuff and showed her the tattoo on his wrist. Three interlocking six-pointed stars, placed there by a shaman. He was about to explain its significance when he felt the stars itching furiously. That meant there was supernatural danger nearby.

A shadow fell across him. Cross felt a hand on his shoulder and looked up into a pair of blazing eyes.

"What are you doing with my sister?" the stranger asked.

Unfazed, Cross affected to ignore the man's tone.

"We were just having a chat over a cup of tea," Cross said. "She was alone, and was kind enough to offer a seat to a broken-down old soldier."

"Who are you?" he asked.

Cross stood, and extended a hand.

"Captain Cross, at your service."

"Jack Edmonds," said the other, responding automatically.

Cross shook hands firmly and held on for an extra moment while he weighed up his antagonist. Edmonds had the same dark eyes and dark hair as his sister. He was perhaps five years older than her, and of solid, athletic build. He might even have been handsome if he had been in a better temper.

When two Englishmen meet, there is a subtle exchange of signals. Edmonds had met someone older than him, and with a military rank, who might be of a lower class but was due a certain deference. A social inferior, but not one he could push around. His anger was redirected.

"You've got some explaining to do," Edmonds told his sister. "You're coming home right now."

The façade of independent womanhood cracked, and a frightened girl sat across from Cross, speechless.

"That's rather up to her, old man," said Cross, quiet but firm.

In reply, Edmonds grabbed his sister's arm and tried to pull her out of her seat. When she resisted, he slapped her back-handedly across the face.

That was enough for Cross. He brought his stick around smartly to strike the back of Edmonds' knees, hard. A Chicago policeman had taught Cross the technique, and it never failed: Edmonds' legs failed under him.

"Apologize to her immediately!" Cross roared, his stick half-raised.

Edmonds, on his hands and knees, crumbled as fast as his sister. He was no longer a man, but a boy, terrified of the blow about to fall on him, half-raising his hands to ward it off.

Around them all conversation had ceased, and twenty pairs of eyes were looking at them.

"I'm sorry," Jack Edmonds said after a second, perfectly self-possessed. Then, in a louder voice for everyone to hear, "I am sorry, Ellen. I lost my temper. That was very wrong. Forgive me."

Ellen, not Seshat anymore, mumbled something inaudible.

"Are you going to behave yourself now?" Cross asked.

The young man nodded, and Cross extended a hand to help him to his feet.

A waitress hovered nearby, perhaps about to ask them to leave. Cross gave her an amiable smile—*we're all friends here*—and asked for another cup for the newcomer. Edmonds brushed himself off and pulled up a chair, all the while looking at his sister.

Conversation started up around them again quite suddenly, a little too bright and loud. Nobody was looking in their direction except the woman with the Pekinese.

"My brothers are very protective of me," Ellen said to Cross by way of explanation.

"How very old-fashioned," said Cross. "I do assure you, Mr. Edmonds, there is nothing immoral going on here, just an act of charity. We had just discovered a shared interest in Egyptology."

Jack Edmonds' gaze moved now to Cross, looking him up and down.

"Quite a coincidence," Edmonds said coldly.

Cross buttoned his cuff and rubbed his wrist. The stars sensed occult powers the way the rest of his skin sensed heat, giving a vague indication of distance and direction. This man was the source.

"Coincidence?" said Cross. "If you believe the world is just a random jumble of happenstance, then maybe you talk about coincidence. In the larger world, we call it serendipity. Or something else."

Cross was enjoying needling Edmonds without seeming to do so.

"Is that so?" said Edmonds.

"I deal in rare books," said Cross. "And, at times, papyri, as I mentioned to your sister."

"Is that so?" said Edmonds again.

"It is indeed so." Cross slid a card across the table. "Your sister hinted that the family collection might be missing a piece, and I wondered if I might be of service."

"What did you tell him?" Edmonds demanded.

"He may know where the missing papyri are," Ellen said, and Cross felt a surge of relief that she was following his lead.

"I mentioned to her that I was looking at a piece purportedly from the tomb of Neferkara a while back. I believe I detected a certain interest."

"Hmm," said Edmonds. He was suspicious and looked down at the business card for the first time. "So, you're peddling something?"

"*Effendi* interested in historic papyrus," said Cross in a faux-Egyptian shopkeeper's accent. "Genuine first-rate quality antique, yes sir?"

Edmonds smiled sourly.

"He might really have something," said his sister.

"We don't want to tell everyone our business," said Edmonds.

"Discretion is part and parcel of my trade," said Cross. "You needn't have any concern on that account. Any discussion with my clients is in strictest confidence, and as of now I regard you as possible clients."

"How come you've found something when we've never managed to?" said Edmonds.

"I like to think of myself as a professional," said Cross.

"Who's the owner?"

"Come, come," Cross chided. "Firstly, I'd be cutting my own throat if I just introduced buyers and sellers to each other. Secondly, many other collectors don't care to let the world know they are interested in the occult either. And thirdly, I'd have to have a look at yours to confirm they were from the same set."

"You don't need to bite him, Jack," said Ellen. "He's just trying to make a living."

Cross adopted the complacent look of a man just trying to be reasonable.

"Well," said Edmonds, tapping the card on the table. "I suppose it might be worth looking into. You had me worried for a minute, Sis, but this might be a stroke of luck. Father will be very interested."

Chapter Two

Cross's dinner suit attracted looks from the café's clientele. His boiled white shirt, black bow tie and the collapsed top hat tucked under his arm could hardly have been more conspicuous among the cheap clerks' suits and stained overalls of the café's clientele. The ensemble might be a little shabby by high society standards, but not to anybody here. There was a sense of amused curiosity: they were waiting for their cue from the king of the Electric Café, who had not yet noticed his entrance.

"Good evening, Mr. Renville," said Cross, "I wonder if I might trouble you for a minute?"

Arthur Renville, the local ruler, was a cut above the rest. He might have been mistaken for a small businessman, or perhaps a bookkeeper, with his correct but old-fashioned suit and a carnation in his lapel. His business was the retail distribution of consignments of goods from the docks which have been written off by insurers. This lucrative trade required many hands at short notice and plenty of discretion, as the legal ownership was often open to question. Renville wielded considerable power in the criminal community and did not like any sort of disruption that might attract official attention, as Cross had discovered during a previous escapade. It did not do to annoy Renville.

Renville had been engrossed in a conversation with a companion. When Cross addressed him, he looked up, and seeing the Captain, his face split into a smile.

"Captain Cross," he said cheerily. "You don't have to dress up for us here at the Electric, you know."

"Thank you, I'll bear that in mind," said Cross, taking the chafing in good part. "As a matter of fact, I'm going on somewhere."

"How very topping," said Renville, affecting a superior accent. His companion, sensing Renville's wish, vacated his seat with a polite nod. "So, what brings you to our neck of the woods, Captain. Business, I presume?"

Renville was smiling as Cross sat down, but there was to be no small talk. They were not yet on friendly terms after Cross's transgression on what Renville must regard as his "manor" a few months previously.

"I've been invited for dinner up on Central Hill. Sir John Edmonds wants to talk about a papyrus."

"Sir John—That would certainly account for the get-up," said Renville. "Evening dress would be obligatory in those circles, I imagine. They're not much in town, the Edmonds. They have a country estate somewhere in the shires and just leave a housekeeper or two in the old place here."

"You're very well-informed," said Cross.

A cup of tea appeared in front of Cross. He recalled sitting in an Arab tent where the hospitality had been similarly formalized.

"Not exactly a *pied-a-terre*," continued Renville. "But you don't get privacy in a mansion flat in North London, and I hear Sir John likes his privacy."

"I haven't met him—do you know him?"

Cross's peerage had informed him that Sir John Edmonds, baronet, held large estates in Somerset, Lincolnshire, and Northumberland. He had lost his deposit in three elections and given up on politics, but was a Magistrate and Deputy Lieutenant in his county, and Colonel of a Home Army unit during the War.

"He drives past," said Renville. "I hear he gambles in some swanky places in the West End, but he wouldn't mix with anyone out here. Too good for the likes of us... though I do hear his wife ran away to the South of France with a jazz musician, and he pays her to stay away. So maybe not so very good as all that."

Cross had not heard that detail.

"I hope he can be trusted in a business deal."

Renville studied Cross and weighed where his interests lay in sharing information.

"As I say, he likes his privacy," said Renville. "They say the place is done up inside like an Egyptian temple. There used to be a maid who worked there, a local girl, who dropped hints about strange goings-on. She disappeared one night. The family said she's stolen some silver and scarpered, but we never got to the bottom of it." Renville leaned forward. "There's some people telling me wild stories about 'human sacrifice.' What would your professional view be on that, now, Captain?"

"Highly unlikely," said Cross. "But not impossible."

"I suppose you're there about buying or selling books about such matters?"

"Exactly so. I might be able to put a certain papyrus his way."

"And are you armed?" Renville asked.

"I'm afraid so," said Cross. "Nothing much though, just a little .25 for self-protection."

"Expecting trouble?" Renville asked.

"Let's say I have an abundance of caution," Cross said. He had some ideas of his own about the Edmonds family and why Ellen was in danger.

"I give you full credit for having the good grace to come and tell me about it," said Renville, leaning back as if delivering a verdict. "And for a man known for going about like a walking battleship, one little pistol is very restrained of you. Now, I'm not going to take you to task for bringing a firearm into this tranquil corner of the metropolis, and I'm not going to cut up rough about it. But I am going to put you on your word not to make trouble, to think before you act."

"You have my word as an officer and a gentleman," said Cross.

"Very good," said Renville. "If I'm frank, it's only because Harry Stubbs speaks very highly of you. Otherwise, I might not give you the time of day."

"First-class chap, Stubbs," said Cross. "I'm proud to call him a friend."

Harry Stubbs was Renville's protégé, someone he counted on for odd jobs—sometimes very odd ones. Cross had helped him on several cases, and vice versa. The former boxer was a formidable ally. Cross had half expected that Renville would insist that Stubbs went along to nursemaid him, as he had done previously, but apparently it was not necessary.

That was just as well; Cross could hardly turn up at Sir John's with a large and irretrievably lower-class pal in tow.

"Everyone around here—and I do mean everyone—" Renville glanced around the café, and beyond, " —relies on business running smoothly without undue interruption. Gunfights attract altogether the wrong sort of attention, if you catch my drift."

"Understood," said Cross.

"All I'm doing is trying to nip trouble in the bud, same as I have to do every day. The world is a drab old place, and having a few colorful individualists such as yourself livens it up. But I must consider the bigger picture. Every day, I just try to keep the lid on the chaos, keep things running smooth."

"I did not come here to disrupt your business."

"For Stubbsy's sake and mine—as well as your own—try to avoid any rough stuff. But watch out for that Edmonds mob, and a gun is a wise precaution for the just-in-case."

"Heard and heeded," said Cross.

"Incidentally, do I infer that you were here the other morning?" Renville asked.

"I had an appointment at the Crystal Palace, and I thought I'd better drop by, but you weren't in. I left my card."

"You did," said Renville. "Very correct. Not many gentlemen leave calling cards here. Mario was a little confused. A verbal instruction will do next time."

"Certainly," said Cross,

"Cheerio then, Captain," said Renville. A pleasant dismissal, but a dismissal.

"Pleasure to see you again," he said, but Renville was already exchanging hushed words with two confederates who had appeared at his elbow.

Cross expected one of the workmen to call after him on his way out with a fruity "Toodle-pip, old chap!" but there was nothing. Renville's stamp of approval was set invisibly on his brow, protecting him from all hostility, physical and verbal. A man coming in held the door back respectfully to let Cross pass.

Cross hoped that he would not disappoint Renville. Also, that he would survive the evening.

Chapter Three

Pins and needles danced across his wrist as Cross approached the grand house on Central Hill. The tiling around the front entrance had a scarab motif, the first sign of the family's love of all things Egyptian. Those protective scarabs looked more than just decorative; it looked as though the whole house was sealed against spirits and magical influences. Sir John really did like his privacy.

The biggest risk was ambush as soon as he crossed the threshold, hence the pistol concealed where it would not easily be found. He did not trust Jack Edmonds one bit.

Cross took a breath and reached for the iron knocker, shaped like a turtle. A liveried servant opened the door smoothly before he reached it though, and Cross stepped over the threshold without hesitation.

The servant took his hat, gloves, and overcoat. Cross held onto his stick.

A moment later Jack Edmonds himself appeared. He was immaculately dressed and met Cross with the absolute socially acceptable minimum of politeness. As he suspected, Cross was never likely to be forgiven for humiliating him at the Tea Gardens, but here Jack was on a leash and not free to bark or bite. The holder of the leash was now approaching.

The son was an arrogant bully, which set Cross's expectations of the father. Sir John's face was lined, he was greyer at the temples and thicker about the waist, and a little more commanding in his manner, but otherwise a match to the younger Edmonds. He wore a dinner suit with the relaxed air of one who dresses every evening with a valet to ensure every detail is impeccable.

"You're not a specialist on Egypt, Captain?" asked Sir John.

The three stood at the door to the dining hall, from where a low buzz of conversation was audible.

"Not at all," said Cross. "But a few items from the land of the Nile cross my path from time to time."

"Your name is mentioned in book collecting circles," said Sir John, making them sound slightly disreputable.

As an aristocrat he could look down on a commoner, as a colonel he could look down on a Captain, and as a man of means he could look down on someone who was in trade. As one with two good legs he looked down on one who walked with a stick. Now he knew he could look down on Cross on matters of Egyptian antiquities, completing the set, and seemed satisfied.

A butler appeared with a tray of glasses of the inevitable dry sherry. It would probably take another decade or two for pre-dinner cocktails to catch on in these circles.

"Let's take our drinks to the library," said Sir John. "I'd like you to take a look at something before we start, Mr. Cross. We'll need the family archivist—Jack, get Ellen."

"Is that her official job?" asked Cross, half joking.

"Everyone in the family is assigned a role from the Egyptian pantheon at birth," said Sir John. "A custom instituted by my grandfather. Ellen is Seshat, responsible for written material."

Cross followed his host to a spacious, book-lined room with two long reading tables. A papyrus was stretched out on each, the corners held down by paperweights in the form of coiled snakes, illuminated by a green goose-necked lamp.

"Captain Cross," said Ellen from the doorway behind them. "So nice to see you again."

Her words were as flat as though read from a script, giving no clue whether she was overjoyed or angry at his having accepted the invitation. She did not offer her hand.

"Pleasure to be here," Cross said briskly.

"Ellen tells me that you might have found the missing pieces from our set," said Sir John. "She thought casting an eye over these two might be enough for you to confirm it?"

"I'll take a look," said Cross, extracting a notebook from his pocket. He noted a slight twitch from Sir John. Had his host expected him to pull out a weapon?

"This is the Fourteenth Scroll," said Ellen, passing him a magnifying glass. "It is one of the best-preserved and has some of the clearest text. The other one is the Seventeenth Scroll, which has some very unusual formations—or at least, I believe they're unusual..."

71

Cross leaned over the first papyrus, careful not to touch it, and began to compare the hieroglyphs with what he had recorded in his notebook. Writing styles changed from century to century, and every scribe brought their own stylistic flourishes. The spacings and alignments of characters, their angles, the presence, or absence of figures in the margins, were all useful identifying marks. Mainly, they were an easy way to tell genuine originals from later fakes, but with enough time and patience they could confirm whether two scrolls were part of the same set.

There were more obvious clues. The dark snakes coiling down the margins were a perfect match for the ones on the scroll held by his collector. But it would not do to speak up too soon.

"Obviously Third Dynasty," said Cross. "Just as you said. The Eye of Horus here…and these characters are one of the later Pharaonic titles."

"They continue here…" said Ellen, indicating with a wooden pointer.

The hieroglyphs obviously meant nothing to Sir John, and after a few minutes of pretending to follow the technical conversation, he drifted over to the other side of the room to peruse *Horse & Hound* magazine.

"Why did you come?" Ellen murmured angrily when her father was out of earshot.

"You needed help," Cross said. "It was all I could think of."

"You can't help me!" Ellen said. "If they even suspect I'm up to anything they'll punish me terribly. I'll be chained up in the attic naked like great-aunt Cora."

"I understand," said Cross. "but that doesn't mean —"

"You don't." Ellen sounded bitter, angry, and upset, but still composed. "I can't get away from the family, not ever. Jack told me — they can follow the tattoo."

"There must be something we can do," Cross said.

"No," Ellen said. "And you're in danger!"

Her tone caused Sir John to glance up in their direction.

"Maybe so," Cross said, as though carrying on an argument, and pointed to a hieroglyph. "But that symbol is not a cobra, is it?"

"A horned viper," she replied. "It forms part of the name of a high priest—I read it as 'Neb-net-uru'."

Sir John returned to his magazine.

"It's the only mention of him," Ellen added. "It says the pharaoh had him executed for heresy."

"Such is the way of pharaohs," said Cross.

There was no further opportunity for private conversation, and when they had finished the inspection Cross was ushered to the grand dining hall.

The library and the hallway had been lit by electricity, but here it was all candlelight, with a chandelier overhead, candelabras on the dining table and dozens more lights set in niches. The tall shadows made the room look even larger than it was.

In addition to Sir John and Jack there were two other young men both groomed and polished to the same high gloss. Paul was Jack's brother, Jeremy was a cousin. Paul had a moustache, and Jeremy was missing the little finger on one hand, though he tried to hide it. Apart from that they were indistinguishable. They might have had blues in rowing, or rugby, or one of the other virile pastimes encouraged in university men.

Two other women were present in addition to Ellen. Dame Elizabeth was Sir John's sister; she wore a turban, and her face was set in lines of disapproval. Ellen's sister Margaret had bare arms and an absurd amount of silver jewelry, laden with amethysts. Her eyes were bright, and she smiled and laughed in a way that immediately made Cross think of drugs. But it was the room which captured his attention.

"It's quite a place," said Cross. "I've seen plenty of Egyptian rooms...but this tops them all. Better than the Egyptian Hall at Crystal Palace."

The great dining hall was a paean to Old Egypt. The wallpaper was patterned with Nile lilies copied from an original decoration, and painted plaster columns that imitated ebony pillars pretended to hold up the high ceiling. Instead of paintings, a large section of fresco, cut from some ancient tomb and encased in glass, hung on each wall. The two that Cross glanced at were familiar scenes: the Sun-God Ra setting out on his daily journey above Apophis, the serpent of the night; and Set in the underworld, battling Apophis.

Egyptian religion, and Egyptian society, was built around the idea of a divine order which ensured that the sun rose every day and the Nile's life-giving waters flooded the dry fields every year. It was the continual triumph of order against the chaos which Apophis represented.

More niches in the walls held a rich array of small sculptures and other items which Cross could not make out by candlelight. The floor was covered by several enormous rugs, and Cross did not doubt that every one was a handwoven antique worth a king's ransom.

At one end of the room was a fireplace and a full-sized wooden sarcophagus standing upright which faced them.

"I suppose it has become fashionable to imitate the style," said Jack. "But of course, this is all original."

How annoying it must have been for this family, which had so decorated its halls for generations, to find itself suddenly in the middle of a craze for all things Egyptian. Suburban families now had fake papyri hanging in the hall, miniature obelisks flanking their fireplaces, of course those ubiquitous miniature Tutankhamun sarcophagi of tinplate and ormolu, the largest of which opened into cocktail cabinets.

"What fashion demands, industry supplies, all in the name of profits rather than prophets." said Cross. "'Tis the great god Mammon—Syrian, rather than one of yours, I think,"

Margaret laughed brightly, and a few of the others smiled, while Jack frowned. It looked like it would be a long evening.

At least the wine was poured as soon as they sat down.

"By family tradition the first toast is always to him," said Sir John, indicating the sarcophagus. Cross followed the others in raising his glass towards it. "I'll tell you more about him later."

The sarcophagus had no face. Cross could not tell if it had been scratched out, or whether the mass of black lines where a face would be was the original artwork.

As Cross feared, the dinner conversation consisted of Sir John alternating between holding forth and cross-questioning his guest.

There were some quiet side conversations, but nobody else addressed Cross. Not that Sir John gave them much opportunity.

"Some people have got hold of the idea that my grandfather fell under the spell of Egypt when he arrived there, and that he dropped English customs and even religion to take up local ones," Sir John told him as a servant went around distributing soup plates.

"Funny how rumors start," said Cross.

"But theology was his hobby long before that, the book of Exodus and the tug-of-war between Moses and Pharoah over the Children of Israel. Jehovah smote the Egyptians with plague after plague to make them release the Israelites; but each time He hardened Pharaoh's heart so he did not yield. What do you make of that?"

"I'm neither a theologian nor a biblical scholar. But as a student of human nature, I'd hazard a guess that He wanted to increase the dramatic effect of His intervention. Twelve escalating plagues are more impressive than one. I say, may I have one of those?"

The servant with a basket of bread rolls had been about to miss Cross. When stopped, he smiled nervously and placed a roll on Cross's side plate with wooden tongs.

"Jehovah is the puppet-master, controlling Moses and Pharaoh and everything in between, putting on a show," said Sir John. "It all makes sense once you realize that."

Sometime later the soup—a very passable lobster bisque—had given way to a fish course of turbot with champagne sauce. Sir John still on his biblical exegesis. Cross was getting used to the sarcophagus facing them, menacing the gathering like a specter at the feast.

"One of the most telling incidents is Moses throwing down his rod so it becomes a snake to prove his power. A snake, mark you. Pharaoh's priests matched his feat, transforming their own staves into serpents. Rather odd, wouldn't you say, that worshippers of a false god should have the same power? Involving snakes?"

Cross, who had seen some remarkable feats without any divine involvement, merely nodded.

"Because the god of the pharaohs was the same as Moses'," continued Sir John. "Hence the similarity between the ankh and the cross, the parallels between Horus and Jesus, and a hundred other seeming coincidences…"

"I'm familiar with some of the ideas in that direction," said Cross, as close to interrupting his host as he could manage politely. Wearisomely familiar, in fact. There was no end to the religious crackpots with explaining how the Egyptian religion prefigured, paralleled, or supported the Biblical narrative.

"And that is what impelled my grandfather to Egypt: to discover traces of the original, uncorrupted religion."

"I see," said Cross.

"What the hell d'you think you're doing?" demanded Sir John suddenly, and Cross saw he was talking to a servant who had spilled some wine while serving Paul.

The man quailed but, wisely, did not reply, beyond a mumbled, "Sorry, Sir."

"The price of that bottle is coming out of your salary," Sir John told him. "And the cost of cleaning the tablecloth. Wasting my good wine! Benson, make a note of that."

"Certainly sir," said the imperturbable head butler, gesturing for the unfortunate offender to leave the room and taking the bottle. "A bottle of the '05. And a mark against his name."

Paul drained his glass and held it out to the butler, who refilled it with perfect steadiness.

"Can't get the staff," muttered Sir John. "Can't get men like Benson these days. Where was I?—the Book of Exodus."

Sir John went on to talk about the willful, unpredictable, cruel, almost random being and how he fitted in with Egyptian beliefs.

Cross, while listening with half an ear, noticed from the corner of his eye that while Sir John was talking, Jack put his hand on Margaret's leg in a decidedly un-brotherly fashion. She moved the hand away, but not quickly.

"In the afterlife, they say your heart is removed and weighed against a feather, and if your heart is heavier, you are damned," said Sir John. "Isn't that the very definition of caprice, leaving cheating as the only possible strategy for any players?"

"Capricious indeed," said Cross. The turbot was very good, and the white wine was excellent. He drank sparingly. Across from him the others were also restrained, though both Paul and Margaret's glasses were always empty and being continually topped up by the serving staff. Those two were set on quietly getting as drunk as they could get away with. Jack was more set on pawing at his sister, but shot the occasional venomous look at Cross.

"Can anyone looking around the world today really still believe in a benevolent deity?" asked Sir John.

"Some people seem to manage," said Cross. Politeness forbade him from telling Sir John that he was bored with cut-price imitations of the Manichean Heresy, that man creates god in his own image and that if his grandfather had discovered that the divine being was a cruel, unreliable bully then he was probably one himself.

"*Credo in un dio crudel*," said Sir John. "I believe in a cruel god."

"*Othello*," said Cross, recalling that the words were part of a creed spoken by the villain Iago to justify his villainy.

"Most religion is eyewash—bells and smells and empty platitudes to keep the people happy—but my grandfather was interested in the actual entities which the Egyptian rituals could contact."

"Entities you say," said Cross. "Not divinities."

"Quite," said Sir John. "Especially one being who is not necessarily divine as we understand the term, but who should be treated as such. One of inconceivable power, but vain, one who needs to be flattered, and placated. But who is absolutely, demonstrably real. As we will show you—"

Sir John sounded proud, excited, ready to show off the power of his brand-new motor car to a guest who had never been in one.

"It's still light outside," Dame Elizabeth reminded him. "These long summer evenings."

"Yes, of course," said Sir John, seeming to rein himself in. "We'll leave all that until after dinner. Now we will enjoy our roast pheasant and talk of other things. Have you visited Egypt yourself, Cross?"

"As a matter of fact, I was there a few months ago," said Cross, taking up his cue. "Alexandria is still something of a lodestar for the book trade—and a chap there wanted me to look at a copy of the

Colophon Aureus. It seemed pretty rum to me that he wanted to pay my fare just for a valuation, but there was supposedly this curse…"

The pheasant came with juniper sauce, roast parsnips, braised cabbage, and boulangère potatoes cooked to a perfection of crispness. It was accompanied by an unusually good Rhone.

Cross swapped stories with Sir John; nothing too sensational or unfit for the dinner table, and he was careful not to top his host's tales with more dramatic exploits. He did notice though, that Sir John's were all second or third hand, while Cross's stories all came from personal experience, though he attributed some of the more outlandish ones to "a friend."

The conversation took an unexpected turn when Paul, by now pretty merry, suddenly turned to Cross.

"Quite a risky procedure, having your foot amputated, what?" he asked without preamble.

"It's a matter of the lesser of two evils," said Cross.

"Still, dashed dangerous, what with the risk of infection an' all that. Gangrene, though!" He chuckled. "People still do it though."

"Paul is referring to a hypothetical case we were discussing earlier," said Sir John. "About how someone might remove a foot, if they felt they really had to."

"Why on Earth would they do that?" asked Cross. "It's a deuced inconvenience, I can tell you."

"Inconvenience!" said Paul, nudging Ellen. She tried to smile, but turned red and looked into her plate, obviously mortified.

"And if thy right hand offend thee, cut it off, and cast it from thee," quoted Sir John, looking at Ellen.

"Yes, if you decided your foot was unholy, you might want shot of it," said Paul. "But infection's a racing certainty without proper medical care, wouldn't you say?"

He looked about for agreement. Cross decided to take the conversation back to safer ground.

"As a matter of fact, I do know a man who cut off his own thumb with a hatchet once, miles from anywhere. He lived to tell the tale thanks to a case of bourbon whiskey."

"His own thumb!" said Paul with a laugh. "Careless, what?"

"Not at all. You see my friend was prospecting for gold in California, and his companion had gone for supplies. In those parts there is a notoriously deadly breed of rattlesnake known as the diamondback, whose lethal venom travels quickly from the affected site…"

The anecdote was a good one and drew appreciative noises from the men and gasps from the women at the appropriate points. As Cross suspected, the story prompted Sir John to tell a story of his own about his father's encounter with an Egyptian cobra, the fabled asp of the Nile. Cross did not believe a word of it.

They were back onto Egypt, it's fauna and flora, real and imaginary, when the elaborate trifle was served. An iron gate clanged outside as someone left. It sounded again a minute later and then again; the kitchen staff were departing, and the number of servants was dwindling. When coffee was served, and the brandy and port decanters set out next to the humidor of cigars, Sir John bade the butler good night and dismissed him.

Cross judged that he might have twenty minutes before serious business would begin. Between now and then he would need to excuse himself and transfer his pistol from its hiding place to somewhere more accessible.

"You might ask why any higher being would be interested in mankind," said Sir John, launching back into his main topic.

"It would be like a man wishing to be worshipped by ants," said Cross.

"Ants, yes, that comparison always comes up," said Sir John, a little acidly. "But rather than ants, perhaps you had better say we are His bees. If we collect honey for Him, our little world continues.

"Our ancestors believed that prayers repeated endlessly in a chantry would please the almighty. In the East they believe the gods love the smell of incense. The Mayans tore out the hearts of captives just to ensure the sun rose every day…they superstitiously believed it worked.

"Recall the ten plagues? We have had a world war, a pandemic of influenza the like of which the world has never seen, Bolshevism in Russia, a general strike…do you think these travails are coincidence?"

79

"Unlike Pharoah, Mr. Balfour is doing everything to help the Children of Israel return to their homeland," said Cross. "Jehovah should be pleased with us."

"You can be flippant," said Sir John. "The truth is, this world is burning. But my family has prospered—prospers—and will continue to prosper. I test my luck at the gambling table, and it always holds. Thanks to our family rules and the rites discovered by my grandfather, we are pleasing in the sight of the One who deals out catastrophes. The hand of chaos falls on others, but we are spared. Generation to generation."

Sir John sipped his coffee and looked complacently around the family group. It was not uncommon for the wealthy to be inwardly convinced that they were the gods' favorites. You just rarely heard it spoken out loud.

Cross was struck by the family likeness. The pharaohs married their sisters to ensure the purity of their bloodline. That way they would have suitable vessels to be reincarnated into, and their souls would endure forever. They believed themselves to be gods. Neferkara though, was said to have practiced abominations which were unspeakable even by the standards of other pharaohs.

"Some might call us depraved," said Sir John, seeming to read Cross's thought. "But how much good does their Church ever do those sheep? They die by the million, and we thrive."

Margaret giggled loudly, putting a hand over her mouth to try and stop herself.

"And that is why you want the papyrus," said Cross. "To better please Him."

"I'll give you a hundred guineas for the name and address of the owner of that papyrus, here and now."

It was Sir John's house, and his dinner table, and his right to talk about whatever he wished. But to raise a sensitive matter of business while the ladies were still present was crass by any standards. Far worse though, was the offer itself. Cross made light of it.

"That's very generous of you, but I'm afraid the business does not work quite like that," he laughed. "Many of my clients would be, shall we say, somewhat embarrassed if their little interests became public knowledge."

Sir John made an irritable gesture.

"How much then?"

He was trying to put a price on Cross's professional reputation, on his honor. Cross was quite used to dealing with men who were not gentlemen. He had hoped for better from Sir John.

"I'm sure that we can negotiate something with the seller that won't cost you nearly so much," said Cross. "It would be dishonest of me to take your money."

Sir John looked blank, as though a brick wall had suddenly materialized in front of him. He was not used to being thwarted. He had spent too much of his time on his estate, surrounded by servants, subservient tenants, lackeys, and his compliant family. Cross doubted that anyone had said no to him in a long time. He was puzzled rather than angry.

"The servants have gone," Dame Elizabeth reminded him. "And it's dark outside."

"Yes, yes," said Sir John, a smile lighting his face. "I will change your mind, Cross. Paul, Jeremy, Jack—the catafalque."

Cross had not expected that. Things were moving too fast.

Chapter Four

The three young men set up a wooden stand with folding legs, then reverently picked up the sarcophagus and placed it horizontally on the stand. It was a weighty object, although when Paul removed the lid, there was no mummy inside. The interior was densely decorated with hieroglyphs.

Sir John posed with one hand resting lightly on it.

"The word sarcophagus means literally 'flesh eater,' as you probably know," he said. "It was meant to speed the dissolution of the flesh. That idea was corrupted into a bizarre, misguided cult of bodily preservation and mummification in the later dynasties."

"So we are given to believe," said Cross.

"Mortal remains might be used by an enemy to torture the soul or perform other acts of mischief," Sir John continued. "Total disintegration is the only answer." He looked directly at Cross. "I don't think you're such a sceptic as you pretend to be. You've seen things. But this will astonish you."

The three younger men positioned themselves on three sides of the sarcophagus. Sir John took up the fourth side, and at his signal all four started up a low murmur. Cross could not make out the words, but on the second repetition they started moving their hands, palms down, as though warming them above a fire.

The three women sat still, mute. Ellen's knuckles were white, and she did not look at Cross. Lady Elizabeth was alert; Margaret looked dreamily into the distance, rubbing her leg where Jack had touched her.

If he had been younger and had two good legs, Cross could have bolted from the room for the front door before matters went any further. But the front door was probably locked, and he knew that behind the curtains the windows were barred. Instead, he sat back, sipped his coffee, and kept his eyes peeled.

The gestures of the four men standing around the sarcophagus had changed subtly. It was difficult to tell by candlelight, but they appeared to be snatching dust from the air and tossing it into the sarcophagus. After a minute, the air seemed to shift. The candlelight flickered for a moment and there was a faint whisper from the direction of the sarcophagus which grew steadily louder until it sounded like the hissing of a hundred tiny snakes.

Dust to dust…his wrist burned as though stung by a nettle.

A little learning is a dangerous thing. Cross hoped his host knew how to manage the powers he was summoning. He doubted it.

The chant faded and the four men stepped back. The hissing continued.

"Take a look at this if you will," said Sir John quietly.

Cross rose to his feet and came over to the sarcophagus. It was no longer empty. At first it seemed to be full of swirling black smoke, or was it liquid? Cross squinted and the liquid took on shape, resolving itself into dozens of snakes, each as thick as his wrist. But he could not see any heads, no eyes, or fangs, nor any tails. It was as though the thing was one enormous serpentine loop coiling around and around on itself.

"Primordial Chaos," said Sir John. "That from which everything arises—and to which everything returns."

Now Cross could see the very scales on the body glittering in the candlelight. Apophis, the serpentine symbol of night, was recognized as a deity, but there were no temples to it. It was the enemy of all order, all civilization, all life. Nobody worshipped it, except, if the rumors were accurate, Neferkara. Everything within Cross said it was unnatural, an unclean thing.

The hissing was continuous. It might have been from the coils rubbing together.

"I'm afraid conjuring snakes doesn't inspire the same kind of religious awe it used to," said Cross in his driest voice. "You can blame the music halls for that."

This was not Apophis, but perhaps some tiny extension or corner of it, a hint of a toenail, the shadow of a shadow. But Cross sensed danger.

With a superior smile, Sir John took a plate with the remains of a pheasant carcass and tipped it unceremoniously into the sarcophagus. The hissing intensified and the writhing forms became smoke for a moment as it closed around the meat which simply vanished. The carcass had not been eaten so much as ground up by a machine of rapidly whirling cogs.

"So-called holy communion unconvincingly turns wafer into flesh," said Sir John. "Our communion transmutes flesh back into nothingness."

He tossed in a second carcass, and a third, which vanished without trace one after the other. The thing's appetite must be infinite. Cross could not detect any change in size or shape.

"A good trick," said Cross.

"I told you it was the eater of flesh," said Sir John. "See how it moves."

The black surface had a hypnotic quality. Coils of scaly black slithered against each other in endless motion, but however close he looked Cross could not see how they were all joined and how they managed to move like that.

Cross felt something pulling him towards the swirling shadows. It seemed simultaneously to be completely flat and without depth, and at the same time to contain an abyssal depth. The draw was what the French called *l'Appel du Vide*, the Call of the Void , the temptation to throw yourself off a cliff or any great height if you approached too close. Except this was more powerful than the pull of any earthly drop.

Cross pulled his gaze away from the sarcophagus, and looked up at Sir John.

"Let me ask you again," said Sir John. "Will you tell me who has that papyrus?"

"I've already said—what? Get your hands off me!"

Jeremy had stepped close and taken hold of Cross' right arm while Paul had taken his left. They had moved in while he had been staring too intently at the seething form in the sarcophagus. It was the most basic of errors and now they held him fast.

"Search him!" ordered Sir John. Jack patted Cross down while the other two held him, but found nothing,

"Look in his false leg," said Sir John.

Clearly that little ruse was becoming well known and Sir John had heard the stories. But Cross did not resist as Jack pulled up his trouser leg and, after some fumbling, found the hidden compartment in the wooden shin. It was empty. Jack shrugged, empty handed.

"No weapon, Captain?" said Sir John. "That's most unlike you, from what I hear."

"You can't believe everything you hear," said Cross. "Are you going to offer violence to one who has eaten bread and salt under your roof?"

The rule of hospitality was a powerful one. The symbolic power of bread and salt could not easily be broken by one who followed the Old Ways. But Sir John laughed.

"We'll see! Paul, get a good hold of his left forearm so you can put his hand in it—he's going to struggle now. You wouldn't want to lose a finger like poor Jeremy, would you? That was a little sacrifice that had to be made."

Jeremy colored but knew better than to answer back. Cross did not struggle, not yet, but paid close attention to how his captors were standing and where they held him. They were both big, muscular fellows. Paul smelled of drink and was not alert; he was the weak link, the one to snap.

"A few years back Margaret was quite willful," said Sir John. "And I had to put her rabbit into the sarcophagus. Mr. Floppy-Ears went bit by bit."

Margaret made a choked sound which turned into another giggle.

"You'll never get away with this," said Cross, a line from a thousand melodramas which usually bought him a few seconds.

"You'd be surprised what we get away with," said Sir John. There was that rumor of the wife—probably not living on the French Riviera with a jazz musician—and that missing maid. And perhaps others. The sarcophagus would be an excellent way to dispose of evidence.

"Now, unless you're about to cooperate, your hand goes into the sarcophagus—and then I'll ask you again."

Cross had no illusions about them letting him go. They meant to disintegrate him, bit by bit or all at once. He would never be allowed to tell anyone about this. Was it revenge for humiliating Jack at the tea gardens, or was getting the papyrus the important thing? Or both?

Cross relaxed, preparatory to making his move.

"Let him go!" shrieked Ellen, throwing herself at Jeremy, stabbing at her cousin with a knife. It was only a table-knife with no sharp edge, but Jeremy let go of Cross to defend himself.

Freed, Cross promptly struck Paul's nose with the heel of his hand, pulling himself free and staggering backwards. Paul was stunned, unable to work out what had happened. Cross found himself off-balance and went back two paces before coming down on his backside. His prosthetic leg twisted at an awkward angle.

Fortunately, his stick was within easy reach, and as Jack came forwards Cross swung it and cracked him smartly on the kneecap. As the pain hit, he whacked the side of Jack's head, sending him reeling backwards. Jeremy was struggling with Ellen and Paul was holding his bruised nose stupidly.

Cross had won a few vital seconds. He fumbled at his shirt, sending buttons flying, tore it open and reached under his armpit to the small automatic held there with bandages. Jack was stepping forward again when Cross levelled the gun at him, and he backed quickly away.

"Everyone stay where you are," Cross said, moving his aim to Sir John.

"Shoot a man in cold blood—I don't think so," scoffed Sir John "Over a prank? Nonsense."

Sir John sounded as confident as ever. Cross noticed he was edging over so Paul and Jack would screen him from Cross's line of fire.

"Put the gun down," ordered Dame Elizabeth. She had extracted an automatic of her own from her handbag and was aiming it at Cross. It looked like a .22, and from her grip she knew how to use it. That certainly made the situation tactically more interesting.

Sir John was quite right in that Cross would not shoot an unarmed man, tempting as the idea was. Remove the old man and the others would give way. He was the kingpin holding it all together, though Dame Elizabeth might be more influential than she seemed. But Cross could not simply kill the man. That would make him as bad as them.

Cross might have tried to shoot out the lights. The chandelier was held by a single rope—but severing it would be almost impossible, and there were still plenty of other candles. There were no convenient boxes of ammunition or bottles of flammable material that might be ignited by a bullet.

Cross was never afraid to take chances, and he had noted one other possible target.

He fired two quick shots through the nearest leg of the catafalque.

Nothing happened for a moment, then the sarcophagus toppled over, spilling its contents. Cross thought it might spill out like black paint, but the contents remained in a compact, writhing form and spread out to form the shadow of a man on the floor. A shadow made of black worms. The entire company seemed to leap backwards, far more distressed by the liberation of the shadow thing than the shooting.

"N-n-nobody move!" shouted Sir John, his eyes wide.

"John, send it away!" said Dame Elizabeth.

"I can't," he said, anguished. "Just stay still, for God's sake!"

Absolute bloody amateurs, thought Cross. The very first rule of this sort of magic was never to call up that which you could not dismiss.

Dame Elizabeth fired three times. The shots splashed into the shadow without effect. She was a good shot, but directing pistol fire at what must be semi-material at most was the act of an idiot.

It was a thing of Apophis, of darkness. Gold, sacred to the sun god Ra, suitably purified and consecrated, might have some effect. If he had known in advance, Cross might have had an instructive session with a friend who was a practicing alchemist and brought a golden bullet. But all he had were homemade dumdum bullets, tremendously effective against flesh but useless against animated darkness.

"Take her!" Jeremy shouted.

Ellen was struggling with Jeremy, the two swaying together. Cross thought Jeremy was simply trying to restrain her, then he saw he was trying to throw her down.

"Take her!" Jeremy shouted again. "Leave us, but take her!"

"Jeremy, no!" Sir John said, but it was too late.

Jeremy partially succeeded in shoving Ellen down, but she caught hold of an armchair and stayed on her feet. Jeremy lost his balance, flailing, catching hold of the tablecloth as he fell. The cloth came off the table with a great clattering of plates and cutlery as Jeremy slid to the floor.

The Crawling Chaos surged forward, losing its human shape as a wave breaks and throws a sheet of water surging up the beach. Jeremy was on his hands and knees, and as the shadow broke around him with a rushing sound, he seemed to sink into soft sand. It was only when Jeremy tried to get up that Cross saw his hands and wrists had dissolved. Jeremy had only a moment to emit a cry of horror before he slid into the seething black mass, a sandcastle melting before the onslaught of the sea.

And then he was gone.

The black form hissed like sea foam dissolving on the beach.

Laughter rang out, loud and harsh. Margaret was laughing hysterically, viciously, gleefully rejoicing at the death of her brother. Lady Elizabeth slapped her once across the face, but Margaret only laughed louder.

"My god," breathed Jack, looking at where his cousin had been. Something silver glinted in the darkness.

"I didn't do it," said Ellen. "It was him."

"His own stupid fault," said Margaret, taking a step forward to get a better look at where Jeremy had been.

The black shape on the floor swirled, became a hundred shining black eels, glided towards Margaret. She jumped up onto her chair, giggling like a maniac.

Where Jeremy had been, some metallic personal items lay scattered—a cufflink, a watch, a cigarette case, a lighter. The rug was undamaged and the wooden floor unmarked.

The blackness stopped under Margaret's chair, formed itself into a shadow again, the shadow of a woman. Margaret moved her hand experimentally and it moved in response.

"Look," she said. "It's waving at me!"

"Stop moving," ordered her father through gritted teeth.

Margaret waved both hands and laughed as the shadow waved back.

It blurred and surged, and the chair began to sink noiselessly into it as though being lowered through a trap door on the stage.

"Oops!" said Margaret, holding on to the chair back.

Cross was taking advantage of the distraction to adjust his prosthetic leg, getting ready to flee. Margaret bent her knees. It looked like she was about to leap clear.

"Come on everyone," she shouted. "The water's lovely!"

Still laughing, she jumped into the seething black shape as though it was a pool, and with a flurry of limbs disappeared into the roiling surface. The laughter seemed to continue disconcertingly for a second after Margaret had gone. The pull of the void had been too strong for her…or maybe she had her own reasons for wanting a quick and easy death.

The sizzling rose to a crescendo and faded as the last of Margaret disappeared.

Sir John was the first to move, bolting for the door, followed by Ellen and Lady Elizabeth. Jack and Paul were slower to react and got in each other's way as they tried to get out the door. Paul ran into the doorframe and took a step back, but managed to get out as the black shape glided towards him.

Cross took hold of his stick, pulled himself up and staggered through the door that led to the kitchen. The shadow was pursuing the others and he estimated he had at least ten seconds. That was more than enough for a man keeping a cool head to find his way out.

The kitchen, pantry and scullery were large and well-lit, and the back door was obvious. It was also firmly locked. The key was nowhere to be seen. The windows were secured with heavy bars. As Renville had noted, the place was often left empty and had been made into a fortress against burglars.

Cross could not help noticing the protective scarab motif in the tiling around the door. The thing would not be able to leave the house…but at present, neither could he.

The front door boomed shut at the other end of the house.

Cross quickly retraced his steps to the dining room. A puddle of simmering darkness appeared in the hall. Cross froze, and watched the shadow cross the hall and slide underneath a door.

"Hmm," said Cross to himself, thinking fast, looking around at the candles, the litter on the floor where the tablecloth had been pulled off

89

the dining table, the niches full of Egyptian relics, and the sarcophagus on the floor.

Cross knew a few protective spells and charms, but nothing he trusted to keep a manifestation this powerful away. It would be like trying to stop a raging bull with a flyswatter.

The sarcophagus though…the sarcophagus was certainly imbued with power that made it impermeable to the Apophis-thing. Any port in a storm, as the old saying had it.

"Here goes nothing," said Cross, and stepped gingerly into the sarcophagus. Then he sat and finally lay down. It was a close fit. The sarcophagus had not been made for a large individual, and if Cross had enjoyed many more good dinners he would never have been able to get in.

He thought about pulling the lid over the top, but that would be altogether too final. Above him the candles cast an uncertain shimmering light on the ceiling.

A distant sizzling—wind in a grove of pine trees, the whine of a thousand insect wings—told Cross that the thing was approaching. The sound grew louder, and now it reminded him of machinery again, the spinning of many tiny wheels in some complex and dangerous apparatus.

It was not easy to judge the direction, but he sensed it flowing around, circling. The sound grew suddenly louder, a torrent of rushing water.

Cross felt like one of those daredevils who trusts a barrel to protect them from Niagara Falls, or who sets out to cross the Atlantic in a bathtub.

The sibilance rose to a crescendo as it seemed to race around him. He did not dare raise himself—there was no telling how far the protective effect extended upwards—but he felt sure the pool of shadow had surrounded the sarcophagus and was lapping in on all sides, looking for the slightest flaw in the hieroglyphic shield.

Cross held his breath, hoping the dry, ancient wood had not been damaged during the evening's events. The thick sarcophagus seemed suddenly very insubstantial.

After what might have been a few seconds or half an eternity, the hissing subsided. The protective charm held. Cross slowly released his breath.

"Well, here we are then," he said conversationally. "Not the most comfortable place to spend the night, but I've had worse bivouacs."

At least he was warm and dry. And Cross was certain that all he needed to do was to stay put for a few hours. Sir John did not know how to dispel the shadow but had conjured it many times previously. There must be some time limit, and Dame Elizabeth had mentioned that they could not start while the sun was up.

Cross felt certain that the serpent of the night could not abide sunlight even for an instant. As soon as the first rays of dawn arrived, the shadow would dissolve like a bad dream, turning back into dust.

The situation was unnerving to be sure. But with a little courage and fortitude, Cross would come out unharmed. He would hold back on his self-congratulation until dawn though. He suspected that the shadow, like so many emanations of chaos, was not simply a mechanical being but possessed a malign cunning and might have a few more tricks to play before it gave up on him.

The hiss rose and fell, and for a moment Cross fancied he could hear whispering voices inside it, calling to him. He blocked them out. Those were dangerous fancies, even if they were entirely imaginary, and infinitely worse if their reality were true.

Cross guessed that the shadow might be attracted to any flesh, living or dead, as it appeared to be heading for the kitchen. Maybe the Egyptian ancient priests used the thing to guard their catacombs. It would absorb tomb robbers for centuries, until they left an entrance big enough to let daylight in…

Assuming he could survive the night, there would then be the matter of Sir John and the rest of the Edmonds. Cross guessed they would have bolted quite some distance—they had probably gone to the station and taken a cab into the West End. They were rabble, Cross decided. The way Sir John had fled and left his family behind spoke volumes.

His musings were interrupted by noises from the front hall. He caught Sir John's barking voice, a female cry. Then a hefty boom: the front door closing again, and the clacking of the lock turning.

Chapter Five

"Captain!"

Cross's eyes flew open.

"Are you there, Captain?"

"Miss Ellen!" he called. "I'm in the dining room. Be careful, it's roaming about."

"My aunt forced me back at gunpoint," she said, glancing over her shoulder. "Hiding in the sarcophagus was a clever move."

"By rights the sarcophagus is yours," Cross said, moving to get up. "Where—?"

"I can hear it in the kitchen," she said. "You stay there."

"I can't possibly—"

"For one thing I'm far more mobile than you," Ellen said. "I always won running prizes at sports day. For another, I grew up here and I know every nook and cranny of this house. And thirdly, it's my own jolly fault."

She was back to being the independent woman. Gallantry would be wasted.

"Are there any other ways out of the house?"

"The French window in the drawing room is shuttered," Ellen said. "There's a kitchen door, but—"

"—also locked. Can you get out of an upstairs window?"

He had not paid much attention to the exterior, whether there were drainpipes that a person could shinny down. A young, able person.

"The problem is—" Ellen said, then darted a look towards the kitchen, from where Cross could hear distant waves. "I've got to go, but I'll circle back here."

Ellen disappeared back into the front hall, footsteps receding rapidly. The shadow flowed towards him from the door to the kitchen, now looking more like a compact block of army ants in the shape of a man. Thousands of legs rustled as it moved.

Cross hastily lay down again. The sound grew and faded, and human feet sounded on the stairs. It would be fatal to be cornered, but the house must have a back staircase for the servants. Ellen should be able to keep some distance between her and her pursuer.

In the quiet he could hear her movements, opening and closing doors, footsteps crossing the room above, and then the tread on a different staircase.

"It's not very fast," Ellen said as she came into the room again, cheerful but breathless. "So long as I stick to rooms with connecting doors I can get away. But no, in answer to your question, the windows are all barred." Her voice dropped. "I was prisoner here until I convinced them I would behave."

Cross was not so sure that the thing was always so slow. Being insubstantial, why should it be limited to a crawl rather than the speed of light? Why could it not split itself into two or more? It might be playing with them, or maybe it was sticking to some rules of its own devising.

"We need tools," he said. "Is there a handyman on the staff? Where does he keep his tools and suchlike?"

"Can't you shoot out a lock?"

"Not without an elephant gun. Are there any tools in the house?"

She tapped her chin, deep in thought.

"They keep them in the garden shed." She glanced up suddenly at a sound. "Oops, got to go!"

Ellen seemed calm enough under the circumstances. Perhaps a little too calm. One slip or trip and she would be ground down to atoms like her cousin—or brother, as Cross suspected—and sister. There was also the distinct possibility that the thing would change its tactics to catch her by surprise. In Cross's experience, even supposedly unintelligent summoned beings had a degree of malevolent guile. One could not afford to be casual.

Cross racked his brains to help her. If only the sarcophagus was bigger...

His mind went back to a similar situation, many years before. He had been trapped in the catacombs beneath San Roque with a slithering nightmare, quite different to the shadow but equally slow and remorseless. Two other members of the party had succumbed to the endless pursuit of the boneless, once-human thing. Cross, the slowest but wiliest member of the group, had survived, after correctly decoding the clues in the manuscript that had guided them there. Running around was seldom the answer.

This time Ellen went up two flights of stairs. That might be unwise; having found a circuit that worked, it might be safer to stick to it. She should be pacing herself for the long haul.

Then Cross remembered something. He could see it quite distinctly in his mind's eye: a telephone set standing on a table in the hall. Ellen and her pursuer would be gone for at least a minute. Cross raised himself, took his stick, and made his best speed, still not sure whether he was really remembering or if it was wishful thinking.

The phone was there, solid, and real. Cross picked up the receiver and spoke rapidly.

"Hello, operator? Can you put me through to West Norwood Fire Station please? It's something of an emergency."

It would never do to call the police, but Cross was sure he could concoct a tale for the firemen about how he had come to be locked in and get them to break the door down. It might take a little explaining, but…

"Operator? Hello?" Cross asked.

"Doesn't work," said Ellen, coming down the stairs two at a time. "The General Post Office has been been promising to fix it for weeks."

"Damn and blast," Cross swore.

"What about the kitchen?" she asked. "Is there any sort of acid or something that could eat through the bars?"

"Not likely," he said, shaking his head. "What we need is a hammer and chisel, a file, a crowbar—anything that might serve as one?"

She was leaning on the banister, looking up the stairs.

"There isn't anything," she said, and almost sobbed. "There just isn't! And it's coming down."

"What about the library?" he asked, making his way back to the sarcophagus as the fizzing grew closer.

The library was full of papyri which must contain everything they needed to know about the thing they faced. Given a few months, and perhaps some help from an able translator, they might find what they needed. All they were likely to get were a few snatched minutes.

95

As he lay back down, he heard Ellen ascending the back staircase. The sarcophagus creaked alarmingly under him. He had accidentally rested his weight against one side, and the dry wood protested.

White noise filled the room, louder this time. It grew louder still. As Cross lay rigid, he sensed the thing pressing up against the other side of his wooden fortress, inches away. It was seeking a split or crack, somewhere the hieroglyphics had been scratched or flaked off. This time it seemed to make a more thorough investigation.

Cross turned his head, scanning for any signs of darkness seeping through. How long would he have? If it started to come through, would he be able to fling himself clear? Probably not, but Cross was not the man to just lie there and be dissolved like an acid-bath victim.

The hissing continued, but no black tendrils penetrated the interior of the sarcophagus. Cross breathed again.

"No luck this time either, old chum," he told the shadow. "Cavalryman is off the menu tonight."

The hissing subsided. It was receding, going towards the servants' staircase, resuming its relentless pursuit of Ellen.

If there was a clear view of another house, Cross could try shooting out a window. That usually got some attention and brought the police around double quick. Renville would not like it, but this was an emergency. But the house was screened by trees; Sir John liked his privacy. Cross considered several other equally fruitless courses of action and discarded them.

"I'm certainly getting plenty of exercise this evening," Ellen said, but her breezy manner was unconvincing. "I'll work off dinner in no time."

"Does your father have an inner sanctum?" Cross asked. "A private study or a house shrine? Because that might also have a protective circle around it. Like the scarab hieroglyphs around the doors and windows"

"There's nowhere like that."

"Hmm. Well, do you have some scarabs here?"

The little beetles, carved from stone or cast from bronze or copper, were worn as protective amulets by all classes in ancient Egypt. With enough of them it would be possible to build some sort of barrier. The scarab represented a beetle that rolls the sun as a dung-beetle rolls its ball of dung. Sacred to the sun-god, it was the obvious symbol to repel Apophis.

"Two that I can think of," Ellen said. "One in the upstairs hall, one in the music room. Are we going to chuck them at that thing?"

"We could try," he said. He had been hoping for more; he expected to need more than two to block a doorway. As for throwing them, that was a desperate move. Protective magic was just that and could not be used offensively. But it was far better that she should be active and have some hope. Perhaps he might be able to think of something else in the meantime, even though it seemed that their avenues of escape were slowly being shut off one by one.

"I'll get them," Ellen said.

Cross's conviction they were being toyed with grew. And whatever Ellen might have to say about the matter, Cross's conscience would not let him lie back in safety while she was devoured by that thing. Of course, that was probably exactly what the shadow wanted, but he would find some way to fight it…he ran his eyes over the relics arrayed on the shelves, hoping for a miracle.

An urgent rapping attracted Cross's attention. It came from the dining-room window.

Ellen and the shadow were on the floor above. For a moment Cross contemplated staying put, given the risk of damaging the sarcophagus. If he left it now, there was a real risk that the wood might split, and he would never find sanctuary in it again. But he rarely took the safe option.

Ellen came into the room panting just as he reached the curtain. Each of her hands was closed around a small object. She opened them to show him two scarabs, one glazed green pottery, the other gold.

"It almost cornered me then," she said. "There was only one door, and …. What's that?"

She opened the curtain and jumped back with a small scream at the huge, ugly face looking down on her.

"Stubbs!" said Cross, delighted.

Harry Stubbs, former heavyweight contender, debt collector, sometime paranormal investigator, and agent of Arthur Renville, raised a hand and pointed towards the kitchen.

"Stubbs will get us out," said Cross. "If anyone can, he can!"

The sound of breaking waves from the direction of the hallway grew closer, and the thing rolled towards them like a rug woven of ebony snakes.

Without hesitation, Ellen bowled a scarab towards it with an underarm motion.

"Go back," Ellen ordered. "You may not pass!"

The thing recoiled from the scarab, and for a moment Cross was hopeful. But a second later it came forward and flowed around the amulet, as though the beetle was surrounded by an invisible glass globe the size of a football.

Ellen prepared to throw the second, but Cross was not waiting.

"Come on!" he said.

Instead of following him, Ellen went through the side door that led to the servant's staircase. She was distracting the shadow away from him.

Stubbs was at the scullery window, two hands gripping one of the iron bars at the base where it was sunk into the windowsill. He braced one foot against the wall and heaved with all his considerable might. The bars here were thinner than those in the dining room, but substantial.

"Get a crowbar!" said Cross. "You'll need some leverage!"

Stubbs, straining hard, managed to smile at him through the window. The stonework groaned and screeched, and two seconds later it gave way. By heaven, that Stubbs was strong. In the time it took Cross to open the sash window, Stubbs had loosened and removed a second bar.

"Be careful, Stubbs," he said. "Oh, damn and blast!"

Cross picked up the pieces of scarab tiling broken by the removal of the bars.

"I take it that's bad?" Stubbs asked.

"It makes things more interesting," said Cross. "But Stubbs, you're a sight for sore eyes! Did Renville send you?"

"He suggested I come over and keep an eye on the house," said Stubbs, now working on the third bar, and freeing it with a grunt of effort. "Which I did. He said you might appreciate some help round about the third act and this seemed an opportune time."

So, this *Stubbs ex Machina* was Renville's doing. Perhaps he had more of an inkling of how dangerous Sir John was than he had let on.

"Sharp fellow, that Renville," said Cross, then shook his head as Stubbs offered him a hand to get out. "There's a woman here too."

"Yes, I saw them throw her back in the house before they went off the second time," said Stubbs, sliding himself through the open window with remarkable agility considering his bulk.

Cross explained in rapid, clipped phrases about the flesh-eating shadow pursuing Ellen around the house, its powers, and limitations.

"For heaven's sake don't try to punch it. It'll dissolve your fist," said Cross.

"All we need to do is distract it for long enough for you and her to get out," said Stubbs.

"Yes," said Cross. "Except for the small matter that, due to the broken seal, the shadow can now also leave the house."

"How bad would that be?" asked Stubbs.

"It would be a massacre." Cross envisaged the thing gliding down the street, absorbing patrolling policemen, assimilating workers coming back from late shift, and consuming folk returning home from the pub. Or insinuating itself under doors and taking whole households. How many could it get before dawn?

Steps were coming down the stairs at speed. Ellen was in a hurry, racing down the corridor toward them.

"Don't wait" she said. "We have to get out, *vite, vite!*"

"There's a small problem," said Cross. "Stubbs damaged the warding around the window."

"Damn," she said, glancing back over her shoulder. "That's bad."

"It's coming," said Cross, as a dark shape flowed down the corridor towards them.

They were cornered, but the window was open behind them. There might be time for Stubbs and Ellen to get away, but there were not enough seconds for Cross to get out too.

Stubbs picked up a butcher's block, a piece of wood the size of a paving slab, and before Cross could tell him this was futile, flung it down on the thing as it advanced into the room. The shadow splashed like viscous liquid, flowing around the wood.

"It doesn't—" Cross started, but Stubbs launched himself forward and, using the butcher's block as a stepping stone, leaped over and down the corridor on the other side of the shadow. A hundred fingers reached up from the shadow, but too slow to do more than touch his shoe.

"Over here!" Stubbs shouted from beyond and waved his hands.

The shadow reversed its motion and slid towards him, forming itself into the shape of a large, bulky man. Stubbs, now in a boxer's stance, backed away from it, keeping his exact distance, and the shadow mirrored him.

"Out the window, Miss Ellen," said Cross, but she hesitated.

"What about you?"

"I have a better idea," said Cross, putting his hands to his mouth to make a loud hailer. "Get the scarabs, Stubbs—the little beetles! We can use them to block the window!"

"I'll try!" came back the reply.

Some seconds later from the dining room: "Might I have some assistance?"

Ellen was already heading down the corridor, and Cross followed. This was his show, after all, and it was his responsibility to see it through.

"Coming!" he shouted.

In the dining room a curious scene was playing out. Stubbs danced about as though facing a human opponent in the boxing ring. The shadow followed, more hesitantly than it had pursued Ellen. Rather than attacking Stubbs, it seemed intent on blocking him.

"It's not letting me get past," said Stubbs.

"Stand still, Stubbs," said Cross, leaning on his stick.

When Stubbs stopped moving, the shadow remained in place. When Ellen edged around to the further wall, the thing shifted slightly.

"It's trying to stop you from getting to the scarabs," said Cross. "If it goes after one of us, another one will be able to get them. If we stay still, so does it."

"The scarabs, or the sarcophagus," said Stubbs.

"Impasse, old boy," said Cross, speaking to the shadow. "But I think you'll find we can outlast you."

The shadow took the shape of a man with a stick but did not move. Was it his imagination, or did it pulse and seethe, as though thinking to itself? It emitted a low hiss all the while, like a steam engine idling.

"We can't get past it, but it can't get us without letting someone past. Do we just stay here until dawn, Captain?" asked Stubbs.

"That's the ticket," said Cross. "Just don't look at it closely, Stubbs. It's not healthy to stare into the Skagganauk Abyss."

"If it wants to get out, why doesn't it go while it can?" asked Ellen.

Cross shook his head. The thing was playing a game, and he did not understand the rules. There was something they did not know which was keeping it here.

"Do you think I might sit down?" Ellen asked.

"So long as you do it slowly," said Cross. "We have a nice equilibrium, try not to disturb things. Nice and easy."

She leaned over, and with one outstretched arm, pulled a chair towards her and sank into it.

"That's better," she said, stretching out her legs. "I'm bushwhacked with all this running about."

"Don't get too comfortable," Cross warned. "I don't trust our shadowy friend here one bit."

"Me neither," said Stubbs. "Don't go falling asleep, Miss."

"I won't," said Ellen, opening her eyes. "Much as I would like to."

"One of us could go up the back stairs and get around it," Stubbs said, looking at Ellen.

The shadow flexed, changed its outline, briefly becoming something like a starfish, then a tall man, then lapsing into an indeterminate shape. It sounded like frying bacon, a whole row of gas burners at work.

Cross had warned them against looking directly at it and had taken his own advice. The hypnotic swirling, the Call of the Void, was not something that one could be immune to.

Cross stole a look. A narrow filament of darkness, like a black tendril, was snaking its way from the nearest extremity of the shadow, winding stealthily towards Ellen down the edge of the rug.

"I say," said Cross. "Watch out!"

Ellen shrieked and jumped backwards in one movement, sending the chair flying. At the same time Stubbs took another chair and used it to vault over the shadow in an acrobatic leap, landing with a roll and crouching by the sarcophagus.

The shadow turned, a wave of breaking black foam rushing towards Stubbs, filling the room with hissing.

Stubbs did not hesitate. Taking hold of the sarcophagus firmly in both hands, he turned it over, so the open side was facing the onrushing shadow. Sweeping the box as though it was as light as matchwood, he swung it along the ground and scooped the dark semiliquid into it.

"Allez-oop!" Stubbs called, flipping the box over and, as the shadow boiled and lashed out with black serpent's heads, placed the lid firmly over the open top and stood smartly back.

Cross and Ellen both watched open-mouthed.

Cross could not quite believe what he had just seen. He replayed it over in his mind a couple of times before he was able to speak.

"Damned good show, Stubbs," said Cross. "Miss Edmonds, are you hurt?"

"Perfectly fine," Ellen said faintly.

"Will the coffin hold it?" Stubbs asked.

"Undoubtedly," said Cross. "So long as the hieroglyphics are intact."

They checked the sarcophagus for leaks, walking all the way around it. The interior fizzled and crackled but it seemed sound.

"Well," said Stubbs, rubbing his hands together, "That was a little hair-raising, and I nearly lost some fingers. I decided it must be staying because it was scared of us getting the sarcophagus and figured the rest out from there. You know, it has no weight at all. It's just black fog."

"Still quite a trick catching it though," said Cross, offering his hand.

"There's something else," said Ellen, approaching the sarcophagus. "My ankle tattoo."

"What of it?" asked Cross.

"As long as I have it, the family can find me anywhere." Her voice was sad and distant, and Cross felt Stubbs looking at him. He recalled that conversation about cutting feet off and knew what she had in mind. "They will not let me go."

"Now don't go doing anything foolish," he said. "Stubbs, restrain her!"

Ellen had reached over to lift the sarcophagus lid, but Stubbs placed a meaty hand over the cover and held it firmly down.

The hissing grew suddenly louder, as though snakes had been agitated.

"The tattoo can't be cut out," she said. "It's part of me. Believe me, I don't want to lose a foot, but if it's the only way I can be free, so be it. Please, Mr. Stubbs, you have to help me."

"Let's not be hasty," Stubbs said nervously.

"I don't believe it's very painful," she said. "It cauterizes the wound perfectly cleanly."

"Let's see what the Captain has to say."

From a certain view point she might be right. The shadow might be the quickest and most hygienic way to remove a limb. But Cross had a well-earned distrust of using supernatural powers to solve problems, especially when chaos was involved. Things always had a way of not working out as you intended.

He needed a counter-suggestion. When he opened his mouth, he did not know what he was going to say.

"Look here," said Cross, "you are the family scribe, are you not?" She nodded. "And you know hieroglyphics and more. I assume you know something about the tattooing process?"

"Obviously," Ellen said, "Since I was subjected to it. We did my baby niece last month. It's a ritual, there's a chant, and the ink and the needles are blessed—it's all in the Sixth papyrus."

"I don't see why you should not do some tattooing as well." said Cross. "With some help from us."

"Make a decoy or two?" said Stubbs. "Tattoo some sailors before they go off around the world? Those blokes will do anything for a few drinks."

"That won't work," Ellen said.

"But maybe we could modify your tattoo," said Cross, still thinking aloud. "Into...I don't know. Something else." He glanced around at the walls for inspiration, while Ellen looked at her ankle. "Their magic will not be able to find you. And if they find your jewelry on the floor —" he gestured to where Margaret's silver trinkets were scattered. "They'll think you were consumed."

"The pattern could be a lotus flower," Ellen said, tracing it. "Two points could be the stem and the rest made into petals. The star of Seshat would be gone."

"The lotus is a symbol of the Goddess Hathor," said Stubbs. His program of self-education was obviously progressing. "Representing music and dance."

"I suppose it could work," Ellen said. "Alright, we'll try it. I'll get the needles and ink, they're in father's study."

"Stay here by the sarcophagus," Cross said to Stubbs in a low voice. "Just in case she's trying to trick us."

"She isn't," replied the big man, but he stood sentinel by the hissing sarcophagus while Cross made a turn about the room. "But afterwards—what about you? They'll know you're alive, unless—"

"Oh no, I'm not afraid of them."

Sir John had proved himself to be a coward, as most bullies were. He was a dangerously incompetent practitioner of the occult and had lost a nephew/son and a daughter in one go. "I don't need to disappear. But if your Mr. Renville could find someone to fix those bars first thing in the morning before the servants come back it would be helpful. I will have mysteriously teleported myself out of a locked house using my mystic powers."

Cross chuckled at the thought. He would pen a thank-you note to Sir John for an entertaining evening, regretting that he had had to leave in such a hurry and suggesting another meeting. That would terrify the old fraud. A man who knew of the reality of occult forces but lacked the skill to control them would be most fearful of what an enemy might do.

"I'll ask Arthur," said Stubbs "You didn't shoot anyone, did you? No mess to clear up…he should be pleased. And I suppose we'll be able to tell him what happened to poor Miss Roberts."

"The maid, of course. I expect he'll be jubilant. His man rescued a fair maiden from an evil wizard and defeated the monster guarding her, saving the whole neighborhood."

"But I almost let it out…," said Stubbs.

"In the army, it was customary to omit that sort of detail in dispatches," said Cross.

The hissing from the sarcophagus seemed to fade, a pot going off the boil.

"Not that it is defeated," said Stubbs, contemplating it. "Not really."

"Of course not. With chaos, one merely postpones the inevitable." Cross poured himself a large cognac from the decanter. It was not theft; he was merely making up for Sir John's lapse in hospitality. "In any case, you and I were a side issue—snacks, beside the main course. For decades, Sir John's family thought they were the favored few. In fact, they were just being allowed to grow to a certain height before they were cut down."

"Because that was more fun?" Stubbs asked.

"Who knows," said Cross, sipping his brandy. "I was just picked as the instrument of destruction."

"But the family is still pretty much intact," said Stubbs. "Still just as dangerous."

Cross shook his head. Dame Elizabeth would be furious at the loss of her son. Margaret and Ellen were probably her daughters too; she might not mourn those losses so much, but the sudden depletion of the family was a disaster. Sir John was to blame, and Dame Elizabeth seemed handy with that little pistol.

He also suspected Ellen would not flee into anonymity. She had scores to settle with her family, and she knew something of the occult. Too much, perhaps. There would be more casualties to come.

"Hathor of the blue lotus also happens to be the goddess of vengeance," said Cross. "I suspect the family may have cause to regret not disposing of Miss Ellen properly."

The hissing from the sarcophagus sounded very much like laughter.

The End

Andrew Doran and the Curse of Nephren-Ka

An Andrew Doran story

By Matthew Davenport

Chapter One

A nd when am I supposed to do this?" I slapped my hands on the stack of papers on the edge of my desk. "These papers won't grade themselves and I have reason to believe that the Dean is going to send this entire university into another reality."

"W-what?" The small man on the other side of my desk looked confused. He also looked like a small breeze would knock him over. "Doctor Doran, I don't know how to impress this upon you, but this is an unprecedented find. I am not even certain that the Arkham Historical Museum is supposed to be in possession of it."

"You said it is a sarcophagus?" I hadn't really been paying attention when this wiry man with thin glasses had jumped me in the hall. I still wasn't sure why he needed me and had bigger concerns seeing as I hadn't been telling a story when I had mentioned the current Dean of Miskatonic University.

"Burial urn," he said. "Recovered from a previously unknown tomb. No record of it exists and we are concerned that it could be a fake." He pulled out a slip of paper, not for the first time, and waved it in my direction. "We are concerned that we purchased something that shouldn't be in our possession, and we need to know as soon as possible if this has been a scam, and we must go to our investors and beg their forgiveness."

"You want me to verify it?" This was annoying. The Arkham Historical Society had spent more than they should have on something that was likely to have been a mistake and now they wanted to waste my time fixing their problem.

"Is this something that you could help us with, Dr. Doran?"

"Call me Andrew," I said, as I rubbed my temple. "And I'm sorry, what was your name again?"

"Derek," he stuck his hand out robotically, "Derek Michaels. I am an assistant curator at the Arkham Historical Museum. It was our understanding that you were the Dean of Miskatonic. Are you saying that's not the case anymore?"

I shook my head at Derek but didn't look him in the eyes as I answered.

"Just a professor of anthropology, now." I didn't know this man enough to be sure if he would understand that an evil cult had managed to seduce the Board of Trustees and had taken over as the people in power, relegating me to being a teacher if I wanted to collect a check. Instead, I said, "Campus politics aren't my subject of interest. So," I moved the conversation forward, "you have an urn in your possession that was dug up and you're worried that it might not be the real thing? Do you know anything else about it?"

"If the person who sold us the urn is to be believed," Derek explained, "they recovered it from thieves in the desert just south of the Valley of the Kings. She tracked them from what she believed to be the lost tomb of the Black Pharaoh."

"The Black Pharoah?" The name sounded familiar, but it wasn't triggering anything specific in my mind. Then something nagged in the depth of my thoughts.

"Wait," I said. "Isn't that what they called Nephren-Ka?"

Derek shrugged.

"I would not know. That is why we need your aid. We would like to verify our purchase and better understand what we have."

"Why me?" I asked. "I have already shown that I don't know much about the Black Pharaoh, if anything at all. There must be someone in this department that has a better grasp of what you might have." I indicated the papers on my desk for a second time. "Or one who's less busy?"

"Of course," Derek was obviously dejected. "I only thought to find you per the seller's instructions."

"Instructions?" I was confused. "What instructions?"

"To find you," Derek explained as he pocketed the receipt again. "Their instructions were clear. If anything were in question, Dr. Andrew Doran of Miskatonic University was to be requested as a consultant at once."

My attention was piqued.

"Who was the seller of this mysterious urn of the Black Pharaoh?"

"Bethany Coombs," Derek said.

I met with Derek Michaels at the Arkham Historical Museum, clear on the other side of town, at eight o'clock that evening. It wasn't a lie that I had a lot of work to catch up on and midterms were not going to grade themselves.

It didn't matter how busy I was, though. I wasn't going to pass up on anything sent my way by Bethany. In the past, she and I had worked together on a hundred different projects and, for whatever reason, lives always seemed to be at stake. She obviously knew something that the museum didn't, and I was going to need to be the person to figure that out.

The other tidbit that caught my attention was that she had liberated this urn from thieves. Bethany and I only ever hunted artifacts and people who worked in occult circles. She had obviously dealt with the people, and that left me with the artifact.

The Arkham Historical Museum was a large building that received much of its funding from private investors and patrons of the school. The shared interest meant that the two organizations collaborated when possible. Mostly, that involved field trips for the students and free examinations of the artifacts for the university staff. Every museum was desperate to discover that they had a secret relic in their collection that would bring in many visitors from all around.

Unfortunately, this was Arkham, and the secret relics were more likely to melt faces and devour souls than to bring in large crowds. The museum was a single-story building with short columns on either side of the entrance. At this hour, the museum was closed, and the dark evening gave an ominous look to the place.

I had only ever been to the Arkham Historical Museum once before and I never made it through their entire collection. Living in Arkham meant, at the very least, that you were apt to have seen something odd. The city seemed to attract the weird and macabre at best, and at worst you didn't want to walk the streets at night unless you had memorized a few spells from the *Book of Eibon* or the *Necronomicon* itself.

It was obvious that the curator of the museum had seen some dark things in his days, but he took the same stance as the board of directors at Miskatonic University. They all saw these dangerous artifacts as something that needed to be on display, as if showing off these items was meant to say, "These are powerless. Please buy a copy in the gift shop."

There was something to be said about robbing magic of its power by teaching the truths surrounding it. It could happen and sometimes did, but that was never quite the case with the stronger and more potent magics. Sometimes telling someone about the cursed book just made them more excited to read it and tell someone else. Most of the time, the cursed book was waiting for just that moment.

The front lobby of the museum was gorgeous. It was wide open with a vaulted ceiling that was all glass. In the center of the room was a small desk with a chair behind it. As it was after hours, no one was sitting there. The exciting, and beautiful, parts of the lobby were everything surrounding the edges of it. The circular room had cuneiform tablets from the Mediterranean, stunningly preserved and on display. They were only receipts for shipping routes, but were perfect examples of the birth of writing in the ancient world. There were obsidian swords from the Aztec empire, shards of the black glass-like stone wedged between slabs of wood. A strong swing from one of them could take off an entire limb and they only served as examples of

110

how, if they hadn't trusted the Spanish, nothing would have stopped them from eliminating the invading forces.

So many beautiful examples of history, ripped from their original settings and on display in the Arkham Historical Museum, yet none of these were what they appeared to be. The cuneiform tablets held a small symbol on the bottom corner of each, referencing the early development and spread of Nephren-Ka's influence.

The obsidian from the blades of the Aztec swords were sourced from a meteorite that brought with it a poison that corrupted the life forces of a cenote west of Tulum, Mexico. The men who carried these swords became abominations that their own people had to destroy or risk letting their entire civilization fall two centuries too early.

Everything was darker in Arkham.

From the far side of the lobby came Derek Michaels, waving as I came in.

"Doctor Doran," his energy was both contagious and too much, "I am so happy that you were able to join us. Since our meeting earlier today, we have had several inquiries to look at the object in question. They were tenacious, but we made it perfectly clear that we needed our own liaison to confirm its provenance before we allow anyone to view the collection."

"Inquiries?" I was confused. If Bethany hadn't been the one to tell Mr. Michaels my name it would have ended there, but my confusion was laced with suspicion. "Who was asking about it? How did they even know you had it?"

Derek eyed me as my concern infected him as well.

"Now that you ask, I am not entirely sure. They offered to pay for a chance to inspect the artifacts. When we made it clear that you would need to review them first, the person on the line wanted to know who the archaeologist would be. I gave them your name."

I sighed. "Did they hang up?"

"Not immediately," Derek shrugged. "They doubled their offer for a showing as soon as possible and gave me a number to return their call if I changed my mind."

"Can I have the number?" I asked.

111

Derek went to the desk and scanned about until he saw the piece of paper he was looking for. He copied the number down and handed it to me. I eyed the phone on the desk for only a moment before shoving the number into my breast pocket.

"Take me to the collection," I said.

Derek led me to a side door hidden behind a collection of the *Pnakotic Manuscripts* recovered from an Australian dig that Miskatonic University had been on several years back. A few weeks ago, my assistant, Nancy Dyer, had been sucked into an alien world by forces outside of my control. She had been the daughter of one of the men who led that expedition for these manuscripts. According to him, it was an alien city of ancient origins.

The memory still hurt. I still planned on retrieving her the moment that I knew how to open a gate to that world, but my connections to the veil and its magics were closed off to me and my research had hit a dead end.

Shaking my head to clear the memories, I stepped past the display and into a long hallway. The ceiling was high to let in the odd, oversized artifact when necessary. Marks ran parallel on the floor where carts had been wheeled in regularly over the years. After less than a hundred yards, Derek turned and unlocked an unmarked door.

Inside were shelves covered with boxes overflowing with bags of artifacts, their labels from various places all over the world. Between the myriad shelving units was a length of tables for the museum staff to work on.

The closest table held an urn. To be more specific, it was a canopic jar. Canopic jars were used in ancient Egypt to store the organs of the pharaohs. At least that was what they were traditionally used for. There were the rare occult uses that the general public had no idea about. It was nothing to find spirits of long forgotten demons trapped inside the air-tight containers or the starved larvae of a Venusian traveler secreted away and awaiting resurrection at the hands of an unwary archaeologist.

Neither was anything that Bethany couldn't have handled on her own. As I stared at this seemingly normal piece of history, I couldn't help but wonder again at what horror she must have sent my way.

Even if it hadn't come from Bethany, the jar was already giving me a shiver up my spine. The lid of a canopic jar traditionally had a design, most regularly that of an animal or human head. This one was no exception. Its lid bore the head of a jackal, more than likely meant to be a likeness of Anubis, yet the eyes and muzzle of this creature were entirely sewn shut. The symbology was dark, yet a mystery to me. Was this saying that the jar was meant to seal in death or was it saying that the contents of the jar were something that could mute the gods? There wasn't enough evidence.

I approached the table and squatted, bringing my eyes level with it. There was a black substance that had leaked from the lid and had puddled onto the table. I followed the puddle to where it had dripped off. A pool of the stuff had coalesced on the floor.

I spun on the curator.

"I told you not to let anyone touch it," I pointed at the slime on the floor. "This is the exact opposite of what I told you."

Derek shrugged. "My apologies, Dr. Doran, but I can assure you that the standing order has been for these not to be touched. That," he paused as he indicated the same black trail, "stuff, whatever it is, was not there an hour ago when I came in here to reference another project."

Turning back to the canopic jar, I leaned in and sniffed it. The smell was horrid. It seemed to be a mix of excrement, a sour odor that made my eyes water, and some sort of plant material. The fact that the entire room hadn't smelled like this gave credit to the curator's statement.

"Do you mind if I pick it up?" I asked.

"That is why you are here," he nodded his approval.

Pulling a handkerchief from the curator's jacket pocket, I focused on not touching the odd ooze that had secreted from it. Aside from my earlier observations, it was clear that something was different about this jar than other canopic jars. Instead of the usual tan or light brown that the aged ceramics tended to have, this was a dark brown. Almost as if the color had been bled out of a black ceramic jar. The even distribution of the brown coloring disproved my first theory that perhaps this was obsidian glass. If that had been the case, many more questions would have been created instead of answers.

113

The entire thing was the length of my arm and just about as thick. It weighed as much as a vase about that size should, which had me concerned. I wasn't feeling any weight inside of it.

My first examination was a focus on the odd lid. While general studies in archaeology and anthropology had given me a good basis for Egyptian study, it was not my focus. I tended to spend more time on occult studies these days. If this weren't Anubis, I would be surprised.

Normally, there would be an airtight seal made from wax that would keep the contents "fresh" for when the pharaoh made his return. Except, this time, the wax seal was obviously broken. I looked over the outside of the jar one more time, looking for any sort of writing or indication of what its intended purpose had been and found nothing. There were no writing or labels of any kind. It was a smooth, oddly brown jar with a very ominous lid.

"If the scent of this gunk is any indication," I said, "then the inside is not going to smell pretty. Prepare yourself."

"Normally," Derek said with a smirk, "I would take the handkerchief from my pocket and cover my face. It would seem that I no longer have that option."

He covered his face with his arm as I pulled open the lid.

For reasons entirely nonsensical, I expected it to hiss or let out a gasp as ancient air escaped. That was not likely to happen, as the wax was already broken. The inside of the canopic jar was covered with the same thick, oily substance as was on the outside. The smell was wrong. It smelled rancid, which I had expected, but it wasn't rot. It had an odor of unnatural life, copper and fresh blood mixed with the horrible other smell.

The jar was empty.

"Are you certain that no one was in here?" I asked again.

Derek shook his head.

"That's a problem," I said.

"Why?" Derek's voice was weak as he asked.

I held up the jar to show the lack of contents.

"Because someone either stole what was in here," I explained, "or it escaped."

Chapter Two

"Escaped?" Derek shook his head, the disbelief on his face shifting to disappointment. "I heard the rumors, Andrew Doran, the Mad Archaeologist. Even so, you were the most highly recommended person in the entire Miskatonic University archaeology department. I figured that, combined with your being requested by our procurement specialist, meant that you weren't as mad as the rumors implied."

I surged forward, my eyes on the floor as I looked for more examples of the viscous brown slime. When I got closer to the museum director, I grabbed him and started looking around his face and neck for any points of entry a foreign creature might have made.

"We don't know what we're dealing with," I said as he yanked out of my grip. "What do you know about the Black Pharaoh?"

"Get off of me." Derek pushed away from me and turned toward the door. "This was a mistake. I am going to have to ask that you leave, immediately."

When he tried to turn the handle, the door was locked. "What?"

As he let go of the door, it shook in its frame.

"We're too late," my voice was quiet. "What do you know about the Black Pharaoh?" I repeated.

"Fine, Dr. Doran," venom dripped in his voice when he said my name. "I will play your game. Nephren-Ka, the dark man. The last pharaoh of the Third Dynasty, although that is contested by several other records. It is believed that he helped develop the hierarchy of animal headed gods."

"What about his deal with Nyarlathotep? Do you know anything about that?" I asked.

"The Mad Archaeologist indeed." A sad smile came to his face as Derek tried the door again. "The deal is only part of the very large myth surrounding his dark relationship with the fictional deity. Nyarlathotep promised Nephren-Ka the gift of prophecy, the only thing that all of the pharaohs craved, if Nephren-Ka slaughtered everyone in the city of Irem." Derek shrugged. "He did."

115

"That's not all of it, though, is it?" I asked. "He would later go on to defeat mortality as one of Nyarlathotep's avatars."

Due to recent events, Nyarlathotep was someone that I had done quite a bit of research on. A few months ago, the Dream Lands had served as a source for an ancient alien god to fill our world with some of our worst nightmares. At the same time, I was manipulated by Nyarlathotep into both saving the world and damning myself and my companions to a dark path. It was this manipulation and my subsequent research that led me to believe that Nyarlathotep might have considered me a prime candidate for one of his horrific avatars.

"I have a theory." I wasn't really speaking to Derek anymore, looking for another way out of the room as I worked through my thoughts out loud. "What if he didn't give him the gift of prophecies, so much as he gave him a … I don't know. A phoneline? Or maybe some other living thing in symbiosis with him?" I turned back to Derek. "Didn't Nephren-Ka think that he knew he was nearing the end of his life? Didn't he supposedly reincarnate years later? What if that was just this," I pointed at the canopic jar on the table, "whatever it is, being found by the next person? And what if it had a more corrupting influence than your average long-distance call?"

"Certainly, I am still playing your stupid game," the director said. "If that was the case, why hasn't anyone else found this 'telephone,' in the years since? While not everything is known about Nephren-Ka, there is enough that at least someone should have found his connection to the divine." He held his hands up in the air to indicate the lack of substantive news. "No new Nephren-Kas around."

"But we did find it," I argued. "Bethany found it. She sent it to you under strict instructions to find me." I pointed at the door that had seemingly locked itself. "And Nyarlathotep might be looking to acquire the next Nephren-Ka now."

I shook my head and returned to searching for a solution to our predicament. People like Derek were a dime a dozen. It would not matter if I summoned Nephren-Ka from the realm of the dead and had him explain what was going on here to the museum director. The deluded man was a part of the masses and ignorant to the darker realities living in the cracks along the sidewalk or just past his reflection.

The plaster wall behind the shelf furthest from the door seemed like a possible point of escape. I reached through the shelves and pushed. The plaster demonstrated some flexibility. I could work with this. "What's behind there?"

"Another room." He looked around as if to remember his location in the building. "The janitor's office, I believe."

My eyes went wide. "Was he here, tonight?"

"You and I are the only people in the building," Derek said.

"It isn't the people that I'm worried about," I mumbled.

Against my better judgment, I had left anything that would have been of use to me back in my office. It would hurt me spiritually, but what I did next had to be done if we were going to survive.

I pulled the shelf down. It crashed into the one across from it, knocking it and both of their contents to the floor. Bags and boxes of artifacts spilled out, covering the floor. A moan of despair rose from behind me.

A loud sigh was how I answered it. I had just undone who knows how many hours of work. The museum would be cleaning this up for days.

If we lived.

"Help me move this away from the wall," I demanded. "We're going to need some room."

"No, Dr. Doran," Derek turned away from me. "If anything, we should be focusing our attention on the door, not on creating new holes in the walls."

It was obvious that he hadn't looked at the door during much of our conversation.

I rushed toward the door, beating him to it before he could grab the handle.

My hands slammed against the door just as whatever was on the other side crashed into it.

I bounced off before scrambling back and pushing my full weight against it.

The door was not going to hold.

"Get the table!" I shouted at the entirely useless museum director.

Derek moved, slowly and with more confusion than assistance, to begin pushing the table toward me and the door. Before he got there, my battle with the door was already lost.

Another crash from the other side was all that it took. The door splintered with a loud crack and broke at the latch. The considerable force sent me into the air. I landed partially on the table Derek had failed to collect in time. I grunted in pain and slid to the floor as a yelp came from the likely still confused museum director.

"Thomas?" I heard him ask.

I rolled over and saw a man at least twenty years my senior come into the room.

His face was red with exertion, and he was gulping in air.

"Are you from the university?" the man asked me.

Aside from his exhaustion, he looked like the standard academic or museum employee, with a plain brown suit.

Getting to my feet, I brushed myself off and kept my distance from him.

"Yes," I nodded. "Dr. Andrew Doran of the Anthropology Department."

"I thought you were the dean?" Thomas raised an eyebrow.

"I was," I answered and chose not to provide any other information to this newcomer.

"Well," Thomas pointed at Derek, "I don't know what he told you or what you're doing in my museum, but that man does not work here."

Chapter Three

Derek's eyes went wide.

"Thomas, what—" Derek shook his head in an attempt to clear the confusion, "What are you talking about?" His eyes went to me. "Thomas retired and moved to Georgia a month ago. I bought you a watch."

"Dr. Doran," Thomas ignored Derek, "whatever this charlatan has told you is a blatant lie. He was fired for stealing artifacts two weeks ago."

I rolled my eyes in annoyance. I didn't care who was lying because the lie wasn't the words, the lie was the persons themselves. Whatever had been in the canopic jar was loose and either controlling one of these men, acting in place of one of these men, or some other horrific thing that I didn't have the time to contemplate.

"It would seem that you both have a lot to discuss," I said, careful to keep my distance from either before continuing. "I will return to the university and when you have this ironed out, perhaps you can give me a call."

There was no intention within me to leave, but I made for the recently opened door anyway.

The thing that called itself Thomas stepped into my path. "Your presence is still requested, Dr. Doran."

His face was passive, as if this were something that we all should take at face value, but it obviously wasn't. Derek hadn't even moved and was still wearing his look of confusion. He would have let me leave and perhaps chased after me in hopes of salvaging my visit, or to curse me out for wasting his time. Thomas had no reason to keep me here and had just identified himself as the impostor.

I was wary to touch him, but my options were limited. I leaped at him in an effort to tackle or push him to the side for Derek and I to escape.

Instead, when our bodies met, he started to absorb me.

Being consumed by a being not wholly of this world was, oddly enough, not new to me. A chemical breakdown and absorption of nutrients was how shoggoths, the bane of my existence, consumed their food. This was different. This didn't feel—yet—like I was being eaten. One moment, I was sinking into the mass that looked like a man in his late fifties, the next I was in a warm, dark space and could not breathe.

I want to say that my mind worked furiously to figure out what this creature was. It had been something small enough to fit in the canopic jar, only the size of an average vase, yet had somehow converted or replaced someone of a vastly different size. I would also like to say that once I had it narrowed down to what it likely was, the idea of how to defeat it sprung to mind and the thing regurgitated me onto the floor.

I would also like to say that I was able to fully eradicate the alien influence that held sway over our planet, and I could retire to digging Clovis points in the lower western states.

None of what I would have liked to say happened, however.

The reality of my situation was that I was suffocating and couldn't think beyond my own panic. There was a moment where a thought, entirely not my own, echoed throughout my mind as if in a shout.

"Wrong," it said.

Then I experienced what I could only assume was how bad food felt when it was regurgitated. There was intense pressure, a ripple, almost like a massage, up my entire body, and then I was ejected, much in the same fashion as I was originally consumed.

In hindsight, the telepathic complaint of my taste made sense. My many dealings with the alien influence over this world had left my flesh tainted with their magics, their energies, their ... ick, and many of their kind didn't enjoy the taste. There were some that would say I had become more monster than man over the years and given my recent adventures, I couldn't help but wonder the same thing.

The Thomas-thing was split from his hairline to his groin with an enormous mouth that coughed and gagged as I wheezed in gulps of air.

Derek was weeping.

I didn't have much in the way of time while the thing gagged to get the taste of me out of its mouth. I grabbed the bedraggled curator by the arm and dragged him toward the door.

120

In the past, before I had lost the use of the power beyond the veil of reality, people and monsters alike had referred to me as a wizard. That was not the case at all. I was a man who knew things—more than most, less than some—about how the world really worked and I was good at using that to my advantage. While the veil had been closed to me, that didn't change what I knew. When you close one book, you still have an entire library in front of you.

Or, in this case, a museum.

Never come at an archaeologist when he's in a museum.

"Wh-what is happening?" Derek was useless and I was beginning to think that not only was the museum director entirely innocent, but that he also had no idea what he had in his collection.

"What's happening," I said, "is that you have accidentally released an ancient creature of chaos into the museum." We rounded a corner and came out into the Egyptian exhibit. It wasn't exactly where I wanted to be, but safe and comfortable in my own bed wasn't an option. "Right now, it is weak. It just woke up and we need to stop it before it has its first cup of coffee."

Derek Michael stopped in his tracks. "I saw it eat you. How are you still ... alive?"

"I'm not very tasty," was all that I offered as an explanation. "Do you want to wait and see if you are?"

Derek took a moment to understand what I was implying and then rushed ahead of me. "What do you need?"

After all the cajoling of the mad archaeologist, it was the threat of digestion that got the director moving.

"I don't suppose you have a book specifically on how to bind an alien avatar of Nyarlathotep, do you?" I asked as I looked through the glass cases for anything that could assist us.

"Unfortunately, no," Derek said.

"Then, we are going to need to wing it." I waved my hand around at the exhibits. "We need a focal point. Something that we can use to channel our energies into the binding. We'll also need a vessel. The only vessel that we know will work is the canopic jar it escaped from." As if in response to my binding recipe, a loud crash signaled the beast behind us. It sounded larger.

"I'll get the jar," I explained. "The hand of a priest would work well for the focal point."

I wasn't entirely unfamiliar with the Arkham Museum and knew that they had the mummified remains of Har-shaf. He was nobody in his day, but his fame meant nothing compared to his faith. Finally, we came upon his corpse. It sat on a raised table, decorated with the usual meaningless hieroglyphs used to sell the exhibit. He was bound tightly and in a plain stone sarcophagus. When I say plain, I am not being glib. Har-shaf was no one of note, and if not for a small cartouche found on the base of his tomb wall, his name would have been lost in time.

The lid to his coffin was standing and on display against the nearest wall, for which I was grateful. I didn't know if we had time to remove it, or if Derek had the wherewithal to assist me. Skipping all ideas of propriety, I reached into the coffin, whispered a quick thank you, and tore off the priest's arm at the elbow.

"Dear God," the director gasped. "You c-can't. H-how d-dare you?"

Using the arm as a pointer, I gestured back toward where we came, indicating the large amount of noise that was crashing toward us. "Would you prefer we argue with it?"

Derek shook his head.

I thrust the arm at the director, and he took it with only a momentary hesitation.

"I am going to distract that … thing and get the jar. You need to find me a book or something with the oldest language in it you can find. Mesopotamian would be ideal." I started to turn and run, but then stopped, remembering something, "Not R'lyehian," I shouted.

In most situations, the words of ancient R'lyehian could do just about anything in magic, but we were talking about the avatar of a much older being. Something that old, that powerful, would laugh at the words of the dread Cthulhu's sunken continent. It would be like singing a nursery rhyme in front of a jury. They would give you an awkward look, but you were still going to jail.

Derek Michaels only stood there.

"What are you waiting for?" I shouted. "Go!"

Taking my own advice, I headed back toward the archival room. While the jar was my goal, I had to admit that I was still curious as to what this thing could possibly be. If my concerns were correct, I was also an avatar of Nyarlathotep, and this thing might hold some answers to questions that I didn't even know to ask.

I didn't have far to go. Where Derek and I had exited the archival halls and entered the Egyptian exhibit, the creature loomed.

It still held a mostly humanoid shape, but it now stood twelve-feet-tall. Instead of looking like a person, it reminded me of shoggoths that I had fought in the past. Specifically, a proto-shoggoth, their ancient and more formidable ancestors, with lumps of flesh and bubbling masses of oozing ichor covering it. In place of a face was only that impressive sideways mouth that had tried to consume me, having remained the same size that it had initially been. The avatar's hands ended in razor-sharp talons that dripped more of the chemical that its body was creating.

There were no eyes on it, or other defining characteristics. Only the mouth, the talons, and the sheer mass of the thing, but what more did you need? I still believed it to be some sort of alien parasite, likely to have inhabited the body of Nephren-Ka, but it had obviously not found a worthy host, yet. Perhaps it wanted to get its strength up before deciding how to confront this new and incredibly different world.

What I wouldn't have given for one of those Aztec swords I had seen near the entrance. The Aztecs weren't unfamiliar with the alien influences in our world and their swords had small amounts of magic to make them at least mildly effective against those powers. Even this many years later, one of those swords would be better than what I was currently carrying.

Which was absolutely nothing.

"What is your name, beast?" I demanded loudly.

It spoke, but its mouth didn't move.

"Avatar," it addressed me, "I desire no name, but if you require a need to address your assassin, you may call me Nephren-Ka."

The thing shifted, making me nervous, but it didn't advance. Perhaps it starved for more than just food and was looking for information as well.

"What do you want?" I asked. "Why do you chase us?"

Even though Nephren-Ka had no facial features, I sensed sadness in its reply.

"Trapped as I was, I longed for a chance to once again dance in the glow of the acid font beneath the maw mists of Roa La, while devouring the cartilage of the glorrkin tinge on the planes of the frozen moments. Home is what I desire, Avatar. That path is forever barred to me and, I feel, you as well. Instead, I search to fulfill the purpose that our god has demanded of us. Chaos. But, unlike you, I seek chaos through leadership. I wish to be the head of the torgtinu and lead this world to its fiery demise while riding a wave of corpses." I could feel a smirk form in Nephren- Ka's voice. "What is it that you seek, Avatar?"

"To better understand why you call me that," I answered. "You were declared Avatar and given purpose and design. I have been called many things. Prophecy called me the Bringer, your god called me an Avatar, and the people I serve call me mad. I am given titles without purpose or reason while I try and save this world from the likes of you," I paused before adding, "or myself."

"No purpose?" Confusion filled the mental voice of the monster. "The lord of chaos and fury, the messenger, gave you purpose by putting his mark on you. What greater purpose is there?"

"You speak of leading this world into chaos, but no goal was given to me," I explained, taking my time on every word to try and buy Derek as much time as possible. "He raised me from death and said nothing to guide me." I paused again, as I wanted Nephren-Ka to understand my meaning and to emphasize the next bit. "You also serve him willingly and with fervor, whereas I will do everything in my power to see this leash that he claims on me cut. I was the Bringer, and I put that prophecy to bed. Being mad has not deterred my course. Now, you call me Avatar, but here I stand, between you," I nodded over my shoulder, "and the world. If I work for him, if I am his Avatar, what does it benefit the lord of chaos for me to stand in your path?"

Anger was the emotion that poured off Nephren-Ka next.

"Yours is not to understand the whims of gods, Avatar," it spit the last word and actual spit leapt from the unmoving mouth and hit the floor. "If the messenger king demands you be his agent in this world, then his plan demands that you stand where you stand and I," every gross muscle on Nephren-Ka's body rippled in an alien flex, "stand where I stand."

This entire conversation had been happening while I slowly circled the thing claiming to be the ancient pharaoh. I hadn't made it any closer to the hall that it blocked, but I had been dropping something while I moved.

My hands were covered in the dry and desiccated flesh of a long dead Egyptian priest. That's the thing about dehydrated flesh. Any moisture, even that of sweaty palms from running from an alien avatar of Nyarlathotep, makes it stick to you. I put it away in my pants pocket and hoped it would be the difference between life and death.

Somewhere between where I started walking and where I now stood was a small trail of faithful flesh. Nephren-Ka's muscles flexed again, and it leaped at me.

"*Mg'nglui*," I shouted as I ran back the way I came.

R'lyehian wouldn't do to bind the beast, but I wasn't trying to bind it. The scattering of decayed cells combined with the R'lyehian word for "barrier," put a weak, invisible wall between us. Yet it was enough.

Nephren-Ka slammed into it with a roar of frustration.

I turned and sprinted back through the exhibit and, hopefully, the opposite direction of the museum director.

Chapter Four

I needed to get back to the archival room, but the damned monster was in my way. Instead, I shifted to the next exhibit with haste.

My goal was to find something that I could use to slow or stop the beast. To be completely honest with myself, I didn't expect to stop the thing at all. Slowing it down wasn't likely either, but I had its attention and leading it around seemed like a good enough idea until something else made itself obvious.

One of my ideas was to put us both into some sort of dream state. Every culture gave credence to the power of dreams and dream spaces. I had traveled to the Dream Lands on multiple occasions in the past, but I couldn't do that without an artifact or spell that didn't require me to use the magics of the veil.

A loud collapse of an exhibit behind me let me know that the parasite was not far behind. I needed to double back to the Egyptian exhibit. There was some hope that what I needed could be found there. Something other than the mummy's arm. Much of Egyptian mythology was steeped in conversations with the gods through the world of dreams. Unfortunately, most of those conversations were initiated by the gods themselves and that wasn't what I had in mind. If I was going to pull this thing into a dream world and battle it there, I was going to need to be the one making the call. It wouldn't do for Nyarlathotep to call us.

I didn't think he would be on my side with this.

Even if I could find something to traverse us into dream, I had to be specific with it. If I didn't have absolute control over our destination, we could end up in the Dream Lands, which was not a better solution than downtown Arkham. The Dream Lands were a universe inhabited by billions of lives and this fleshy construct would find a way to do the same amount of damage there, and it would only be a matter of time before it found someone who could bring it back here. Or worse, brought an army of the Dream Land's finest to subjugate our reality.

I covered the American Indian exhibit and considered the collection of dream catchers on display. I had seen wizards and shamans alike use the power of dreams with dream catchers to imprison beings of lesser power and the idea appealed to me. Unfortunately, I had reason to believe that this thing chasing me had more power than the dream catchers could contain. If it burned out, in the effort I would have spent too much of my own energy to attempt again or escape. The next exhibit dashed that plan to cinders as a new idea came to mind.

While the beast tore through the American Indian displays with no regard for the cultural importance of what it was destroying, I examined a unique display of the Knights Templar. Before the occult had fully consumed my existence, I had been obsessed by the Knights of the Cross and their adventures throughout the Crusades. They were a mix of heroes and bastards with as many moments of pure heroism matched by just as many of pure barbarism. As a young boy, you played either knights in shining armor or cowboys. I leaned toward knights.

The display in front of me held two things that might be of use. The first was a full set of armor. Metal shined in places where age had failed to tarnish it. Even through my fear and adrenaline, the younger Andrew's heart leapt in my chest in excitement at seeing the chainmail, helmet, shield, and, of course, sword.

I slammed my elbow into the glass and grabbed the sword. I knew from experience how to handle one, as, until recently, I had carried a non-commissioned officer's Cavalry Sword. This was heavier, but that might be beneficial against the thing chasing me.

The other thing in the case that I hoped would be useful was a bronze key. It wasn't this key, specifically, that mattered to what I had planned, so much as the lie that I intended to weave around it.

The mass of flesh, muscle, and talons crashed around the corner. He slid across the tile floor and slammed into the case that I had already broken. I swung the sword up and rested the blade on my shoulder while holding out my fist. In my hand was the key. I held it so that he could see that it was a key, but kept it mostly hidden.

For this to work, I needed the monster to think that this tarnished bronze was black. That meant that I needed this creature to be colorblind or at least not see it very well.

The thing righted itself and squared off about ten feet from my newest position. The tiles and the lack of friction meant that I could have a moment to escape if my plan didn't work.

"More tricks, Avatar?" Nephren-Ka's voice reverberated in my mind. I briefly wondered if it was a broadcast to all nearby minds or if this thing had the power to focus its attention on only me.

"What do you know of the Obsidian Key?" I asked.

Nephren-Ka's voice was steeped in mirth.

"I know that," his head tipped in the direction of my fist, "is not it."

Show time.

My features hardened with the rage I felt for this thing, and for all things that hoped to bend the wills of man and subjugate humanity as if it was a lower species. That rage focused me, and I pushed that focus into my half-truth.

"How certain are you?" I asked almost too quietly to hear. Quiet or not, I projected confidence with every word. "How do you know that I did not track down the *Historiae Tenebras*? Can you be certain that I didn't find the unmarked map in the *Book of Eibon* and compare that to the tales of the Dark Histories?" I let a smirk cross my face. "How could a puny human then take that knowledge and track the Obsidian Key to Greece..." I paused as I saw the monster's foot slide back from me. An indicator of fear? Nephren-Ka's talons scraped across the tile. Was it situating for a better launch at me or was my plan to actually scare the horrific monster starting to work? "How certain are you that I did not challenge the guardian of the key and fight the unresting Knights Templar?"

I pumped my fist in the air. "The key can send anyone anywhere with a simple wish. They had been banished by the church for trying to find a secret back door into Heaven, cursed to protect it as one broken beast made of six men. How do you know that I don't have the ability to toss you into the very pits of Hell itself?"

Nephren-Ka made no movements. A shudder, more heard than felt, radiated throughout the room. "Our god chose well in you."

"I could do it," I said as I pumped my fist again. "I could send you anywhere else, but I don't want to make you someone else's problem. I would prefer a more peaceful solution."

The vibration twisted into a chuckle. "A solution that saves your civilization, perhaps?"

"Something like that," I nodded.

"No."

"Wait, what?" I was caught by surprise. I thought this was going an entirely different direction. Hope that my stupid gambit with a bronze key would save all of humanity had begun to form and in that one word, Nephren-Ka had shut it all down. Nyarlathotep was a creature of chaos and he had also chosen well in this thing, his other avatar.

"Do it. Do your worst, Avatar. My lot is to rule, be it here or in the depths of whatever star that you wish to send me." Nephren-Ka wanted to win or lose spectacularly, and our world wouldn't survive either.

Well, damn.

I had absolutely no idea what to do next and did not have the time to sit here and figure it out.

That was when a bit of motion behind Nephren-Ka caught my attention.

The museum director was standing behind the ancient thing and was pointing to his left.

At a light switch.

This dumb plan kept getting dumber, but it was still the only plan that I had.

I thrust the key as high into the air as I could reach and shouted.

"Very well, but the pits of a star are not where you are destined to traverse. Yours will be to suffer in the darkest crevices of the largest black hole. You will rule over a realm of darkness."

Derek took that moment to hit the lights, providing me a much needed distraction.

Chapter Five

In my life, I have faced elder gods, serpent kings, the reanimated dead, ghosts from other universes, gods of nightmare, and horrors that shattered greater men and women than me. So, when I say that there's almost nothing quite as terrifying as a monstrous parasite charging at you while screaming alien obscenities with sword-like talons stretched out to kill me, you will have to take my word for it.

All those previous encounters had helped me fortify against the fear, but I still had an almost life-ending moment of frozen terror. To my credit, I came out of it and brought the sword up in a two-handed block that caught the beast's right appendage talons. I swept it to the side and rolled under the swipe of the other hand that would have cleaved me in two.

When I came up, I dragged the sword in an arc that passed through Nephren-Ka's left arm. Nephren-Ka twisted and kicked out, hitting me in the chest before I could bring the sword back down.

I hit the near wall at the same time as its arm hit the floor.

I grunted with the impact and watched as the parasite's arm released tentacles of flesh that reattached the arm. It swung at me with its right arm again as I managed to find my breath. The sword was in place just in time to protect me from the talons slicing through the plaster wall I was against. The force of the attack carried through the blade and threw me again. This time, I landed down the hall and further from the archival room.

Nephren-Ka must have enjoyed its rageful roars because it let loose with another one, this time opening its body-length mouth. The thing had no lungs or other features that would allow spittle to fly with its roar, but thick, gray globules of some fluid like what we had found in the bottom of the canopic jar dripped from his maw.

My breath was hard to catch, but I had already pulled an emotional response from this creature once and needed to keep doing it.

"Is that it?" I wheezed. "How are you supposed to subjugate nations when you can't smite one asshole with a sword?"

Nephren-Ka changed tactics, dropping to all fours, and running at me like a twice-sized bear.

I charged him. As we came within feet of each other, I swung and twisted the sword in my palm. When the point was aimed directly at the alien, I threw it like a spear. Nephren-Ka and I were moving too fast with too much mass to adjust our trajectories.

The blade hit the mark and pierced Nephren-Ka right where a human's brain would be. It tumbled, pain causing it to lose a step and grasp at the blade's handle while it continued forward, sliding across the floor.

My momentum was no better an ally than Nephren-Ka's. I leaped as it slid and struggled across the tiles to remove the sword. I wish that I could say my fall was with grace that I landed on both my feet prepared for a fight.

That was not at all the case. I landed on the thrashing Nephren-Ka with what equated to a bellyflop. Its feet came around with a talon piercing my thigh. I let out a scream of pain as it kicked up, sending me into the ceiling.

The ceiling buckled from the impact, and I fell back to the ground with more speed than I could prepare for.

The ground came up fast and my memory of what happened next was fuzzy at best and mostly nonexistent.

When I was conscious again, Nephren-Ka had figured out how to remove the Templar sword. It was holding something. What was that?

Oh, it was me.

It was holding me off the ground by my chest, one hand entirely engulfing my middle as though I was a child's toy. "You have failed, Avatar."

"Stop calling me that," I grunted through the pressure of my lungs being squeezed tighter than I would have preferred.

"If you did not have the taint of," it grunted an alien word that I had no translation for, "I would use you as my next host. Together, we would be mighty."

"Mighty stupid." I admit that was not my best comeback, but I had just suffered a head injury. Tainted or not, I was only human. "I doubt that you will curry favor with your god if you kill the current avatar."

131

"Current?" Nephren-Ka made that noise I associated with its laugh. "The Crawling Chaos has many avatars over many centuries. The fact that he chose one so weak and human is perhaps a test for me. Perhaps by wiping out the meekest of his chosen, I can curry more favor." Its grip tightened and all air fled my lungs. "Your death might grant me much power."

"Excuse me," a quiet voice said behind the monster, "would you be interested in this?"

Nephren-Ka's body shifted to take in what was behind it. I wondered what this thing used for eyes that it needed to adjust to see things. Behind it stood the museum director, Derek Michaels holding up his closed fist.

"Welp," Nephren-Ka said. "You will make a fine host."

Derek puffed his cheeks and opened his palm. A red dust puffed out and onto the surface of the parasite.

Nephren-Ka spasmed and jerked about wildly. It tossed me to the side and sent me skidding across the tiles back toward the archival room.

Before I was airborne, I saw the dust had caused Nephren-Ka's flesh to blacken and putrefy where it had touched.

Derek was beside me in a moment, pulling me up by the arm and leading me back to our preparations.

"What was that?" I asked, surprised that this seemingly useless academic had managed to hurt the monster.

"Chamomile that I had brought to have with my lunch," he said quickly. "I said a quick Hail Mary over it."

That made a surprising amount of sense. Chamomile was considered a sacred spice in Egypt. Even though the prayer might not have meant much, blessing it in any faith that was felt by the practitioner would have provided it with a power of its own. While the thing claiming to be the ancient pharaoh was really an alien parasite, things of our world powered by belief, faith, and the powers of dream tended to have a negative effect on the things that claimed the power of gods over humanity.

Like Nyarlathotep.

That being said, a sunburn wasn't going to stop Nephren-Ka. We would need to move quickly. I only hoped that Derek hadn't been having his lunch while I fought the fleshy beast.

"Thanks for the save," I acknowledged. "Did you find a word?"

Derek winced and my heart plummeted.

"Yes," his answer surprised me. "At least I think so. The word that I found was used for measuring out amounts of spice, yet when transliterated, it could be used by modern English speakers to mean 'hold.'" He pointed at a tablet on the table next to my already drying puddle of blood. "This here is a symbol that means 'pinch.' Do you think that this will work?"

There was a lot to be said about the meaning of a word in its original language and how we use that word in our current tongue. A lot of spellcraft was about symbology and words were just symbols meant to convey sounds and ideas. Symbols, much like ideas, change over time. If this word meant to pinch like we use it, as in a pinch of salt, then the original meaning, transliterated through our own internal interpretations of how we use the word could work. Either way, we were out of time.

"It doesn't matter now," I pulled out the desiccated hand of Har-shaf and used it to point at the canopic jar. "Grab the jar and some of the blood. Get ready to draw it on once Nephren-Ka is inside."

Those words seemed to summon our enemy, with its talons tearing the hole in the doorway wider as it stepped through and faced us.

Once upon a time, I could use my willpower to summon powers that no magician could counter. As that was no longer the case, I was worried about my part in the plan. Using the priest's hand was meant to close the gap in my lack of power.

I pushed my willpower out and into the hand of Har-shaf. I was rewarded for my efforts as I saw the ancient priest's fingers crack as they stretched open. Without hesitation, I aimed it at Nephren-Ka and focused my will on grasping it.

Har-shaf's fingers clenched and Nephren-Ka screamed.

The parasite lifted off the ground, floating as it began to shrink.

"The jar!" I shouted over the psychic screams of the alien. "Derek, prepare the jar!"

Nephren-Ka was not making this easy. Its will pressed against mine. The Crawling Chaos had no dog in this fight, and it was only one beast's alien mind versus my own. Will versus will required more power than Nephren-Ka could afford to sustain its bulk. As it shrunk, the raw flesh color faded to white, and its shape began to resemble a snake or worm.

The arm was growing hot in my hands as I turned my body, dragging it toward where Derek had heard my cries and prepared the jar. The museum director stood with the jar almost horizontal, waiting to catch the thing that had plagued our evening.

Veins of some sort became visible as Nephren-Ka continued to shrink. Or at least I thought they were veins, but they quickly turned out to be something else.

Each of them became tendrils that launched off the parasite and toward the only viable host in the room.

The tendrils stretched for Derek as he held the jar farther out, hoping to keep his distance from those probing arms while still doing his part.

As I brought Nephren-Ka closer to the jar, Derek couldn't avoid them. They latched onto his head and groped around the various orifices.

"Ignore it," I shouted. "We almost have him."

Derek tried to vocalize something of his disgust, but the tendrils filled his mouth and nose. We had to do this quickly.

The world was a dark place, and I wasn't naive enough to assume that the heroes would win and there would be no victims. Against this avatar of an ancient god, my assumption that failure was a likely option was just a realistic understanding of our situation.

So, at that moment, I made the potentially dangerous decision to divide my focus and memorize the symbol that the museum director had shown me. It was likely that Derek wouldn't be able to draw it once we had the creature contained and knowing it would be hedging my bets.

Nephren-Ka sensed my division of attention and pressed, filling my head with images of those who I had failed in the past, my assistants, my family.

Leo Dubois. My friend and assistant in my war on the unknown. Dead to our world, his soul is forever imprisoned in the Dream Lands. Imprisoned by me to save him from dying in our world.

William Dyer. My colleague at Miskatonic University. Driven mad by his studies and dead by the magical projection of my split psyche. His death was a tragic accident in an ancient alien city.

Nancy Dyer. She took the place by my side when I lost Leo and we fell in love. That love cost her as she fought to save our home from an invading alien god. I did not know her fate as she was locked away in the distant world of Hyperborea, perhaps left as the plaything of that same nightmare-inducing god.

The hand of Har-shaf failed me.

Or, more appropriately, I failed the hand of Har-shaf.

Nephren-Ka burst from my mental grasp and plunged into the mouth of Derek Michaels.

The museum director gagged, bones broke somewhere in his head, and I could hear flesh tearing as blood sprayed from my one-time savior's nose.

The release of the telekinetic grip was sudden enough to rock me back. My butt hit the ground hard, but I barely noticed as I watched Derek cease to be and the new incarnation of an Egyptian pharaoh who ruled absolute take his place.

Chapter Six

Nephren-Ka was using his new, blood-covered mouth to smile. It was a man now, if only because of its stolen form. It was somehow more horrifying than the creature he had shown himself to previously be.

"Poor Avatar," he used real words in Derek's voice. "You have failed."

Laughing at me, he looked down at the canopic jar still clutched in the museum director's hands. The same jar that was his prison for a thousand years and we sought to use to imprison him again. He crushed it. The shattered pieces fell to the floor of the archival room.

His eyes bore into me.

"Is there any feeling better than destroying one's cage?"

I raised the hand of Har-shaf and focused my will again. Har-shaf's fingers clutched at the air and I could feel the beast within the museum director gripped in my mind.

I pulled with everything I had. It was not enough. His hold on Derek Michaels was complete. He would not leave that body against his own free will.

Time for Plan B.

I leaped to my feet and threw the dead priest's hand at the pharaoh reborn. He batted it away as if it were nothing, but failed to see my fist coming in to connect with his jaw.

His head knocked back from the blow and I saw him take a step back in an effort to recover. I needed to keep him off balance if I intended to keep landing blows.

My left hand came in for his nose as he straightened himself, but the avatar of the Crawling Chaos would not be surprised again. His hand shot up and batted my own away with little to no effort.

Faster than I could bring up my next punch, Nephren-Ka thrust out his open palm and struck me in the chest.

I flew back, bouncing off the edge of the shattered door frame and landing on the floor between the archival room and the hall.

The Templar sword lay in the hall not far from where I had landed. Nephren-Ka must have thrown it when he had managed to extricate it from his flesh. I dove for it, standing and running back into the room.

Lunging forward, I skewered Derek Michaels, regretting it on a sympathetic level, but knowing that the man was no longer in there.

Nephren-Ka did nothing to stop my attack with the smile on his face never fading.

Pushing with all my strength, I drove him back. When he hit the wall that, only a short while earlier, I had considered trying to dig my way through, I pressed the blade through him and to the hilt, pinning him.

I released the sword and spun to grab the nearby table that had previously housed the canopic jar. With an effort, I slid the heavy table toward Nephren-Ka and shoved it into the monster. I had no fantasies that it would hold him for long, but I hoped that it could hold him long enough.

The entire time, Nephren-Ka was laughing at me.

I pulled the sword out of him and, in the same movement, swung it around and down. His arm fell to the table.

Remembering what had happened the last time that I had cut an arm off the creature, I grabbed it by Derek Michael's wrist and tossed it across the room. I could already see where the flesh at the cut was stretching out in tendrils to regrow the arm. It wouldn't be an instant fix, but my time to act was limited. The second arm took two swings before it fell off. I tossed that one too.

"Do you understand what they needed to do, the effort that it took for those hundreds of mortal men to destroy the body of Nephren-Ka, weaken me, and bind me to that vessel?" He hung his head, shaking it in some mockery of sympathy. "Cities burned, armies died, generations wept before I was weak enough for them to even try."

I bent over and scooped up a shard from the broken Egyptian jar and stepped up to the beast who had killed what, likely, had been a good man.

"Where are your armies, Avatar? How does the 'mad archaeologist' hope to succeed where entire civilizations have failed?" The blood dripping from his wide grin as he spat the words at me made him look madder than anyone had ever accused me of being.

Nephren-Ka's arms were already growing back. My time only grew shorter. I climbed onto the table and knelt to get a better angle.

"Do you know what I am wondering?" I asked the monster in a man's flesh. "I am wondering why they bothered pulling you from the body of Nephren-Ka in the first place. It seems to me like that's a step that can be skipped."

I grabbed the former museum director by the hair and held his head still. Using the shard, I carved the cuneiform word for pinch into the demon's flesh.

Nephren-Ka did not stop laughing, although I could see that where I had cut the symbol his flesh was not growing back. At least there were some limitations to his abilities.

"Because," he offered as an answer, "when I get free, I will tear this face off, destroy you, and find a new host. I am forever."

It was my turn to grin. "Then I will have to make certain that you do not get free."

The fleshy veins that had been the regrowing arms, flexed and slammed into the table. They were far from completed, but they were more than enough to toss me and the table across the room.

Nephren-Ka was not wrong. I needed to find a way to contain him permanently and, again, I needed to do it quickly. Preferably in the already dead body of the museum director.

Nephren-Ka was thrashing his new tentacle arms around, knocking down shelves of artifacts as he attempted to direct his rage toward ending me.

It was everything in my power to weave and avoid the attacks. Even with my considerable experience fighting, it seemed like forever before I was able to grab the Templar sword again from where it had landed in the thrashing and present myself as a worthy opponent.

With the sword in my hands again, I was able to remove the stump-tentacles again, buying another moment or two before he grew them again.

"All I need to hold you," I said between exhausted gasps for air, "is the Bracer of Har-shaf."

With that said, I turned and ran out of the remains of the archival room and toward the Egyptian exhibit.

I heard Nephren-Ka call after me in confusion, obviously searching his host's mind for what I could possibly be referencing.

"The what?" he shouted.

He would find no answers in the director's mind.

I had made it up.

Where I had failed to dig through the wall for escape, Nephren-Ka succeeded. As I rounded the corner toward the exhibits, Nephren-Ka burst through the wall in a shower of wood and plaster. He glanced at me in a fit of rage and confusion before racing ahead of me.

I chased after.

As I reached the exhibit, Nephren-Ka had already leaped up onto the casket and was digging through it.

"What bracer?" he bellowed.

Never slowing, I swung the blade as I ran by, taking off both of his legs. Nephren-Ka collapsed into the coffin of the dead priest. I hacked off both of his arms as good measure.

Then I ran to the heavy lid standing up nearby.

Too heavy, I realized. I couldn't move that. It would take at least three men to move that coffin lid and by the time I found someone to help me Nephren-Ka would be gone and wreaking havoc on my world.

Laughter echoed from inside the sarcophagus.

"Face your choice, Avatar. Now is the time to decide your role in this world." He was enjoying this as if it had been his plan all along. "No man could lift that lid alone. Do you embrace your destiny as the tool of the mad god, or do you let me free to collar humanity so that you can save your precious soul?"

There was no choice. Ask every single one of those people that the monster had forced me to remember. Those people that I let down and had left for dead or lost forever would tell you that I will always choose humanity over myself. Damn the consequences to me as long as humanity gets to continue.

I grabbed the lid that was leaning back, and forced it away from the wall and upright before closing my eyes.

I focused my will and looked toward the place where at one time I would find the power from beyond the veil. Instead of the odd alien energies that could drive a person mad, I found only darkness. The darkness was not empty. In it I could sense a presence, something that, when I concentrated on it, came to me as a strange and alien music. A foreign piping, carrying between the stars and bearing the weight of reality on it. From my own studies, I knew that what I heard was only my interpretation of a power beyond any mortal being's understanding. The reality of that song was much more horrific.

Then a thought struck me. Not from the darkness, but from the back of my exhausted mind. Why was it so easy to tip the lid?

I opened my eyes and forced my consciousness back to the here and now. Stepping back, I examined the lid a little more thoroughly. The damned thing was on a dolly. The wheeled cart had been tied to a stake in the wall, stopping it from rolling away, but otherwise, the entire stone slab was set up so that a lonely museum director could move the piece into place by himself.

Thank you, Director Michaels.

It only took me a moment to grab the sword and cut the rope. Then, with more effort than I had expected it would require, I put my shoulder against the slab of stone and wheeled it into place.

Once in position, I leaned it against the coffin. Nephren-Ka's tentacle arms were already regrowing. I could see nubs at the ends that would reform into digits if given enough time. He was beginning to use them to shift toward the edge of the coffin.

I took a break from my efforts with the lid to chop them off again. Now that I had him, I wasn't going to lose him.

The problem with the lid hadn't gone away, though. It had only shifted to a different issue.

The lid was still too heavy to move. I could tip it and let it fall into place, but the fulcrum that was the dolly would combine with the weight of the lid and break the stone slab. Then I would have no more options.

"All of your efforts are useless!" Nephren-Ka was spitting as he shouted at me. "Lay down and die if you will not take your rightful place as his chosen."

Only one option was still available to me. The same option that was always there. Again, I would damn my soul, but when Leo died, I had stopped an ancient horror. When William had died, I had killed my madness and set my soul free.

And when Nancy had been pulled into the horrible cold of an alternate world, she had saved all of reality from a god of reality-warping nightmares.

"Derek," I shouted back at the monster, "he hasn't had the time to completely burn you out of there. Not yet." I was pleading with the dead director. "Help me save Arkham. Help me move the lid into place. We can still bind him."

Nephren-Ka's yelling quieted. "Poor Avatar. He is gone. I have consumed him entirely."

The beast's tentacle, already growing back, reached down and underneath itself. My frustration was flooding me with defeat.

"Please," I started to say when the tentacle came back up and threw something at me.

The other hand of Har-shaf. It hit my chest and I caught it and then realized what had just happened.

"You're a genius," I shouted, before turning back toward the lid and focusing my will through the dead priest's hand and Derek's last gift to our reality.

Nephren-Ka wasn't laughing any more.

The lid to the sarcophagus of Nephren-Ka lifted into the air, only inches at first. Then the dolly fell away, clanging to the floor. The noise almost made me lose my mental grip on the stone lid, but I stopped it from slamming down and instead guided it gently into place.

When the lid was in place and I could no longer hear the ancient pharaoh, I dropped the hand and used the sword one more time to cut a fresh wound into my palm. I leaped on top of the coffin and used my blood to write 'pinch' in cuneiform. Then I collapsed to the floor and laid there for probably way longer than I should have. I had a lot of very heavy thoughts to consider and the silence of the museum at night became an echo chamber for my fears.

How close had I come to giving up my humanity and my ties to this world? How warped would my perceptions become if I had? Would I turn into the next Nephren-Ka? Would dipping into the powers offered by Nyarlathotep condemn my soul or had my soul already been condemned?

Perhaps it was, but there was no reason to race down the hill of the damned if I was already gently sliding down it. They were dark thoughts, and in the end I decided that I was still me and remained as free as I ever had been from the influence of the Crawling Chaos. Some day he will come and collect what he thinks is his, and hopefully I will have the strength to say no.

I had to call my former secretary and friend, Carol Berg, to assist in the cleanup of the museum. She was the only person I knew of that had the resources and that I could trust with this kind of thing.

Unfortunately, I had to cover up what amounted to a murder. I also had to make certain that Har-shaf's sarcophagus never came into contact with anyone else.

Carol forged some papers that showed that the museum was loaning the sarcophagus of Har-shaf to Miskatonic University's archaeology department to conduct research into a recently discovered connection between Har-shaf and the pharaoh, Nephren-Ka.

While she organized the clandestine movement of the sarcophagus to a more secure location, I did the most despicable thing I have ever done.

I poured out several bottles of booze down the sink, after finishing one, of course. There was no way I was going to do this sober. Then I walked around the museum and left a bottle here, a bottle there, and threw two of them into the archival room so that they shattered and matched the recent redecoration.

When I was done, I went to the office of the museum director. I placed a bottle there and found a glass in the desk. I set it up so that it looked like Derek Michaels had been drinking in the office. Then I pulled out his typewriter and wrote a very short note.

It is too much for one man.

Thomas understands.

Formerly,

D. Michaels.

It was horrible. I was tarnishing the reputation of a man who had saved this world in his last moments. From beyond the grave, he had stopped the avatar of the Crawling Chaos and I was implying he had surrendered to the weight of his responsibilities.

Thanks to Derek Michaels, the world was free from the sway of an ultimate evil. I thanked him by sacrificing the last of who he was so that the world could sleep at night.

Perhaps I had sold my soul after all.

The End

Blackwood Relic

By Andrea Pearson

Travis Blackwood hurried to finish hooking the plow to the tractor, refusing to allow even the trees from the forest to distract him from his chores. He was already late, and Pa would tan his hide if he didn't get the fields done today.

He couldn't help but cast a worried glance at the forest before hopping up onto the seat, though. The shadows were deep and long, even with the bright sun overhead, and he was glad Pa and Ma forbade him from ever entering that forest.

Travis was in a hurry for another reason, though. Cassidy, his girlfriend, was coming over in a few hours, and he wanted to be done before she got there.

Throwing the stick into gear, he pulled onto the field. Once he settled into the familiar motion, he started to daydream, and all thoughts of the forest skittered from his mind.

Cassidy … He sighed, grinning stupidly as the bumpy ride shifted him back and forth on the tractor seat. *She is so purdy she could make a hound dog smile. Besides that, she is the best thing that ever happened to me. Boy, I sure love her, and I'm gonna marry her.* He still couldn't believe he'd somehow snagged her. And not just her attention; her *heart*.

Travis frowned. Pa and Ma wouldn't like that news. Pa didn't have anyone else to help with the farm, and Ma had always been way too protective of Travis. In fact, he knew she'd be real upset to find out he even had a girlfriend. She and Pa had always been so bossy about the girls he dated. It drove him nuts. Why they got to have a say in such a big part of his life was beyond him. And so, he'd held off on telling them about Cassidy as long as possible—he wanted to enjoy the relationship before they tried to ruin it.

On the other hand, he also couldn't wait to introduce her to them. They'd be so surprised that he, scrawny Travis, could get a girl like her.

Well, he *could*. And he *had*.

A sudden bump jolted Travis from his daydreams, and the grinding that followed was rough enough to make his teeth chatter. The tractor stopped moving and the engine whined as it attempted to keep going.

"Oh, no, oh, no," Travis said, popping the thing out of gear. A cold sweat rushed from his scalp and down his back. Only one thing would stop the plow.

The stone.

Pa is gonna kill me. Travis jumped from the tractor and rushed around to the side of the plow where the sound had come from.

"Doggonit," he said, yanking off his hat.

He'd run over that dang rock, and the blades on this side of the plow were ruined, all tangled up around the stone.

Why Pa insisted on keeping it there, in the middle of the field, was beyond Travis. And the stupid part of the situation—Pa didn't even know why they couldn't get rid of it, just that Ma's folks had told him to leave it. They'd been gone for years, and yet Pa still insisted it stay and everyone leave it be.

Well, Travis had had it. It was time to get the thing taken care of. And now was the best time to do it, seeing as how Pa and Ma were out on an all-day date. They always got back late on date night, so Travis had several hours to dig.

"This stinks to high heaven," he muttered, rubbing his chin. "I'll get whooped for sure now." He couldn't get his chores done without a proper plow.

Travis scratched his head. But how to get the plow unstuck? He bent and grabbed the twisted metal, prepared to tug as hard as he could, but the moment his hand brushed the rock, all thought fled his mind. His joints froze and his heart stopped beating. A dull ache spread through his body, starting in his chest.

145

He gasped for breath, struggling to regain control, but a sudden terror seized him. The sound of a flute drifted to him from the forest, accompanied by beating drums, and he felt someone—or something—approach. He pulled his hand away from the rock and looked around, barely able to move his head, but didn't see anyone. The pressure became unbearable, and tears sprang to his eyes.

What the heck is going on? he thought.

The pressure gradually disappeared along with the sounds coming from the forest, but the feeling that someone watched him remained. That sensation came from all directions, as if the persons—or beings—surrounded him.

"God?" he said out loud, looking up at the sky. But the feeling in his heart was far from the warmth Ma always said came from God.

Something else was out there.

Travis's breath caught. His hands slipped off the metal of the plow, his palms clammy. His heart pounded, making his ribs ache.

No, nothing was watching him. That was stupid. Only the plow was there, and plows don't watch humans. They don't watch animals or trees or objects, either.

"'Cause they don't watch nothin'," he whispered to himself, wishing his courage would return.

He was *definitely* going to dig up the rock.

Travis's phone rang just then, making him jump. He pulled it out of his pocket, nearly dropping it as he fumbled to see who was calling.

"Oh, Cass. Man, you scared the bejeebies outta me!"

"Why? What's going on?"

"I feel horrible, and it's freaking me out. It's all on accounta this here stone." He dropped his voice, shielding the phone with his hand, hoping that whoever was listening wouldn't hear what he would say next. "And I gotta do something about it. Gotta get rid of it. I have to start as soon as possible 'cause it's gonna take all day 'n night."

Cassidy made a little pouty sound. "What about our date?"

Travis slapped his forehead. "Oh, Cass, I'm so sorry. I totally forgot. But there's no way I can go bowlin' when I know this evil is around. Ma and Pa are gone until at least ten, so I only got now to do it. Pa'll

146

get so mad if he comes home and sees his field all dug up. Nope, gotta get rid of the stone today, then make the field right as soon as I can."

"Oh, well, okay." Cassidy sighed and paused. "Could I come help?"

Something in the forest caught Travis's attention, and he glanced that way. A sigh echoed across the field toward the stone.

"Shhh," Travis hissed. He crouched down, looking at the trees, trying to see what had made the noise. Nothing happened, but he continued waiting, glaring in the sunlight, trying to ignore the prickly sensation on his skin.

Realizing that Cass might think he was a coward if he didn't do something, he jumped to his feet and shouted. "Whoever you are, you ain't scarin' me!"

They were, but maybe they wouldn't know he was bluffing. "Trav, you're freaking me out."

Travis waited, and when nothing more happened, he passed a hand across his eyes.

"It's freakin' *me* out," he muttered. "What did you ask?"

"If I could come over."

Travis thought for a bit. He didn't want to put her in danger, but he could really use her help.

"I guess so," he said. "But we gotta be careful, and we gotta go fast."

"Okay! I'm good at digging. Between the two of us, we'll get it done."

He couldn't help but smile at her enthusiasm. He was so lucky she'd decided to date him.

"Bring a shovel. And thanks, Cass. I appreciate it."

He ended the call, tucking his phone back into his pocket. Talking to Cassidy always lifted his spirits. It didn't take long, though, for the pressing sensation of being watched to put him out of sorts again. He glanced at the forest as he got back to work. He'd never once set foot in it, on account of the stories. Stories he was sure weren't true, but regardless, he had never wanted to know for sure.

It took him almost two hours to unstick the plow and get the tractor back to the barn. The job would have been much easier if he'd asked Pa for help the next day, but there was no way he'd do that. Not when it for sure meant Pa would learn what happened.

Of course, he'd learn about it eventually. Travis couldn't hide something like that forever. But at least when he did learn, that stone would be long gone, and Pa would be too grateful over the clear field to get his knickers in a knot.

Cassidy spent twenty minutes trying to decide what to do with her hair once she'd finished curling it. She couldn't wait to meet Travis' family, and she wanted to make a good impression. Hopefully, the style she chose would last through the digging she and Travis would be doing.

After finally deciding to pin up half of it, she grabbed her purse and a shovel and hopped in her car, heading for Travis's place.

Cassidy had no idea what stone Travis was talking about, but she didn't care because he was something special, someone she'd wanted to get to know for a long time. And he was cute—his eyes were the perfect shade of chocolate brown, a beautiful contrast to his wheat-colored hair.

She sighed, a grin crossing her face.

Cassidy pulled up to the farmhouse, admiring its clapboard shutters, blue siding, and white trim. Very cute. The yard was littered with odds and ends, only some of which she recognized, and an old RV sat along the fence that separated the front yard from the pasture.

Before she could even get out of the car, Travis appeared at her door, opening it for her. Cassidy smiled up at him as he pulled her to her feet and threw his arms around her, a shovel in his left hand.

"Thanks for coming," he whispered in her ear, causing tingles to erupt down her back.

She closed her eyes. "Wouldn't miss it."

Cassidy knew how grateful and surprised he'd been when she'd said yes the first time he'd asked her out. True, he wasn't as built as her last boyfriend—or most of the guys in school—but he'd always been able to make her laugh, for as long as she'd known him. And he was kind. And his eyes were beautiful. She'd always had a thing for brown eyes.

"Let's get started." Travis pulled her shovel from the trunk.

He led her past the fence and pasture near the RV, then down a small dirt road by the big, faded barn, and finally to a field. "What are you planting?"

Travis glanced back at her. "Corn. Same as everyone else."

She nodded. Made sense. There was a lot of government money in corn.

They'd almost reached a big stone jutting from the soft soil when a dark feeling dropped over her, originating from the forest just south. The forest seemed to be pulsing, straining its borders.

Cassidy shuddered, her eyebrows knitted. Was it like that all the time? She'd never been to Travis's place before.

"That always been there?" she asked, staring at the dark and withered trees. Was she imagining them reaching for her?

"Ya mean them trees? Long as I can remember."

"No, the feeling."

Travis squinted at her, a worried expression crossing his face. "What feelin'?"

"That they want to eat us." She glanced at him, hoping she didn't sound crazy.

Travis swallowed, his Adam's apple bobbing, and a slight tremor made his hands shake. But then he shrugged and laughed. "Trees don't eat people."

"Yeah, I know," Cassidy said.

Better change the subject, she thought. She motioned to the stone.

"You sure you want to do this?"

"Heck, yeah." He handed over her shovel, and then began digging, his mouth set in a straight line.

"Have you told your parents we're dating yet?" she asked after several minutes of silence.

Travis hesitated, his shovel poking into the dirt. "Not yet."

"Why not, Trav?"

"I guess I'm nervous. I want to avoid the type of reaction your folks had to the news."

Cassidy's parents had been furious. They'd forbidden her from dating him. Now that she was eighteen, though, she made her own choices. "Digging her own grave" were the ironic words her dad had yelled at her, considering what she and Travis were now doing. But she'd figured it was because they didn't approve of her choice. What would Travis's parents have against her? Daddy was a successful business owner, and it could be said that Travis was dating up.

They hadn't been digging long before Cassidy noticed that Travis refused to touch the stone, so she asked him about that. "I accidentally did earlier, and weird things happened."

"What sort of weird things?" Travis flushed, making Cassidy even more curious.

"Just things." He looked at her. "It freaked me out. And I don't wanna talk about it. Or nothin' else about the forest." His eyes flicked toward the dark trees.

"All right," she said. Something was obviously bothering him — she'd never seen him so uncomfortable. She set her shovel down and stepped up to him, lacing her fingers behind his neck. "What would you like to talk about? Or … is there something you'd rather do than be digging up a stupid rock?"

"'Course there is, you vixen." Travis leaned over and kissed her. "But we gotta get this done, and before my pa finds out. He hates a job that's only part finished."

"Can't blame me for trying." Cassidy sighed.

Travis looked down, then grinned. "No, I can't. This body is irresistible."

Cassidy giggled, wishing they could spend the rest of their time kissing. But she would do whatever it took to remove that worried look from his face, so she picked up her shovel and got back to work.

After another moment or two, Cassidy recognized something.

The more of the rock that was uncovered, the more she felt the forest reaching for it. Even the dirt underfoot seemed to shift and move, eager to reveal the stone it had covered for who knew how long. The sensation was disturbing and brought to mind what standing in a pit full of earth worms might feel like.

150

About two hours after they started, they realized the rock wasn't just some ordinary stone. It had weird designs and figures carved all over it, plus foreign words and what looked like Egyptian hieroglyphics.

Trying to decipher the inscriptions, Cassidy brushed her finger against the surface. She felt something flow over her, then shift away, as if she'd been dismissed. She bristled for a moment when Travis suggested that maybe she wasn't as important.

"To a stone, Cass. And who wants to be important to a stone?"

She had to agree with that, and rather than argue that stones weren't intelligent and didn't view people as important or not, she continued working.

The task grew easier the deeper they dug. The dirt seemed to lighten until it practically rolled away from the rock on its own. But still, she and Travis worked up enough of a sweat for a swarm of gnats to permanently hover nearby.

"I hate gnats," Cassidy said.

"Gnats?"

She pointed to the swarm up above. "They're really coming in now."

Travis frowned, staring at the hovering insects. The lines on his forehead deepened and he bent over, shoveling faster than before. He muttered to himself, quiet enough for Cassidy not to understand what he was saying, but she caught the intent from his tone. Something was wrong here. His unease started rubbing off on her, and more than once, she caught him staring up at the bugs, as if their presence offended and scared him. Why, though?

Just as the sun was about to set, they'd uncovered enough where Travis was sure they could pull the rock up and out. Cassidy leaned against the side of the pit to rest, grateful to be nearly done. The gnats had multiplied until it was impossible to see more than five feet in any direction, and she wanted to leave as soon as possible.

"How are we going to move the stone without equipment?" Cassidy said.

Travis rubbed the back of his neck.

"Didn't think that far ahead." He bit his lips. "The tractor. I'll go get the tractor and a bunch of rope, and we'll pull it out that way."

"Where are we going to take it after that?"

He exhaled in exasperation. "I don't know, okay?"

Cassidy glanced away, trying not to be hurt by his impatience, and saw headlights flash across the field. Travis's parents were home! She turned to him.

"Babe—" she started.

"Them's not just figurines," Travis whispered. "Them's writing." He stepped forward, following the biggest inscription with his finger hovering over the surface. *"Utco kag're tuthr."*

He glanced back at Cassidy. "Wonder what language this is."

"Sounds like Spanish." She frowned, her eyes on the surrounding gnat swarms that had swooped in closer as he'd read. "And I don't think reading it is a good idea. We need to hurry. Your parents just got home."

Travis hesitated, following her gaze to the insects.

"Darn it! Pa and Ma are early." He chewed his lip. "I suppose we should keep goin', though."

"Yes, please." Cassidy rubbed her hands across the sudden goosebumps on her arms.

But Travis gasped, pointing at the stone. A dark liquid bubbled from the inscription he'd just read.

"Holy …" He scrambled back, bumping into the dirt wall. "There's somethin' definitely wrong with this thing, Cassidy."

She whimpered. "Can we go now?"

"What're we gonna do with it? We can't just leave it like this."

Travis said something else, but Cassidy was no longer paying attention. The liquid had dribbled down to the dirt, and something was wriggling its way out of the soil there. A hand! A hand crawled out of the ground where the liquid puddled. Using its fingers, it climbed toward Travis.

She pointed, trying to find her voice to scream.

Long, mangled fingers grabbed ahold of Travis's ankle. He shrieked, jerking away, but the hand held on, a wiry arm revealed.

"Zombie!" Cassidy shouted. She jumped away, expecting more of them to come up out of the dirt.

Instead, the skin on the hand began bubbling and steaming. The steam had a weird hue to it—a greenish orange Cassidy had never seen before. She watched with morbid fascination, barely aware of the insects buzzing around them, clogging the air.

The steam rose, covering Travis, smothering him. He screamed again, his eyes wild with fear. The gnats thronged him, coating every inch of his body. Cassidy wrung her hands, whimpering.

His cry ended, and he geared up for another, but the moment he began inhaling, the steam rushed into his mouth, choking him.

"Oh, no!" Cassidy screamed.

The buzz of insects surrounding them rose to a fevered pitch.

Travis grasped at his throat, gagging. The zombie hand fell limp, and Travis began gurgling, convulsing, foam flowing from his mouth.

Finally, he collapsed, unconscious. A sudden silence dropped over the field.

Cassidy whimpered again, then cautiously approached.

"Trav?" she whispered. "Are you okay?" She touched his arm, then gently shook it. Dead gnats fell to the dirt and others rose, hovering silently a few feet above. The silence pounded against her.

"Travis, wake up!" Cassidy started crying.

When he still didn't respond, she pulled out her phone, fumbling to wake the screen so she could call 911. But Travis suddenly coughed, spraying foam. He looked around, dazed, blinking slowly.

He glanced down and saw the zombie hand still attached to his leg. He bent and pried the hand off his ankle. The gnats flitted around him.

"Oh, my gosh, Travis!" Cassidy said, sobbing. "That was horrible! Are you alright?"

He didn't respond. He didn't even look at her.

She grabbed his arm, nearly falling, unable to control her shaking limbs. "Travis, we have to go."

"Shut up, girl," Travis said, finally turning to her. He clamped his hand over her mouth, breathing heavily, pushing her into the stone behind her. "I've waited far too long to be stopped by some imbecile and his whore."

The eyes that stared into Cassidy's showed no kindness, no spark to which she was accustomed.

What is going on? she desperately thought.

Finally, Travis released her. He wiped foam from his mouth and turned and waved off the gnats. "Your work is finished."

The insects flitted away, leaving the air clear.

Cassidy slumped to the ground, jaw slack. *Travis commanded the bugs?*

She watched as he stepped up to the stone and rubbed his hand across the surface, eyes closed, a reverent expression on his face.

He muttered words Cassidy couldn't understand. She stood, placing a hand softly on his shoulder, not wanting to anger him, but desperately needing to leave before things got even weirder. "Come on, Travis baby. Let's go."

Travis ignored her, so she tugged a little harder. "We have to—"

He whirled on her, and the expression of hatred in his eyes was distracting enough for her not to notice his hand as it flashed through the air and connected sharply with her cheek.

Cassidy stumbled backward, unable to see as lights blared across her vision. Tears sprang into her eyes again. *Travis would never hit me!*

Cassidy cradled her cheek, stepping away. Something was very off, and she had to get help.

As she raced almost blindly away, she heard Travis whispering more words behind her. They rolled smoothly off his tongue, as if he'd said them before.

Travis struggled and fought, screaming. His body refused to obey him. Powerless, he watched his hand lash out and slap Cassidy. He cried out but couldn't hear his voice.

"Cassidy!" he yelled again, unable to understand why the sounds weren't coming from his mouth. "I didn't do it—I'd never do somethin' like that!"

She obviously couldn't hear him, and the hurt expression that crossed her face made him ache to comfort her.

"Oh, Cass—" He gasped to himself. Something foreign was in his mind, something capable of thinking. Images of a dark man dressed like an Egyptian Pharaoh flashed before him until the other entity seemed to realize he'd noticed. Then the images disappeared.

Someone was trying to take over his body! He had to kick the other person out—had to free himself. Get his body back.

Travis stretched, pushing with what used to be *his* arms. They didn't respond. He jumped, struggled, and tried to force himself to move. Again, nothing happened. He tried screaming once more. He tried thinking hard against the being in his brain, trying to push it out.

Nothing.

Travis watched, helpless, as Cassidy stumbled away from him. His mouth was talking, saying things he didn't understand. His hands moved of their own accord, caressing the stone. It began glowing.

Suddenly, a faint light shot from the side of the relic, pointing into the forest, and Travis's body crawled up the side of the hole, following the stream of light.

Travis screamed, thrashed even more.

No way in heck am I going into that creepy forest! Realizing his efforts weren't getting him anywhere, he changed tactics.

"Please, whoever you are, let me go 'n I won't tell no one what you done."

No response, and his body continued following the stream of light. It seemed to lead deep into the forest, where not even Pa had gone before.

Where no one ever went.

There were stories about this forest. Legends and myths. People a hundred years ago used to do awful things there. Sacrifices. Of virgins. And the spirits that still lived there supposedly still carried out those sacrifices.

I am a virgin! Travis gasped. *Am I about to get sacrificed? Curse my inability to get a girlfriend before Cass!*

His legs continued forward, climbing over fallen trees, and rather than fight now, Travis was forced to concentrate on keeping himself

155

calm. The panicked feelings—the fear—from earlier cascaded over him as he realized that bugs were chirping again, leaves moving. And not only were they moving, but they were reaching for Travis, caressing him as he passed.

No, not him—the being that possessed his body.

Who's inside of me?

"Hello?" Travis didn't expect a response and he didn't get one. He wasn't even sure whatever had possessed him was human.

That hand had been human, though... It was time to change tactics again. Instead of trying to force the being out, Travis would have to logic his way through the situation. Use reason and smarts against whatever it was that had taken control of him.

Unfortunately, smarts had never really been his thing. And Travis was having a hard time ignoring the foliage surrounding him. His body continued forward confidently, and the plants allowed him. Branches moved, fallen trunks lifted themselves. A path was cleared, leading to a petrified tree stump.

Travis's hands groped at the tree, and the side of it became mushy. His hand dug into it—he could feel something inside.

His hands pulled out the object. It was a small stone, a replica of the one he and Cassidy had dug up.

Travis's hands turned the relic toward the stream of light. His mouth uttered more unfamiliar words.

Maybe he wasn't paying attention earlier or maybe the words this time were more powerful because the moment they left his lips, he felt a tugging sensation in his belly, and cold air that made him shiver.

There was power behind those words. Power, and something ugly. Travis suddenly felt like he'd been rolling in horse crap all day. A weird, vile smell—like rotted vegetables and burning rubber—encompassed him, seeming to originate from the stone in his hands. And instead of turning away, the being that possessed him breathed in deeply.

"Oh, Nyarlathotep," Travis's lips muttered. He turned and pressed the small stone into the side of the petrified stump. "Return. Return, for your servant awaits. And this time, with a multitude of hands, ready and willing to perform your work."

The tugging in his belly grew stronger, and suddenly Travis felt another, darker presence in his mind.

"I come now," the presence whispered.

Cassidy ran blindly, stumbling across the field, tears streaming down her cheeks. That look in Travis's eyes—it wasn't him anymore. It couldn't be.

She reached the farmhouse and lurched up the steps of the porch, then pounded on the door. No one answered, so she pounded again.

The door to the RV behind her opened, and a large woman in a bathrobe, rifle in hand, stepped out. A man appeared behind her, doing up his overalls.

"What do you want?" The woman peered at Cassidy.

"I'm looking for Travis's parents."

"Them's us," the man said. "Who are you?"

"Cassidy McKay, Travis's girlfriend."

"Oh, boy," the man said.

What was that supposed to mean?

"We've done something stupid."

"Yer pregnant?" A panicked expression crossed his face.

"What? No! Travis—we dug up the stone."

Pa cussed. "That's even worse."

Ma nodded, and Cassidy was inclined to agree, judging by Travis's situation. A baby or being possessed by a zombie? Not a tough decision.

"Where's my boy?" Ma asked.

"Um... He's not doing so well," Cassidy said. She quickly explained what happened, ignoring cusses from Pa as he got more frustrated with the situation.

"We need ta git there now," Pa said. "I don't know what's 'posed to happen after that stone gits dug up, but your pa always said it wouldn't be good."

Ma nodded, and after grabbing a revolver and flashlight, Pa led the way across the field. But Travis wasn't in the hole anymore.

Instead, a pale light shone into the forest.

"The forest?" Pa gaped. "We ain't followin' in there. No boy on the planet is worth it."

"Clay, we're goin' in and you're leadin' us," Ma growled. "Or I'll burn the trailer down. That's my baby, and he needs savin'."

Pa glared at her.

"Fine," he barked before clambering out of the hole with Ma and Cassidy following.

As they headed across the field, Ma put her hand on Cassidy's arm and whispered,

"I love that man, but he and my family have always held some weird beliefs about this here forest. It's why they loved him so much — he fell into step with everything about them right away. So much where *he* took on *my* name instead of *me* taking on *his*."

"What beliefs?" Cassidy glanced at her.

"Well, apparently, both our kin used to come and perform rituals. For the gods who created humans." Her tone of voice left no doubt how she felt about all of that.

"What sorts of rituals?" Cassidy asked.

Ma shook her head. "Pa and my parents never told me much, but I know it involved sacrifices." She looked at Cassidy and away again. "Of body parts."

"Not the whole body?" Cassidy asked.

"Most of our ancestors had missing limbs. And toes and fingers. You can see it in the pictures back in the farmhouse." She crossed herself. "One of the only blessings a' livin' in that trailer instead of the house is not havin' to look at them pictures all day long."

Cassidy tilted her head.

They live in the trailer? she thought. *When there's a perfectly good house only steps away? Why?*

She was about to reply when Pa held up his hand, shushing them.

He peered through the dark trees. At first, Cassidy couldn't see what had caught his attention, but then she noticed that the pale stream of light led into a small clearing, where it connected to a stump with a tiny glowing thing on it. The trees around the clearing were bent toward the stump, shivering almost excitedly.

A figure stepped into view, coming around the stump.

Travis.

"That's only Travis, girl," Pa laughed. "From what you was sayin', I was expecting Algernon Blackwood hisself."

"But that's the point—there's something wrong with—"

Pa waved her off and strode into the clearing. "Son, ain't I told you not to come into this here forest?" He grabbed Travis's arm, pulling him away from the stump.

Cassidy's heart nearly stopped when she saw the expression of hatred on Travis's face.

"Mr. Blackwood," she said, "we need—"

She hesitated when Travis suddenly smiled.

"All right, *Father*. We may go. It'll be several days before he arrives anyway." He glanced at Ma and Cassidy. "But I will be requiring a physical donation from one of you—call it payment for letting you live on my land for so long."

"Yer land? *Yer* land?" Pa bristled. He whacked the back of Travis's head. "I have a mind to tan you right now, in front of your *girlfriend*."

Travis glanced at Cassidy. "Ah, yes. The girl."

"We'll be having words about you datin' her later. But not tonight. You've upset your ma enough already." He shook a finger in Travis's face. "And don't think I ain't furious about you diggin' up that stone."

He and Travis led the way out of the small clearing, arguing about the rock.

Cassidy hung back, not wanting to be close to them. She glanced at Ma.

"It's not him," she whispered.

"He's talkin' weird, I know," Ma shrugged, "but that don't mean he's possessed or somethin'." She patted Cassidy's arm. "But don't you worry. I'll keep an eagle eye on him."

Cassidy was afraid that wouldn't be enough.

When they got to the trailer, she couldn't help but ask why they lived there and not in the farmhouse. At first, no one answered, and she began stressing that she'd been too forward. Pa shuffled his feet, then put the revolver and flashlight away. Ma watched him. Travis stared at Ma, seeming to want to know as well.

Ma finally sighed. "Pa's got too much stuff in there. He keeps starting them DIY's—do it yerself projects—and never finishes. The last one was the kitchen. The sink and stove are out back, behind the house. He never installed them again."

"Oh. Well, um. Okay."

After standing around awkwardly, Cassidy finally decided it was time to go home. She knew she'd be back first thing the next morning. With everything that was going on, she'd been surprised to find she was starting to love Travis, and she really didn't want him to be lost forever. Besides, who knew what that body-snatching zombie had in mind? Someone who knew what had happened needed to be on watch.

The drive home seemed to take much longer than it should have. The darkness was too dark, the air too still. They pressed against her, even through the doors and windows of the car, making her feel like she was suffocating. Like they were aware of her. It put her nerves and senses on fire.

She felt something approaching, but every time she looked out at the fields surrounding the road, nothing was there.

———

Travis tired real quick of trying to force his visitor away or to take over his body again. Whoever it was had a grasp that was too tight.

Ma had shown Travis's body where he usually slept, above the cab of the RV, when Travis acted like he was too tired to figure it out on his own. If she suspected anything, she didn't let on. And by that point, Travis was exhausted from his attempts to get other people to hear him, so he didn't even try to clue his visitor in.

Travis's body got ready for bed, then made himself comfortable, and Travis no longer had anything to think about.

Boredom quickly set in.

At first, he spent the time thinking about Cassidy, how their date should have gone, if he'd only left the stupid stone alone. After that, he played his video games in his thoughts before going through the plots of all his favorite movies.

His thoughts returned to Cassidy again and he was daydreaming about their first kiss when Travis's visitor finally spoke. "If you spend one more moment thinking about her, I give you my word, she'll be dead the moment I see her again."

"Oh, so you're finally talkin' to me?"

"Lamentably."

"Who are you? What are you doin', and why *me*?"

Travis's body sighed.

"My name is Algernon Blackwood. I'm your ancestor, Travis. And I'm shocked at your antagonism toward me, especially after voluntarily allowing me use of your body."

"I didn't allow nothin'!" Travis sputtered. "I only wanted to get rid of the darn stone."

"You didn't read the entries in my journals about Nyarlathotep's test?"

"What journals? I don't know anythin' about no journals."

"The ones I left in the attic."

"Pa said he'd tan me if I ever went up there."

"And you obeyed?"

"Have you seen him? He's got a hundred pounds on me!"

"Wonderful." Algernon growled. Then he was silent for a moment. "I expected my descendants to make more of themselves than they have, and I'm afraid Nyarlathotep is going to be exceptionally disappointed. I may need to prove to him that I'm still worthy with worldly treasures. Yes, I like that idea. It should work. I'll purchase riches and items of interest. Surely, I could get my hands on some Egyptian runes or relics."

"You're going to *buy* somethin'?" Travis scoffed. "With what money? There ain't never been money in this family, far back as I know, and I'm not loanin' you nothin' from my bank." Besides, he only had a couple hundred saved up.

Algernon growled, then cussed. "Apparently, it's all been squandered. It was with the journals. I'm assuming someone down the line from me must have found it and spent it all—probably on whiskey."

"Grandpa was a drunk. And no one knew where he got the money for the booze. He died real young—'fore I was born."

"The scoundrel."

Travis hesitated. "So... now that you know you ain't welcome, how 'bout you leave?"

"And miss the arrival of the outer god? Not a chance. I planned for this my whole life."

"Who is this outer god?" Travis asked.

Algernon paused. "You'll see when he comes."

And that was the last thing Algernon would say, regardless of how hard Travis tried to get him to talk. So again, Travis was alone in his thoughts. This time, though, he made sure not to think about Cassidy. It was hard, though. He'd never felt so isolated from reality or people in his life, not even after he'd played a new video game for twenty-seven hours straight.

After all the lights had been out for a couple of hours, Algernon stirred, then carefully climbed down from the bed.

"Whatcha doin'?" Travis asked.

Algernon didn't respond. He crept down the hall to Ma and Pa's room and pushed the door open, and stood in the doorway.

"I'm serious. What are ya doin'?" Travis asked. He started to get scared. It was a weird experience to feel fear without his body telling him he was feeling fear. "Please, don't hurt them."

Algernon ignored him. He stepped farther into the room, then hovered over Ma. He remained motionless, apparently watching her sleep. He waved a hand in front of her face, then did the same with Pa. After several minutes, with Travis not daring to say anything, Algernon finally left the room. But instead of returning to his bed, he exited the trailer.

"Look, man, I'm not comfortable with you wanderin' my property," Travis said.

Algernon headed to the farmhouse and carefully opened the door, then stepped inside. Once his eyes had adjusted, he began cussing up a storm.

"Yeah, the place is a wreck, I know," Travis said. "It's not just upsettin', it's embarrassin'. It's why Ma insists on livin' in the trailer now."

Algernon picked his way slowly through the rubble, fingering things that must have been there since his time. He eventually made his way up to the attic, where he dug out the large wooden box Travis had been forbidden to touch. He easily broke the rusted padlock and sifted through the books inside. He froze, then flipped through them quickly, as if searching for something.

"We haven't touched the box ever. I swear," Travis said.

Travis wondered if Algernon regretted letting him know he could talk. He definitely didn't seem to want to do it again.

Algernon once more dug through the box, pulling out a journal that was a little smaller than the others. He sat back on his heels and flipped through it, using the moon for light.

Travis cringed at what he saw in the book. Pictures of half-maimed people with descriptions of the sacrifices that required the maiming. Loss of an eye to grant the donor sight of the dead. A finger removed to help a person win at cards or to encourage more milk from a cow.

Practical uses, in other words. But there were also uses with what seemed like little to no relation to the body part being sacrificed. A leg or toe to grant a child a wealthy marriage or to gain favor in the town. Several of the sacrifices came with the promise of receiving magical powers, along with the hope of dwelling with the Old Ones. Popularity contests, basically, but with creatures that were conjured up in Algernon's and the others' imaginations.

Algernon continued flipping, and Travis saw that only the first half of the book had images. The last half looked like journal entries.

Algernon abruptly shut the book tight at a certain point, glancing around the room as if worried someone had seen what he was looking at. Apparently satisfied that he was still alone, he tucked the journal into his pocket. Then he put the box back where it had been and returned to his bed in the RV.

Travis tried to relax, but now he was too wound up.

What was Algernon lookin' for? Why did he git so jittery at the end?

Cassidy knocked on the door of the RV, a plate of biscuits in hand.

Ma opened the door a crack, then all the way when she recognized Cassidy.

Cassidy followed the larger woman inside but didn't say anything when she saw Travis playing video games. She slumped onto the couch in relief. He couldn't possibly be possessed anymore—no one but Travis could tolerate the games he played.

"Hey, Travis baby. I brought some butter biscuits."

He ignored her.

She rolled her eyes, then curled up next to him, willing to put up with his silly games so long as she had him back.

"Sorry 'bout him," Ma said. "Apparently, he ain't got no home trainin'."

Cassidy knew the woman was apologizing for Travis's lack of manners.

"It's fine," she said, though it really wasn't.

After watching him play for only a couple minutes, Cassidy's heart sank. This person had never touched the controls before—it was obvious. She hadn't ever been to Travis's home before, but she knew he loved games. There was no way he'd be this unfamiliar with them. His character in the game kept running into walls and easily dying in ways Cassidy herself would have survived.

Cassidy stood and asked to speak with Ma alone. Ma led the way down the hall and to the bedroom at the back of the RV. She turned to Cassidy, an expectant expression on her face.

"I just wanted to know what's going on with the stone." Cassidy had help dig it up, so she felt obligated to help get it covered again.

"Pa went out to bury it hours ago." Ma shrugged. "He should be comin' along any minute." She glanced at a clock on the wall. "I'm headin' to the store now. You're welcome to come along, if'n you like."

Cassidy declined the offer, instead heading out to the field to help Pa. She was a little disappointed that Travis didn't notice her leave, but unsurprised. It wasn't him—she was even more convinced of that now.

164

She realized it was stupid to leave him alone, as they had no idea why he'd been possessed or what the person who possessed him wanted, but she had a feeling this was leading to something much bigger than she could imagine.

They needed to get to the bottom of things. And it was looking like she'd have to be the one to do it.

It didn't take long for Cassidy to reach the pit. Pa wasn't immediately visible when she arrived. Shouldn't the stone be buried by now?

"Mr. Blackwood?" She circled the hole, at first hoping to avoid having to go down into it, but when she saw Pa slumped over, unconscious on the other side of the stone, she quickly slid down to him.

"Mr. Blackwood?" She hesitated before shaking him, realizing he might have been possessed too.

He stirred when she touched his shoulder, then rolled over, squinting in the sunlight.

"Wha ...?" He put a hand to his head. "How long I been out here?"

"A few hours, according to Mrs. Blackwood. What happened?"

"I was tryin' to bury that dumb rock. Don't remember nothin' after I picked up my shovel."

Cassidy nodded.

"It doesn't want to be buried." She frowned at it, thinking. "Why was it covered up in the first place?"

"I don't know. My pa always said it needed to be hid from the world cuz it was unsafe and brought bad things. Them journals in the attic say more. It's too late, though, to stop—"

He suddenly jerked backward, scrambling away from the stone.

"Because he's comin'," he whispered.

"Who's coming?"

"The one them sacrifices was did fer."

"Oh, that's just not true, Mr. Blackwood." Cassidy worked hard to keep her voice from quivering. "It's not possible. No one's coming."

Pa didn't respond, but he allowed Cassidy to help him up and out of the hole.

165

Despite her words, Cassidy was freaking out. She couldn't feel her hands or feet, and she was having a hard time not hyperventilating. It was too late to bury the stone again. She could feel something coming too.

She had to stop whatever it was.

But first, she needed more information. This was a big job to do on her own, but something told her that Travis's parents wouldn't listen to her.

They would listen to those journals, though. At least, she hoped so.

Cassidy returned to the trailer. Once Pa was settled in next to Travis—who was still playing video games and didn't seem to be in a hurry to get anything done—Cassidy headed to the farmhouse.

She opened the front door, unsurprised to find the place full of stuff—broken garden decorations, a few toilets, tires, cinder blocks, and lots of other things she ignored. She stumbled through the entry and up to the attic.

Cassidy hesitated when she saw fresh footprints and scuff marks in the thick dust coating the floor. Someone had been up there recently.

She sneezed, then covered her nose against the dusty air. She hesitated before continuing. The feeling that permeated the room was slightly familiar, and her thoughts immediately flitted to the stone in the middle of the field. A presence was here—or had been recently. The same one that had flooded over her when she'd brushed the surface of the rock.

This room had been guarded nearly as closely as that stone had been. But by whom? The being that now possessed Travis?

Cassidy took a step toward the corner where the footprints led. She wiped her sweaty hands on her pants, trying to ignore the prickly sensation on the back of her neck. Regardless of how she felt, no one watched her now, she was sure of it. But how long would Travis's possessor stay away? Would he suspect her of wanting to find and read the journals?

She'd better hurry.

After digging through several cardboard boxes, she found a wooden box full of leather journals. She probably should have started there—the footsteps had mostly centered around it—but she'd wanted to be thorough.

The journals were stained and smelly and she cringed just touching them, hoping those dark marks weren't caused by blood. She leaned back on her heels, starting with the earliest dated book and scanning through it and the other journals until the stone was first mentioned.

The journals were written by a man named Algernon Blackwood—Travis's ancestor. He was a professor at Katon University when it was first founded. Cassidy had never heard of Katon University, but it seemed that Algernon taught about myths and legends of supreme beings who claimed to have created humans. He'd become infatuated with these beings, especially when he learned that at one point, they'd planned to grant magical abilities to humans.

During his studies, Algernon uncovered rumors of an ancient relic that would call a specific being back to earth—one Nyarlathotep, an "outer god" who would come, test Algernon, and grant him magical powers if he were found worthy. He immediately struck out to locate it, eventually succeeding to everyone's surprise, and brought it home.

Algernon claimed he'd been called—chosen by Nyarlathotep—to guard the stone and protect it. He was disappointed to learn that the stone could only be used once every five hundred years. A hundred and fifty years remained until the next opening would arrive.

Rather than allowing one of his posterity the opportunity to call back the outer god, Algernon became obsessed with being the last protector the stone would ever need. A permanent guard.

Cassidy could see from his journal entries that he slowly went mad, a thirst for power, prestige, and magic nearly overtaking him. She was sickened when he started suspecting his family of jealousies and began writing of ways to keep them permanently away from the stone.

Cassidy perked up when he mentioned a book of spells that had an entry that could help him stay with the stone until the hundred and fifty years had ended. Maybe the book would have other spells in it? Like, one that would get rid of whatever possessed Travis?

She continued scanning the journal entries, becoming more and more sick over the man's behavior. After a while, the madness took over, and he wrote about how he'd killed his entire family, except for his oldest son who was away at college.

The next entry was his last.

The final step is about to take place, wherein I shall bind my flesh and bone to the soil surrounding the relic and my soul to the relic itself.

Alfred, my eldest. Please don't hate me for the things I've done. As you read through these journals, you'll come to understand the importance of my mission and why I had to be the one to fulfill it.

I leave you with a command to forever guard the relic, and a command that your children do the same.

Read the book of enchantments. Memorize it. When the time is right, one of our descendants will use it to unlock the spell and allow my spirit to inhabit his body so that I may call Nyarlathotep. What an honor and a blessed situation for that individual! To be the vessel of my soul, a servant of the Crawling Chaos!

Cassidy looked up from the journal, sickened by Algernon's wickedness. She couldn't believe he'd killed nearly his entire family. And he thought it would be an honor for him to possess a person's body. Ridiculous.

And poor Travis. To be the "lucky" one.

Needing answers, Cassidy quickly scanned more, hoping to find something that would bring Travis back.

Nothing was there.

She started digging through all of the boxes, trying to find the book Algernon had mentioned—the one with the instructions in it.

Cassidy didn't find it or anything else written by Algernon, but she did find a few journals written by Alfred, his son.

"Man, what's with these people and journals?" she whispered, opening up the first book.

Alfred's writing style was like Algernon's, and Cassidy found that scanning through the pages was an easy task. At first, she was hesitant, steeling herself for a personality like Algernon's. But Alfred was kindhearted and a hard worker. He immediately wrote of the situation with his father, touching on the pain Algernon's actions brought him before showing everything he did to try to rectify the situation.

First, he buried the book of enchantments in the forest. He gave instructions on how to find it, if the need ever arose, but warned against seeking it to satisfy curiosity. Only for the worst situation imaginable — that his father had possessed the body of a descendant — should it be recovered.

Cassidy snorted. Check. She took a picture of those instructions with her phone, then continued reading.

Second, Alfred had buried the huge relic in a separate part of the forest. This task was apparently very difficult, because the relic didn't want to be covered.

"As poor Mr. Blackwood discovered today," Cassidy whispered. She wondered at what point of the farm's history the forest surrounding the buried relic had receded.

The third thing ended up being a failure. Alfred tried to find the stone's replica to destroy, as it was the final piece in calling Nyarlathotep.

Cassidy frowned when she read that part. Algernon's journals hadn't said anything about a replica. How had Alfred learned of it? He must have had access to other writings of his father.

That was everything Alfred mentioned about the relic. Cassidy shut the journal, determined to find the book of enchantments.

Something dashed across the attic's floor, making her jump. A mouse. She put a hand over her heart, breathing deeply, trying to calm herself.

Not wanting to spend another moment in the attic, she jumped to her feet and dashed down the stairs. Then Cassidy headed toward the forest.

Travis wished he could yawn, but apparently his body wasn't tired. He'd never thought it was possible to get bored of every single video game he owned, but his visitor had somehow managed to get Travis there.

169

And why's Algernon playin' them dumb games, anyway? He's nuttier than a squirrel turd if'n he thinks it'll do him any good. He's evil through and through.

Pa stormed from his room at the back of the trailer. Travis knew it was him because of the heavy boots Pa always wore. Algernon, of course, didn't turn to see.

"Travis, get off that skinny butt a yours and get outside and do your chores! I'm sick of seeing you wastin' the day away."

Algernon started. *"Chores?* Excuse me?"

"Yes. Them cows still need milkin'. I did it for you last night—don't make me do it again."

Algernon put down the video game controller and folded his arms. "I do *not* do chores."

Pa's mouth dropped, and Travis couldn't blame him. He hadn't contradicted Pa like that in years. Pa recovered quickly. "Do I have to make you, boy?"

Algernon stood, hands balled into fists. "How? What could *you* do to *me?*"

Pa again looked shocked. Then he drew himself up to his full six feet, four inches, towering over Travis, who was several inches under six feet.

Travis panicked. "Algernon, buddy. He's got a hundred pounds on you. Look at yourself. There's no way this body is gonna win against him."

Algernon looked down, seemingly shocked to see someone else's form there. He was smart enough to recognize reason, and he wavered, not meeting Pa's eyes. "What do you want me to do?"

"Yer chores, boy!"

Algernon nodded, then stepped out of the trailer. Travis expected him to ask for help, but he didn't. Since it was Travis's body that would receive the punishment, though, Travis gave Algernon the information anyway, teaching him how to gather eggs and milk the cows.

"Ya know, I don't get somethin'," Travis said. "Why are you okay with pretendin' to play video games, and yet chores are beneath you?"

Algernon didn't respond, and Travis didn't expect him to. He sighed, watching his ancestor gather eggs. He wished Cassidy could talk to him, could see him, and know he was still there.

He was lonely, but on the other hand, and for the first time in his life, Travis didn't mind doing chores. He wasn't really doing them anyway.

———————

Cassidy headed to the barn to get a shovel, but ran into Ma, who was standing outside the door, staring in with a confused expression on her face.

"Mrs. Blackwood?" Cassidy hesitated.

Ma shook her head. "I'm beginnin' to agree with your assumption that he's not quite in control a hisself."

Cassidy investigated the barn, following Ma's gaze to the other side of the large building where Travis sat on a stool, swearing at the cow he was trying to milk.

"Looks like he's having trouble," Cassidy said.

"Trouble? He done forgot how to milk! She kicked him once and stepped on him twice. Travis ain't had problems with them cows in years." Ma looked at Cassidy, tears in her eyes. "Help me get ma baby back."

"I will. Watch him and make sure he doesn't do anything dangerous. There's no telling what he's capable of. I'm going to the forest to get something that'll help. I'll be back fast as I can."

Cassidy crept around the barn and pulled a shovel from where it hung on the wall. She breathed a sigh of relief when Travis didn't notice her.

She ran to the forest, energized and feeling optimistic now that someone was on her side. Two against Algernon wasn't good, but it was better than one.

Before she reached the trees, Cassidy pulled out her phone, opening the picture she'd taken earlier of Alfred's instructions. It occurred to her that Ma wouldn't have minded if she'd borrowed the journal, but who knew what Pa would have said if he'd found out.

The instructions talked about many landmarks she'd need to follow to find where the book was buried. She paused before entering the forest, staring at the dark trees that seemed to forbid sunlight from entering.

The moment she stepped into the forest, she could tell she wasn't wanted there. The heavy branches loomed over her and the undergrowth bunched up, making it impossible to tell where to place her feet. She started forward, and more than once she got snagged in brambles and had to break her way through.

If the physical difficulty of finding the burial site was the only thing she had to deal with, it wouldn't have been so bad. But the feelings that assailed her were especially upsetting. A few times, she swore she saw someone watching her, but when she turned to look, no one was there. She couldn't tell if whomever it was that watched was friendly or not, but it didn't matter. The feeling of several pairs of eyes on her was enough to make her nearly cry with joy when she finally found the huge, moldy boulder Alfred described.

Cassidy tucked her phone into her pocket, then jammed the shovel into the soil. An abrupt silence fell over the forest, and the wind stopped playing through the leaves.

Something gently caressed Cassidy's cheek. She jumped, turning to defend herself. But no one was there, and still nothing moved, not even the branches. It seemed as if the forest had been frozen.

Her breath hitching in her throat, Cassidy began digging in earnest, trying to ignore the pressing sensations that flooded her. Were the spirits she saw from the corner of her eyes the victims of the sacrifices that had been performed?

"I'm here to help stop Nyarlathotep from coming," she whispered, taking a chance that those who watched wanted him to be stopped.

She knew not to expect an answer but was still disappointed when one didn't come. The deeper she dug, the more she felt like she would suffocate from the silence.

This book was dangerous. And so was the forest.

About an hour after starting, the shovel clunked against something solid. Cassidy dropped to her knees, pulling the rest of the moist soil away with her hands.

Once enough dirt had been moved, the wooden box was visible, its metal clasp almost completely rusted away. She lifted the box, setting it on top of the mound of fresh earth.

Cassidy pried at the lock. It didn't give. She whacked it several times with the shovel. The old metal finally broke enough for her to open the lid, revealing the leather journal inside. The cover was rotted, the words engraved on it almost impossible to read. She picked up the book, nearly dropping it, disgusted by the slimy texture of the leather.

She turned the cover, then gasped. More than half of the pages were in tatters. Had the spell been destroyed? She looked at her phone, reading in Alfred's description that the spell was about halfway through the book. She carefully turned the moist pages, grateful that later pages were in better condition than earlier ones.

Finally, she found it. A large portion of the writing on one page had bled from the humidity of the soil, but she couldn't read that section anyway—it was written in the same Spanish-like language she and Travis had encountered before. The other side was apparently a translation into English.

Cassidy scanned the instructions. The "recipe" called for a locket of hair from someone not related to Algernon, a fingernail, blood, and bone shavings from Algernon's corpse. She'd have to make a poultice of the stuff, tie Travis to the stone, then press the poultice between him and the stone. It would supposedly force Algernon's spirit to leave Travis and reenter the stone.

Algernon had been dead for ages—did his bones even exist anymore? She really didn't want to have to dig around for them.

The spell on the next page was obviously the one Algernon had used to get himself in this position. It was nearly the same as the one Cassidy would be working with, but instead of bone, he had to use shavings from the stone. And like the other one, he had to tie himself to the stone and put the poultice between himself and the thing. Judging by where his hand had come up from the ground, he must have died, tied to the stone, long after the poultice had fallen. What a horrible way to go.

Cassidy took a picture of the spell before returning the book and box to the hole and covering them with dirt. Algernon wouldn't know that she had the antidote on her phone, but if he spotted that book, he'd immediately be suspicious.

When something again caressed her cheek, Cassidy jerked to her feet. She picked up the shovel and ran back the way she'd come as fast as she could, only tripping a couple of times. The moment she cleared the trees, she dropped the shovel and bent over, breathing heavily.

She'd never go back into that forest again if she could help it.

Cassidy headed toward the barn. When she neared, Pa and Travis were yelling at each other just outside the door. She approached cautiously and replaced the shovel, relieved they didn't notice her.

Ma must have seen her from a window because she came out of the trailer and stood next to Cassidy, staring at her husband and son, arms folded.

"What's going on?" Cassidy asked.

"Pa wanted Travis to finish plowin' that stupid field, and whoever it is that possessed the boy blew the tranny on the tractor." She sighed, glancing at Cassidy. "What did you find?"

"The remedy." Cassidy couldn't help but smile in relief. "But I'll need help."

Ma looked over Cassidy's shoulder at the men before inviting Cassidy inside. "It's just you and me, girl. I tried talkin' to Pa. He didn't believe me."

Cassidy nodded. She was grateful to at least have Ma's help.

The two women sat at the table, and Cassidy opened the picture of the recipe. "We need bone, blood, a fingernail, and a locket of hair."

"Does it say what kind of bone?"

"It has to come from Algernon's corpse."

Ma raised an eyebrow. "Algernon?"

"He's the one who possessed Travis." Cassidy nodded. "He's Travis's ancestor."

174

"About Travis," Ma frowned, distracted. "We need ta discuss you two datin'. I hate to hurt your feelin's, but it's just not a good idea." She flushed. "I mean, I don't think ya mesh well."

Cassidy rolled her eyes. "If it's because of my dad and his business, I don't want to talk about it. In fact, I don't want to talk about anything at all except Travis's current situation. Once we get him figured out, we can discuss other things. Okay?"

Ma bit her lips, obviously still concerned. But she relented.

"I suppose you can't go kissin' him now, can ya?" She motioned to the phone. "Where are we supposed to get the fingernail from?"

"It doesn't say."

"What's goin' on, and why's it happening now?" Ma pressed her hands against her eyes, obviously feeling the stress of the situation.

Cassidy filled Ma in on what she'd read in the journals, realizing Ma probably hadn't read them herself. She didn't enjoy the expressions of shock that crossed the older woman's face.

"I come from a truly monstrous family!" Ma spoke, horrified.

"No, I'm willing to bet Algernon was normal for the area ..." Cassidy flicked her gaze to Ma. "When Travis and I started dating, he told me about these weird rituals that used to get performed by the townsfolk."

Ma nodded.

"Yeah, they quit when Bob and I was little." She took a deep breath. "Let's get to work." She looked at her manicured hands. "I don't have much use for these anymore. Time to donate one to my little boy." Before Cassidy could ready herself, Ma ripped off half of one of her long nails. She didn't make a sound, even though Cassidy was positive it hurt like the dickens.

Why didn't she just use fingernail clippers? We're in a hurry, but not that much.

Cassidy jumped to her feet, grabbing some paper towels for Ma to hold against the bleeding nail bed. Then she rummaged through the cupboards until she found a glass bowl for them to put the ingredients in.

Cassidy snipped off a lock of her own hair with scissors she found in the bathroom, adding it to the bowl. Then she returned to the kitchen area and held the bowl out to Ma. "Drip some of that blood in it."

"It's not going to be enough, I don't think."

"The recipe doesn't say how much we need."

"It says to make a poultice. A poultice ain't gonna come from just a couple drops of blood."

"Okay." Cassidy pulled a knife from a drawer, prepared to cut her palm, but Ma stopped her.

"Does it have to come from a person?"

Cassidy shook her head. "I don't know—it didn't mention anything specific."

"Then we're not using your blood. There's some raw hamburger in the fridge. We can use that."

Cassidy bit her lips. "I hope it works."

"If it don't, we can take blood from you. But it's worth a try first."

Cassidy didn't want to say it, but she agreed. The thought of cutting herself made her stomach curdle. She removed the wrapping from the hamburger and poured about two tablespoons of blood into the bowl.

Cassidy returned the beef to the refrigerator. "Now, the bone."

Ma nodded. "That's gonna be hard."

"We'll have to dig it up."

Just then, the door swung open, and Travis and Pa entered the trailer. Both their gazes landed immediately on the bowl.

"Whatcha got there?" Pa asked.

"I'm fixin' some fried chicken for dinner," Ma said as she slid the bowl out of sight.

"Country fried, right?" Pa grunted. "We're starved."

Cassidy felt Travis's eyes on her, but she refused to look at him. With Ma now rummaging through the cupboards, Cassidy knew getting Algernon's bone was up to her.

"Well, I'd better be going now. Gotta get back home."

"So soon?" Algernon asked.

Cassidy finally glanced at him. His eyebrows were drawn together, and an expression of distrust was on his face. It caused prickles of fear to stab her in the stomach. Did he suspect she was up to something? He had to—he'd seen the bowl. "Yeah. I need to get some homework done."

Pa tilted his head. "School don't start for several more weeks."

Ma elbowed him. "Cassidy's in summer school. Ain't that right, sweetie?"

"Um … Yeah, that's right."

Feeling Algernon's gaze on her, Cassidy picked up her purse that was still on the couch where she'd left it earlier, slipped her phone into it, and exited the trailer, glancing at Ma one more time. The bowl was completely out of sight. Hopefully, Ma would be able to keep it away from Algernon while Cassidy went digging.

She planned to do that right away, but Algernon decided to escort her out to the car. He held the door for her. "Sorry I've been so distant today, uh, darling."

Cassidy tried to smile. "It's fine—everyone has off days."

"What were you doing with Ma while I was milking the cows?" Algernon asked.

"Oh, having girl talk," Cassidy said.

"Really." His tone of voice made it clear he didn't believe her. Algernon's hand suddenly whipped out and grabbed her wrist. "You're not planning something stupid, are you?"

"Babe, what sort of thing could I possibly be planning?" Cassidy hoped her bright tone would hide her fear. "Are we still on for tomorrow night?" Their date was supposed to have been last night, but hopefully, Algernon didn't have access to Travis's memories.

Hopefully, Travis was still there inside him.

"I'm looking forward to it," Cassidy said.

He finally released her, stepping back from the car. Cassidy hopped inside, slamming the door, barely breathing as she drove away.

She couldn't help but look at him through the rearview mirror. Algernon watched until she turned out of view.

Algernon growled as the car disappeared around a bend. "Your girlfriend is up to something."

Travis breathed a sigh of relief. If Algernon was addressing him directly again, maybe Travis could convince him to leave Cass alone. "I doubt that. She's really behind in school and... and has stuff she needs to do."

"I didn't miss the bowl on the table, but perhaps you did. There was blood in it. And hair," Algernon said.

"So?" Travis had no idea what the significance of that was.

Algernon snorted, turning back to the trailer.

"Boy, you must not have had a brain in your head before I got here." He laughed lightly. "Don't worry—I'll take good care of your body. And your little girlfriend."

Travis refused to respond. Doing so might anger Algernon into following through with his threat to kill Cassidy.

Algernon entered the RV and sat next to Pa, who was watching football. Ma wasn't in sight.

Travis hoped Cassidy wouldn't return that night. Even if she was coming up with something to help him get rid of his visitor, it wasn't worth her getting hurt or killed in the process.

Rather than drive home, Cassidy headed straight to a nearby hardware store and bought a shovel. She didn't want to waste the extra twenty minutes it would take to get to her side of town and the shovel she'd used the night before.

She returned to the Blackwoods' farm and pulled onto a small dirt road that divided the forest from the field.

Cassidy emptied her purse—she'd need a place to put the bone once she dug it up—then, shovel in one hand and purse in the other, she walked across the field to the hole.

She found where Algernon's hand had shot up from the ground, but the hand wasn't there anymore. Had it pulled itself back into the dirt?

Cringing when she thought about the shovel hitting the old man's rotted flesh, she dug slowly at first.

And found nothing.

Maybe Algernon had come out here and removed his body.

She kept going, digging faster. Her arms ached from the work she'd done the night before, and her hands were on fire, blisters erupting on the tender skin.

Finally, the shovel hit something that wasn't dirt, something that didn't have as much give.

No longer caring what she might touch, Cassidy dropped to the ground and scooped away the excess dirt, revealing a skull.

It had to be Algernon's.

The smile gaped at her, teeth missing, eyes empty and dark. No flesh remained except for a patch on the head where some hair was still attached. How had it survived the many years since Algernon's death?

Cassidy dug the skull out the rest of the way, then picked it up, nearly heaving. She'd never touched human bone before. Sure, she'd seen skeletons plenty on TV and in movies, but actually touching a part of it—something that had been inside a person, full of matter and brain—made her stomach roil. She placed the skull in her purse and stood.

"Now that you've found my body, perhaps we can do a proper burial," Algernon spoke.

Cassidy gasped, nearly falling into the hole she'd just dug.

Algernon grinned down at her, his mouth reflecting the smile the skull had given her earlier.

"Allow me." He offered a hand.

Cassidy backed away, hitting the relic. She tried to ignore the sensations touching the stone brought, but with Algernon there, it was difficult. Unseen eyes pressed in on her from all sides, and the feeling of something big coming nearly overwhelmed her.

She took a deep breath, trying to clear her mind. "I'll stay here, thank you."

"For how long? Until Nyarlathotep arrives?" Algernon glanced up at the sky, an expression of wonder on his face. Then his eyes narrowed, and he looked down at her. "I can't allow you to continue with your plans."

"Oh?" Cassidy tried to control the quiver in her voice. "What plans?"

Algernon barked out a short laugh. "Stop playing games, girl."

He suddenly jumped into the pit, landing next to her. Before she could react, he backhanded her.

Cassidy's head flipped to the side, her body following. She slammed into the dirt several feet away, her vision fading before she tried to push herself up. A sharp pain radiated through her jaw and head.

Her hands sought for her purse, but she'd dropped it. Ignoring the deep ache, Cassidy scrambled to her knees, holding her temple with one hand, trying to reach her purse before Algernon did.

He was faster.

Algernon pulled out the skull, holding it, an expression of awe on his face. "How often can an individual say they've held their own skull?"

A shadow fell over him—Pa and Ma had arrived, Pa with a rifle pointed at Algernon, and Ma behind him holding the bowl in one hand and a rope in the other.

Cassidy gasped when she looked more closely at Pa's face. Purple bruises were blossoming across one eye, and his cheekbone sported a fresh cut.

He cocked the rifle. "Drop it."

Algernon raised an eyebrow. "You kill me, you'll be killing your son."

Ma whimpered, mirroring Cassidy's feelings, but Pa didn't waver.

"I never had much use for possessed family members anyways." He kept the rifle trained on Algernon. "And I'm positive if I blow them brains away, you ain't comin' back a second time."

"You have a point." Algernon nodded. But he didn't put down the skull. "Why don't we talk through this? Even if you kill me, the Crawling Chaos will still be coming. What will you do when he arrives?"

"He ain't gonna come."

180

Algernon snorted. "You don't know that."

"Yes, I do. Cuz you're gonna tell him you've changed your mind."

"I'll die before I do something so ridiculous." Algernon pulled a knife from his pocket, holding it to his own throat.

"That don't work, you idiot," Pa scowled. "I got a gun on you—you can't hold a knife to yerself. It don't work that way."

Algernon's gaze flicked away. "Yes, I see the irony in the situation. At this point, it'll be a miracle if he even deems me worthy with how ridiculous my progeny have become, but there's still a shard of a chance I'll pass the test. I'll not be asking him to change his mind."

"And I'm not gonna change *my* mind," Pa said. "You ruined ma tractor and upset ma cows."

Just then, Ma touched Cassidy on the back. Cassidy nearly screamed before realizing who it was. How had the woman gotten around the hole without anyone noticing? Ma held the bowl in her hands and motioned to the pit where Cassidy had pulled the skull from.

"There more bones in there?" she whispered.

"Let's find out."

Cassidy turned to start digging, but Ma put a hand on her arm. "Yer hurt. Watch them men and keep Algernon's attention off me. I'll git it."

Cassidy nodded, trying to think through the pain that reverberated in her head.

Ma dropped to her knees, pulling out dirt. Cassidy was grateful when not once did Algernon glance Ma's way. He continued arguing with Pa, holding the knife in one hand and the skull in the other.

Moments after she started, Ma finished, and Cassidy helped her to her feet, a bone from Algernon's neck in her hand. Ma pulled a disposable razor from her pocket and shaved several flakes of the bone into the bowl. Then, using the other end of the razor, she mixed everything together.

The poultice now ready, Cassidy and Ma turned to the heated conversation the men were still having. Pa had come into the hole, and they were now fighting about the eggs Algernon had dropped while in the coop.

181

Ma removed the rope from her shoulder, unwinding it. She handed one end to Cassidy, motioning to Algernon.

But right as the women jumped for him, he lunged at Pa with the knife.

Pa's gun went off.

Algernon spun from the impact, slamming into the rock.

"My shoulder!" Algernon screamed, holding it with his hand.

Cassidy and Ma froze, then rushed to him. Travis had been shot!

"Travis, baby," Cassidy said, reaching for his cheek.

"What are you doin', girl?" Ma shouted. "Tie him up!"

Cassidy nodded, biting back her sobs. Tears flooded down her cheeks, making it difficult to see. At least he was alive.

Pa dropped his gun and helped. Pretty soon, Algernon was completely immobilized.

Ma retrieved the bowl and approached.

"I want ma son back!" she screamed in his face. She glanced at Cassidy. "How's this supposed to work?"

"Put the poultice between him and the relic," Cassidy said.

Ma smeared it between him and the rock, then stepped back.

Nothing happened.

"What's wrong?" Pa asked.

"I don't know," Cassidy said.

"You missed something," Algernon mumbled, his dark expression lightening.

Cassidy shook her head.

"No, we didn't." She pulled up the recipe on her phone, then lowered it. "Unless we needed human blood? We used cow blood."

"It should not have mattered where the blood came from," Algernon said.

Cassidy whined. "Then we did everything it said. Everything! We created a poultice made from a fingernail, blood, bone from Algernon's body, and hair from someone not related."

Pa swore and Ma's face blanched.

"What was that last thing?" Ma asked.

"Hair?" Cassidy hesitated. "From a non-family member?"

"Where did you get the hair?"

Cassidy lifted her hand to her head. "Me."

"Oh, no," Ma groaned.

Pa cussed again. "I *told* you we'd never get past this."

Algernon started laughing. "The girl is family, isn't she?"

"No, I'm not," Cassidy cried. She glared at Algernon. "That's a horrible thing to say. Stop trying to goad us with your lies."

"Cassidy, sweetie," Ma said, her eyes filling with tears.

Why wasn't she arguing with Algernon? "Come on, Mrs. Blackwood. Tell him."

"Your pa ..." Ma shook her head.

Cassidy's heart nearly stopped beating. "What are you saying?"

"Your pa and I ..."

"No. No." Cassidy's hands fluttered to her mouth. She looked at Travis and backed away. "I don't believe it."

"There ain't nothin' to believe," Pa said. "Travis's ma stepped out on me, and Travis came along." He held out his hand, motioning for Cassidy to give him her phone. "Here, let me see the recipe. We'll do it again. If it works with *my* hair, you'll know we're tellin' the truth."

Algernon opened his mouth to say something, but fainted instead—probably from pain and loss of blood.

Cassidy handed over the phone, hands shaking.

This isn't possible. I kissed Travis how many times? We held hands? Stared longingly into each other's eyes? Why didn't Dad tell me when he yelled at me about dating Travis?

Her stomach roiled, the nausea from earlier returning. He'd tried— he'd said he needed to talk to her, tell her about mistakes people make when they're placed in compromising situations. She thought he'd been trying to tell her about the birds and the bees, not about an affair.

"Oh, gosh," Cassidy said, sinking to the ground, hands on her mouth, unable to think as she watched Ma and Pa gathering the new ingredients.

Ma donated another fingernail. Pa soaked up blood from the place on Travis's shoulder where the bullet had gotten him. He yanked hair from his own head and added it to the bowl while Ma put in more bone shavings.

Then Ma placed the poultice between Travis and the relic.

183

This time, they knew immediately the recipe had been followed correctly.

Algernon's eyes opened, widening, and he struggled for a moment.

"Nyarlathotep …" he choked out. The stone glowed brilliantly, and he slumped, steam billowing from his mouth, eyes, ears, and nose.

The steam dissipated. Everything was still.

Then Travis's body gasped, and he looked around himself.

"Ma? Pa?" He met eyes with his girlfriend. "Oh, Cass," he whispered.

Cassidy started crying.

———————

Two days later, Pa let Travis dump the last of the dirt onto the relic. His shoulder stung with even that much motion, and he leaned against his shovel, catching his breath.

He hadn't seen Cassidy since the other night, and he hoped she was okay.

Travis couldn't believe she was his half-sister. He refused to think about all the sweet, intimate moments they'd shared. Why neither set of parents had told them anything was beyond him.

"That should do it," Pa said. "And we'll let the irrigation water flood the field—put a nice pond here instead of corn."

"And like I already said," Ma responded, "we should have forced Algernon to stop that thing from coming—he could arrive at any moment."

"He ain't comin'. The man was lying about that."

Travis turned to Pa, feeling his anger rise with the same argument they'd had multiple times over the past two days. "And like I said, burying the relic ain't gonna be enough. You know I felt him comin'—heard him talkin' to Algernon. He's gonna test us and see how we do. And if we fail …" Travis didn't want to know what would happen then.

"Yeah, well, I think we shoulda tried destroyin' the relic again. I coulda bought another stick a dynamite."

Ma snorted. "And what makes you think it would do any better than the first three?"

Ma had a point. The relic was indestructible. And so was its miniature in the forest. The faint beam of light that led from one to the other seemed to be a permanent addition to the farm.

"I coulda gotten my hands on twelve sticks, then," Pa insisted.

Ma scowled at Pa. "And we would've said goodbye to our property."

Travis tuned out their argument, deciding it was time to go home and deal with his aching heart. Regardless of whether or not some ancient being—outer god—was on the way to earth, he had to find a new girlfriend.

The End

Cookies for the Gentleman

By C. T. Phipps

I live alone. I had a wife, once. Her name was Rebecca. You wouldn't remember her, even though she lived right next door to you. You see, she never lived next door to you. Not now. Not ever. One day, you woke up and the next-door neighbors you remember lived there and had always lived there. You don't remember talking with Rebecca, gossiping with her, or the fact she asked you to our wedding.

That's because the Gentleman took her. I see him every night, usually when I can't sleep. I walk to the window of my apartment and stare out into the parking lot. There, he's always standing perfectly still. I would say he's looking at me, but he doesn't have any eyes. At least, eyes I can see. No, instead there are only shadows where his face should be and too many arms where humans have two. He dresses well, in a suit I'm sure someone gave him, but I've never seen his feet.

Sometimes, when I go to sleep, I can hear the Gentleman crawling around my room. He's too tall for it, you see, standing half again as tall as a man and he must slouch over. That doesn't prevent him from moving through cracks and stepping through walls. He plays with my cat, Whiskers, who can see him like me and doesn't seem the least bit afraid.

I wish I wasn't. It's rude and I'm always worried he's going to take offense, but it's hard not to be afraid. The Gentleman's shadow brushing up against you makes you unable to move, your hands shaking palms sweaty, and your mouth dry.

I used to fear nothing, happy to spit in the face of men twice my size and never losing a fight. That was before I lost half my weight and I ceased to ever sleep completely. He's waiting for me in my dreams too, you know. I won't tell you about what he does there, though it's nothing *ungentlemanly*. It's just he might hear and decide to visit yours too.

The proper thing is to remember the Gentleman is lonely and the best thing to do is be polite. He doesn't speak, I don't think he has a mouth or a tongue or vocal cords as we know them. However, he *understands*. Don't scream at him, threaten him, or insult him. I made the mistake of doing that when he first showed up in my apartment. I didn't realize it was his and everything which resided in it belonged to him.

That's when he took my parents.

Now, now. I know you're going to say that my parents died when I was very young. They disappeared in a fire, and I was moved from foster home to foster home. That's the thing, though, I met with them just a day prior to their disappearance. They were speaking about my baby brother and how very proud of him they were. It turns out he was never born. The Gentleman left me a picture of him, though, and sometimes brings him to visit.

My brother has no eyes or tongue anymore, only shadows. I think he's happier where he is now.

Now, you can imagine my reaction to all of this as event after event piled up. I panicked and pitched a fit, calling the police, the National Guard, the exorcist, and even professors of the occult. Funny thing, no one could remember doing any of that within minutes of me doing it.

My wife believed, though, perhaps because the Gentleman let her remember my parents. We decided we'd rabbit for the state lines and go as far West as we could go.

Too bad the Gentleman decided we weren't allowed to leave. I won't tell you what he did to us but there are other places I went to when I tried to go leave his influence. Merciful God—if merciful he is— has wiped my mind of most of the sights I saw, but in the corner of my eye I still see the terrible place of all-corners that I only briefly glimpsed. The place where the things which mustn't be and never were stay and I WILL NOT TALK ABOUT IT ANYMORE.

Ahem.

The thing is that the Gentleman only wanted to be loved and I was foolish not to realize that. My wife, on the other hand, comprehended it first. She was foolish about it, though, cutting open poor Whiskers and tossing her parts about around the room. I think she must have read it in a book that gods like the Gentleman appreciated animal sacrifice.

They don't.

I still see my wife every day in the bathroom mirror. I don't know if she's behind the reflection like Alice or whether whatever was done to her burned an image inside it. She doesn't move, though, only occasionally opens her mouth as if she's trying to say something but I can't make it out. Sometimes, I think about asking the Gentleman for Rachel back. I don't think that's a good idea, not since he so dearly loves Whiskers. He was nice enough to return Whiskers to life. But Rachel? He did not like Rachel at all. No sir.

The worst punishment, though, was when I decided to escape the Gentleman the only way I knew how. I tossed myself off the top of our building and hoped to God that I would end up in Hell, because surely that would be better than the apartment belonging to the Gentleman. I landed in my apartment, with the Gentleman waiting for me.

There is a worse punishment than even the place I WILL NOT SPEAK ABOUT, at least for good Christian folk. A punishment I am even now living and would warn you about, if not for the fact that all will become clear in time.

In the end, knowing I could never escape the Gentleman and that I had been a terribly rude man, I remembered a story of my grandmother. She was from Appalachia, you see, where stories were passed down from mother to daughter straight from Scotland where people came from looking for a new life. All that's forgotten now, replaced with strip malls and gas stations, but she remembered the stories. The stories she'd shared with me.

Oh, I don't know if the Gentleman was the Black Man who made pacts with witches, the God with a Thousand Faces, or the Worm that

Walked, but I *remembered* the tales. The ones I heard in my dreams that were the true stories behind the Brothers Grimm. The frightening ones she used to share with me when she babysat, where princesses had their feet cut off for dancing in the glen and peasants' eyes were ripped out for seeing too much.

In the old tales, though, there is the lie that the supernatural can be appeased. If you believe a lie enough, in the Dreamlands, maybe a cat will make it real. I remembered hearing that somewhere, maybe when I walked the streets of a city made of stories and the Gentleman left me alone for a night. Maybe he whispered it to me as I screamed in terror for my wife and my neighbors called the police. For a bit of sour milk and some treats, the supernatural would leave you alone for a time. They wouldn't rip your babies from their cribs and leave someone else in their place, they wouldn't skin your husband alive and wear him like a suit, nor would they take you away to the Unspeakable Place where the headless men and living whips holds court. So, I needed to bake cookies for the Gentleman.

Oh, you have no idea what fear and trepidation accompanied this perverse realization. No child hoped to bribe Santa Clause or placate the monster under the bed more than I, when I had the terrified realization this was the only way I could get the Gentleman to spare me further torment.

I was not afraid of death, indeed were suicide a possibility I would have welcomed it even then, but the thought of being forced to do my "penance" was sanity tearing. I hoped, foolishly, that if I managed to placate my new master then he would not make me go through the horrible thing he'd forced upon me.

I'm sure you must think me quite mad or a great liar. Indeed, by the look on your face, I suspect you are already thinking of calling the police or at the very least asking me to leave. A part of you, however small, thinks I'm either telling the truth, or more likely deranged enough to believe I am. You possibly think I'm violent. I beg you, however, indulge me a few more minutes. I do not have any ill-intentions to you or your household.

I swear by HIM.

Now where was I?

Oh yes, cookies.

The belief that cookies—sugary crumbly pieces of baked flour—could set me free from the hands of a being able to dance between the spaces of God's own kingdom was a mad, mad thought but one I latched on with force beyond measure.

Unfortunately, acquiring them wasn't as easy as it sounds. I had never been a baker and knew precious little about the kitchen my apartment contained. My wife and I subsisted on take-out and sandwiches, ignoring the fineries of the culinary arts. I also knew—perhaps instinctively—that nothing could be so easy, that store-bought cookies would only enrage the Gentleman. Given his earlier actions towards me were spurred on by only, I think, mild irritation, I did not have any desire to test the being's patience further. No, I would have to master the art of cookie making on my own and create such a spectacular confection as to delight the taste buds of a creature with no mouth.

The Gentleman was kind enough to let me out of the apartment for this journey, perhaps sensing I was going to make him an offering he'd appreciate. For the past week, I'd been trapped in my apartment. The door to the outside led to my bathroom and the windows opened to an apartment identical to my own.

Several times, even, I caught a glimpse of myself entering said apartment only to look over at me as I looked over at him. I feel for my doppelganger and occasionally wonder what he did to incur the wrath of the Gentleman.

But we were discussing my inability to make a decent tasty treat.

Oh, the *desperation* at the grocery store counter when I realized my escapades had drained my finances dry. I had not been to work in almost a month and overdue bills had long since obliterated my meager savings. At the grocery store counter, I considered killing the woman behind and making away with my supplies before I remembered there was still a little money left on my credit card.

I didn't want to do the cashier harm, of course, but hope is a more dangerous beast than despair. A man who despairs cannot be harmed and, truth be told, I wish I'd fallen to it completely. Unfortunately, I saw an escape and that makes monsters of all of us.

Whatever the case, I bought enough supplies to bake cookies for an army. I also acquired books of recipes that were as precious to me as any spellbook. Ugh, you should have tasted the first of my creations. Vile, disgusting things with too much sugar and burnt from top to bottom. I spent hours retrying the recipe, reading through the literally dozens of cookbooks I'd checked out of the library as if they were sacred scripture and trying them all. Several times I threw up, not having eaten in days only to fill my belly with sweet but nutrition-less confections.

I didn't sleep for almost two days until I came up with something I believed which would satisfy the Gentleman. It was hubris, of course, a madness shared by Perseus and other great heroes who thought they could walk amongst the gods without being struck down.

Oh, the agony! The pain! The terrible *things* he did to me. It was minor compared to my penance but so much more *physical*. All the torments and fires of Hell could not match the Gentleman's wrath he inflicted on me without saying a word. Even now I feel like curling into a ball and crying, I who used to brag about my ability to take a punch without flinching.

Where was I? Oh yes, the Gentleman did not care for my cookies. At all.

A more foolish individual might have concluded that it was the fact I was offering him cookies and not something more substantial that offended him. Since that time, I have occasionally been allowed to walk the crossroads with the Gentleman and I have seen what other people have left for him: gold, shoes, wildflowers, infants, and the hearts of young women. The Gentleman seems to prefer the flowers, putting them on his lapel as one might a boutonnière but is indifferent to the others.

The cookies, though, I was sure were the key to his heart.

I drank myself silly after my failure, indulging in two bottles of whiskey the Gentleman had allowed me to purchase, which I threw up before they killed me. I could sense the Gentleman was growing bored with me and that terrified me more than the prospect of his wrath. You see, across the hall, there was a happy couple much like my wife and I had been. Arguably, they were more so because they had a five-year-old daughter.

Now they don't. They never did, citing the expense and hardships of raising a child. I think the Gentleman must have taken a fancy to her and took her with him to the nameless realm he calls home. Perhaps her young developing mind is not so caught up in the mundane aspects of things like physics, cause and effect, or people should have all of their parts when they speak. I like to think so. The other option is simply too terrible.

In the old stories, the Gentry simply cooked and ate the children they took.

It would be a mercy compared to the alternative. I poured over my recipes like a deranged alchemist, tasting the cinnamon and sugar each to see what might have been the problem. I tried combinations which ranged from the ghastly to the sublime, struggling to see where I went wrong. My landlord gave me an eviction notice during this time, only to be replaced the next day by a kindly old woman who said I could stay as long as I desired. I do not like her very much. She has no shadow and I can see things moving under her skin when she thinks I'm not looking.

Whatever the case, I was halfway to embracing whatever punishments the Gentleman could devise when inspiration struck me like it must have struck Edison when he created the light bulb: the milk! The Gentleman was a creature beyond the scope of time and space; he wouldn't want cookies made with artificial ingredients. No, he would want *raw* milk for his cookies and the drink to wash it down. Straight from the cow and fresh! I seem to recall having heard raw milk was much tastier, simply possessing a higher possibility of germs.

Finding a dairy willing to cater to my unusual request wasn't that difficult. Many of the local farmers resented the government's regulations against raw milk and were willing to sell it to me in bulk, especially once I revealed my willingness to pay exorbitant sums I'd acquired from pawning my wife's jewelry. Adjusting my recipes to the new, stronger taste, took some work but I could tell I was on the verge of something masterful.

By that point I hadn't eaten or drunk anything but my creations in days. But, determination kept me alive—determination or the will of the being who was now the arbiter of my fate. Whatever the case, I finished a batch of what I felt were the single greatest cookies ever made by man well after midnight and laid them out with a fresh glass of raw milk by my doorstep. From there, I climbed into my bed and collapsed.

I had hoped—rather foolishly in retrospect—that the Gentleman would let me die. I never entertained any ridiculous notions of him returning my parents or my wife. Such thoughts had long since left my head, along with any idea that the Gentleman cared about such things as humans might. I'd compare him to a lion amongst gazelles, but lions are closer to humans than the Gentleman is. Better to compare him to a star or a gaseous cloud than anything which evolved on planet Earth.

Instead, I simply lay there, unable to sleep. I felt the Gentleman creep into my room and pick up the plate from the ground. I could imagine his sickly, spider-leg-like fingers lifting each of the cookies and making them disappear into the shadows where his face should be. I doubt, now, that the actual composition of the things mattered to him. He could have eaten the molten metal of the Earth's core without grimacing. No, instead, it was the suffering and desperation of my struggle to please him that made the cookies good.

You see, he really is just lonely. Once he finished the plate, making it disappear along with the glass, I knew he would never be satisfied with simply one order. From this day forward, I would be expected to prepare my magnificent feast of wafers every night. They would all have to be as perfect as this batch, never the slightest mistake or error. I do not know if the Gentleman will allow me to age, but I do know I am still expected to do my penance.

Yes, my penance.

I mentioned it earlier, that terrible thing that is worse than the place of all-corners. I tear up and scream inside every time I think of it. Yet, as bad as it is, I promise you I would return to it rather than do this. I have no choice, though, because if I didn't comply things would get worse. I don't know how they would get worse, I lack the imagination, but I know in my withered belly and sleepless mind they would.

The Gentleman is lonely you see, and he has a delightfully karmic sense of justice for those who are rude to him. I was terribly rude to him by not showing him proper respect before and the only way to pay him back for my discourtesy would be to find him new friends. People who could show him the love and affection he so richly deserves.

I've chosen you. Now, now don't panic. Your friend panicked. What friend? Oh dear, this is going to be a long story.

Cookie?

The End

Coolidge and the Enchanted Dagger

A *Mosaic Chronicles* Story

By Andrea Pearson

Coolidge clenched his hands together, trying not to fidget as he waited for the man sitting across from him to deliver the report. This was the third doctor he'd seen regarding two separate sets of MRIs. With how his luck had been recently, it would yet again end up being a complete waste of time and money.

He closed his eyes.

Please, please, please, please.

If only the man would say, "Your scans are clean. I have no idea why you haven't received your powers yet." But Coolidge knew better than to hope for that. What he *did* hope for was that whatever the doctor ended up telling him would be something fixable.

Finally, Doctor Hess broke the silence and met Coolidge's eyes with a grave expression. "I'm sorry, but ... I agree with my colleagues."

Coolidge swallowed, his stomach dropping. "In which way do you agree with them?"

"Your pineal gland is underdeveloped."

He waited for Doctor Hess to continue, but the man didn't say anything else. "And what ... does that mean to you?"

"The same thing it does to everyone else." The doctor removed his glasses, folding them up before putting them in his front pocket. "Your magic will never develop. It's physically impossible. Arete powers

195

originate in the pineal gland, and without proper development, magical growth is permanently prohibited."

Coolidge's shoulders slumped. Why had this happened to him? After the first doctor's diagnosis, he'd spent hours reading up on the condition. He'd refused to believe it was *his* condition. He'd found and interviewed others who'd received the same diagnosis. Nothing fixed it. No hormonal therapies, no medication, nothing.

Nausea built up in Coolidge's stomach, threatening to enter his throat.

"But ... I don't understand. How is it possible? Both my parents are magical. My mom got her powers when she was fifteen, and my dad when he was sixteen. I should *already* have my magic!"

"I'm sorry, son. I really am." The doctor only shook his head.

"Can we do a transplant of some sort?"

Doctor Hess blinked. "Of course not. It would have to come from a magical donor with the same blood type as yours and the same age. It would also need to come from someone who hasn't gotten their magic yet. The chances of us finding a person who fits *that* criteria are very slim. Not to mention the fact that magic is inherited. Yes, a lot of it is physical and originates in how your brain developed as a child, but some of it does come from ancestors. We would never find the right pineal gland."

"There's nothing I can do?" Coolidge felt the back of his eyes burn. He would *not* cry right now. He was nineteen, not seven.

The doctor shook his head. "If something else develops— headaches, dizziness, sudden weight gain, problems sleeping too much or too little—that sort of thing, we can set up an appointment with an endocrinologist and figure out if there's any medication that would treat the underdeveloped gland." He raised his hands, stopping Coolidge from responding just yet. "But no treatment exists that would address the magic problem."

Doctor Hess got to his feet and shook Coolidge's hand, pulling him up in the process before stepping to his door and opening it. "Again, I'm sorry. I hate delivering bad news. If you have any questions after you've churned my answers over, feel free to set up another appointment."

196

Coolidge mumbled a thanks and left the office, feeling like everything had crashed down around him with a finality that hadn't been there after the first or second appointments.

He really would never do magic.

Coolidge got into his car, locked the doors, and buckled up before resting his hands on the steering wheel and staring out the windshield. What was he going to do? How was he supposed to move forward? Everything he'd ever desired and expected revolved around magic. Every career he'd considered, every place he wanted to visit, even almost every friend he'd had—it all had to do with magic.

It was what he'd dreamt about growing up. Partly because of his own hopes and plans, but also because of his parents. They were some of the most powerful Aretes alive, and they were so excited for their son and a future for him that brimmed with magic.

No, he didn't worry they'd be upset. They weren't those types of parents—the ones who expected and pressured children to be just like them. But they would be disappointed *for* him.

He couldn't tell them just yet. He wasn't ready to deal with his frustration and disappointment and theirs. Luckily, they were at home, halfway across the country from his university, and he could put off letting them know for a bit longer.

Coolidge shoved a fist against his eyes again when he realized the day hadn't ended. He still had to meet with the Magical Items 101 TA. Because a D wasn't close enough to passing for his jerk of a professor. Not that he'd expected it to be … but still. The guy had been very rude about it.

And actually, he'd been a jerk since Coolidge's first assignment, and Coolidge had no idea why.

A glance at the clock told him he'd be late for the TA appointment if he didn't leave right then. Coolidge turned on the car and pulled out of the parking lot, pushing his diagnosis to the back of his mind. He'd have to deal with it later. *After* he dropped out of college.

The thought made his stomach clench.

197

The first five or so minutes with the TA went fine, but soon, Coolidge's attention drifted back to what the doctor had said. Transplants weren't possible. Hormonal treatments wouldn't help. His magic literally had no way of coming.

He'd never felt so powerless and out of control in his life. Every avenue had been shut to him, his future now gone.

It didn't take long for the TA to notice his distraction. She did her best to pull him back to the conversation at hand.

"You've really got a knack for this stuff," she said, motioning to the table full of toys, household things, and random knickknacks, all of which had been charged magically at some point. "I know you haven't received your powers yet, but magical items are attracted to you."

He glanced at her, feeling himself intrigued despite his dark thoughts. "They are?"

"These things don't respond to just anyone," she said, encouraged by his response. "In fact, I've never seen them reach out for *anyone*. Warm up, yes, but not reach for. Not even to people who have all their powers. I can sense excitement from these objects when you're around. It's really cool."

"What are you saying?" Coolidge knitted his eyebrows.

"You have a gift." She fully met his gaze. "You might not have magic, but you're definitely talented." A concerned expression crossed her face. "You can't let Professor Wilson get in the way of your success. You guys butt heads so much, more than anyone I've seen, and it's slowing you down. It's taking away all your focus."

Coolidge tossed his pen on the table, realizing she had no idea what was really causing his distraction. "It doesn't even matter. *None* of it does—this magic stuff."

"What do you mean?" The TA tilted her head, frowning.

"I got an MRI—two, in fact." He put up his hands. "I know, I know. Nineteen and not having magic yet isn't exactly rare. But my parents both got their powers much earlier than normal, and I wanted to make sure there wasn't something wrong. Well, there is. Apparently, my pineal gland is underdeveloped."

"I don't understand how that affects anything." The TA frowned.

He wasn't surprised. He hadn't known either, at first. "Magic comes from the pineal gland, right? If that gland isn't developed, magic can't develop."

"Is that possible? I don't believe it. Did you get a second opinion?"

"Yes, and a third. And two MRIs, like I said. And I did a lot of my own studying. The answer has been the same across the board. I will *never* be able to use magic."

The TA got to her feet and paced, obviously agitated. Coolidge struggled with tracking her movements—he was too depressed from what he'd learned to get agitated along with her.

When she spoke again, it wasn't words of sympathy she uttered. What she said totally took him aback.

"I've heard of something that might help. A magical dagger. I don't know, though, Coolidge. It's dangerous." She paused, taking a deep breath. "Once every thousand years, the dagger supposedly grants an Arete magic they wouldn't have otherwise. From what I've studied in my advanced magical items classes, it's due another granting soon."

She leaned over the desk in front of him, staring directly into his eyes. "Go talk to Professor Wilson. Ask him about it. I *know* he has information on it."

He opened his mouth to respond, but she lifted a hand, silencing him. "It's not going to be easy."

Coolidge raised an eyebrow. "Yes, I know. He and I don't exactly like each other."

She gave him a confused expression before smiling and shaking her head. "No, no. That's not what I'm talking about. This enchanted dagger... From what I've read, you have to be willing to do crazy things for it to work. You have to get tested, and by powerful beings."

"There isn't *anything* I'm not willing to do," Coolidge said, getting to his feet. "Is he in his office now?" He wasn't sure if he should believe her about the dagger, but he was desperate to follow every avenue.

"Professor Wilson? I think so." She looked at her watch. "He should be there for another twenty minutes."

"Good. Thank you."

Coolidge left the room, heading toward the professor's office. He knocked on the door and ran a hand through his hair, trying to maintain a pleasant expression even though he absolutely did not want to see the person on the other side.

With a bit of satisfaction, he noted the look of frustration on Professor Wilson's face when the man opened the door and saw him. The feeling was mutual.

"Mr. Coolidge," Professor Wilson said, opening the door wider. "What a pleasant surprise."

Coolidge didn't miss the sarcasm in his instructor's voice.

"Come on in," he said, returning to the chair behind his large mahogany desk. "What can I do for you?"

"Your TA was just telling me about a magical dagger that can help me get my powers."

The professor raised his eyebrows and stared at his student. "And why would you need to use an enchanted item to get your magic?"

Coolidge explained about the diagnosis all three doctors had given him. "And you believe a dagger would resolve this dilemma?"

"I don't know—I only just heard about it, so I haven't had time to study. But I'm willing to do anything. Besides, your TA said it's possible."

"Of course it is." The man shuffled papers on his desk. "I'm not inclined to let you use it, though."

"Wait, *you* have it? And why wouldn't you let me use it?"

"Because you're lazy." The words rolled so smoothly off the man's tongue that Coolidge wondered if he'd rehearsed them. "You don't push yourself."

"I don't have powers. How am I supposed to 'push' myself?"

Professor Wilson looked Coolidge in the eyes for several moments. "It doesn't matter. You should be getting at least a B in my class *without* magic. I don't know what's going on, but you have a huge amount of potential and you're not doing anything with it." His frown deepened. "You probably wonder why I seem hostile toward you. I know who your parents are. I know where you come from. And I also know that children of parents like yours tend to be spoiled and lack self-discipline. You have so much potential, Coolidge, and you're wasting it."

"I'm not wasting anything. And I don't lack self-discipline."

"Then why aren't you getting a better grade?"

Coolidge gritted his teeth. He was about to say, "Because my teacher is a jerk," but he stopped himself in time. He knew better than to be disrespectful like that, and besides, it wouldn't get him any closer to what he wanted or needed.

"I've discussed you with your other professors," Wilson continued. "You're not doing well in any of your classes."

"You *what*? You *talked* about me?"

"We regularly discuss students who show potential but do nothing with it. You want to know why? Because it drives us nuts. No one likes having a possible prodigy on their hands who squanders their talent."

Coolidge's mouth fell open. He'd never been talked to like this before. He didn't know whether to slug the instructor or sling insults in return. Obviously, he wouldn't do either, but the temptation was strong.

Professor Wilson steepled his fingers, and all sense of frustration left his face and voice.

"There's something about you. A difference around you. Something that tells me you'll have plenty of opportunity to help a lot of people during your lifetime. But not if you don't learn to apply and discipline yourself. To direct your talents and abilities."

Coolidge leaned his elbows on his knees and stared at the threadbare carpet. Something about the earnestness in his professor's voice calmed his angry emotions, and he felt the need for honesty.

"I get bored. I go down rabbit holes, studying things that are only briefly mentioned in lectures. I know a lot more than what is being taught, but because it doesn't follow class outlines, it doesn't help me with tests and assignments." He raised his gaze to his teacher. "I'm not lazy—I just want to focus on things that interest me."

"I understand," Professor Wilson nodded. "I was that way too. But I also learned how to make it work with what I studied, and my grades didn't suffer as a result."

Coolidge shook his head slowly. "Either way, my 'potential' doesn't matter if I can't develop my magic. Don't you see? I want to be good at all of this. I want to learn what is being taught. And I definitely don't want anything to hold me back. But my magic is never going to come. I can't graduate or move forward if I don't have powers. Call me crazy, but I feel like my entire future hinges on this, like I won't ever fulfill my life calling if I miss out on something most magical people take for granted."

Professor Wilson stared at Coolidge for several moments, as if he were weighing his opinion on the current Coolidge versus what he thought of Coolidge's future.

"I don't know if I believe you." He got up and walked to the corner of the office, unlocking and opening a huge armoire. "It doesn't matter if *I* believe you, though. It only matters if *she* does."

"She who?" Coolidge asked.

Professor Wilson turned to face him, holding a beautiful dagger with a brilliant red rose at the top of the hilt.

"This is what my TA was telling you about." He stared at Coolidge for a moment. "Did she warn you it would be difficult? I hope so."

"Yes, she did."

"Good. And this is why—in order to access its powers, you must stab yourself with it. And not just anywhere. You must stab yourself in the heart."

"Wait, what?"

"If you survive, you'll know you were found worthy, and you'll be granted your magic."

"Are you *kidding*?"

Professor Wilson didn't blink. "Of course not."

Coolidge swallowed, his eyes straying to the red rose that seemed to practically grow out of the hilt. It was a beautiful weapon, and the closer he looked at it, the more he realized the handle was made of delicate glass. "What are the chances I'll survive?"

How did that question even leave Coolidge's mouth? Was he *really* considering doing it?

"That's up to her." Professor Wilson took his seat again, setting the dagger on the desk in front of him before meeting Coolidge's eyes. "You said you were willing to do anything to gain your magic. Were you telling the truth?"

"I ... I think so." He just hadn't thought it included suicide.

"Go ahead, pick it up."

Coolidge hesitated for a moment before reaching across the desk and grasping the dagger by the hilt. It was lighter than he expected it to be, and he realized the glass hilt must be hollow. The dagger warmed in his hand as all magical items did.

"As I expected," the professor nodded. "I've noticed, and not just because my TA pointed it out, that magical items call to you. If you applied yourself, you could be very successful with them."

Coolidge inspected the intricate designs and the beautiful blade, feeling the weapon warm even more. The workmanship of the rose was especially good—the glass was a blood red, and it shone even under the awful florescent lights of Professor Wilson's office.

As he looked at the dagger, Coolidge felt something he'd never sensed before. A presence in his brain. Without asking, he knew it came from the enchanted item.

Do you really want this? a low, gravelly voice asked.

I... don't know. I don't know if I'm willing to kill myself. The moment the words had been formed in his brain, Coolidge knew he would do whatever it took. Determination filled his heart, and he gritted his teeth. *Yes, I do want it. I need my powers.*

Very well.

All fear and hesitation drained from Coolidge's system. Without thinking, his hands raised of their own accord. More determination flooded his system. He couldn't tell if the feeling came from himself or the dagger. Just who was controlling him? And did it matter?

Before he could finish following that train of thought, he plunged the blade into his own heart. Shock widened his eyes at the pain. His body stiffened, and he fell to the floor.

The last thing he saw was a worried expression on Professor Wilson's face.

And then the world turned black.

———

Coolidge opened his eyes. It took a moment for him to focus on his surroundings, and when he did, he scrambled to a sitting position.

He was on the edge of a massive cavern in the dead of night. The sound of beating drums echoed from the cavern, pounding against his now whole and dagger-less chest. Faint moonlight showed craggy rocks and small withered trees, barely gripping the side of the cliff that housed the cavern.

Coolidge lurched to his feet, startling a group of rats that had been chewing on something not far from him. The rats ran into the cavern. For a moment, Coolidge was tempted to inspect the mound of flesh they'd been devouring, but something about the cavern called to him, and instead, he turned to follow the rats.

The way was rocky, and he pulled out his cell phone, trying to get it to shine on the faint path, but it refused to power on. He tucked it back into his pocket, figuring the battery had died.

Either that, or he'd been transported to a totally different dimension.

That thought spooked him almost as much as the thought of stabbing himself with the dagger had. He really hoped he was still on Earth.

He hadn't been in the cavern long before he realized he had no idea where to go or what to do, or even why he was there. Had he failed without knowing the trial had begun? The drums beat so loudly now that he felt as if his skull would burst from the pressure of the sound.

Coolidge pushed forward, trying to find his way, but only became disoriented. He froze, unsure of what to do, and deep laughter sounded behind him, barely audible above the drums. He turned.

A man stood behind him. He was tall and slim, and his clothing consisted of a shapeless robe of heavy, black fabric. Despite the lack of light in the cavern, Coolidge saw the man's face perfectly well, and he stepped back. The man immediately reminded him of a pharaoh of Egypt. His features were commanding and sharp, and he had an intense air of authority about him. He looked like he came from long ago and far away.

"Who are you?" Coolidge asked.

The man raised a hand, and the beating drums slowed, then stopped all together.

"You may call me Nyarlathotep."

204

Coolidge swallowed against the fear that threatened to choke him. Even just the man's voice had turned his insides to mush. He didn't need a college degree to recognize that this being was powerful.

"My dagger brought you to me," the man said. "And now, your heart must be weighed to find if you are worthy."

Nyarlathotep reached for him, but Coolidge stepped back again. "How can I trust you? Professor Wilson told me the dagger was from a *woman*."

The man grinned at Coolidge, his dark eyes narrowing, making the expression sinister. "I take on many forms. Thousands, even. I chose the form I thought Wilson would appreciate most. Would you like to see it?"

Without waiting for a response from Coolidge, the man's body began to bulge and expand in places, shrinking in others. Coolidge's stomach flipped at the sight of moist, red and pale pink flesh, twisting and roiling. Bones shifted under taut skin, warping the man's appearance until he was barely recognizable. His clothes and features changed colors—his face turning into a deep purple as boils swelled, exploded, and shrank. Then the flesh settled into a recognizable form, the skin supple and healthy, the body no longer repulsive.

And the most beautiful woman Coolidge had ever seen stood before him. She practically glowed with health and vitality. Everything about her was magical. Her long, golden hair. The elaborate, beautiful blue dress she wore. Even the diamonds that sparkled at her throat and wrists. She was otherworldly.

Despite an undercurrent of fear—this creature was far too powerful to take lightly—Coolidge couldn't help but relax. How could he *not* trust this woman?

No, Coolidge, he thought. *It's not a woman, it's a creature with enough power to destroy you.*

Not even reasoning with himself was enough, though. Surely, there was nothing to fear from this being—she was a goddess, perfect in every way.

"You respond better to me now, as well," the woman said, her voice light and bubbly. "And as I was saying, your heart must be weighed to find if you are worthy."

Before Coolidge had a chance for the words to sink in, the woman pounced on him, flinging him backward onto the cold stone. His head snapped against the rock below him and for a moment, he couldn't see anything. Pain radiated through his skull and down his spine. He struggled to breathe through it, struggled for awareness of anything other than the agony.

It took several moments for Coolidge to realize the woman was perched on him, her features hawk-like. Her eyes were demonic. They bored into his. She shifted her position until she straddled him. Her gaze dropped to his chest, and she ripped his shirt open.

Despite the pain, Coolidge began to feel hope. But before he could formulate a thought, the woman raised a hand. Her nails grew an inch, and she plunged them through the skin over his heart.

Sharp pain shot through his torso, and he screamed. He felt ribs break as her hand went deeper. The woman pulled his heart out of his chest cavity, and the breath sucked out of his lungs. She jumped to her feet, not looking at him.

Coolidge stared down at the gaping hole in his chest. There was no blood, no gore. Just pain. That, and the heavy feeling of suffocation. He gasped for air, but only a little came. It was barely enough to maintain consciousness. How was he still alive?

"Hhh …?" He couldn't get his question out, though, and the woman didn't even turn.

An old-fashioned scale appeared next to her, and she placed Coolidge's heart on one side of it, causing both sides to tip and teeter.

She watched for a moment.

"You are … shall we say … *pure* in heart." She laughed, and Coolidge knew her choice of words hadn't been a compliment. "Are you *worthy* of the power you so strongly desire, though?" She glanced at him, still facing the scales, and her voice dropped to a whisper. "What are you willing to sacrifice?"

He swallowed. He'd already stabbed himself in the chest and had his heart ripped from his body. Everything else paled in comparison. "Anything."

The woman raised an eyebrow. She knew he was lying.

"Okay," he gasped, still struggling for air. "I don't want to do anything illegal … Like, murder … Or rob."

"Are you sure?" She scowled.

He didn't flinch or back down, and she rolled her eyes. "Pathetic. Nevertheless, I will still find use in you." She turned to him fully. "I can see your future, Coolidge. You will have the opportunity to sacrifice yourself and your time by mentoring and helping people who struggle. By collecting them to your group, so to speak. They will follow and revere you. Do you swear to help them?"

Coolidge warmed with conviction. He knew he didn't need to promise this creature anything—he would have done it anyway. "Yes. I do."

The scales tipped heavily in his favor.

"Very well," the woman said.

She picked up his heart, wrapping her fingers around it before glancing at him. "Can you feel that?"

Oddly enough, Coolidge could. He nodded.

"Good." She grinned, staring at the organ in her hand. "I'm tempted to have some fun with you before returning it." She squeezed, her fingers whitening. "Odd sensation, isn't it?"

Coolidge gasped when pain shot through his chest.

"What are you doing? Stop!" He could barely think through the pain. "Please."

"As you wish." She shrugged, then dropped to the stone floor beside him.

The woman thrust his heart back into his chest, then held her hand over the hole. He felt the organ warm and start beating, and the residual pain from the injury she'd caused melted away.

He relaxed into the stone below him.

"Thank you," he panted.

But the woman wasn't finished. She grabbed his arm and yanked him to his feet, then gripped his face with both hands and stared into his eyes.

Coolidge began to tremble. A cold sweat shot through his system. What more did she want?

"You, as many before you, have passed the test. You shall gain your powers. Congratulations are in order." Her grip intensified. "You will not remember the following when you awaken. Know this—despite the fact you won't remember, I want you to keep it in your heart—I'll expect you to return the favor someday. I'll find you down the road when you have gathered followers. And then, I will take those followers as my own, along with you and all others who have passed my test. You shall become my servant."

She smiled, dropping her face close to his. "I thank you for your sacrifice."

The woman increased the pressure on Coolidge's head until he blacked out.

———————————

When Coolidge awakened, he was lying on the ugly carpet in Professor Wilson's office. Something was different this time, though. He couldn't figure out what.

Professor Wilson was working at his desk, marking, and shuffling through papers. He yelped when Coolidge sat up, then laughed. "Looks like I didn't waste the dagger's thousand-year use."

Coolidge looked down at his chest. The only thing that remained of his experience was a ragged hole in his shirt. The skin underneath was completely healthy. But still, *something* was different. He felt complete, as if he were in pieces before and had been mended.

Professor Wilson watched him expectantly.

"My... I..." Coolidge couldn't get anything else out.

A strange pulsing waved over him, becoming stronger, energizing the cells in his body. It originated from Professor Wilson. Goosebumps erupted all over his arms when he realized what he'd just sensed. His jaw dropped.

"I can feel your magical pulse." He closed his eyes for a moment, sensing his own powers swirling around him, begging him to release them, to use them. He had access to his magic!

When he opened his eyes again, he saw that his professor was smiling.

"Congratulations on your Restart." A serious expression settled on the older man's face. "As long as you do as you promised, your gifts will always be available. Don't misuse them, and don't forget that you gave your word. To both me *and* the woman."

Be a better student and help those who need help. Got it.

"I won't," Coolidge said, thinking better of informing the professor that the woman was really a pharaoh-type man called Narlathetip. Or was it Narlothal? Narmathotip? Nar-something, for sure. He couldn't remember, and therefore, it couldn't be important. Because Coolidge always remembered the important things. What made him grateful was the fact that the god was a benevolent one, and that had to be rare. Why else would he want Coolidge to help people? His plan was far too intricate, far too elaborate to…

And just like that, the thought was gone.

Coolidge blinked, then shook his head. A sensation of déjà vu crossed him—something once familiar was now forgotten, wisps of it wafting through the air around him like a word that remained just out of grasp.

Professor Wilson stood and opened the door, ushering Coolidge out. "You've got a lot of work to do to get caught up. You'd better get going."

Coolidge agreed, tucking his thoughts aside. They'd been fleeting anyway, and specific details about the god were unimportant, as he'd originally decided. He left his professor's office with a bounce to his step he hadn't had for a long time. He would focus on his studies. He would graduate with a 4.0 GPA. He would study magical items and find out what made them yearn for him.

Nothing would stop him from becoming the most powerful Arete the world had ever seen. His future had finally opened before him, and he found his entire body warming with the thought of helping others find their way too.

He couldn't wait to get started.

The End

To read more about Coolidge and his future "followers," grab your copy of *Discern, Mosaic Chronicles Book One*, a modern, young adult retelling of Lovecraft's *At the Mountains of Madness*.

In Its Shadow

By Eric Malikyte

January 25th, 1980

I can feel the cold in my bones. My limbs are heavy due to the drugs the orderlies stuck me with. The memories from the dream play on the concrete walls of my cell like the silent movies my parents told me about as a child.

Doctor Webber doesn't like when I call it that. My cell. But that is exactly what it has become.

They tell me I'm here to get better. That I'm unwell. That I'm serving my country by being here.

But all they ever want to know about are my dreams, and the drawings made through me.

Growing up, the doctors always said dreams were my brain trying to tell me something important.

Sometimes I wonder what they would say of my dreams now.

But I wouldn't wish them on anyone.

They give me tools to write and draw with. Without calendars and clocks, I used them to keep track of the days and months.

Most of the time, writing keeps the voices and dreams away…

They would rather I use these tools to draw, but no matter how much I tell them I'm not an artist, that I couldn't draw a stick figure to save my life, they still insist.

Sometimes when I'm writing these entries, my hands start to itch. A creeping, gnawing thing crawls out from the depths of my gut. Tears well up in my eyes. And the movies playing on the walls, they close in. And I can feel its touch. Its sickly, slimy claws on my hands.

Grabbing them. Squeezing them. Taking them.

And the next thing I know, my hand is turning purple and I'm staring down at an image frozen in time, ripped straight from the movies that play in my mind's eye when the lights go out and shadows come out to play. A thing I've seen. A thing from beyond the reach of even my worst nightmares.

Sometimes I'm not even sure if I'm really alive, or that this pen in my hand is real. Wouldn't it be ironic if I died on my mission six months ago?

Maybe this is just what hell is like.

Wouldn't Mom just love that?

January 31st, 1980

They came for me again. This time it was Doctor Webber's orderly.

He grabbed me by my arms and dragged me down to a new room.

Used to be, when they wanted answers from me, they'd just visit me in my cell, set up a tape recorder and ask their questions.

This one is different. The walls are the same type of cement as my cell, but there are red stains in odd places and large holes in the plaster where bricks show through. The door looks like it's made of solid steel and has a small window where they can look in on me, make sure I'm still chained to the floor.

I'm not alone.

The orderly's not looking at me. Not directly, but his hands are never far from the set of hypodermic needles he keeps on his belt.

The shackles hurt my wrists. But they always let me take my notebooks. That's good at least, even if I know all they want are the pictures…

There is something new, too. A big camera, like the ones they use to make the news.

Once upon a time, I wanted to be a TV host, or a newsman. But my parents always shot that dream down. Said I was only good for one thing.

What would my parents think of me now?

My mother always expected me to wind up dead in a ditch somewhere, my soul rotting in Hell like the sinner I was. My father always told me I'd end up in prison.

And I guess this place isn't much different than that, is it?

The door creaks open like its hinges are full of screaming, tortured things. It's Doctor Webber.

He's a young man, but shadows corrupt his eyes. A voice in the back of my head tells me he's seen things. A voice I'd rather not hear from.

He's holding a brown folder with the Office of Extradimensional Intelligence's seal stenciled into it, featuring a label that spells out Subject 105 in big serif letters.

They love their serif letters.

He doesn't waste time greeting me and ignores the fact that I'm writing all of this down.

The doctor takes a seat across from me; he does not smile.

He directs the orderly to start rolling and opens his notebook.

The camera clicks and clacks, drowning out the buzz of the fluorescent lights above me.

"Subject 105," Doctor Webber says. "How are you feeling?"

I don't answer. He only cares because the camera is on.

He's staring at me. I'm trying to ignore what the voice is telling me. Trying to avoid his stare by writing in my notebook.

The doctor sighs. Like a reflex, my eyes flinch, and I look at him.

For a second, he looks as old as The Crypt Keeper from those old horror comics. His skin is gray, wrinkled, and I can see his skeleton cutting through, like he's slowly melting.

His eyes, though.

Despite the unnatural, yellow sheen, they don't betray the stare of a madman.

A voice tells me he's intent to open the way. If only he could find the key.

All it takes is a blink for me to see that he's not the sickly, mad creature I've seen in my dreams, but he does look like he's losing patience with me.

"You don't have to do that anymore," he says, pointing to the TV camera, "that's why we're taping this. For posterity."

I shake my head. If I stop writing, the dreams will get their way. That's how it always happens.

"Can you hand me the notebook, Subject 105?"

I shake my head again. "If I stop, the dreams win."

"We've been over this before. We need to see what's in your notebook."

"Please, please don't."

He's sighing, rubbing his eyes. "Orderly, take the notebook from Subject 105 and hand it to me."

I can hear the smack of the orderly's boots on the hard floor bouncing off the walls. I can smell the fermenting oils souring on his skin. The tartar of his teeth festering into rot.

I can feel him reaching.

I need to keep writing. I need to keep writing. I need to—

There are pages missing now. Webber's got them aligned on the table. Staring at the drawings one by one.

He's smiling. I hate that.

"See, Subject 105? That wasn't so bad."

I don't want to look into his eyes again.

"You can even keep writing if you'd like. Write every word we exchange if it makes you feel better. All I wanted were the drawings."

Don't look into his eyes.

"Do you know why I wanted these drawings?"

I shake my head, careful not to look at him.

"Subject 105, can you tell me how you got here?"

No! Not this again!

"Please answer the question. Tell me how you got here."

"Why?" I ask him. My voice sounds strange to my ears. Like it's coming from someone much older.

That's not what I sound like, is it?

214

"No questions. The less you know about why, the better it will be for you."

"You always say that…and I always…I always do what you tell me, but…"

"But what?"

"But it never gets any better."

"I promise there is a point to all of this, Subject 105."

"That isn't my name. Can't you just call me by my name?"

"I'm sorry, you know that I can't. Now answer the question. You know what will happen if you do not cooperate. And I know you don't want that."

No. No. No. No. No! No! No!

Not that. Never again.

Doctor Webber leans over and looks at what I've written. He smiles. I look away.

"Now, answer the question."

I'm nodding. Then I'm shaking. And then my mouth is running almost as fast as I can jot it all down.

"It was…it was a year ago. I think. Needed a job. The army had kicked me out of basic."

"And why was that?"

"I didn't measure up. Too weak. Too skinny."

"That's not the real reason, is it?"

"I…"

"What was the real reason?"

"Medical…"

"And what was the diagnosis?"

"I get rashes…bad ones…"

"And what causes this?"

"Leather…citrus…soaps…and certain kinds of metal I think…The doctor called it contact dermatitis. Told me I had to avoid all the things that cause the rashes."

"And that was too much for the army?"

"Yes."

"And then what happened?"

"I packed my things. They were going to put me on a bus back home. The other guys were making fun of me, making up stories. They thought I wasn't right. I didn't want to go. Not back to Mom. She'd know I was a failure. But my C.O. He saw how hard I was trying. Told me I didn't have to go home if I didn't want to."

"And? How was that going to be possible?"

"You know how it—"

"Answer the question."

"He told me there were places in the private sector, places that did important work for the government, that needed people to do dangerous things for the security of the country. He told me if I was willing to trust him, he'd send me somewhere where I could be useful. Where I'd be important."

"And did he say anything else?"

"You know he didn't."

"Yet, you trusted him. Wasn't it his decision to have you sent home?"

"Yes."

"Amusing."

The doctor's laughing at me. Not physically. But I can see it in his grin. "What happened next?"

"He told me he couldn't tell me where I was going, but that I'd know when I got there, and put me on an unmarked bus in the middle of the night. I was the only passenger, but any time I asked the driver where we were going, he just ignored me and kept his eyes on the road.

"With no one to talk to. I fell asleep.

"And that night I dreamed of a man in a tattered doctor's coat with wrinkled, graying skin. A man whose bones protruded through his flesh like dull butcher knives slowly ripping through a carcass. His hair, an unnatural white, set aglow by a black sun burning eternally from the open ceiling.

"He was walking through an endless series of hallways. Hallways that were three times as tall as any man and made from a material that reflected the light in strange ways, betraying impossible, dreamlike angles. He clutched at something in his bone thin arms.

216

A book with a tattered leather cover. I don't know how long that dream went on for. It seemed like I was watching him for days when he finally stopped marching and turned back."

"And what did you see then?"

"He was looking right at me."

"And did he say anything?"

"He said I wasn't the right one and kept walking."

"And that's when you woke up?"

"Yes."

"And how long had you been asleep?"

"The entire trip. The driver was no longer in his seat when I woke up. It was dark. And there were three men in black uniforms standing in front of me.

"They told me to come with them. So, I did.

"When I got off the bus, the first thing I noticed was the sky. It was full of stars. The air was biting cold, and I could almost make out mountains in the distance. A clock I saw told me it was 14:00. 14:00 hours and it was still dark. That narrowed down where I might be.

"The men led me to a room with what looked like school desks. They told me to sit.

"At first, I wondered if others would join me, but I was alone.

"I waited for what felt like hours for another man in a black uniform to come out and hand me a brown folder, like the one you're always carrying. He told me to fill out the paperwork, sign, and initial it all."

"And did you ever think that was strange?"

"A little. But I figured this was a really top-secret outfit. That they meant business."

"Continue."

"When I was done, I waited for another man to take the folder from me, and this one stayed. He spent some time looking over my paperwork before he walked over to the blackboard at the front of the room and pulled down a white screen.

"That's when I noticed the film projector at the back of the room. An old one too. Not like those new tape players some people have.

"The film started rolling and a woman's voice echoed through the room."

217

"We already know about your briefing, Subject 105. Let's get to your mission."

I'm shaking my head. I don't want to talk about this part.

"Subject 105, if you don't cooperate, we will take your notebook away and return you to your quarters. You don't want that, do you?"

I start rocking back and forth. I can't stop. I don't want to. I don't want to.

No. No. No. No. No! No! No!

"Very well, have it your way."

The man is coming toward me. I hear his footsteps again. Constantly rapping on the church's rotting floorboards—

February 10th, 1980

"Subject 105," Doctor Webber says. "Do you know why we're here again?"

I shake my head. The pen feels heavy in my hands. The camera is running.

A whisper tells me that everyone will see what they're doing to me. But that whisper is a lie. No one cares. No one is coming for me.

"In our last session, you suffered sudden onset of psychosis. You started hallucinating. Do you know why?"

I'm shaking my head, rocking back and forth. I can't stop.

"I believe that it is tied to your first mission," Doctor Webber says. "Can you tell me what happened?"

I shake my head. I shake my head. I shake my head.

"Subject 105, please answer the question. With your words."

"No. Please..."

"I will take away your notebook if you do not. I will turn out the lights in your quarters, and you will be forced to relive it anyway."

"Why are you—"

The orderly. He's walking toward me, hand reaching for my notebook. I need to hold it tight. He can't have—

The orderly is walking away. Good. Stay away. This is mine.

MINE!

218

"Do we understand each other now?" Doctor Webber asks. He's grinning. There are more creases in his skin today.

"Yes. Please don't take it away."

"You know what I want. Give it to me, and I will allow you to keep your notebook."

I'm nodding to him. But inside...

"It was the middle of the night when you put me on the bus. You were there, smiling at me. Telling me about what I needed to do. Then you gave me a folder and a small black box.

"I looked it over. It was no bigger than the palm of my hand. You told me that I was heading to a small village south of where we were. That the target of my mission was in that village, an old church.

"You told me that all the information I needed was inside the folder and that once I read all of its contents, I was to burn it."

"And did you?"

I'm nodding. I hope he believes me. "I did. I burned it as soon as I arrived in Tiergetown.

"I arrived while it was still dark, but the moonlight was bright enough that I was able to see the buildings. The bus came to a stop, the tires crushing pebbles and dirt—the loudest sound for miles.

"The driver said nothing, but I knew I had to get off. I clutched the folder you gave me tight to my chest and made my way to the front of the bus and down the stairs. It struck me immediately.

"It was like traveling back in time. The buildings were wooden things with ancient, peeling paint. Everything was lit by gas lanterns. There wasn't an electric lamp or sign in sight.

"No one was out and about, but that wasn't strange. It was 00:00 hours. Most people were probably in bed, I figured. Besides, in a place like that, who could be blamed for not having a nightlife?

"Then, it finally caught my eye.

"The lantern lights at the edge of a building that looked older than time itself, built from wood sourced from the first trees. I could almost smell the rot of the place piercing through the cold in the atmosphere. Could feel the place's immense presence as if the single-story wooden building swelled in size before my very eyes, drawing me closer to it.

"The sound of the bus leaving me alone in that horrible town broke my trance, and I figured I'd check in at the local bed and breakfast before it got any later.

"The staff was expecting me, an older lady and her son. She directed me to my room, which was a small chamber no bigger than my cell here. There was an old bathtub with yellow stains running down the side, a twin sized bed that looked like it had been stuffed with straw, and a small fireplace.

"The old lady had rules. She told me I was never supposed to go out at night. That the sheriff would have words for me if I did. And under no circumstances was I supposed to go near the old church.

"I asked her about it, despite the gnawing feeling that I shouldn't have, and she glanced at the folder clutched tight against my chest.

"She said that under no circumstances was anyone in Tiergetown to mess with the lanterns around the building or step foot inside.

"The look on her weathered face told me I shouldn't ask any more questions.

"The old lady's son stayed behind to help me start the fire.

"He kept looking at my folder. So, I asked him about the church.

"At first, he stayed silent. I noticed dark circles running beneath his eyes.

"After a while, he told me not to go there.

"My heart felt like it was beating a little faster. My skin running cold with the fire having yet to warm me.

"The boy turned from me. Half of his face plunging into the dark, hidden truths burning at the edge of his twisted tongue."

"And what did he say?" Doctor Webber asks.

"You always go in. And it always gets you."

"Let's move to the next day."

I'm nodding. My hand is getting sore from writing, but something is compelling me to keep going.

"I didn't sleep a wink that night. I stashed the folder under the mattress. The old woman made breakfast when the sun came up. The smell was almost enough to drown out the stench from the church. She placed an old clay plate on a decrepit wooden table. Reindeer sausage, two eggs, and a piece of toast.

"It was better than the food here at least."

"I'll be sure to bring that up with the chef."

"After breakfast, I went upstairs and grabbed the little black box I'd hidden under the mattress, placing it in my coat pocket. I went downstairs and before I could get to the door, the old lady said that I should enjoy the day while I could, because once the sun went down, that'd be it for the season.

"I left without saying a word.

"The sheriff, or whatever passed as law enforcement in that tiny, forgotten town, found me before I could even think about going near the church.

"He greeted me and asked me what my business was in town. I said I was on vacation and the look on his face told me he knew I was full of it. But he made no effort to call me out.

"The sheriff was a weathered old man. The weight of his age seemed to drag his torso forward, as if death was slowly tugging on his soul, threatening to yank it into the Astral Lands.

"The old man told me the same thing the old woman had, spat at the dirt, and left me to wander.

"The town was small. The sign out front had a population number in the triple digits that had been crossed out several times. Now it was down to eleven.

"Though I feigned interest in the other buildings, the homes that some of these people had built for themselves, I could not help but return to the old church.

"Even with the sun blazing high overhead, the lanterns remained lit. Pacing around the town, I counted them from the corner of my eye.

"Thirteen. There were thirteen lanterns.

"Occasionally, the sheriff would approach them carrying a large canister. Carefully, he would refuel each and every one. As the day wore on, I noticed that the lanterns seemed to keep the shadows from touching the ancient building.

"Curiously, the doors and windows of the church had been completely boarded up.

"There was no way for me to see inside. At a distance, at least.

221

"Not daring to get too close to the church, I told myself that I would return in the middle of the night.

"I made my way back to the bed and breakfast and retreated to my room, poured myself a glass of scotch, and lit a fire to keep myself company.

"I sat on the bed staring into the flames for what felt like hours, waiting for darkness to grace my window. Eventually, my hands found their way beneath the straw mattress, to the brown folder.

"I opened it and read through the mission parameters again. And again.

"Local legend suggested that the old church in the town was cursed, that it drove the residents of the town out into the world one by one, until only a few remained. The briefing papers told me that the town had been mentioned in many grimoires with forbidden knowledge of interest to the OEI. I was to get inside that building at all costs and use the black box to collect any data that I could.

"I didn't know why a government agency was looking to books on magic for places to investigate, but I couldn't deny my fascination with the old church.

"Eventually, I fell asleep with the brown folder in hand.

"And in that sleep, the door to the old church loomed before my sweaty palms.

"I ripped the rotting boards from the doorway, tossing them aside with wild abandon. What was left before me was the most extravagantly carved wooden door. Strange symbols stretched up and down its surface and I found myself caressing them, running my fingers through every angle and curve.

"Somehow, I knew that this was something of a seal. A powerful thing that kept whatever lurked beyond the door from entering our world.

"The doorknob was hot to the touch. But despite how much it burned, my grip held firm as I twisted.

"The door swung open and dark winds carried me inside."

"And what did you see?" Doctor Webber's expression is odd. The smug, malicious grin that was plastered on his face mere moments ago

222

is gone. When I make the mistake of looking into his eyes, the voice tells me that it is *hunger* that I see.

"I don't remember," I tell him. And for once, I'm telling the truth.

"You're telling me you don't remember anything?" Hunger is quickly transforming to anger. I'm not giving him what he wants. I could make something up, but he would know…he always knows.

I shake my head. "Yes. I'm telling the truth. I can't remember more than bits and pieces."

"Try harder."

"I can't give you what I don't have, Doctor."

"There are other ways to make you remember." Webber is looking at my notebook. He's going to take it from me if I don't tell him.

I need to tell him.

"Please, Doctor, I can't…I can't…"

"Orderly," Doctor Webber says, not breaking eye contact with me. "Take Subject 105's notebook and return him to his cell."

The floorboards are creaking.

Foul winds caress my skin.

The stench is unbearable, like rotting things and primordial worlds under black stars.

I must hold on. I must hold tight.

"Oh, and be sure to turn out the lights when you—"

February 29th, 1980

I've missed you so.

The orderly brought you back to me today.

I've been in that place so long I almost forgot what this twisting concrete maze looks like.

The orderly takes my arm and forces me to my feet. He's leading me back to the interview room, but no matter how hard it is, I know I must keep writing.

Writing keeps me from seeing what *it* sees.

The orderly makes sure to keep hold of my chains as he opens the door. Then he's yanking me along and shoving me back into my seat.

223

Doctor Webber is already sitting across from me.

"Are you ready to tell me what you remember?" He asks.

I nod.

"Then begin."

"What I said before. I was telling the truth. I did not remember. But...being in the dark. I saw it. I saw it all play out like a movie. I saw other things too. Hidden things. Things that this notebook was supposed to protect me from."

"What hidden things?"

I'm laughing. I can't help it. It's all so funny now.

"When I opened that door in the dream, I was pulled inside a vast mansion, one older than the very Earth on which we rest.

"I knelt upon a tattered red carpet that stretched up a twisting flight of ancient stairs.

"Though it seemed I was the only one there in that place, oddly enough, I felt as though something was watching me. Waiting for me. As if it had always been waiting for me.

"I walked up the stairs, taking one crooked step at a time. The proportions of the things inside that place, they weren't like they are here. I am not an artist. Not really. But the perspectives seemed odd, like they didn't follow the same rules things do in our world.

"Perhaps that's to be expected of a dream house? But this was no dream.

"I came across a vast corridor, one beyond the dimensions of the abandoned church. The red carpet stretched up to a circular chamber. At the center of that chamber was a four-foot-tall slab with strange markings embedded in it. A wooden box was resting upon its jagged surface.

"Fear gripped every morsel of my being. It commanded me to flee from that place, back to the safety of my room. Yet, with a fresh stream of piss spilling down my legs, still I was carried forward. I think through a force not totally my own.

"The stone slab was a kind of altar. Surrounding it was a white circle, painted upon a wooden floor with the texture of black marble. Along the circle's boundary were other, smaller circles. When my legs stopped moving, I looked down to see that I was standing in one of them.

"My body was not content with remaining there.

"No.

"The box loomed before my eyes; my hands itched to caress it.

"Before I knew what was happening, my digits were toying with the latch, my palm gently pushing the lid back.

"What I saw perplexed me. Inside the box was a small stone with dozens of flat polished edges. So dark it was nearly black. Those flat edges reflected the light from unseen torches in odd ways.

"The stone was not allowed to touch the bottom of the box. Instead, it was held aloft by two thin metallic wires that stretched across the center and two other supports that extended horizontally at an angle to the box's walls.

"At certain angles, it looked almost like the stone was floating between those wires.

"I could not take my eyes off of it; nor could it take its eyes off of me.

"It showed me things. I saw visions of places beneath all manner of colored skies; black suns burning above vast cyclopean cities; the dreaded depths of unknown space and terrible beings, some of which eclipse the might of the largest stars. I saw worlds die from wars waged by giant winged things that descended from the skies, eyes burning red, tentacles for mouths. And I saw vast, dead worlds, floating amongst a place where there are no stars to light their surfaces, where time was forgotten like the dead…

"…And then I saw you."

"Me?" He seems surprised.

"Not you. Not as you are. But a different you. One whose skin was ragged and graying much like mine must be now. One who clutched a book to his bosom, waiting for the right person to come along to start the cycle of corruption all over again.

"Yes. I saw you. Or someone just like you. After all, when Azathoth created our dream, its blind, idiotic screams splintered them like a mirror cracked into a thousand shards. In his eyes I saw the same hunger I see in yours. Do you know what that other you told me?"

225

"That you were not the one he was waiting for."

"Yes. It seems you have met."

After staring into my eyes for what feels like an eternity, Doctor Webber pulls out a tattered book from his lab coat and places it on the table; his dry, thin lips parting into a smile.

"Is this the book you saw?"

I nod.

"Interesting. I had a feeling I might be needing it today."

My eyes. I can't stop staring at the book. Its tattered, handmade leather edges. The crude markings that read MESSAGES FROM THE ABYSS.

"Would you like to hold it?" he asks.

How many secrets does it hold? Could any of them be the secret to my salvation?

Yes, the voices tell me.

"May I?"

I reach forward, the clink of my chains echoing through the chamber. Doctor Webber holds the book just out of my reach.

"I'll make you a deal," Doctor Webber says. "If you tell me everything I want to know. I will let you read it for as long as you want. Does that sound good to you, Subject 105?"

I nod.

"Then I suggest you continue your story."

"Promise me you'll let me read it."

"Of course."

I do not believe him…but what choice do I have?

I take a deep breath. Close my eyes. Pen to page. And focus on the rest.

"I saw myself standing before the box, my countenance twisted in total horror. That's when I knew something was wrong. I could see myself screaming, as if my unconscious self had witnessed something so terrible that it had paralyzed me. But still, I did not awake in my body, in the bed provided to me by the old woman. Still the nightmare did not end. I saw from something else's perspective, I saw a thing bobbing up and down, and I could hear a great flourish of wings in that desolate space.

"I watched as fight or flight finally took over my body, as it stumbled into a witless, frantic sprint toward the staircase.

"The thing got so close I could smell its rancid, protoplasmic flesh. I saw it reach out with claws made of twisting trails of smoke and I watched helplessly as my foot missed one of the steps. It is a strange thing, watching yourself fall down a staircase.

"I thought I was dead.

"The next thing I remembered, I was naked, on my knees, and facing the sealed door to the abandoned church.

"In my delirium, the Sheriff came and snatched me off my knees, dragging me to the edge of town. We came to a trap door in the snow and after he unlocked it, he led me deep underground.

"As we marched through a winding series of cavernous, torchlit tunnels, he told me a story. And I was lulled into passivity by his words.

"His story began in Providence, Rhode Island.

"There was a place there. One of the first Gothic cathedrals ever erected. Like Tiergetown's lonely, evil church, it too sat desolate and abandoned throughout most of the 1800s. The church was operated by a cult known to the locals as Starry Wisdom before they were chased out of town by an angry, God-fearing mob.

"They left behind their great work, and their most prized possession. The Shining Trapezohedron.

"Despite what the locals might have thought, Starry Wisdom did not create the device. Something much older fashioned it through a science that is as much magic to us as today's technology might be to prehistoric man. The device gave the high priests of Starry Wisdom the ability to see other worlds, the future, and even the connecting tissue between infinite universes.

"But it also came with a price. All those that used the box's gifts were cursed. Hunted by a thing made almost entirely of shadow. Light could keep the thing at bay, but if there is one truth about this universe that cannot be escaped it is that light is fleeting.

"Eventually, the shadows would get their way, and the being would take their lives—leaving their faces stricken with horror.

"It was seen as a great honor, to open the box and be gifted a brief glimpse at the secrets of the Great Old Ones.

"The locals boarded up the cathedral and surrounded it with lanterns to keep the shadow thing from leaving. But a severe thunderstorm left Providence in darkness, and not even the town's elders and torch wielding mob could keep the *thing* trapped inside from fleeing into the night and finding the one who so recently communed with the Shining Trapezohedron.

"It took Robert Blake's life and maybe his soul that night.

"The locals, fearing a great evil in the box, tossed it into the lake. But that was not the end.

"Narragansett Bay slowly carried the box out into the ocean, where it sank to unknown depths, eventually finding its way to the tribes of Dagon. The fish people, however, quickly learned that the dark depths of the ocean were no place for the Shining Trapezohedron and returned it to the surface.

"Grover, Delaware was a town and that's all anyone can really say about it today. There isn't a map made after 1920 that features it and no living roads to take you there now.

"One day, a girl found the box, believing it had washed up on the beach. Legend has it that its people were consumed by it.

"And they were.

"Their story would have been lost, but Grover, Delaware was also one of the last places where the descendants of Starry Wisdom had fled. A single woman whose name is now lost to time. She alone had the ability to resist the box's call to view its wonders.

"With the box secured, she traveled, eventually making her way to Alaska. As far as she knew, she was the last of her order. The last member of Starry Wisdom.

"And she was determined to keep the order's legacy alive.

"In Alaska, she would be safe.

"The old man said that it was in Tiergetown that she started a family. And she wasted no time in passing her order's secrets onto them.

"But, her husband, being a God-fearing man, resisted. He claimed that she was doing the devil's work and in the dead of night, attempted to murder her.

"The woman had other plans.

"A glimpse inside the box was all that was needed. The Haunter of the Dark took him. Over time, the woman's family grew, and Starry Wisdom was reborn.

"The woman would send her children out into the world to attract visitors by spreading vague rumors about an old church and a haunted village. And once they arrived, dreams would tempt them to enter the church to accept the box's gifts.

"The shadow thing would eventually take them, but not before the woman could absorb their knowledge for her order. To make a new book. A book of knowledge to rival even the *Necronomicon*'s reputation.

"The old man's voice stopped; it echoed off the cavernous walls. It was the end of the line. We stood before a massive staircase made from putrid, emerald stone that descended deep into a blackened pit. Foul, decaying winds assaulted my senses as we descended into that abyss, leaving the comfort of the caverns behind.

"Soon, even the furthest cavern wall was replaced with total darkness. With only the faint glow of those emerald stairs to guide us, all sense of time left me, and the world behind us was swallowed by the abyss.

"By the time the faint image of something glowing in the distance crept into my vision, the pain in my legs was so great it was like burning alive.

"The staircase ended and beyond it was a path to an emerald altar. Where the altar's phantom light could not reach, the vague outline of a thing with too many limbs writhed. Something which had overcome the mortal confines of this existence. As we drew closer, I could see it more clearly. Its skin was slightly translucent in the dark, a protoplasmic glow echoing off what I could only assume was a body covered in eyes.

"It could not have been human, but something told me that like the tribes of Dagon, through transformation, the limits of human physicality can sometimes be overcome.

"The old man told me to step onto the altar and obey her commands.

"HER.

"Could she have been the last descendant of Starry Wisdom? A voice that I would become all too familiar with in the future told me yes.

"I stepped onto the altar and the thing beyond it commanded me to kneel before HER in a voice and tongue totally alien to my conscious mind.

"Yet, I obeyed.

"I knelt down in a small white circle before HER unknowable girth.

"At the center of the altar, a tattered book with Starry Wisdom's seal etched into its cover lay open before me.

"HER voice commanded me to behold HER gaze.

"And I did.

"Dripping, slithering things crept in the dark, caressing my mind and probing the depths of what the box had shown me.

"In a way, as my physical body screamed into the depths of the abyss, it was almost comforting.

"When it was over, the old man dragged me back up the staircase and through the caverns, tossing my naked form onto the cold Alaskan earth.

"He told me to run. And to not look back. And I did."

"And what of the device we sent with you? Did you plant it inside the church?"

"I don't remember."

Doctor Webber takes in a deep breath and exhales slowly. He rubs his eyes and writes something down on his notepad.

"That's unfortunate," he says, "had you done as you were told, I might have had more incentive to give you what you want. Unfortunately, it seems as if we'll get more data from your termination than anything else."

"What? But you promised that—"

"You'll be doing your country, and humanity, a service, though. So, I'm sure you can take comfort in that."

"You're…"

The voices. They were right all along. He was never going to give me what I want. He wants it all for himself.

Webber snaps his fingers, and I can hear the orderly's boots smacking against the concrete, but he's not getting closer.

I hear the ruffling of Doctor Webber's coat as he stands up. The voices are demanding I look at him.

I can't.

He's walking away.

They're both at the door.

The voices are screaming.

They're going to leave me in here. They're going to leave me in here without the light.

I NEED THE LIGHT!

There's a click.

And the lights go.

The End

Dream Math

A Scion Cycle Story

By Matthew Davenport

Two Months After the Events of Miskatonic University: Elder Gods 101

The shades were drawn, and Sheryl Mason's room was filled with the calming sound of flute music from the computer speakers. The addition of incense filled the space as well, but not for its calming effect so much as Carlos's feet stunk like Hell.

Sheryl sat cross-legged in a sort of triangle with her friends Carlos Davies and Stephanie West. Each of the three Miskatonic University students had their eyes closed and were attempting to clear their minds of all clutter.

They were attempting. Sheryl was failing.

Carlos broke the silence.

"You won't figure it out if you don't practice."

That comment was enough to shake Sheryl from continuing. She opened her eyes and glared at her friend, even though his remained closed.

"Not all of us are naturally gifted Dreamers, Carlos," Sheryl replied. She scrunched up her face and tried to get her mind into the same headspace that Carlos had been preaching all day. The vast nothingness, or perhaps a cluttered table, where she could imagine removing each of the stray thoughts she had and putting it in a nearby receptacle. For Sheryl, it was a duffle bag.

Unfortunately, it was no use. You couldn't make yourself not focus on the things in your life and, at least for Sheryl, focusing on removing items from your "table" only made her focus on those things and why they were on her table in the first place.

Carlos opened his eyes.

"This has nothing to do with being naturally gifted at anything," Carlos frowned at Sheryl. "Besides, I am still learning too."

"Yes, the Dreamer speaks facts." Stephanie had seemed to master the concept of meditation and her face was one of complete peace as she spoke almost too quietly to be heard. "Carlos nearly left me in an alien hellscape last week. It was quite terrifying. I even took notes. Let's not give him too much credit."

Recently, Stephanie had begun blogging as a way to help compartmentalize her trips into the Dream Lands with Carlos. Her blog was gaining steam as a fiction horror blog, even though everything she described was painfully factual. At first, Carlos had been against it, not wanting to draw attention to himself, but she had pointed out that no one who read the blog believed it, and besides, she was getting a decent penny off of ad-revenue from the site.

"I said I was sorry." Carlos winced. Quieter and mostly to himself, he added, "I would hardly call it a hellscape. You had the little cannibals interested in adding you to their group of royal elders."

Stephanie's eye opened and she retrieved her glasses, putting them on as she asked, "Really? Royalty?" She stretched. "That is interesting. Although, I found their stench slightly worse than your current foot situation."

"Foot situation?" Carlos asked, shaking his head. "We're off topic. Sheryl," he turned back to his other friend. "Stress increases sleepwalking and if you can't figure out a way to clear your mind, the random trips won't stop." His look turned grave. "They could get worse."

Carlos was referring to Sheryl's problem with her power. She was a math witch. By focusing on the geometries and equations that built our reality, or other realities, she could alter or travel between those

233

realities. The problem was that she was entirely new to these powers with no mentor available to her. Before she had discovered who she was, Sheryl had suffered accidental trips into other, horrific, realities. They had mostly gone away as she learned what she could do, but had recently resurfaced in her sleep.

When Carlos said she was sleep-walking, he meant that Sheryl was opening gateways to other realities in her mind. If Sheryl lived alone, it likely wouldn't be a problem as her powers tended to protect her from the worst of those foreign lands. But the math student didn't live alone. She lived in a dorm room that she shared with Meredith Johnson. Meredith was an anthropology major at Miskatonic University. She had woken up too many times already in the wrong reality or on the wrong planet. It was only a matter of time before Sheryl came back while still asleep and left Meredith behind.

Sheryl threw up her hands and stood. Grabbing the game controller from the end of her bed, she booted up *Wicked West* and started in on a caravan mission.

"My mind obviously can't handle being at rest. If it could, I wouldn't be trying to solve dimensional mathematics in my sleep. This just isn't working."

Sheryl's disinterest in continuing to search for answers to her problems frustrated Carlos, who truly believed that a little bit of practice at meditation would solve this for her.

"Alright then," Carlos said, "what would you recommend?"

Sheryl shrugged, not taking her eyes from her video game. She was trying to act like none of this was bothering her, when all her friends knew that it was.

"I don't know," she said. "Maybe it's a phase?"

"Can you bet Meredith's life that it's just a phase?" Carlos demanded before smirking. "Or Stephanie's patience? She never wanted a roommate."

Stephanie stood up slowly, shaking the blood back into her limbs.

"Meredith, though pleasant, is too inquisitive for my comfort. She will either get herself hurt or her over-abundance of questions into my research will lead to me hurting her." She tilted her head to the side, "I would prefer to avoid that."

Sheryl let out a roar of frustration and tossed the controller onto a pile of laundry under the television. Stephanie walked over and picked it up, switching the gaming account to her own before she started playing on her character in the western-themed game.

"I don't know what to do, Carlos," Sheryl said. She was somewhere between feeling helpless and angry, and it was showing no matter how hard she tried to hide it. "I can't just not sleep and there doesn't seem to be any other alternative at this point."

"Exhaustion wouldn't make this better," Carlos shook his head. "Who knows what you would have to run your mind through just to try and stay awake, and the moment you fell asleep we might not be able to wake you if an event occurred."

"Then we're entirely out of ideas," Sheryl said, falling back on her bed and pulling a pillow over her face.

"We could speak with Nyla," Stephanie said.

"Who?" Carlos and Sheryl both asked at the same time.

Stephanie didn't look up from what she was doing as she answered them.

"Nyla Smith. She's an older medical student, working on her graduate degree. She did a presentation on her upcoming thesis for my class with Dr. Werner. The lecture was on inducing REM sleep chemically in braindead patients. She hypothesizes that if she can stimulate a dream state in the deceased mind, forcing the brain into a safe place of its own choosing, it would be easier to coax that brain back to full consciousness."

This idea seemed mildly offensive to Carlos, who didn't like the idea of using the realm of dreams to attempt to resurrect the dead. If these people were connected directly to the Dream Lands by this chemical process, their bodies could be vessels for other things and not the intended patient.

Then again, Carlos wasn't even sure if that's how it all worked, and at that moment he would gladly pass off Sheryl's problem to someone else.

"How could she help, though?" Sheryl asked. "A theory isn't going to help me knock out."

"I said a hypothesis." Stephanie frowned without taking her eyes from the video game. "Until the paper is done, she does not have a theory in place."

"Sorry," Sheryl murmured from under the pillow.

"Nyla's demonstration," Stephanie explained, "included her pharmacological recipe for the drug that would induce REM sleep. Specifically, deep sleep. Perhaps she can assist in giving you a stationary night's rest."

Nyla had given the class her campus email address in case they had any questions about her work. It took Stephanie a moment to find it before an email was sent about Sheryl's predicament. It was almost an hour later, and noticeably only ten minutes since the last class of the day, when Stephanie received a reply. Nyla wanted to meet at the Student Union.

The Student Union housed several restaurants for lunch as well as a decent cafeteria for everyone to sit, but Stephanie had chosen the coffee shop just inside the northern entrance to meet. In the afternoon it wouldn't be too busy, and it had only a handful of tables, so even if it were busy, there wouldn't be a lot of people present.

When the three of them arrived, Stephanie made introductions and then excused herself.

"If this turns into a dimension hopping disaster," she gave as a farewell, "please let me know. Otherwise, I will be doing my best not to murder my temporary roommate."

Nyla Smith had midnight black hair. It was so dark that Sheryl assumed she must dye it and Carlos was mildly put off by it as if it sucked you in. He didn't understand why. She looked a few years older than them and wore jeans with a black t-shirt. The t-shirt had Neil Gaiman's *Sandman*'s Death on it. She also had a silver ankh necklace around her neck. Aside from her hair, there was nothing about her that should have been setting any of his alarms off, but he couldn't look at her without being concerned.

Much as he had in the past, Carlos stretched his mind into the place he only recently realized was a connection to the Dream Lands. Normally when he did this kind of thing, he could get a fact or two about the person's life and who they were. It was never anything too world-shattering, but always something that was at least mildly useful. When he searched his dream-wiki for Nyla Smith he got nothing. That wasn't entirely unheard of but was still rare. Carlos did his best to file that in the back of his mind and continue forward. He was here for Sheryl.

Carlos and Sheryl didn't know where to begin, but before they could start, Nyla spoke up.

"Stephanie says that you're having sleep problems?"

Sheryl nodded. "I have a problem with, uh, sleepwalking."

"Waking up in strange places?" Nyla crossed her arms. "Your keys are never where you put them? Friends claiming that you've had entire conversations with them that you don't recall?"

"Something like that," Sheryl agreed. "Except, it's getting dangerous. I keep waking up in places or situations that aren't safe."

Nyla shook her head. "Normally, your subconscious will keep you from the more dangerous stuff. Do you mean, like, a busy street or something?"

"Exactly," Carlos answered for his friend. He knew he was looking suspicious but he couldn't help it.

"Is this a drug thing?" Nyla leaned back, frowning as she did. "Because if you're—"

"Ugh," Sheryl let out in disgust before focusing on an equation she had been using lately for when she needed peace and quiet.

The room around them was gone, except for the table and chairs that the three of them sat at. In its place was a space of angles carved into the black of nothing. Light came from nowhere, but they could still see just fine. The entire place had a hum that they could feel in their bones. As they resonated with it they were flooded with calm.

Despite the calm energy of the place, Nyla started. "What is this?"

"This is my problem," Sheryl said. "I can use math to go places. That part is cool. The problem is when I am sleeping."

Nyla was staring at everything and nothing as she finished Sheryl's explanation. "So, when you wake up in dangerous places, you mean entirely new places."

"Yes," Sheryl was smiling.

"We can't just show normal people this kind of thing," Carlos admonished her.

"Dude," Sheryl said, rolling her eyes, "she thought we were trying to buy drugs off of her."

Carlos was still upset, but the bridge had been burned and there was no point dwelling on it.

"So," he asked, "do you think that you could help her sleep without running dangerous math problems in her head?"

Nyla shrugged. "My studies have been around putting REM sleep into dead minds. This," she waved her hands around, "is entirely different."

"Would it hurt to try it on a living mind?" Sheryl asked.

Nyla shook her head. "There's nothing about the process that is harmful, or it would defeat the purpose."

"Can we test it out?" Sheryl asked.

Their new friend hesitated. "It's an untested drug, not approved by any organization. I don't even know what the potential side effects could be."

It was Carlos's turn to cross his arms and lean back.

"You designed it, you know what goes into it. What effect do the chemicals in the drug, historically, have on a person?"

Nyla leaned forward and opened the folder that she had brought with her, turning it to face the two friends.

"Nothing. Each chemical, in its original form, is sourced naturally and has no history of negative side effects. Generally speaking, most of the chemicals are meant for inducing sleep or regulating dream cycles. There is no reason, in my opinion, that together they would cause any sort of reaction in the average person other than the desired effect."

"How long would you need to make it?" Sheryl was having trouble holding back her excitement.

"I might already have some." Nyla smiled as she reached into her pocket and pulled out a small, clear vial with a cork in it. The substance inside was red in color and thick, like a cough syrup.

"That's convenient," Carlos mumbled.

His mumble didn't go unnoticed.

"I was hoping to show this to my professor this afternoon," Nyla pocketed the vial again.

"Sorry," Carlos said. "I don't mean to be suspicious, I just can't help it."

"You guys came to me," Nyla said. "If you don't want my help, just get us out of this thing," she waved her hands around, "and I'll gladly be on my way."

"No," Sheryl gave Carlos an angry look. "We want your help."

Nyla nodded looking at them both. "Fifty bucks."

"Oh," Sheryl hadn't expected Nyla to approve at all, but agreeing to help them and then also having a fee attached was a direction for which she hadn't prepared.

As a means of apologizing to his friend and their potential savior, Carlos offered to pay. Once Nyla had the money, Sheryl focused on a different equation and the world shifted again.

This time, they weren't in the coffee shop. The table and chairs had returned to their home, but the three people involved had landed in Sheryl's room, each of them sitting on her bed.

"That's trippy," Nyla said under her breath. "As this isn't my room, I guess that you want to get started immediately?"

Sheryl nodded. "What do I do?"

Nyla reproduced the vial, holding it up to the light.

"This is about two doses. Drink half of this and lie back. Then you just wait. If everything works, you will sleep the best you ever have. The only side effect should be that your dreams are more vivid than ever before. Then, I will monitor you to make sure that you don't go skipping across the universe."

"I want to take the second dose," Carlos spoke up.

"What? Why?" Sheryl asked, mostly concerned that if Carlos were to take the second dose and it works, then she wouldn't have a dose to take later.

"You know why," Carlos was trying to be secretive, which Sheryl had already explained he wasn't good at.

"Ugh," Sheryl grunted before turning to Nyla. "I've got a funny thing, so does he." She hooked her thumb at her friend, still sitting next to her on the bed. "He can walk in dreams."

Nyla frowned. "Like a Native American thing?"

"No," Carlos said, annoyed with Sheryl for sharing more of their private information with someone they'd just met. "Well, maybe. I guess it depends on what they actually did, but that idea kind of works. I can leave my body and go places. I want to go wherever Sheryl goes and make sure she stays safe."

"Uh-huh, sure," Nyla wasn't believing it. "Whatever, it doesn't matter." She uncorked the vial and handed it to Sheryl. "Let's get this over with, I want to start recording the results."

Sheryl drank what she felt was about half of the vial and handed it to Carlos. It tasted like a smoky meat stick, both good and weird, as that flavor should be in a liquid form.

Carlos stepped over to Meredith's bed and already felt the world tipping as he walked.

He laid down and saw that Sheryl was already under.

"Don't you need a notebook or … something for studying us?" he asked.

"You just worry about keeping up with Sheryl." Nyla smirked.

Carlos's head hit the pillow after he was already unconscious.

He opened his eyes to a storm. He was in some sort of cloud cover, thick and full of lightning jumping between the clouds. His feet felt like they were on something solid, but there was nothing beneath his feet that he could see.

He called out to Sheryl and started "walking" in a direction. When traveling through the worlds as a dream construct, which he figured he still was—even if it was chemically induced—intent and perception were more important than actual movement. The movement of his feet became symbolic, but his desire to find his friend would, hopefully, push him in that direction.

The storm shifted as he walked through it and he found himself in an ancient city. The sky under his feet faded into squared stones covering a path with buildings on each side. The entire road seemed only just wide enough for a car to get through. The buildings, ancient in design, with elaborate doors and weathered faces carved into the walls, rose up high enough to almost hide the sky. It gave him a very claustrophobic feeling.

He approached one of the walls. It flexed under his pressure but didn't break. It still felt like stone, but it flexed like rubber.

He had seen odder things while traveling between the worlds, so Carlos took this in stride and kept his focus on finding Sheryl.

———————————

Sheryl was in a deep forest surrounded by trees that had already shown themselves to be made of something that had a violent reaction when touched. Out of curiosity she had reached toward the weird, red-speckled bark and each of the speckles turned out to be an eye that all opened to look at her in that moment. Then the tree started thrashing and slamming its branches into the ground in an attempt to destroy her. The entire forest around her joined in as if rallying an army in the single tree's defense.

It was only by luck that she found a clearing without too many trees within "crush Sheryl" distance. She stood there, not sure which direction to move in and hoping that, at the very least, she wasn't subconsciously sucking the entire dorm into a similar danger-forest.

Sheryl sat there on the purple-colored moss that made up the forest floor for what felt like hours when she noticed the moss was shifting form to her direct right.

Sheryl jumped to her feet as the trees in that same direction parted and changed into stonework and shaped itself into buildings. As the moss solidified into a stone road, Sheryl saw Carlos walking up this new path and to her.

"Odd," Carlos said, "don't you think?"

"What is?" She was looking around her. "Do you mean the forest that eats people? To be honest, my small experience with dreaming makes this seem on par."

Carlos stepped up to her and put his hands into his pockets. The world shifted and his path into her corner of this universe disappeared, and the trees came back.

"Except, how are you supposed to leave?" he asked. "We aren't in the Dream Lands, not really, but we're someplace that seems to operate by the same rules. No matter where you go in the Dream Lands, you only end up trapped if that was the intent of the Dreamer."

"You're confusing me," Sheryl said.

"I should be scaring you," Carlos bent down to examine the grass. "I walked here to you by wanting to come to you. It's easier for Dreamers to direct their thoughts into molding the world, but that doesn't mean you can't do it. Did you want to be trapped in an angry forest?"

"No," Sheryl said. "Of course not."

"Then why are you?" He pointed up to the clouds. "I appeared in the sky, mostly because I expect to after so many trips into Dream. What do you want to do?"

"I don't want to suck everyone I care about into a mathematical portal," Sheryl said.

"Bingo," Carlos snapped his fingers. "How does this do that?"

"It … doesn't?" Sheryl wasn't getting what Carlos was trying to lead her to.

"That's my point. It doesn't," he said. "That tells me that you didn't make this place."

"Then who did?" Sheryl didn't have enough answers to ask the right questions, and Carlos could see that.

"I think I know, but I need more information," he said. "You will have to wait here, but I can go and check on my body now that I know where you are."

"Hurry," Sheryl said. The normally tougher of the girls in the group seemed distraught by her surroundings. "This place feels like it wants to eat me."

Carlos focused his mind and drifted back toward where he knew his home, his body, his anchor was.

Ralph, Carlos's Innsmouth born roommate, was in the room and feet away from his and Sheryl's bodies. For whatever reason, Carlos couldn't get back into his body. Carlos didn't know how he got there or what he was doing. His astral projection stood next to his friend as Ralph looked to be raging and yelling at a calm Nyla standing exactly where she had been when he fell asleep.

Noticing that he couldn't hear them, Carlos focused on centering himself more in his home reality.

"—them go," Ralph was shouting. "I will tear you apart!" Then Ralph slammed his fist forward and hit a solid mass that Carlos couldn't see.

A barrier.

Shifting his focus again, he saw as the barrier came into view. It glimmered a faint gold only inches from Ralph.

Suddenly, Meredith, Sheryl's roommate was coming through the door with her pistol, gifted to her by the occult administration of this school.

"Watch out," she brought the pistol into place and took aim at their would-be sleep savior. Before she could fire, Nyla raised her hand and both Ralph and Meredith were tossed back through the doorway and into an unprepared Stephanie.

The door slammed shut.

"See?" Nyla turned to face Carlos's ghost. "That's why I didn't want you drinking the second dose." She shrugged. "Couldn't be helped, I suppose."

"Holy crap," Carlos freaked out. "You can see me?"

"Obviously," was the only explanation he got. "You had better get out of here, I'm almost ready to invite my friends over and they can tear apart spirits as well as people."

Carlos looked at where Nyla's eyes had glanced. It was at Sheryl. A faint purple tunnel of light was stretching from Sheryl's chest to Nyla's.

"What are you doing? Are you going to possess her or something?"

"No, Little Dreamer. I won't be possessing anyone. Your friend can open doors, so I have her mind running some of that fancy math she knows so that a very specific door can be opened."

"Miskatonic University has protections," Carlos argued. "You can't just bring other things here."

"Yes, it does, but she doesn't." Nyla raised an eyebrow. "Haven't you connected the dots? Your friend isn't affected by the protections that the school has. You can anchor all of reality and it still won't have any effect on a math witch. They are the loophole." She sighed. "Look at me, doing classic villain monologues. Begone you, I've had it with your stupidity." She thrust her hand forward and Carlos could feel his essence being shredded into oblivion.

For Carlos, reassembling who he was took eons. He had to find where each piece of his mind and soul had been, collect it, and then figure out how to add it again to himself. He did this over and over again until he was whole again. Then he went back to Sheryl.

For Sheryl, wrapped in the magic of a prison made of someone's dreams, Carlos was gone for about fifteen minutes.

He explained what he saw.

Sheryl rolled her eyes. "Are you kidding me? The only person we find who might be able to help me and they turn out to be a witch or something trying to use me for my powers?"

Carlos nodded. It was weird how this kind of stuff was drawn to him. He recalled what the school administrative staff had said about the Scion Cycle and how he and his friends were instrumental in keeping the world as safe as it could be. This was probably part of that.

"Imprisoning you in a dreamscape show so she could use your body sounds like more than just a quick plan to take advantage of us." He rubbed his face while he thought, exhausted from the eons that were already fading from his memory. "If you were the end goal, we're talking years in the making. She had to know you would be here, with these gifts, and she had to put herself in a believable position to have access to the cover story that would have got her in place. It's too complicated."

"Unless you had mastery over space and time?" Sheryl offered.

Then they both remembered their secret class that they were taking, with only a select group of students in the know.

Elder Gods 101.

"You think this isn't a group or witch, but something less human." It wasn't a question, and he was starting to agree. "Knowing which less-human thing it is would help us out a lot, but there might be a less obvious way to stop her."

"And that would be?" Sheryl was still eyeing the scary trees.

Carlos couldn't help but notice that they seemed closer than when he had left. "Whatever Nyla is, we can stop her entire plan by getting you back to your body."

"You think?" Sheryl asked.

"It isn't for you to escape, but she also admitted that I wasn't supposed to take the second dose. She probably thought that I would be stuck here, too."

"And you obviously aren't," Sheryl said. "Get out of here and wake me up."

"We're getting out of here together," Carlos's mouth turned up in a smile. "I don't think she was as prepared for you as she thought either."

"What do you mean by that?" Sheryl had stopped looking at Carlos and was staring at the encroaching trees. They could now see them actively shifting in the moss toward them.

"I can get us out of here, but she's already shown me that she can keep us from getting back to our bodies," Carlos explained. "We'll need you for that, I think."

"Get a move on," Sheryl said. "The trees are almost in smacking distance."

Carlos grabbed Sheryl's hands and focused his will, pushing his mind into the powers of dream.

Almost instantly, the road to the ancient city opened. Not letting go of Sheryl's hand, Carlos led her as they ran down the new path and to freedom.

"This is somewhere actually in the Dream Lands. It looks a little too Roman for Ulthar, but I haven't been there in months." Carlos shook his head. "It doesn't matter. This is where you come in. I need you to

245

math us back to our world, and specifically, as close to our bodies as you can get us. She has a shield to keep me and our friends from interfering. Can you still do Dream Land math?"

Sheryl nodded, but she still looked frustrated. "It would be easier with a calculator or my phone."

Carlos shrugged.

Sheryl closed her eyes and started moving her finger in the air. After what felt like ten minutes, she opened her eyes. "I think I've got it."

Carlos's eyes lit up. "Let's hit eighty-eight miles per hour and get out of here, then."

"*Back to the Future* doesn't work here," Sheryl said. "This is more of a TARDIS thing."

Carlos let out two slow and deep groans. "Is that better?"

"*Allons y!*" Sheryl shouted and then mentally pressed on the space in the math that made the most sense.

A fissure in that reality tore and they could see Sheryl and Meredith's room on the other side.

Stepping through, they were standing behind Nyla. She sensed them somehow and spun to blast them with whatever force she had used to scatter Carlos earlier. A quick glance showed the friends that their companions were on the other side of the door, already cracking through it.

Sheryl surprised Carlos by running right at Nyla. As a spirit and not a dreamer, Carlos wasn't sure what she could do. Nyla, on the other hand, freaked out.

She dove out of Sheryl's reach and continued to leap around the tight space to avoid the spectral grasp.

Which gave Carlos enough time to get back into his body.

He stood up and slammed his open palm into Nyla's forehead.

Darkness engulfed him. He was floating in a fathomless void.

A voice spoke to him.

The words hurt.

"You've bitten off more than you can chew, Dreamer." Pain coursed through every fiber of Carlos's being. "I should destroy you completely... except this would cause me different complications."

"Leave us," Carlos shouted through gritted teeth.

"The battle is yours," the voice said. "I seek to win the war. Your friend has earned her peaceful rest."

Carlos was back in Sheryl's room. Sweat drenched his clothes and his hand was still held up to where Nyla's head had been.

Except that she was gone.

Ralph burst into the room with Meredith and Stephanie behind him.

Sheryl sat up.

"Hey guys," she smiled weakly.

Ralph was panting while Meredith searched around the room with her magic pistol.

Stephanie gave a small wave to Sheryl.

"Nyla was a monster?" her question couldn't have had less excitement in it if she had asked about the weather.

"Yup," Sheryl said.

"Something worse than a monster," Carlos said, not wanting to use the g-word but having a distinct suspicion of who Nyla really was now.

Stephanie looked at Carlos. "And you dispatched her?"

"Yes," he nodded.

Stephanie turned to her friends. "Shall we get dinner?"

The End

The Siege of New Ulthar

A *Cthulhu Armageddon* adventure

By C. T. Phipps

Chapter One

D oom had come to New Ulthar.

New Ulthar was, in simple terms, a shit hole. It was a cattle town—if you stretched the definition of the mutant steers sold here enough to call them "cattle"—but also a place where every vice imaginable was permitted. Nay, even welcomed by the locals. Gambling, prostitution, and murder were indulgences permitted in every town from here to New Arkham, but New Ulthar took the next step. Here, the townsfolk were willing to overlook eyes where they should not be and the worship of things that should never have their names uttered.

If you wished to marry something that barely qualified as human, then you didn't have to hide it in the basement unless it was going to eat someone. It was a town where minding your own fucking business extended well past virtue into a kind of selective insanity. In the last days of humanity, when the Great Old Ones had risen, and hope was a distant memory, New Ulthar was the sign that humanity would go out with not a bang but a whimper. A ragged, twisted, deranged bunch of oddballs and degenerates who were barely kept in line by their appointed dictator of a sheriff.

That was me, by the way.

Yes, New Ulthar was a shit hole, but it was my shit hole, and I was sure as shit not going to let some scumbag living dead, fungus-ridden bandits come to loot my town. If this was the last days of humanity—which it almost certainly was—I was not going to abandon my little piece of Purgatory to a gang of raiders come to burn it to the ground.

"John, you're being stupid," Mercury said, standing beside me as I laid out the various weapons I'd prepared for confronting the Yellow Raiders.

Mercury was my partner in most senses of the word, a redheaded Eurasian woman who was wearing a dirty white linen shirt and a pair of black, stained slacks. She was currently holding a rifle as she looked up at me. It was a ridiculous weapon since I knew she could do things with sorcery and monsters that could lay waste to far more than any gun could ever do. I just wasn't sure that would help in this situation.

The two of us were in our shared business called The Wages of Sin, a half-saloon and half-brothel that I'd inherited by the oldest law of the Wasteland: you kill the owner then you get their stuff. The customers had been cleared out and I was now trying to assemble what broken weapons, idols, and amulets we had in hopes of figuring out something that could repulse the swarm of locusts about to descend on our Biblical Egypt.

The building was the remnant of an old Pre-Rising hotel/motel that had been patched repeatedly by me and others over the past century since the end of the world. It was full of old wooden benches and plastic chairs that didn't exactly scream high class, but the kind of customers who drank here didn't care about ambiance.

"Maybe I *am* being stupid," I said, surveying the rows of guns and mystical artifacts on the tables. New Ulthar was half in and half out from the Dreamlands, so things that wouldn't normally have any power now did. Religious artifacts, lucky charms, and personal totems might give a slight edge against the Undying King.

"But smart would leave us running into the Wasteland without anything to our names and that's its own kind of stupid."

"You stupid bastard," was Mercury's only answer to that.

"Yep."

"And for these assholes?" Mercury asked, waving her hand toward the village around us.

"Yep."

There was a time when I had been a United States Remnant Ranger and was supposed to protect the pure-blooded humans of our home base. That was before I found out I wasn't a pure-blooded human myself, but a Kastro'vaal—something closer to shoggoth than man—and that everything about me was just illusion. I was a mad monster pretending to be a human and would have been destroyed by my own people if they'd known the truth. Mercury and Jackie were with me despite the fact we didn't share anything resembling proteins, let alone blood. And yet we were a family, nonetheless. New Ulthar was about the only place that our arrangement would be accepted, though. At least until the last of humanity passed from the earth in fifty years or so. That was a prophecy coming closer every day.

"Do you want me to lay any land mines, Dad?" Jackie asked, gathering supplies from the back room.

"What the hell?" Mercury asked, confused. "Where did you even get those?"

"Remember that guy who tried to eat Becky?" I asked.

"Which one," Mercury said.

"The second one," I said. "He left an entire wagon full of them."

Mercury shook her head.

"I hate this town so much."

"You love it," Jackie said, coming out with two arms full of landmines. "It's the only place that wouldn't burn you at the stake."

Jackie Howard was a ghoul, though she hadn't yet made the transformation into one of the feral lycanthrope race that dwelled underground. Her human mother meant that that she wouldn't begin her transformation until she was about thirty. Theoretically. Even now at twenty, she already was showing signs of her unnatural heritage that marked her as different from the so-called "normal" humans of the Wastes.

Jackie was over six feet in height and extremely muscular, standing above most men, not just women. Her hair was a tangled mess, impossible to brush, and hung down to her waist. She had just the

250

barest traces of fur on her palms as werewolves were once identified by. Her eyes were an iridescent shade of green and her canines pronounced to the point of looking like fangs as the rest of her teeth came to points. Despite her obvious inhumanity, Jackie reveled in the effect she had on others and dressed in cut shorts as well as a shirt tied at the midriff. Sand, dirt, and the acidic rain did not bother her the way they did creatures of mere homo sapiens flesh.

"Burning doesn't always kill witches," I said. "I remember one that exploded into flesh-eating maggots and tore half the town to pieces."

"That's an urban legend," Mercury said, reluctantly taking the mines from Jackie one by one and stacking them. "Probably. You never can tell what's a lie and a truth these days."

"The ghouls of Tremortown say that anything that can be dreamed of by man or beast is true somewhere in the Dreamlands," Jackie said, rubbing her hands. "They said that the Old Ones awoke because Yog-Sothoth tore a hole and let them all come spilling into the world. That's why the ghoul race doesn't fear death because they know life and death are one and the same."

"And that's why I think religious people are all crazy," Mercury said. "Especially when I have proof gods exist."

Mercury had once been a die-hard atheist who had been raised on the lessons of the United States Remnant's dogma that the Great Old Ones were nothing more than humungous aliens with vast psychic powers and incredibly advanced technology. It was our feeble defense against a universe intrinsically hostile to all life.

Unfortunately, even the sad illusion that we could hold our own against the madness of reality had been plucked from her mind when we'd been forced to use technology beyond the grasp of even the mightiest of Earth's minds to bring Cthulhu back to the Earth it had escaped. Mercury had witnessed the legendary Sleeping God in all its glory and had been driven mad by the experience.

I'd done a terrible thing, violating her mind to bind away what she'd seen, but it had left marks. Now I found her praying at night to clay idols with human fat candles dedicated to Old Ones and gods I'd never heard of. That didn't bother me as much as the fact that sometimes I could hear them answering.

"We live in the worst of both worlds," I replied. "The gods are real and they're uncaring assholes. We're the fungus growing on the toes of beings infinitely older and more powerful than us. Beings that will outlive this universe."

"Thanks, John," Mercury said. "Because we really need that before our life and death struggle with the Yellow Raiders."

I grimaced. "You have a point."

No one knew the origin of the Undying King. A scarecrow-looking man with a burlap sack over his head, riding an emaciated, half-dead horse, showed up on the edge of Little Stone a month ago. He had ordered everyone to offer up their children to Hastur. When they didn't, he'd destroyed the entire town. A week later, he'd shown up at Ghostrock with all Little Stone's dead behind him as well as an army of remnants. All of them were covered in a vile, yellow fungus growing in and out of their corpses, spreading a horror that animated them like puppets. This time the local headman had grabbed every child from their parents' arms with his goons and offered them up. The Undying King promptly destroyed the town anyway.

There was no way of escaping across the Wasteland, and destroying an army of the already dead was probably impossible. Nevertheless, the Undying King's actions provided a nice level of certainty to my chosen course of action. If the choice was dying on your knees or dying on your feet, then it was easy to throw yourself into the meatgrinder. Sun Tzu said something about that but, lacking a copy of *The Art of War*, I had to paraphrase it.

"Well, I think that's every weapon we have," Mercury said, staring at the row after row of weapons. "Do we even have ammunition for all of these?"

"Some," I replied, not at all that confident. "A few of these are busted beyond repair."

"Gun maintenance takes a backseat when you become a tentacle monster," Mercury said, insulting me.

"Please don't," I said, still hating every moment of my life when I lost control and abandoned myself to the thing inside me.

Eventually, no matter what choices or desires I might have, the alien mind would consume the human mind and leave nothing left of

John Henry Booth, Recon and Extermination Ranger. In its place would be a far older thing that had lived millions of years in various forms across time. A thing that had as much in common with a human being as a cat. Hell, far less because at least a cat was a creature of carbon and base proteins. The Eyes of Yog-Sothoth, as my "true" race was known, lived outside time and could assume the forms of beings who bathed in lava or drifted across airless voids.

I'd managed to hold onto a semblance of my prior self, though even that I couldn't be entirely sure of, due to the fact the monster had time on its side. Humankind didn't have a future, our world was too hostile, and there were only a couple of generations left until we went extinct. When that happened, if I somehow survived, I would have no choice but to give in to the beast within. It would be better to live wild and free, like the Old Ones, than be the lone thing that remembered mankind when we were nothing more than dust on the road of greater beings' travels.

On the other hand, I was probably going to die today so what was the point in worrying about such things? Death may eventually die but it would probably be after he claimed me.

"I'm just saying that we may have a chance with you," Mercury said, sounding like she was trying to convince herself more than me.

"I'm not immortal," I replied. "You of all people should know that it's not impossible to kill the creatures of other worlds. We've both done it and plenty of them were tougher than me. We were just the wasps lucky enough to sting them to death. Magic tricks or not."

Mercury didn't immediately respond. She'd started as a virtual slave to the Remnant government, doing whatever horrible things she needed to survive. Now she was free and had turned to the sorcery of ghouls and the late Alan Ward to seek power over her life. It cost much of her soul, as such things existed, but provided control over her life. That control was an illusion, though. Even if sorcery could make you the strongest ant in the world, it didn't make you any less likely to be squashed.

"I don't want to die here, John," Mercury said, almost a whisper.

"I don't want to either," I replied.

"Don't you?" Mercury asked.

253

The statement hung in the air with no definitive answer. Life as a monster or merciful death as a man. Was I here prepared to fight against an army of the dead because I didn't want to abandon the twisted little burg I'd set myself in, or because I figured this was a way to die semi-human? After all, stupidly throwing your life away was one of the things humans did best.

The somber, fatalistic mood was interrupted by Jackie's baby, Baby John, crying out above our heads in one of the second-floor rooms. Jackie was a mother now, her child carrying more mixed human as well as ghoulish blood, and watching her rush up to tend to the child caused me to reevaluate my priorities.

"Too bad that kid doesn't have a future," Mercury muttered.

"He does if we win," I replied.

"Will we?" Mercury asked, turning back.

"Yes," I said, deciding we will. I had no way of guaranteeing that and it might be delusion, but if you lost the battle in your mind before it happened then there was no point in fighting it at all. Baby John would inherit a dead and dying world no matter what I did, but the Old Ones' lives were measured in epochs not years or decades. Maybe I could make it so Jackie and her child lived long enough to have a human's lifespan. However short and insignificant that was to a ghoul, let alone the creatures that existed far longer than their entire race had since they evolved in the Neolithic Era.

"Good. That's all I want from you. A lie that we can believe in so this worthless hellhole will have a fighting chance. I'll even give you free rounds with the girls," Mercury said, going over to the table with remnants of our last big adventure: the one against the Unimaginable Horror where seven heroes had set out to save the world and only a few had lived to tell the tale.

"I'll have free rounds with the best girl in the house," I replied, giving a half-smile.

"Don't get romantic, John, it doesn't suit you. Will this help?" Mercury asked, handing me a belt with two holsters. They were Thom Brannan's guns, each emblazoned with the hellish brand of Cthugha the Living Sun that Eats. Things that could kill me. Maybe things that could kill the Undying King.

I pulled out both from their holsters, feeling a malign intelligence inside them that wanted to kill me as much as anything else in the world.

"Yeah, I think these will do nicely."

Chapter Two

I didn't have a chance to think more about my situation because the door to the Wages of Sin opened and let in a few of those poor fools who'd decided to stay. Not that there was any place to flee to right now. The destruction of Little Stone and Ghostrock had cut us off from part of the Greater New England Wasteland. What little "settled" territory that existed was now isolated and perfect for this undead host to wipe us from the face of the cosmos. That didn't mean plenty of New Ulthar residents weren't trying it. I didn't expect to see them again because if they could outrun the Yellow Raiders, they wouldn't outrun the heat and lack of supplies.

The first of these poor brave fools who were joining me in my assisted suicide by undead horde was Becky Khatri, a lovely girl of East Asian descent that was wearing a smudged white spring dress. While formerly a working girl here at the Wages of Sin, she'd somehow managed to move beyond bare survival into one of the few nice homes leftover from before the Rising.

While a savvy businesswoman, I noted that was mostly due to the fact the previous occupants were eaten by something, given all we'd ever found of them was a boot with half a missing foot next to an incorrectly made Elder Sign drawn in blood on the floor. Becky was a crack shot from days when her family had killed mutated but still terrestrial varmints for the other families. Her rifle, made in the last ten years but equal to anything made in the Old World, was slung over one shoulder. A pleasant little hat was resting on her head, as if this were all a summer's eve rather than the end of this part of the world.

Behind her was Matt "Wild Dog" Davenport, a tall man built like an oak tree with a thin goatee and a vest over a blue shirt with black slacks. A pair of thin spectacles rested on his nose and a revolver was holstered awkwardly to his side. Matthew was a writer from Kingsport who had somehow found himself down the rabbit hole of the Wasteland's strangest town. Which was saying something. I fully believed he was only here for Jackie and otherwise would have fled. It was noble. Foolish, but noble.

The third individual rounding out the group was August Bierce, a chocolate-skinned man with a shaved head and a beatific expression on his face. August dressed starkly different from the rest of the town, wearing a robe-like leather trench coat and metal goggles that protected his eyes. August had been driven mad by looking upon Cthulhu as well but while I debated putting a bullet in the head of the wizard as he stared catatonically up at the ceiling, he came out of his deranged state on his own.

I honestly wasn't sure if he were the same man I'd met earlier—and didn't particularly care—his magic was of a different sort than Mercury's. Not necessarily stronger, but he could command the beasts of other dimensions to do his bidding. Things far older and stronger than anything Earth had produced. That was why he was the one man I feared as I always wondered if that included me. Death was better than slavery as I knew what horrible things could be done when a man lost control of himself.

"Sheriff?" Becky asked. "Are those all the weapons you were able to assemble?"

"Technically, I'm a Marshal," I replied. "A Sheriff requires an election in a county."

"Technically, you're neither because you're just the local murderer they've put in charge to kill the people the locals dislike most," August said.

Whenever I doubted he was still the same man as before seeing Cthulhu, he said something like that and reminded me that alien consciousnesses were unlikely to replicate August's peculiar brand of assholery.

"Yes, Becky, these are all the weapons I was able to get out of our little slice of Hell."

"How many volunteers were you able to muster?" Mercury asked.

"Seventeen," Becky said, listing a depressingly small number even for a flyspeck of a town. The world's population was dwindling rapidly but not so much that that wasn't infuriating.

"Do they expect to be spared if they don't fight?" Mercury asked.

"No, they're all holed up in their houses," Matthew said, sighing. "They'll fight to defend their homes and property but won't lift a finger to save each other."

I sighed, not even surprised.

"We need to hang together or surely we'll hang separately."

"I'd rather not hang at all," Becky replied, not getting the double meaning. Language had changed a bit since Ben Franklin's time.

"Seventeen is not enough to cover the town edge," Matthew said.

"No shit," Mercury said, rolling her eyes. "It's not even enough to do a twenty-one-gun salute."

"Yes, that would be twenty-one," Becky said.

Mercury and I looked at her side eyed.

"What?" Becky asked.

"It's not too late to try to escape, sir," Matthew said, looking at me. "There's nothing you can do to stop this, and no one would blame you for not trying."

"Except everyone before they died," August replied. "But they'll be dead, so you won't have to worry about their opinion."

Matthew glared at him then turned back to me.

"At least try to send Jackie and her baby away. She deserves better than to die horribly out here at the monster's hands."

I wasn't sure who exactly he thought did deserve to be torn to shreds by a madman leading an army of fungus zombies, but men in love were stupid the universe over. Even the Kastro'vaal had something equivalent, though they were a race that bred with countless other species, growing their children inside them like parasites. We were a race of cuckoos, and it was hard to say if we were really kin to the races we joined with at all. Then again, I'd changed enough that I tended to think of Deep Ones, serpent men, and ghouls as just other versions of humanity.

"I'm the eighteenth gun in this posse," Jackie said, descending the stairs, holding Baby John. "I'm not going to be abandoning my ma, pa, or friends. Few as I have of them."

Baby John was clearly not Matthew's baby, for reasons of skin color and the fact he hadn't appeared in her life until a few months after the baby's birth, but I could see the look on his face was one of a proud father.

"You have plenty of friends, Dog Girl," Becky said. "I'd happily play fetch with ya if you weren't likely to bite my hand off."

Jackie narrowed her eyes. "Quiet, Monkey Girl."

"I'll have you know that some of your best friends are monkeys," Becky said. "Me—"

"Wrong," Jackie said.

"Matthew," Becky said. "Your mother. I'm not sure about John. He has that worm that walks sort of feel."

"Thank you," I replied, resenting the comparison. The people of New Ulthar were far more accepting of the unnatural than most of humanity's scared scattered remnants, but that didn't mean it wasn't more convenient if they thought of me as a human. Just one that had made some sort of dark compact with eldritch forces. Apparently, that was better than being a wholly alien creature.

Somehow.

"You're welcome," Becky said. "In any case, we don't have much time. It's about a couple of hours until the Yellow Raiders arrive. Old Blind Sue saw it in a chicken's entrails."

"Is that, uh, accurate?" Matthew asked, confused.

"Extremely," August replied. "There's no way for you to escape even if you wanted to. Their rotted horse corpses would track down even the most tireless rider."

"Shit," Matthew said, looking down at the ground.

"It's okay," Jackie patted him on the shoulder. "I promise I'll shoot you before they get to you."

"Uh, thanks." Matthew looked less than reassured by this statement.

I didn't want to think about what that offer to kill her lover meant for Jackie's child. I fully believed that, if the situation came down to it, Jackie would kill her child before she allowed it to be torn to shreds by the Yellow Raiders or reanimated as yet another of their weapons. This was the world now as we lived in it. I needed to find a way to get the child away and cursed myself for not doing it sooner.

"Could we have a moment alone, John?" August asked, putting on a pair of thick leather gloves.

"Sure, August," I muttered. "What is it?"

August led me outside the Wages of Sin into the dirty, shit-smelling, mud streets of New Ulthar. A rain barrel was nearby, catching water that was pouring down from a light thunderstorm. The general store, stables, gunsmith, and butcher were all visible from my hotel doorstep. A windmill farm in a lonely set of hills above our town provided what little power we needed, though it could also catch lightning according to its mad owner.

Most notable about New Ulthar was the fact that it had about four cats for every citizen and the place was utterly littered with strays. They came in every color of the rainbow and were a particularly foul-tempered set of unidentifiable mixed breeds.

It had been a capital crime to harm a cat in New Ulthar by the time I'd taken over as Sheriff and I'd enforced the law since. Not that it had required much enforcing as the locals—at least the ones who had been here before my arrival—had a passionate fear of violating said taboo. Personally, I much preferred dogs, but avoided harming any of the local felines. They always seemed to be *watching*.

"I'm not going to be joining you in your protracted suicide," August said, dryly. "I'll be leaving ahead of the Raiders."

I stared at him, balling my fists. "You heard what they said. There's no way to escape."

"No, there's no way for these poor fools to escape," August said. "I might walk through the spaces of time, send my spirit across the globe to another poor fool's body, or turn into a great nightgaunt that flies far into space on the winds of Azathoth's breath."

"And these people mean nothing to you," I said.

"Absolutely not a thing," August said. "They are one of the most aggressively ignorant and uncultured races in the universe."

"And you know many?" I asked, not even that surprised.

"Oh yes," August replied. "My encounter with the Lord of R'lyeh sent me on a journey to distant Kadath where I awakened many of my past lives. In them, I saw such things as to make the destruction of Earth and its populace seem like a mercy killing."

I stared at him. "I'm so happy to hear that."

"There are other places than this world," August said. "Dreamlands made in the image of Earth and even parallel versions of this world. The past, the present, and distant realms where you could assume the form of a local to live out their lives. If you are so inclined."

"I am not," I said.

August rolled his eyes. "I knew you'd say that."

"Which is why you've wasted your efforts and my time," I replied. "Something that I no longer have much of."

"A strange condition for an immortal being," August replied. "That is, unless he is set on ending himself."

"Death holds no mysteries for me," I snapped.

"How can it when it is an end?" August said. "Life is an illusion and even if consciousness can be picked up by future generations or preserved like a fly in amber amidst the streams of time, how can it be said to be the same thing as it was? The soul is extinguished every second of the day, constantly changing like a river, and it is an interrupted continuity of consciousness every time we go to sleep, let alone die. Life as we know it is but a particular form of insanity that we delude ourselves in having value. Like your whore in there or faux grandchild."

I was tempted to put two rounds into August's stomach and make a pithy line about agreeing his life had no value. Certainly, it wouldn't be the first cold-blooded murder I'd committed just because some fucker had annoyed me. However, I wasn't in the mood for whatever reason. August was his own creature and had never pretended otherwise. Maybe honesty was his one redeeming quality, if it could be called that.

"Then get the hell out of here," I said, making a dismissive wave.

"If it's any consolation, I contacted the forces of the Arkham Republic," August said. "They have weapons that can lay waste to this particular strand of evil. Shells, tanks, flamethrowers, and disposable fools that think themselves to be heroes by throwing themselves into the jaws of monsters."

The Arkham Republic was what the United States Remnant had renamed itself after, ironically, losing New Arkham. They'd spread out

261

into the Wasteland and used their weapons to take over Kingsport, Scrapyard, and a dozen other locations. They were driven by a perverse Manifest Destiny that was even more delusional than believing we had a chance here.

Because they could not accept that humanity was doomed, they sought to conquer and reunite as much of the East Coast as possible. They'd already run into unbreakable walls with the Dunwych tribal nations and the Miskatonic cultists, but they had established dozens of trade routes. There was even talk they'd activated an old power plant managed by ghouls and were laying down track for a revived train system. Not that such a thing was a sane project with things like tunnelers and beasts the size of ruined skyscrapers.

"My daughter and son are New Arkham citizens," I replied. "The ones by blood."

"And doomed to become monsters themselves?" August asked. "I hope they're not stupid enough to join the military like you. Mind you, I would have told them of their destiny. Do they even know you're a monster?"

I didn't answer him.

"How strange you so readily leap to death at the hands of the Undying King but are too cowardly to confront your real family about their coming doom," August said.

I had been married to a woman named Martha prior to my exile from New Arkham. She was a psychic and, at the time of our prearranged union, had been the "freak" of our pairing. We'd had two children, Gabriel and Anita, who had been left behind when I was forced to walk the Wasteland for the crime of surviving an attack no human should have. I loved my children, but I was a catastrophe that had come into their lives. They'd been doomed before they'd even been born, and I simply hoped they were not actually my children or somehow the curse of my alien blood would pass them.

"They would not appreciate a monster," I replied. "Better I stay out of their lives than infect them with the alienness I bring."

"So speaks a man given the keys to heaven and immortality yet complains that they are silver not gold," August replied.

"What?" I asked.

"The look on your face," August said. "Romanticizing humanity and death as if they were things that were worth doing so. Humans are ugly bags of water and meat that smell terrible after just a short time in the sun. They were one of evolution's mistakes and nature is now correcting that delusion."

I smiled and patted him on the shoulder. "I'm going to miss you, August. Some of the time we spent together was almost enjoyable."

August frowned then shrugged.

"Goodbye, John. Before I take my leave, I wanted you to know that there were some Dunwych looking for you."

"I guess they're just out of luck," I said.

"Perhaps," August said. "But I have the feeling you will survive this. The question is will anyone else?"

Chapter Three

I wish I could say that August became a giant eagle, disappeared in a puff of smoke, or even slipped into the shadows. Magic was often dramatic like that, at least since the Reveal, but I just looked away for a moment then turned around to find he was gone. It was said the Kastro'vaal could slip through time and space like that, part of their relationship to Yog-Sothoth, but it was a trick that I couldn't do.

I knew a little magic, a few tricks that I'd picked up from Mercury and the late Alan Ward, but nothing that could mark me as a wizard. It was ironic because as a monster, I probably could do things regular human beings would be torn apart by due to the forces they were channeling. Assuming any regular humans still existed.

Gods and Old Ones, I never stopped complaining, did I? Maybe August was right that I did lionize mortality and humanity more than both deserved.

Heading to the walls that had been erected around as much of the main part of the town as possible, I checked that they were properly secure. They weren't, being made of nothing more than welded together pieces of steel that were as fragile as a wire fence. The people gathered on the platforms—our seventeen—were a mixture of the elderly and the too young. People who had very little to live for or too little experience to know they weren't invincible.

Beyond the walls of Ulthar was a massive mud flat that in better times would be able to grow blood grass. Blood grass was one of the things, like mushrooms, that mankind had been reduced to eating almost entirely due to the inability to digest most other mutated plants. Most plants and animals that humanity had once subsisted on were almost extinct now. We lived on mutated cattle, this peculiar type of weed, things grown in our own shit or corpses, and a handful of other unappetizing things. Now the blood grass had all been harvested and it would be a few more weeks before the next crop arrived, leaving only an endless sea of blackish sludge.

The farms and ranches that tried to grow other than these things were behind us and I wondered if the Yellow Raiders would hit them first. Somehow, I doubted it. They didn't come here to slaughter animals, but the people inside, as little difference existed between humans and their beasts of burden. No, the Undying King seemed only to want to extinguish the race of man and its various offshoots wherever he found it. Or she. Truth be told, I had no idea whether the Undying King was a man or a woman. I'd met plenty enough she-cats and wild women who were every bit as vicious as a man.

In the end, no longer waiting for me back at the Wages of Sin where I'd left them, the rest of our meager posse assembled as the rain went from a drizzle to a full downpour. In the skies above our heads, I could see a strange aurora of weird colors and new stars that reminded me that the world was getting stranger rather than more normal. I wasn't even sure if we could still be a living world anymore. Sometimes I wondered if we'd died at some point, and this was just Hell. It bothered me that I couldn't really find any coherent points to refute my musings.

Mercury came up by my side as everyone else assumed what positions they could.

"I don't suppose you have any tricks left?"

"I radioed for help," I replied. "No response from the Dunwych. The Miskatonic cult flat out said no."

"What about New Arkham?" Mercury asked.

"August apparently took care of that," I replied. "No dice. I think they'd kill everyone here if they somehow defeated the horde."

"You're exaggerating," Mercury said. "They'd give everyone a blood test first and then slaughter all the mutants as well as hybrids. There would be at least one or two children spared. Just not Baby John. Oh, and maybe they'd keep a breeding female or two."

"We were definitely working for the wrong side," I replied, keeping my gaze focused forward on the mud flat. I could feel this was the direction they were coming.

"There is no right side," Mercury replied. "There's just winners, losers, the living, and the dead."

"A very convenient philosophy," I replied.

"The living can afford to debate morality," Mercury replied. "The dead don't have to."

"Morality is usually about rules for keeping you alive and making sure you don't destroy any long-term gain for short-term benefits," I replied. "Also, to provide meaning in a senseless world."

"You know, August is right. You are a depressing bore."

"You're only now picking this up?" I asked.

Mercury chuckled. "So, I'm going to take that as a no on the tricks."

"I'll turn into whatever kind of monster I can," I replied. "But I can't beat an army by myself."

"You killed a shoggoth once," Mercury said. "With magic pistols."

"I got lucky," I replied. "There's not a lot of that to go around. How about you?"

Mercury stared. "I have what magic I could prep."

"What was the cost?" I replied.

"Don't expect to see Old Man Jim Joseph again," Mercury replied. "I saw him trying to leave while his grandkids were holed up in his cellar. His blood didn't exactly give me much to work with, but it was better than nothing. Nodens will provide, though."

I didn't respond, simply noting that I couldn't bring myself to condemn her for what amounted to human sacrifice. At this point, desperation had blotted out most of my old morality and I was willing to forgive almost anything of Mercury. Which was already much as we'd both wronged each other horribly.

"What about Baby John?" I asked, feeling the anticipation in every drop of freezing cold rain.

"Sue is looking after him until we're all horribly murdered," Mercury replied.

"We're trusting the baby to an old blind seer?" I asked.

"I don't think that's the biggest problem we're facing right now," Mercury said. "Besides, if she has any problems, she'll definitely see them coming."

"Unless she offers the baby up to Yog-Sothoth," I replied.

"That's ridiculous," Mercury said. "Yog-Sothoth prefers young, virginal maidens. So, me and Jackie are out."

"Do ancient gods really care about the sexual status of sacrifices?" I asked, not turning from the mud flats but glad for any distraction. "I somehow imagine a guy that occupies all of time and space simultaneously has better things to do with its time."

"Probably not," Mercury said. "As the old joke goes, throwing a virgin in a volcano probably didn't stop any eruptions but was very useful for getting women to loosen up."

I rolled my eyes. "The really sad part is that I'm pretty sure there are plenty of religions that actually had that as a motivation."

Mercury leaned her head on my arm. It was a rare intimate gesture for a woman so guarded. Even if we were effectively husband and wife, as much as such a thing existed without laws or religion to bind us, she kept a close guard on her emotions.

"When I was still a doctor, I had some mild psychological training."

"I wonder what the training for 'go mad from the revelation' was," I replied.

"Drugs, hypnotism, brainwashing, and a bullet to the brain in that order," Mercury replied. "But no, there was a condition called apophenia that always intrigued me. It's the condition of seeing patterns and meaning where there isn't any."

"Like omens in the wind or rain," I replied.

"I'm not sure that's the best example as this storm seems to be following the Undying King," Mercury replied, "but yes. People wanted to find an inherent order to the universe in hopes that they could deduce the secrets of these patterns. Knowledge is power and all that. A belief the gods and immortals cared about every little thing ranging from who you fucked to what you should do when a woman was bleeding."

"And there is no pattern," I replied.

"None that this universe cares about," Mercury said. "No god cares about mortals. Any more than you or I care about ourselves. Whenever a sacrifice is offered to one of the Old Ones' creatures, if they notice at all, it is someone just ringing the dinner bell."

"There's one," I replied.

"What?"

"One god who cares about the activities of mortals," I replied. "Like a child with a magnifying glass who names each and every ant that burns."

"You knew some screwed up kids," Mercury replied, noticeably not asking which god I meant.

We both knew.

An oppressive silence filled the air as Old Man Caruthers coughed, having caught an infection of the lungs that I suspected would kill him within a few months. Perhaps that had contributed to his decision to defend the town, or maybe he was one of the few people who realized it made no difference whether we fought or fled so we might as well die with our boots on. Perhaps I also misjudged some of these men and women and there were at least some among them who believed they could spend their lives to buy more time for their children.

I had a deeply pessimistic view of mankind, but sometimes they displayed a wild and tremendous form of madness that justified their delusions of eloquence as well as courage. Good did not exist save as a salve on the ultimate futility of life but it was a beautiful idea. Perhaps the saddest thing about the extinction of mankind was not the actual loss of its people but that all this wonderful madness would be forgotten.

My name is Ozymandias, King of Kings;
Look on my Works, ye Mighty, and despair!
Nothing beside remains. Round the decay
Of that colossal Wreck, boundless and bare
The lone and level sands stretch far away.

Except it seemed almost silly to compare humanity to the Pharaohs of old when much grander and more powerful species were ending around us as well. The Deep Ones, Yith, tunnelers, serpent men, and ghouls would all be joining us in annihilation. I did not believe they would survive this epoch any better than us. The entire universe was collapsing.

"I miss Jessica," Mercury said, interrupting my increasingly frequent ruminations on the end of everything.

"You hated Jessica," I replied.

Jessica O'Reilly had been a fellow R&E ranger from New Arkham and was my best friend. I'd been more than a little in love with her back during my human days, but she'd been married, widowed, and someone I'd treasured too much to try to have an affair with. She'd tried to kill me after my inhumanity all but consumed me, but I didn't hold that against her. I think Mercury held it against me that my feelings for her had always been different than mine for Jessica's.

"No, Jessica hated me," Mercury said. "She thought I was a bad influence."

"How so?" I asked.

"That I encouraged you to embrace being a horrifying monster," Mercury said.

"You didn't," I replied, remembering how she'd chosen not to have our child.

"What is good for me is not good for you and vice versa," Mercury said. "I know you can't go back to what you were. She thought you could."

"I would if I could."

"Then we'd all be dead," Mercury said. "Now we're just going to be dead later."

"We're always going to be dead later."

"Not for some beings," Mercury said. "Perhaps if I was a stronger magician or you knew how to share some of that immortality."

"I don't, though. I'm sorry."

"Believe me, I am too," Mercury said. "I'm just glad you'll be there to remember us all when the Earth is no more."

That was no comfort at all and was why I was happy to die here. I wasn't able to respond, though, because we were interrupted by an ominous fog rolling in across the mud flats. In the mist, I could see shadowy figures on horseback start to emerge, one by one. The rain intensified and I was glad of my hat. Thunder and lightning accompanied the arrival of the Yellow Raiders as if they were the legions of some foul god, which they might well be.

"Prepare to fire on my mark!" I shouted, barely able to be heard over the din.

I could see some of the riders through the parting of the mist and it was hard to not want to flee at the sight. Their bodies weren't so much animated by the yellow fungus covering their bodies like a second skin and musculature but consumed by it, bizarre and disgusting pustules carrying the dread spores that I recognized as the Fungus that Eats. It gave the forces that were attacking us a nightmarish new dimension as I'd heard stories of these awful things before.

The Yellow Raiders were sporemen and they were directed by a single, unholy intelligence that crawled into the brain of each of these then operated them like puppets. It was a meat moss that ate the flesh of the living and yet could think, reason, and use tools. Sporemen were not so terrifying because of the plague they were to the living, —they were just one of a thousand horrible threats—but of what they represented. They were a sign of the way life was adapting to the brave new world we'd found ourselves in. Humanity had no future, but this crawling psychic evil that I could feel reaching out to touch my mind very much could.

Join us.
Be free.
No longer afraid.
Eternal.

The voices I heard in my mind were soft and melodic with a chorus of the dead. The images and whispers of the previous towns' victims were inside the gestalt and I couldn't help but wonder if they continued to live as a part of this alien hive-mind. However, if the choice was living forever as cannibal bread mold, I'd rather choose death.

"John, I don't think bullets are going to hurt these things," Mercury replied.

"No, they are not," I replied. "Fire would be good right now."

"How convenient there's a fucking rainstorm going on," Mercury muttered.

"Yes, convenient," I replied, pulling out my guns. "If you could work on that, that would be great."

"Because I'm a witch I clearly know how to control the weather," Mercury replied, sarcastically.

"Do you have any better ideas?" I asked.

"Not a one," Mercury replied.

That was when a single rider in black rode out, a burlap sack over his head, gloves on his hands, and a horse that looked like it was dressed in the skin of a dead one. There was a malevolence to the man wholly different from the sporemen descending on us like a funeral procession. Weirdly, when the Undying King approached halfway across the field, I could make out the sight of a half-circle drawn underneath the eyeholes. It added a bizarre comic element to the whole thing as I realized the leader of this necromantic army had drawn a smiley face on his death mask. He had a pair of pistols, a bandolier across his chest, and a rifle on his back that I immediately recognized as my own. Weapons I'd lost in my fight against the Unspeakable Horror.

"You have Mercury Takahashi, doctor, witch, and whore among you. You have John Henry Booth, the Living Death that Walks among you. Bring them out to us, that we may know them!" The voice sounded eerily like my own and could be heard as clear across the thunder and lightning ridden field as if the rider was standing right beside us.

"The Bible reference is cute," Mercury said, showing more knowledge of the subject than I expected. "However, I am offended you get an awesome title and I'm just a whore."

"Also, a doctor and witch," I replied.

"Do you know this guy?" Mercury asked, not even bothering to look at the others who were already moving their guns to us except for Jackie. Even her boytoy looked like he was contemplating it.

"Try it and I will have the ground eat you," Mercury said, staring forward.

Everyone was suddenly interested in something else. Death at her hands was as certain as death at those of the horde's. Mercury had once made a man eat his own fingers and another take three days to die after spontaneously catching fire. Violence was the only language most people understood these days and Mercury spoke it well.

I looked between her and the Undying King.

"Yeah, I have a pretty good idea who it is."

"Who?" Mercury asked.

"Nyarlathotep."

Chapter Four

Nyarlathotep.

The god the Devil prayed to.

I couldn't tell you precisely what Nyarlathotep was any more than an ant could tell what a human being was passing over them. Some speculated he was a kind of gestalt psychic entity that the Old Ones used to communicate among their servitor races. Others that he was the son of Azathoth and Yog-Sothoth in an unholy Anti-Christian Trinity. Others still believed him to be a mortal being who rose to become a god in ancient Egypt or far off Delain—which explained his twisted fascination with mortal beings. Some even believed him to be Satan himself, which said something as that was by far the least esoteric and most provincial of explanations for his existence.

In truth, I had encountered Nyarlathotep multiple times in the past. The Other God had left his mark on me after I'd been left for dead by the late Alan Ward. I'd later summoned him with a spell from the *Necronomicon* and he'd responded, chatting with me in his form of the Black Soldier. I had no idea if I'd summoned the real thing, if such a thing existed, or what my mind believed the Other God would be like. Either way, he'd said he was the answer to human and other races' prayers for the universe to have meaning. A meaning that somehow explained all the horrible, terrible, awful things that existed. I believed him. It. Whatever you wanted to call the thing.

It was possible the Undying King was not actually Nyarlathotep. Nothing prevented anyone with the slightest bit of occult knowledge— and there were a massive number of "learned" religions these days despite humanity's dwindling numbers—claiming to be the god. However, something told me that this was the real thing. It was like a nightmare come to life and there was no escaping that he was the arbiter of my destiny.

That was when Mercury looked to me.

"I guess we better head out, huh?"

"I'm surprised you think that," I replied.

"Well, if we don't then they'll try to throw us down and then we'll have to kill everyone in town."

I stared at her.

"I like those odds."

"Yes, but it's a bit self-defeating," Mercury said. "Especially since the whole reason we're up here is to try to save everyone."

Mine wasn't. I was here to die killing as many of the sporemen as possible. That was another oddity to all this as I wondered why Nyarlathotep had brought such a creature with him. It wasn't like the god couldn't wipe us all out with a wave of his hand or a whisper. Heroes and fools had fought against the cults of the Old Ones for centuries but, honestly, had probably done nothing to change or alter the timeline of their rise.

"We thank you for your sacrifice, Sheriff, Doc!" Becky called over to us. "You truly are the best of us."

"Screw you!" Mercury shouted back.

"I promise to take care of Jackie!" Matthew shouted to us.

"You, too!" Mercury replied.

"Do you want me to come?" Jackie called.

"Fuck no!" Mercury finished what were possibly our last words to the townsfolk of New Ulthar before climbing over the side of the meager fencing we were holding fast behind.

I had to admire her bravery. No, it wasn't bravery. It was more calculated than that. Mercury knew that there was no way to survive by staying on top of the flimsy walls upon which we had erected our hasty defense. Just like I had expected death here, she had stayed behind because of a perhaps unjustified belief that I could pull victory out of the mists of nothingness. It was the mindset of a dedicated survivor and yet it had twists and turns that I could not follow. Yet, in my heart, I knew she was going to walk forward and confront a god because that was perhaps the only way she'd get through this alive.

She is not alive, a familiar voice whispered in my mind. *What was Mercury Takahashi died in the face of Cthulhu's presence. What is left is what you envisioned her to be and crafted with your spells. A corpse walker with a new soul crafted by Kastro'vaal magic.*

I remembered the ritual I'd conducted in Mercury's bedroom in the Wages of Sin, her catatonic form lying on a bed in need of its sheets being changed. I'd threatened the owner with a gun if he'd disturbed

273

us and, in the end, killed him when he tried to buy her. The ritual had involved a human heart, a dozen cats in the room, and a brazier burning incense I'd stolen from a Cthulhu worshipper passing through.

The spell had been magic from the *Book of Eibon* and assembled from papers Mercury had kept under her room's floorboards that I had barely understood. Still, I knew enough to realize that the will behind sorcery was more important than the ritual. I had begged, pleaded, and finally commanded the ether to bring her mind back. I'd focused on what I knew of her personality, idealized and otherwise, then willed it to exist where the mere presence of Cthulhu's psychic imprint had washed it away like sand on a beach. It had worked and she'd opened her eyes with life behind them again.

Lies, I said. *She is who she was.*

No one is who they were. Nor can they ever be again. Life is a river, constantly shifting and changing substance while remaining predictably the same.

What do you want? I asked, watching Mercury and now uncomfortably aware it looked like I was leaving her to face the Undying King again.

You will find out, little Kastro'vaal. Death is a doorway but who says that it is one that lets in who you want? Nyarlathotep taunted. *Or maybe it is your concubine, and you will be betrayed by someone else you want back, my little necromancer.*

There was no response and I reluctantly crawled over the wall myself and jogged up behind her, still a decent way from the edge of the Lord of Chaos' forces.

"I see you're finally coming," Mercury said.

"I got caught up reminiscing," I replied.

"Probably about all the whores you're going to miss once I'm gone."

"We're not doomed yet."

"We were always doomed," she said. "Like Doc Holiday."

"He was a doctor, gunfighter, and brothel owner too."

"He also died of tuberculosis at age thirty-six."

I didn't quite know how many years old Mercury was but didn't think she was much older or younger. Time tended to get away from people these days since the Sun went up when it felt like it and went down erratically. It was the biggest proof the Earth had merged with the Dreamlands and arguably didn't exist anymore.

"He was a dentist, not a proper doctor," I said. "But I didn't want to bring that up."

"And I was a torturer," Mercury said. "Any tips for speaking with a god face-to-face? I've only spoken to them via prayer and ritual, which is to say I was talking to myself."

"They will kill you or spare you regardless of what you do. They are completely unpredictable, inhuman, and insane by human standards."

Mercury paused and I caught up with her, just ten yards away from the Undying King.

"You know he can probably hear us, right?" she asked.

"I imagine he heard our first breaths and is now listening to the sounds of our deaths an hour or a million years from now."

"Ah, so the best suggestion when talking to a god is not to bring you along."

"Probably."

That was when the Undying King stepped off his horse and looked at us. I couldn't make out his eyes underneath the sack, but the silly expression drawn on the sack made the whole thing seem even more surreal.

"Hello, John, hello succubus."

"I'm getting some distinct misogyny here," Mercury said. "I have a name, Man in Black."

"I have many names," Nyarlathotep said. "Many identities. Each stranger than the last. You should be glad that you are no longer a mere person, a candle flickering in the night. You are a dream of a monster consumed with loneliness and bitterness brought back to life. You won't be the last, though, but will be mother of a new race of monsters. Even as it seeds its black bastards across the Wastelands."

"If you mean John, I know he's a lech," Mercury said. "He'd make me richer than Croesus if I charged him for all the play he's had

275

between brooding and murder. But I am not his dream. I dream myself and right now I'm dreaming you're going to take this army of corpses out of here."

It was insane bravado and no more likely to be effective than screaming obscenities into a storm. However, I couldn't have been prouder of Mercury than if she'd thrown a harpoon at Cthulhu while quoting *Moby Dick*. If humanity died tomorrow—hell, if it died right now—it would be at least a defiant death in the face of the gods. Which, perhaps, was what Nyarlathotep had wanted from her.

"You have a hell of a bill for all the times you've been with me too," I replied.

Mercury gave me a sideways glare.

Nyarlathotep gave a deep, malevolent laugh that sounded like several people speaking at once, both male and female. Supposedly he was the horde of demons that Jesus has cast out into a herd of pigs while others said he was the Carpenter himself. I didn't think it mattered.

"What do you want, Dreammaster? Why did you lead this horde of the dead to our feet?"

"These?" Nyarlathotep waved back to the sporemen. "These are the rats that follow my piping song. They seek to know the music of the spheres and hear the whispers of my father Azathoth, as if it was not the gibbering lunacy of a blind idiot god. As for what I am doing, I am giving humanity that for which it begged."

"What is that?" I asked, wondering why gods always talked a great deal or not at all.

"To bring an end," Nyarlathotep said, his voice becoming all too much like mine. "The human race's dwindling elements do not wish to go with a whimper across generations but the bang of horsemen and armies of the damned. So, I am here to bring an answer to their prayers. The thundering of hoofbeats and an army of two hundred million."

I stared. "And if I were to stop you?"

"Do you wish to?" Nyarlathotep said. "Is life so good for someone who desperately wishes death himself versus an immortal life as a monster?"

Mercury stared at me with an accusing look, but it wasn't like it was something that she hadn't known before.

"Yes," I said, coldly. "I'd like that. I'll live a bit longer to save this village."

"Longer or forever?"

"Nothing is forever," I said. "Not even you."

"Clearly you don't understand time," Nyarlathotep said. "But as you wish."

I blinked. "What?"

"The dream is dictated by the sleeper and the sleeper has not awakened yet. I do not speak of Cthulhu or you, but others. I'll let you and your fictious girlfriend survive to have some other stories to tell if you play the role others would have us play."

I shook my head. "I have no idea what the fuck you're talking about."

"John, not helping," Mercury muttered.

"The audience on the wall demands a story," Nyarlathotep said. "The Undying King versus the mighty sheriff and his deputy."

"I better not be the deputy," Mercury said. "Also, he's technically a marshal."

The Undying King chuckled. "How would you like to be immortal, Mercury?"

"Would it be one of those tricky Aesop forms of immortality like making me a rock or something?"

"Yes," Nyarlathotep said.

"Then no," Mercury replied.

"Then be silent," Nyarlathotep said.

Mercury glared.

"Are these games really worth it?" I asked.

"These games are as close as anything that provides this world meaning," Nyarlathotep said. "Without the stories whispered on Carcosa, the plateaus of Leng, the halls of risen R'lyeh, or the tombs of Stygia then there would be no purpose to any of it. I am the narrator, and you are the characters."

It was the piss poor author who wrote themselves into a story. I'd learned that from a writer named Phillips in Kingsport.

"So, how do we give the audience a show?"

"A gunfight," Nyarlathotep said.

"You're kidding."

"Almost certainly," Nyarlathotep said, pulling his gun out. It was black as midnight and seemed to wiggle like a living thing. "But the joke is that if you don't then the horde behind me will pour over your little town and every man, woman, and child will meet their ends sooner rather than later."

"And if I win a gunfight with you then the town goes free?" I asked. "The army of the dead goes away?"

"I didn't say that," Nyarlathotep said. "My legion is made of the crushed consciousnesses of five thousand humans. It might live to populate the world after mankind is destroyed and colonize other worlds. Maybe it'll be demolished by you this evening. However, I won't be the one who leads it to end New Ulthar and its cats."

"Yes, the cats are clearly the ones who matter here," Mercury said.

"Versus their slaves, yes."

"God has a sick sense of humor," Mercury said. "So much makes sense now."

"Most of the gods do, yes," Nyarlathotep said. "After all, they are all faces I have worn. Maybe someday I'll wear yours, if I'm not already."

"So, we handle this high noon style, huh?" I said, hoping that the mad god was telling the truth. "Twenty paces turn and fire?"

"You can simply be the one to walk and turn," Nyarlathotep said. "Unless you're afraid I'll shoot you in the back."

"That wouldn't make a very good story, would it?" I replied, dryly. Nothing prevented the Crawling Chaos from simply destroying us at will. It wouldn't be a fight, no matter how many stories of mortals wrestling with gods there were. It would be like trying to battle gravity or the Sun, except even larger.

"It depends on the religion," Nyarlathotep said. "There are places where cunning and treachery are worshiped in place of fairness or honor."

"Yeah, I've been to most of them," I said. "Will my gun even hurt you?"

"No," Nyarlathotep said. "It might hurt the Undying King, though. You can't kill the god, but you can destroy the mask."

That was as close to a reassurance as I suspected I would ever get out of the monster. Admitted murderer of men, women, and children by the thousands—and those were just the crimes he committed within the past few weeks—it was hard to think of the Crawling Chaos as evil. It was the god that humanity and countless other races had asked for. It tended to the spirits in the Dreamlands of Ra, Vishnu, and the Nailed God along with the small gods of other races. Ones that were close enough to humanity to be actually worth worshiping. He was above good and evil because they were simply irrelevant to him. The same way as the morality of insects would be as inscrutable to those of monkeys or stars.

I pulled out one of my pistols—cheating if we were doing this Wild West style—and took twenty paces before spinning around to fire. He hit me first and I fell to the ground, massive pain in my chest from where I'd been shot. I'd made the stupid mistake of believing I could outshoot the Devil when it was his game.

That was when Mercury drew her pistols and unloaded into Nyarlathotep. The Undying King's entire body caught fire and exploded into piles of insects that spread across the ground as unholy screams escaped each of the thousands of little creatures crawling from his burning clothes.

That was when the sporemen started charging at us both.

"Shit," I said, what was possibly my final word.

Oh, and the sky started raining down fire.

Chapter Five

What followed was wild, chaotic, and insane as I pulled my other pistol and fired into the onrushing horde of sporemen. The Cthugha guns fired bullets made of flame and had an unlimited number of them. Mostly because it wasn't a gun but something else inside the weapons, taking the form of metal and steel while hungrily eating the living with its fiery venom. I chose deliberately to only see the image of the creature rather than the weapon as I unloaded into as many of the enemy as I could despite bleeding to death on the ground.

Each time I managed to hit one of the creatures, they burst into flame and screamed with the wailing of the damned as they were sent off to whatever oblivion awaited sporemen. The Fungus that Eats would keep a copy of the consciousness, if not the souls themselves, in even the tiniest sliver of their existence. It would eventually recover and devour this town unless every little bit of it was destroyed. Given I was dying, I didn't particularly think that was a likely outcome, but I was damn well going to try.

The insanity of my circumstances gave me a perverse sort of hope, though, as the sky continued to rain down fire on the army of the dead. Balls of flame and ruin landed like mortar around us, sending up piles of mud and steam. They were indiscriminate but seemingly centered over the mud flats, so the only victims were the attacking army and, well, us.

"Mercury, I don't suppose this is your doing!" I shouted, continuing to shoot as I experienced intense pain from the bullet that Nyarlathotep put into my stomach. It burned like a hot branding iron shoved into my gut.

"Not unless it's divine punishment for shooting a god," Mercury shouted, slinging lightning as a circle of flame burned around us in a protective ring.

"Could be!" I shouted, thinking it was more likely a parting gift from August from a safe distance. "Now would be a good time for some Johnny Cash!"

"John, shut up!"

An undead horse ignored the protective circle and pushed itself forward, causing its body to burst into flame and become akin to a vision of Hell. The creature thrashed above my head and lifted its hooves to crush my skull. I gave it both barrels, a term I'd always wanted to say, before it exploded into burning chunks. I wondered how it had managed to get through the circle, one powered by the might of the Elder Gods, and realized that it had been Nyarlathotep's horse.

I was close to passing out—a state I wouldn't wake up from—when I saw the sporemen start moving around the protective circle. The Fungus that Eats was not going to keep its focus on us, the only people giving it any sort of fight. It sought to now wash over New Ulthar while we were trapped in our present position. Perhaps it knew that I would leave our limited protection to try to save everyone.

I kept trying to fire into the heavy rain and throng of horrors surrounding us while Mercury futilely threw her spells into the ranks of the Fungus that Eats. We destroyed dozens of the creatures, but there were hundreds—if not thousands—gathered around us. It was like pissing into the wind and I soon found myself having to cover my stomach with one hand, barely able to stand. The bullet was burning through my essence, the creature I was that existed in other dimensions, not just the four that humans dwelt in.

"I have to go," I muttered, unable to cross the flames any more than the rest of the horde could. The circle prevented me from leaving as assuredly as it prevented any of the sporemen from crossing.

"John, don't be stupid!" Mercury shouted. "You'll die!"

I reached my fingers into the wound, feeling staggering agonizing pain as I opened it further to grasp the bullet killing me. It was like grabbing hold of a burning coal, but I managed to keep my fingertips around it until I pulled it out then tossed it into the flames. I almost passed out then and there but lost my sense of slowly burning to death. I was injured but not dying, crippled but alive. At least if I could get the injury sewn up.

Probably.

"Jackie is out there!" I cried out. "We can't abandon her!"

"Does this look like abandoning her?" Mercury said, sweat and rainwater having soaked her even as her hands burned from the supernal powers that she had channeled to try to end this horror.

"I can take more of them down," I said, hearing the pitiful sounds of gunfire in the distance. Weapons that were all but useless against the sporemen and would do little but make noise as the horde overrode them. "I can become the monster!"

"You killed Jessica when you became the monster!" Mercury cried out. "You can't control yourself during it!"

It was like a blow to the stomach, more so than the pulsating wound I was already feeling. I had denied and lied to myself repeatedly about that terrible night in New Innsmouth. I had given myself to the beast within, the alien creature that was the last of his kind in this dimension, in hopes that I could control it. That I could wield it as a weapon against a host of Dagonite Deep Ones purists that had been massacring a community of hybrids.

When I'd awoken, I'd been surrounded by a dead community. I'd slaughtered the attacking army to the last squamous horror, leaving their entrails scattered and their skulls dashed against the ruins of their conquest. My blood rage did not limit itself to the conquerors and murderers, though. It was not that kind of story.

The beast within was not a force for good, it was the mad predator of a different world trapped within the body of another world's vermin. A mouse containing a lion. I had slaughtered my team who had stayed to fight for a people that were reviled by the humans and purebloods of R'lyeh both. I had slaughtered the people who we'd come to defend. Butchered the people who'd fought by my side to defend them.

I was a monster.

"Let me go," I said, whispering. "I can stop this."

"John! Stop trying to kill yourself!" Mercury said. "It's not going to do anyone any good."

I held my gun tight, my finger on the trigger as a kind of madness overcame me. This was my chance, regardless of how little sense it made, to rewrite the past. If I destroyed the sporemen here, then I could save the people I'd gotten killed. I had a whole bunch of lives on my conscience I could name: Jessica, Thom, Stephens, and so many others that I'd choke if I attempted to speak all their names.

"Let. Me. Go," I enunciated each word.

"Are you going to shoot me?" Mercury asked.

No, I wasn't going to shoot her. The thought briefly crossed my mind as the only way to lower the flaming circle around us. I was mad, desperate, and suicidal, but not so much to the point that I would repeat my past. Without Mercury to anchor me to this last lingering remnant of my humanity, I would kill everyone here. If I woke up beside Jackie and Baby John's corpses, then I might as well be like the Fungus that Eats: a creature that would put to death every human it encountered.

That was when a bolt of lightning struck downward against one of the sporemen and it made me realize what I'd been missing. Looking at the flames, I concentrated on the lie of my humanity and walked forward. Magic was mind over matter, will over reality, dream over physics. There were no limits to the level of what it could accomplish any more than a writer was limited in what he could accomplish by putting words on a page.

I was not naturally a wizard, nor a witch like Mercury who exalted in the power of sorcery. She would sell her soul and devote herself to it in order to be able to work miracles. But I was a monster and came from a people for whom magic was as natural as breathing.

Perhaps if humankind had more time, they would have evolved into something similar. The talent for dreaming showed that they had the potential. Combined, monster and dreamer, I was able to construct a very simple spell and made myself human for the second I needed to step through the flames. They did not burn me any more than they would any other mortal that called upon the Elder Gods to protect them. Beings that did not exist until mortals had dreamed them up as a defense against the things in the dark.

"Killer!" I shouted, holding my one pistol in both hands. "I know you! Face me!"

Far in the distance behind me, I could hear the mines that Jackie had placed blow up and take out a couple of dozen more sporemen. The sporemen were also stopped cold for the moment by the fact that the metal sheets erected around the town were covered in the squiggly star of the Elder Sign. It was almost humorous that whatever time was bought to save my little village was due to a few scratches with a knife.

I knew it wouldn't stop them for long, but I was pleased to see them dump every bit of oil in the town over in barrels onto the sporemen before lighting them up. It created a brief moat over part of the town's barrier that continued to destroy more of the murderous fungus. However, unless they burned every bit of it, their toxic substance would rise up to infect them all.

I gunned three more down with my pistol, wishing I'd brought the other one but only able to keep my guts inside because of the hand holding them in. Even so, I could tell the sporemen were ready to swarm me and there wasn't a damn thing I could do about it.

"Brilliant plan, John!" Mercury called from beyond the fire. "You clearly have thought this through!"

"Not helping, Mercury!" I shouted back.

"I feel my last words to you should be bemoaning your stupidity!" Mercury said.

"I know what I'm doing," I said, lying. "It wants to fight me."

I had no idea what the Fungus that Eats wanted, but I could feel it all around me, its consciousness diffused among the hundreds of corpses remaining. Two or more for every single man, woman, and child in New Ulthar, but all centered around one single will. I could hear that will speak, its voice a cacophony of entrapped spirits forced to speak as one but not quite managing it. Instead, it sounded like five or six spirits speaking one after another with different inflections.

You must be destroyed.

All must die.

A new world will be born from death.

I knew I had its attention now and concentrated on trying to speak to it, backing my next words with every ounce of will in my body.

"These people want to live. All you can do is kill them."

They will live through me.

Life is not good as a human.

We must survive.

It was hard to argue with such simple logic once you rearranged reason around the parameters of survival at all costs. It was, after all, the most primal of drives. If you couldn't survive then it didn't matter if you were good, evil, mad, or sane. Lately, sanity was in short supply and as I found myself surrounded by more sporemen as they prepared to tear me apart, I suspected I wasn't adding to it.

I struggled to change in that moment, to become the monster who would tear into all these creatures but leave his loved ones alone. I almost laughed but was in too much pain and aware that the horde was going to tear me apart in seconds. Nyarlathotep's bullet had been more esoteric than practical. As I'd prepared to die heroically as a human, he'd taken away my power to change to a monster.

At least for a time.

"You will not," I replied, looking through the dimensions of man and monster. I may not have been a monster anymore—a decidedly less than comfortable realization right now—but I still had the Sight. That was as much my birthright as any power or secret tentacles.

All around me, I saw the various sporemen crying out with hidden faces and screaming souls. They were all entangled by a psychic web, though, that reached back to a single obese, armless sporeman in the center of the horde. I briefly wondered what his story was. How had he become the first of the creatures to be incorporated into the Fungus that Eats. Was he a good man, bad man, or simply an insane man who'd been blessed as well as cursed with transformation into a monster? What had compelled him to try to absorb all his fellow men? And what role had Nyarlathotep played in it?

I found that I didn't care as I aimed through the descending monsters that piled onto me, one last shot at where I saw all these myriad consciousnesses linked, and pulled the trigger. It was a long shot but one I hoped would prove to be the head of the beast. My bullet struck home and the heart of the Fungus that Eats exploded into flame while the others all reared up at once as if they were the ones on fire. Pain beyond imagination spread through the collective as they were released from the control of the psychic parasite who had created their foul existence.

They didn't all fall to the ground, but they started attacking each other and running in different directions. The central guiding intelligence that had driven them to want to consume the remains of humanity was lost. All that was left were mad, hateful, pained corpses animated by alien mycelium. I felt dirty teeth and hands claw at me even as I fell to the ground under the pile of monsters above me.

It was not the death I wanted, oblivion losing its appeal no sooner than it was upon me, but there was a kind of poetic justice to it all. I'd managed to stick my finger into the eye of the Devil—or at least some fool playing it—one last time.

I didn't know if the meager posse could keep fighting the now-decapitated Yellow Raiders, but I'd done my part. Nothing, not even hunger, motivated them especially against humanity's bitter remnants. Only mindless malice and the desire to reproduce sent forth the once-human throng now. Emptying my gun into more sporemen and feeling the flames licking me as they were blown away by one last spell, I finally lost consciousness. My last memory was Mercury calling upon Yog-Sothoth, the Hebrew God, and another power before a terrifying wave spread out.

I awoke, much to my surprise, with bandages wrapped around stitched wounds and lying on a nasty mattress that reeked of human waste as well as the alcohol used to purify my injuries. It was extremely well-done, implying Mercury had done it, but I did not understand why I was abandoned since this was my room at the Wages of Sin. Except the door was boarded over and there was no sign of life around me.

I did not see any sign of New Ulthar's survivors. The town was normally full of life, and I could not hear anyone around me. Climbing to my feet, seeing a jug of well water beside me, I chugged it down and crawled to the window. There was no sign of the sporemen, but the town was dead.

Empty.

Lifeless.

"What happened here?" I asked, staring out.

"Your lover called upon the power of the Other Gods," Nyarlathotep whispered.

He had taken the form of Mercury. I saw her cold, lifeless face in the reflection behind me.

"She sacrificed the whole of the town to save your life. A few survived like those exploding mines in the distance but the bulk were burned as fuel for magic."

My blood ran cold.

"No," I said.

"Yes," Nyarlathotep said, chuckling. "I love testing humans. You never cease to surprise me."

"I am your plaything," I replied. "Not her."

Nyarlathotep laughed. "All life is my plaything, John."

The god vanished. Then I was alone.

Unaware if the only people I cared about were still out there and unsure if they were monsters worse than the creatures who'd preyed on my home.

The End

All the Way Up

A Cletus J. Diggs and Donovan DeChance Adventure

By David Niall Wilson

Chapter One

Cletus J. Diggs opened his mailbox, just like any other day, and scanned the pile of glossy, ridiculous political ads, offers for credit cards, and invitations to free dinners to hear a pitch about solar-powered windmills. He stopped when he found a single sheet of crude paper. There was no envelope and the writing was cramped, clearly written with a fountain pen. Maybe even a quill? The note was short.

"Somethin' is comin'. If you can reach that magic man, tell him to come. Tell him to bring whiskey." - N

Cletus carried the mail down the drive and around the corner toward the sprawling Pope Plantation. Halfway across the yard he heard a yip and Dog appeared at his heel, following him toward the porch of the old home. Dog knew where the treats were kept, but he also knew that Cletus rarely went inside alone. The two moved in sync, and Cletus shook his head, grinning despite himself. Dog's presence always calmed him.

It wasn't that he didn't like the plantation house. It had a history, but that had been mostly cleansed. It was the way things shifted. The plantation house belonged to Donovan DeChance, who visited from time to time. It stood on what Donovan called a 'nexus,' a place where locations and times intersected. You could walk in one day and it was a renovated plantation house. You could take a leak in the fancy bathroom by the kitchen and walk out into that same home, but a hundred years in the past. Then there was the door that opened beneath the winding stairs that led to the second floor. If you just opened it, there was a closet beneath, coats, hats, never the same, but that wasn't enough to freak Cletus out. There was another way to open it. If you took the right number of steps forward, then back and forward again, and pushed the door just right, it didn't enter a closet. It opened into a hallway in a brownstone in San Valencez, California on the thirteenth floor. Two doors down from the entrance to Donovan's penthouse.

The magic man owned the brownstone, and very few knew that there *was* a 13th floor. Fewer still knew how to access it. Cletus had been watching the Pope Plantation for some time, and he'd had an open invitation to visit *all* that time, or move in, but he'd never been able to go through with it. The note in his hand changed things. Nettie didn't send mail. She didn't ask for help, and yet, he was holding both of those things in his hand, and he knew if he didn't take it seriously, he was going to regret it.

"What do you think, Dog?" he asked. "Want to go visit Cleo and Mo?"

Dog's tongue lolled, and he stared up at Cletus with no more obvious intelligence than any other canine, but Cletus knew better. The two were connected in a way that made no sense and that Cletus found he was better off not dwelling on. He knew he'd trust Dog with his life, and felt it reciprocated.

"Well, hell," he said. "Was bound to happen sooner or later."

Cletus started stepping forward, took two steps back, three steps forward, four back, and then kept walking. As he did, he pressed his hand into the door and it swung inward. He closed his eyes and stepped through, Dog at his heel.

Chapter Two

Deep in the outer reaches of the Great Dismal Swamp, down a road barely worthy of the name, the town of Eternity stood empty as a ten-dollar bottle of whiskey on Saturday night and silent as a grave. There were no businesses, few houses, and those were boarded up. The only building that remained in good repair was the church. The walls glistened with fresh white paint. A few years back, there had been serious trouble, but all evidence of that had disappeared.

The reverend who'd overseen services was gone. The strange twins and the hidden laboratory had been shipped off. The Church of New Light and Starry Wisdom remained and flourished. Come Sunday, the pews were filled, just as they had been. Services were held every Sunday, morning and evening, and though it seemed as if no one lived nearby, the congregation had grown.

There was a new reverend in town. No one knew where he'd come from, or where he disappeared to after services, but they hung on his every word. He was exotic, a man of color with features such as they'd never seen. His skin was dark as night. His voice was low, sibilant, and hypnotic. None of that was important. It was the message... the instructions... the energy that filled the church every time they gathered. It grew and soaked into the swamp beyond.

He'd given them instructions. He'd drawn maps in the dirt that etched themselves into their minds and drew them into the swamp. The parishioners of the Church of New Light and Starry Wisdom were private people. They went to town when it was necessary. Their children married one another, and they lived in the shadow of civilization, just out of sight. When they started wandering the trails leading deeper into the swamp, no one noticed.

And they found things. Forgotten ruins. Statues. Pillars that had once supported unknown idols or framed lost doorways. They returned with their discoveries. They dug stones from the muck and hauled the ruins of something dark down the trails. Sometimes they used pickups, and more than once they used stolen or rented heavy equipment. Their lives depended on routine, but that routine had

290

dissolved into obsession. The garden behind The Church of New Light and Starry Wisdom was cleared, the stairs leading down to the abandoned laboratory below forgotten. Above, an ancient temple slowly materialized from the dust and muck of the past. The entrance to that dark place was flanked – or guarded? – by twin statues, lifted to rest on chipped, cracked pillars. They were enormous frogs with human eyes and lopsided, feral grins.

Through it all, the new reverend, who spoke his name before every service and greeted every one of them by their names, watched. He did not direct them, because they were caught up in something spiritual, something alive and they needed no direction. They were aware of him, they listened to him, rapt, when he spoke, but if you were to ask any of them what the name was that he told them over and over, you would get an odd, far-away stare, or an incomprehensible sequence of syllables they couldn't repeat.

Now and then, he stared off into the trees. His expression didn't change, but his level of concentration did. The Dismal Swamp was old. It had existed before highways and civilization, wars and thousands of churches sprung up like some sort of industrial fungus. The swamp had been home to many beings, some human, others with powers that waxed and waned as centuries passed. The Reverend knew what his followers were building, but he didn't know who or what else was out there. He felt the weight of unseen eyes, and reached out, searching shadows and bogs, trying to sense their intent. Who, or whatever it was eluded him, so he turned his concentration inward. Whatever would come, it would not be boring and entertainment at this level was rare. He returned his attention to the workers, dragging more stones from the line of trees beyond the temple, and he smiled.

Chapter Three

One of the things that Donovan DeChance was least accustomed to was hearing a knock at his door. His brownstone, a fifteen-story building with apartments below and a few penthouse floors above, had everything, as far as the outside world was concerned, except a thirteenth floor. The elevator didn't stop there, and the stairs were protected by a glamour. There was a utility exit in the rear of the building that could only be accessed from a separate stairway. The number of others who could find their way to his door could be counted on one hand, and only a couple of those were welcome.

All this is to say that when the knock came, and Cleo leaped down from his desk to paw at the door, it was one of the rare occasions when he was caught off guard. He rose, crossed the room, and closed his eyes. Then he smiled and opened the door.

"Cletus," he said. "I know you live off in the middle of way-out-yonder, but you do have a phone. Maybe send a text?"

Cletus stepped inside and Dog followed, walking over to Cleo, who rubbed against his snout and purred.

"Meant to," Cletus said, "but didn't think this could wait. Fact is, I walked straight here as soon as I got this."

He held out the note, and Donovan took it, reading it quickly.

"Nettie?" he said.

"Who else would be worried about something bad coming, but certain to ask you to bring whiskey?"

"This must be serious. I can't imagine Nettie asking for help. I mean, think about what we've seen, and then think about how long she's been there. She didn't blink an eye when you had that dinosaur running around the swamp."

"You got that right. Lucky those boys came to help, Mac and Isabella and the rest. I see ol' John Tyler Gault now and then, and he nods, but we don't talk much. It's hard to believe any of that really happened. Every time I turn around, or try to go fishin' with Jasper, all hell breaks loose."

"That reminds me," Donovan said. "I ran into an old friend of ours again. You remember Mr. Whatley?"

"Thought he was gone?"

"He is now," Donovan said. "Give me a minute to gather some things. I believe we'd better get out to that shack and find Nettie. There will be time for stories later. I'm not a man to leave a lady waiting, but I need to let Amethyst know I'll be gone."

Donovan glanced up at the mantel above them. Near the peak, a sleek, sharp-eyed raven glared back at him.

"Can you tell her, Mo? And while I'm gone, can you look out for her?"

Cleo ran over and bumped Donovan's leg. He glanced down.

"You?" he said. Then he smiled. "Of course. You go to her. Mo loves trees and the swamp. Don't' think I'm getting soft though… I don't want to lose you to her."

Cleo rubbed against his calf, purred louder, and Donovan laughed. Asmodeus launched from the mantel and landed on Donovan's desk with a Thunk! Dog gave a sharp yip and rose to put his paws on the edge. Asmodeus glared at him, then circled the desk and hopped onto the old canine's back.

"Seems like we have our team," Cletus said. He glanced around. "I've never seen this many books in one place. Not even the library in Old Mill."

"You probably don't want to see the hall, the other rooms, or the inventory from the database then," Donovan said. He began wandering around the room, picking up small occult items, wrapped scrolls, crystals, and chains. He tucked them into the pockets of a long, dark trench coat and slipped into it. Before they left, he stepped over to his bar. He opened a cabinet in the top and pulled out a small bottle filled with brown liquid.

"Would not do to arrive empty handed."

"You got that right, magic man. Nettie is a lot of things, but forgiving isn't one of them. And I'm not sure she even has a choice. I've been doing some research, and I think, maybe, she's older even than I was thinking. I figure maybe the whiskey is a double-D goddam tribute. Like, she can't just help. Or maybe she needs it, needs people to believe in her and sacrifice, even if it's just a cheap bottle of hooch, so she can stay."

Donovan stopped with one hand tucking the bottle into his jacket and the other on the doorknob.

"You know, Cletus," he said. "I believe I have underestimated you again, and maybe Nettie as well."

Then he opened the door and stepped into the hall. Cletus followed, Dog trotting at his heel. After the door closed, Cleo jumped down, stepped around the far side of the desk, and was simply gone.

Chapter Four

The old shack stood, as it might have for a century. The roof was discolored. The windows were boarded and the door still closed, but at an angle that seemed geometrically impossible when it was closed. Beyond it, the moon dropped slowly behind the trees and the silence was broken only by the bugs and crickets from the swamp.

Cletus drove up slowly and dimmed his lights. Donovan was riding shotgun with Dog's head firmly planted in his lap. Far above, silhouetted against the moon, Cletus saw Asmodeus circle down slowly to land on the peak of the roof.

For a long moment the two of them sat, staring at the porch.

"She gonna do it again, you think?" Cletus asked.

He turned to glance at Donovan, who was pretending to scan the note in his hand, the one from Nettie. When the two glanced back up, a shadowed figure was seated at the rickety table on the front porch of the shack. Cletus grinned and opened his door. Donovan stepped out and Dog jumped down, circling around to fall into step behind Cletus.

"You boys took your time," Nettie said.

"It's a long trip from California," Cletus said.

Nettie laughed. "One of these days," she said, "I'm going to have a talk with the magic man here about those tunnels. You could have been here last week if you knew how to use them."

Donovan hesitated, just for a moment, then stepped up onto the porch and took a seat across from the old woman. Cletus took the remaining chair. There were three aged tumblers on the table. It felt as if they should be coated in dust, or sporting cobwebs that reached to the edges of the table, but they glistened in the moonlight.

Donovan reached into a pocket and produced the small bottle he'd brought from his den. Without preamble, he popped out the stopper and poured three equal draughts into the tumblers. Cletus watched, and marveled at how even they were. The bottle was empty, and Donovan sealed it and tucked it away.

"Something special," he said. "Something old."

Cletus cut in then, blurting the words so the other two turned to him. "I had a sort of… weird vision," he said. "I feel like I should know the words, like there is more to this than whiskey… like there's a ritual. When I think about it, I remember my father, and my grandfather…"

"Words have power," Nettie said, "but they're just trappings, Cletus. You're here. There is some very fine whiskey in your glass. You have honored your ancestors."

"I'm never going to know who you really are, am I?" Cletus asked. "Or her." He tipped his head toward the tree line. "I know she's out there."

"You already know. One day you'll be ready to accept it. Right now, I suggest we drink."

Donovan lifted his glass and tilted it to the center of the table. "I agree. I admit, the idea that there is something threatening this place that you need help with, I'm more than a little concerned."

Nettie took a sip of the whiskey in her glass, hesitated, smelled it, and took another. "Oh my," she said. "That is…"

"Very old," Donovan said. "I realize my usage of the labyrinth is limited, but occasionally I get lucky."

Nettie smiled, but only for a second. "There is something here, magic man. I've never encountered anything quite like it, and like this whiskey, it's old. So old that the meaning of the word in any human context doesn't apply. You know that church in Eternity, Cletus?"

"Couldn't forget it if I tried. But those boys were hauled off by the feds, and the Reverend is gone."

"There's a new Reverend," Nettie said, "and he's dark. I don't know who, or what he is, but he's not human, and he has those folks hauling and building. The things they're pullin' out of the swamp were there before any man or woman. I knew they were there, but I didn't pay attention because they weren't… here. I mean, they were buried in the swamp, but they were sinking, and fading. Somehow, he's brought them back."

"Them?" Cletus said.

"It's not just the stones and the statues. I feel something bigger, something very old, and very dark, growing and pushing against boundaries that aren't meant to be broken."

296

"Have you seen him?" Donovan asked.

"I have, though I'll tell you, he did not want to be 'seen' as anything other than a man, and he's powerful. Some dark creatures have passed through here, some worse than others. This is different. I know the swamp, the Earth, the air. I know what lives and breathes here. That man, or whatever he is? I can't sense him at all. He's *wrong* – like he isn't here at all."

Donovan swirled the whiskey in his glass and closed his eyes, just for a moment. From somewhere high above, Asmodeus let out a cry.

"You tell that old one to stay back," Nettie said. "I got a very bad feeling, Magic Man. I think we need all our options available, and I don't want my calling for help to hurt you, or yours."

"I'll hold him back as well as I can, but he's not mine to control. That is a powerful bird, much wiser than I am, and much older. I just want him close enough to see if he senses anything he might remember, anything that might help. This place... this swamp... draws things. Cletus and I ran into one on a farm not too far from here. The alchemist a few years back, and the stories I've heard. If there is something here that worries you, and you tell me it doesn't belong, I'm thinking this might be a power I'm ill-prepared to face.

"That said, I have access to things, dangerous things, important things. I don't understand all of them. If Asmodeus can give me a hint, just an idea where to look, and for what, it might be the difference between solving this, or failing, and I don't like to think about what that might mean."

"Nor do I, Magic Man, nor do I," Nettie said. "I know a lot of things, but they are all related to this place. I'm a part of it, I feel its pain, and its growth. When a thing comes in from somewhere beyond the swamp, I have to learn, or protect... or ask for help."

"You will always have that," Donovan said. He drained his tumbler. "There is enough for each of us to have another drink, and I would be truly offended if we did not finish this."

He reached for the bottle and started to pour, but his eyes suddenly went wide, and his arm jerked. Cletus, without thinking, reached out and snagged the small bottle from his hand. Then he, and Nettie, stared, and waited.

Chapter Five

Donovan soared high above the trees, his vision suddenly sharp, and intense. The vertigo nearly snapped the connection, but, for the first time in their history, Asmodeus did not allow it. Donovan felt something akin to a slap in the face, and his mind steadied. The moon was bright, not quite full, but the land below was illuminated, and he caught snatches of clear land, the quick movements of nocturnal animals, and the glistening surface of bogs and streams as they flew.

He'd shared such moments before, but never with such clarity, and never with the sense that this time, unlike all the others, it would not be up to him when the bond was broken.

Ahead, just above the trees, he sensed something hovering, something different. It wasn't a cloud, exactly. It was more of a glitch, as if the shades of moonlight rippled and shifted in ways that weren't normal. As he grew nearer, he saw it was a cylinder, darker near the center, and through the gloom that darkness caused, he saw the gleaming white steeple of a church.

Asmodeus wheeled, coming short of the rippling wall and circling, close, but not close enough to touch it. Donovan concentrated on what he could sense and see. There was something about that place, that wall of energy, that made his stomach crawl, and he shared the old bird's revulsion. They made a full circuit, and were about to break away, when something shifted. The darkness moved closer, suddenly, and Asmodeus screamed.

The sickening darkness swelled, stretching toward them and the old raven's strong wings fought for purchase in the air, diving and pulling away, too slowly. Donovan wanted to help, poured every ounce of himself into that contact and that moment, but it wasn't enough. He didn't have the strength, and then, very suddenly, a brilliant white flash of power coursed through him. They were up and away, flying faster than seemed possible, crossing fields and trees, bogs and farms, on an arrow-straight path back to the shack.

Chapter Six

The world snapped into focus, and Donovan reared back, standing, and nearly knocking the chair he'd been sitting in over backward. Hands steadied him. One was thin, but incredibly strong, and the other was callused and firm. He closed his eyes, took a breath, then opened them again. The three of them stood, himself, Nettie, and Cletus, clasping hands. Asmodeus perched shakily on the table between them. The old bird looked dazed, and Donovan had never seen him that way, would not have believed it was possible. He released the others' hands and carefully scooped his familiar up. The connection revived them both, and Asmodeus hopped up to his shoulder with a soft squawk.

He reached back, straightened his chair, and sat.

"Thank you," he said. "Whoever, or whatever, that was, I have never felt anything like it. Even here, I feel as if I need to shower, and as if there isn't enough soap or hot water to clean it off my skin, or my eyes."

"We saw you start to shake," Cletus said, "Kinda like a seizure or something, and Nettie here, she told me to grab you. Then she grabbed me, and I'll be Double-D goddamed if I didn't feel, just for a second, like I was flying. And that thing... that darkness. What in holy hell...?"

"That was as much you as me, boy," Nettie said. "I knew when I saw you and that dog that things were shifting. Should've seen it comin' a long time ago, all things considered. I don't know if I could have pulled the magic man free without you."

"There's another thing," Cletus said. He glanced over at Dog, sitting bolt upright at attention on the floor of the old porch. "That – whatever the hell it was – felt... familiar? I mean, it was darker, and it was strong as hell but..."

"But it was close to what we faced with Whateley," Donovan said. "I felt it too, and I told you I ran into him again. He's gone, but that power, that darkness, is not of this Earth, or maybe it's not of this plane? I don't know. It doesn't belong. Everything about it feels disconnected from reality."

"It doesn't hate," Nettie said. "It doesn't care. It's unconcerned with consequences, other than its own design, and I sense there is more beyond that. As powerful as that thing is, I think it's only a messenger, or a gatekeeper. Whatever that gate's meant for? We have to stop it."

"He, or it, made a mistake," Donovan said. "He came to your swamp to do whatever it is he's trying to do. Pretty sure he didn't see you, or me, or even Cletus here coming. I have a thought. There's someone I met a long time ago, someone I helped. He left me something. I need to get it. In the meantime, I think you should keep an eye on this, but from a very safe distance."

"You'd better be fast, magic man," Nettie said. "He's going to hurt something, or someone under my protection soon, and I'm going to have to do what I can. If it's not enough…"

"I won't be long," Donovan said. He reached out and poured the last of the whiskey into the three tumblers and lifted his. "We need to get back to the plantation house, Cletus, but I think we can all use this." Nettie and Cletus lifted their tumblers, and they all drank. The whiskey was good, and Cletus closed his eyes, savoring the taste. When he opened them again, he and Cletus sat alone at the table, as if they had been that way all along.

Chapter Seven

Cletus and Dog waited patiently as Donovan opened the door to his penthouse, then followed him inside. The lights brightened as they entered, and Asmodeus, fully recovered, lifted off Donovan's shoulder and flew to his perch atop the mantel. Cleo stood in the center of the desk, glaring at them... just for a moment. Then, with an unexpected and for the most part terrifying leap, launched herself at Donovan's chest. He caught her, barely, and staggered a little as she pressed her head hard up under his chin.

"Easy girl," he said. "We're okay. Barely, but okay."

She smacked his chin again, her purr so loud the floor rumbled, but pulled back and let him drop her to the floor.

"Kinda wish she'd been there," Cletus said. "Not sure why, but something tells me that cat might be more than a match for ol' Reverend whatshisname."

"She probably would have told us to keep farther back," Donovan said. "There's nothing on this Earth I wouldn't face with her, or with Mo, or you and Dog, for that matter, but this? This isn't from the Earth. Most of what I've learned and collected isn't going to be much help here. I have a vague notion who, or what we're dealing with, but I've never encountered it before, and those who have did not fare well. All except one."

"You got a cavalry to call?"

"Not exactly. His name was Titus, and I only met him once. He asked me to protect some very rare books, books that are problematic here, but a lot more dangerous in the hands of folks in a different place."

"Different?"

"Remember those doors in the labyrinth? Something like that, but a whole lot harder to break through. He told me if the people in that other place fell, we might be next, or the next after the next. The books he left with me could have been used against them."

"We can't use them here then," Cletus said.

"No, not that, but he gave me something else. Tell you what, let's have a drink, and I'll show you something. We haven't done this before, but I have a way of taking us into my memories. I think to get the full impact of what we're up against, you might need to have 'been there,' and I'm not sure I could do it justice if I just tried to explain it."

"Some sorta magic Donovan TV huh?" Cletus said. "I'm in. I have to say, in all the time we've known one another, all that we've seen, I don't feel like I really know you like I should."

"It's easy for me to forget how long my life has been, and how strange. It's one thing to mention events in the past casually, and quite another to explain what it was like to live through them. Let me get us a drink. I have a particular thing in mind, but I need to call Amethyst, so she can join us. It's a special experience, but I believe this is the time to share it. I need to call one other, as well. I think meeting her is going to be... different."

"In for a penny," Cletus said. "You do what you need to do, but you did mention a drink? Don't suppose you have something less special while I wait?"

"Of course. The bar is over there by the mantel. Nothing in it is dangerous, but all of it is old. Feel free to read if you like. There are a lot of amazing things here, but the dangerous manuscripts are sealed."

"Don't suppose there's anything on NASCAR or WWE."

"There is not, but there are some articles you've written in an album. It's one of the reasons I knew, long before we met, that our paths would cross."

Cletus started to ask a question, then thought better of it. "I'll get a drink and see what I can find," he said.

Donovan laughed, turned, headed down the suite's single hallway and disappeared into one of the rooms. Cletus stood, crossed to the bar, and studied the bottles. There was one label he recognized, and he smiled. He grabbed a tumbler and poured two fingers of Old Crow. From the first sip, he knew it was not the Old Crow that he knew. He glanced up at Asmodeus, still perched on the mantel, and winked. "Here's to you, Mo," he said. "Double-D Goddammed oldest crow I've ever met."

Chapter Eight

The gathering at Donovan's dining table was one of the strangest groups Cletus had ever encountered. Donovan, Cleo, and Mo, who stood in the center of the table, Dog lying at Cletus' feet, Amethyst, whom Cletus had met and actually knew as well as, or better than Donovan after a fairly recent adventure, and one other. Donovan introduced her as Vanessa, and the woman was so beautiful that Cletus had trouble breathing if he looked at her for too long. It felt strange in a way that made him uncomfortable and infatuated at the same time.

"Before we start," Donovan said, "I'm going to explain something to you, Cletus. I know you'll believe me because you've met Kali and Vein. Vanessa is Vein's sire. I believe I've told you the story of her kidnapping."

The name snapped into focus. "You're – that Vanessa, then," he said, feeling clumsy and stupid. "I'm pleased to meet you, I..."

Amethyst rose and circled behind Cletus. With a grin she dropped a chain over his head. A blue crystal sphere dangled from it. The moment it rested against his chest, he found he could breathe, and, though she was still very likely the most beautiful woman he'd ever seen, he could meet Vanessa's gaze steadily.

"Sorry," Amethyst said. "I meant to give you that sooner. Vanessa can be rather imposing if you aren't protected."

Vanessa smiled. "It is a problem, at times," she said. "There was a time when I could tone it down, but that was long ago."

"I'm startin' to feel like a teenager who wandered into an adults-only party. Just how old are you all?"

"Don't worry, Cletus," Amethyst said. "We're in the same boat. I'd say, even the animals included, we're the young ones, but I believe you have me by a few years."

Cletus shook his head.

"Full disclosure," Donovan said, "I've been around since the 1860s. It's not polite to ask a lady her age, but I assure you, when I was born, Vanessa was already turning heads."

Vanessa actually winked at him.

"I wanted you all here for this, because there is something happening in Old Mill that may have far-reaching consequences. There is no imminent danger to us here, but that could change, particularly if what I have in mind fails. The memory I'm going to share is one that involves very powerful beings, and should anything happen to me, that knowledge needs to survive."

"I don't like the sound of that," Amethyst said.

"We have a bond," Donovan said, "and part of that bond was strengthened by your gift, Vanessa. I know Johndrow and the others will listen if you need to warn them of something, and I like the idea of you knowing more about my past. I seldom get a real chance to share it. What you gifted to me, and to Amethyst, is priceless, and I wouldn't want you to experience something through that tie that was unexpected. I hope you don't mind my requesting your presence."

"I'm fascinated," Vanessa said. "I sense you are talking about powers, and beings, that would make me feel much as Cletus feels now. It's been... quite some time since I've felt... young."

Donovan smiled. "Let's get started."

He produced a leather bag and pulled several items from its depths. There was a small tripod carved from a single piece of Dogwood. He placed it in the center of the table and dropped a crystal sphere atop it. The crystal was crazed, laced with flaws and inclusions.

There were several slivers of wood, burned to charcoal, and he took one carefully, using it to draw a circle around the crystal. Then he drew a second circle around that and between the two lines he etched a series of symbols and characters. He took his time, and the others waited in silence. When he was satisfied, he took four small braziers from the bag and placed them at the compass points of the circle.

Cletus watched carefully, and he sensed this, though he had no idea why he believed one was North. He could barely find the far side of a dead-end road, but this one time, he knew he was right.

Once he'd placed incense in the braziers, Donovan lit a long wooden match and looked up.

"This is a moment of sharing. It has to be consensual." He glanced around the table. "Do you accept what I offer?"

They all nodded slowly.

"Then let us begin."

Donovan lit each brazier in order, softly offering an incantation to the wind, fire, water, and air spirits. When the smoke was swirling and twisting above the circle, he sat back.

Cletus was about to break the silence and ask what they should do next, when the room dissolved around him. He blinked, and when his eyes opened, they were in a different place. A different time if what he saw was real.

Chapter Nine

A dark purple Volkswagen van pulled up to the curb, and Donovan stepped out. He was dressed in the familiar long coat, but beneath that, dark, tailor-fitted bellbottom jeans and a colorful silk shirt. Cleo hopped down from the seat to stand beside him, and he leaned to scratch her ears. His boots were dark leather, pointed at the toes. Donovan locked the door of the vehicle and he and Cleo headed up the steps of his brownstone. Cars were parked up and down the street, and, though cleaner and somehow more imposing than the structures surrounding it, the building blended in perfectly.

San Valencez was expanding from the downtown waterfront into sprawling housing developments. Downtown was segregated into industrial, business, and residential areas. Technology drove growth, as always. Donovan did his best to maintain a low profile. His building was safely within the residential neighborhoods, and he'd made certain contracts that would keep it that way in perpetuity.

He opened the door, and Cleo sauntered in. He followed. They headed for the elevators. Donovan pushed the up and down arrows in an intricate pattern, and a moment later the left elevator opened with a soft pinging sound. They entered, and the door closed behind them. There were no buttons.

This was the only way to the 13th floor, his floor. He knew that the other residents were eventually going to question his odd button pushing, and his unwillingness to share an elevator. He needed a private way up, and he had some ideas. For now, it sufficed, and this day, of all days, he had no witnesses. It was an odd time in the world, as well. No one questions an oddly dressed man with long hair and a cat who followed him everywhere without running. He wished he could share with the rest of the city just how strange the times were, or what they might face in the future. Instead, he unlocked the door to his quarters and stepped inside, locking the city out.

The lamp on his desk illuminated slowly, bringing his den to life. The walls were lined floor to ceiling with bookshelves, each crammed with leather bound tomes, hand-bound manuscripts, piles of papers and rolls of parchment. There was a small, cleared section, just inside the door, with a fold-out desk-like shelf. It held several crystals, a brazier, a long, slim decorative dagger, a very old silver cup, and various amulets, stones, and strange objects.

There was a fireplace on the wall to his left, beside which stood a large, polished wooden desk. The lamp was old. Its base was carved metal in the form of a tree. The tree had ten branches, and from each of these dangled a small coin with a hole in its center. A rod ran up the center to a spiked finial, which screwed down to hold the fragile slag-glass shade in place. The glass itself was thick and lustrous. It was violet, giving off a soothing radiance similar to that of a black light. Around the rim of the shade, formed of inlaid bits of colored glass, ran the twenty-two letters of the Hebrew alphabet. Like most things in the room, the lamp served more than one purpose.

Donovan hung his coat on the hat tree by the door and crossed to the desk. He had research to complete, and a manuscript to translate. Cleo leapt to the desk's surface and curled into a large, spotted circle of fur at the corner. Donovan stepped to his bar and grabbed a tumbler. As he poured two fingers of very old bourbon, the hairs on the back of his neck shivered, and he stood very still. The lamp gave off a sudden flash of light, and Cleo spun, arched her back and stared back over Donovan's shoulder. She didn't hiss, but she was alert. Donovan replaced the cork in the bourbon bottle, and slowly turned.

He took a slow breath. What he saw made no sense. Against the bookcase along the back wall of the den stood a very strange, very old grandfather clock. At least, it seemed to be a clock. It had a face, and numbers, but there were too many hands. Four of them, and after only a moment's glance he saw they were out of sync. It was impossible to pin down, but the motion was erratic, each drawing his attention, then giving way to the next.

And then, there was the man. He stood nearly as tall as Donovan's own six foot three. Like Donovan, his hair was long. He was dressed in an antiquarian fashion, but it suited him perfectly. Donovan glanced over briefly and noted that Cleo had settled back on the desk.

"And you are?" Donovan said at last.

The other man stood still, but he smiled. "My name is Titus Crow," he said. "I have come a very long way to deliver something. You are Donovan DeChance."

There was no question in it. "I am, and I know your name, as well. I heard it while visiting San Francisco near the time of the great quake. I was invited by members of The Wilmarth Foundation. They sought my help, even offered me a position, but I have my own mission, and I'm not much of a joiner. They didn't provide details, but if I understand what I was told, you were a part of the group that prevented it becoming much worse."

"Ah," Crow said, "The Wilmarth Foundation and their American Project. That was a tricky business, to be sure. I might have spent more time with them, but we had our own battles, and they were hard won."

"There is a lot I still don't understand about it," Donovan said. "They referenced dimensions and deities I am not familiar with. It was a bit esoteric, even for my taste, so I thanked them for their offer, but declined. Like I said, I am not the type of man to join and follow others. I'm also not fond of having my home invaded."

"I do apologize, but would you rather my clock appeared on the street outside, drawing attention? I will not take much of your time. I don't have time to explain fully why I am here. There is another place, a different world. They are threatened by a power so immense, and so alien, their demise could happen, and their enemy would not even be aware of them. If certain creatures were to get their hands on this," Titus pulled a small bundle from a pocket inside his jacket, "they could open the way for a great evil. They may do so without it, but if they possessed it, the contest would be won. I'm aware that you collect, and protect, objects of power. I ask that you do so with this."

Titus took a step forward and extended his hand. Donovan hesitated. Cleo chose that moment to hop down from the desk brush past him and rub affectionately against the stranger's boot. Donovan watched, just for a second, then accepted the offered package. As he did, his hand brushed against Titus' fingers. A tingle of something otherworldly flickered up his arm and caused him to gasp. Then he had the package and was stepping back.

Titus leaned and scratched Cleo behind her ear. "You have changed," he said softly. Then he returned his attention to Donovan.

"There is more," he said. He reached into another pocket and pulled out an object wrapped in silk. He let that cover fall away so that Donovan could see what he held. It was a stone with a rough sigil etched in the center, surrounded by a circle. Around all of that was a five-pointed star, but rather than solid lines, it was formed of many etched lines that reminded Donovan of the legs on a millipede.

"What is it?"

"A star-stone," Titus said simply. "Your American project was in possession of several similar artifacts. They serve as protection against those powers I have mentioned. The Elder Gods, and their servants. In large numbers, the stones can contain things. Alone, they serve as protection and can sometimes help to close portals or contain things that do not belong in this realm."

"Why do I need this? Is it because of what you have asked me to protect?"

"No. Time does not work for me as it does for you, or for others. I have memories that might be past, or present, and often the context is not clear. I know that you will need this, so I brought it. But I must go. Any time I spend beyond Elysia is a danger. I do not want to attract the wrong attention to you, or to myself. Suffice it to say that I am certain both objects are where they are required to be."

Donovan started to speak again, but Crow had turned. The air in the room thickened, and the lamp flashed again as brightly as before. Everything slowed, just for a moment, and Donovan found himself stumbling forward. All that he faced was his wall, and his books. In one hand he held the star stone, and in the other, the wrapped package.

Unconcerned, Cleo turned, leaped back onto the desk, and started washing her front paw. Donovan sank into his chair but turned it to face the now empty space where the great clock had stood. As he stared, the room faded.

Chapter Ten

Cletus found that he'd closed his eyes at some point. He opened them very slowly and saw the others doing the same. Only Donovan appeared as awake, and aware, as always. Donovan and Cleo, anyway.

Vanessa recovered first.

"That was... remarkable," she said. "I remember that earthquake, of course, but never sensed anything beyond the earth shrugging her shoulders. And that clock. I know this was a vision, but even so, it affected my thoughts. I felt as if staring at it for too long might change... perception?"

"Time was fluid, just for a moment," Amethyst said. "I felt it most strongly when he disappeared. But the stone... you have it?"

"The star-stone?" Donovan said. "Of course. "I wanted you to see that, to experience it, so you might get a small glimpse into what I'm afraid we're facing. I've done more research on Crow over the years. There is not much. Stories here and there, snippets, but all of them involve creatures and powers on a scale that simply can't be comprehended by the human mind. We can hate them, fear them, Cletus and I even had a brush with one of their minions, a Mr. Whateley. They would not recognize us at all. They do not see any encounter with our insignificance as battle, or even threat. Most of what are known as the Elder Gods, as he named them, have been imprisoned, or blocked from certain dimensions.

"They have acolytes constantly working in the shadows trying to set them free. If I'm correct, that is what is happening outside Old Mill. I've never encountered power so... alien. It knows we're aware, but we still have the advantage."

"How in the hell do you figure that?" Cletus said. "I saw what that thing did, what happened to Mo."

"He – it – does not consider us a threat," Donovan said. "We have been considered, measured, and unless we confront him directly, found inconsequential."

"Yeah, but that reverend, that... whatever the hell... kicked our collective butts."

310

"We have a better idea now what we face," Donovan said. "We also have Nettie, and we have this."

He pulled a now familiar wrapped object from his pocket and laid it on the table. He pulled back the silk covering, and they all saw the star-stone. It seemed no more than its name implied. A stone. The carving in its face was visible but seemed crude.

"May I?" Amethyst asked.

"Of course," Donovan said. "This stone is part of why I needed you here for this. That, and the fact that we share so much, I didn't feel comfortable sharing anything with others that you were excluded from. Also, I'm nearly certain this process only works once for any particular memory."

"I thank you for my inclusion," Vanessa said, as Donovan passed the star-stone across to Amethyst. "The council will be very interested in this, and others. We are, of course, aware of such entities, such powers. The religions of men have come and gone. Not all of them were benevolent. Not all of them were without real danger, or power. As a rule, cults have been unkind to those like myself and Johndrow."

"Men and religion are a poor mix," Donovan said. "Most of the gods they pretend to worship don't exist, but when they find one with real power that will direct them, they fall in line like puppets."

"You got that right," Cletus said. "We got more churches in Old Mill than we do people, but somehow come Sunday they are all full. Those people, most of them are old, rich, and mean as snakes. They come in their Sunday best and drop money in the collection plates, but it's more like some sort of weird cabal controlling local politics and acting like the Civil War never happened. For all that, they aren't the ones to watch out for. The ones that are scary are like the previous Reverend out in that swamp and his Horned God, or the crazy ones with their snakes and speaking in tongues. You want an Elder God coming around? That's how you get one."

Everyone turned to stare at him, and Cletus felt a little heat rising around his collar. Then Vanessa laughed, and that sound, that voice, filled the room. "You are a very wise man, Cletus Diggs," she said. "I have never heard that put quite so simply and eloquently."

"I have one more thing to ask," Donovan said, and the somber tone in his voice quieted the room. "Cletus and I are heading back to face this thing. We can't take the rest of you with us, even if you were to want to go, because, if we fail, you are now the only ones who might mount a defense, or an attack. The three of us," he nodded at Amethyst and Vanessa, "are bound. Whatever happens to me, you will know. We're asking Cletus to be part of this."

"I know you both realized his connection to Dog is significant."

Amethyst snorted, waved her hand, and laughed. "I'm sorry. I know his name is Dog, but what you said…"

Donovan hesitated a moment, fighting back his own smile. "It is significant," he said, "because, as we've suspected for some time, there is more to Cletus than he realizes. I have learned some of it from Nettie, and the girl…"

"What in hell are you talking about magic man," Cletus said. "And that girl…"

"She is your daughter," Donovan said. "That is all you need to know, and more than it's my right to tell, but this is a strange circumstance, and I need you to understand. You, your father, your grandfather – you are tied to the swamp as surely as Nettie herself. You see her as an old woman, but she is so much more, and that is simply the way she presents herself to the world. None of that matters now; it's a subject for another time. For now, I'm asking," he turned back to Vanessa, "to add you to the bond we three share. It will lend you strength, and clarity."

"You have the bottle?" Vanessa asked. "It has been some time since any tasted."

"There is enough," Donovan said, "for four."

"One condition," Vanessa said. "If this is to be a bonding, I ask that it go a step further. Each of us will add one drop."

Donovan met her gaze, measured it, and nodded. "I agree. I can't speak for the others."

Amethyst smiled and nodded. "Of course. Your gift is something I can't repay."

"What in the double-D goddam hell are you three talking about?" Cletus asked. "Drop of what?"

312

Vanessa smiled at him, and he felt his heart nearly melt.

"Oh…" He glanced at Donovan, and Amethyst, and then, just to be certain, down to where Dog sat watching him. Then he turned back. "Right. I'm in, then," he said.

"It is good," Donovan said. He reached into another of the many pockets in his jacket and pulled out a small bottle. It was about half full of a deep brown liquid.

"It's brandy," Donovan said, smiling. "But not just brandy."

He rose, crossed to a cabinet, and returned with four small snifters. Then he produced a long, slender needle. He very carefully uncorked the bottle, held his finger over the opening, and pressed the needle through his skin. A quick pinch of his finger produced a single drop of blood. Cletus noticed how Vanessa's eyes grew dark and very deep as she watched. Donovan handed her the needle. With quick, graceful ease she pierced her own slender finger and added another drop. Cletus thought she'd slide it over to Amethyst, but she didn't. She caught him staring and held his gaze as easily as twirling a string over a cat. She slid the bottle close to him, but she didn't hand over the pin.

Cletus meant to ask her. He meant to reach out and take that pin, but instead, he held one finger over the top of the small bottle and felt the needle slide into his skin. He sensed her touch, very light, and the world slowed. He saw the drop of blood form, saw it grow heavier, and heavier, and finally, as if reluctant to fall, drip from his finger into the bottle. He heard it strike the brandy but could not move to pull his hand back. The room swam back into focus, and he saw the bottle had already moved on to Amethyst.

"What…?" he said softly.

"I want you to understand what I have shared," Vanessa said. "I want you to understand how rare, and how powerful it is. You are a good man, Cletus Diggs. I give this gift freely."

Amethyst handed the bottle to Donovan, who took it gingerly and poured an equal amount into each of the four snifters. Cletus took his as if he was afraid it would shatter in his hand. Amethyst raised hers first. "To family," she said. Vanessa flashed an odd smile but lifted hers as well. Cletus and Donovan joined them, and they all drank.

Chapter Eleven

Cletus shook his head groggily. He was lying on his back, staring at an unfamiliar ceiling. Donovan leaned over him and lifted his head carefully from the floor.

"What…?"

"Take it easy," Amethyst said. She stood on the other side smiling down at him.. "I guess we should have warned you that drink had a kick."

Cletus sat up slowly. His memory returned along with a throbbing ache where the back of his head had hit the floor. He was about to say something when a wet tongue lapped at his face, and Dog hopped onto his chest.

"Dammit," Cletus said, laughing, "get off me. He pushed Dog gently off and started to rise. He was still shaky, so Donovan offered a hand, and he took it. "I gotta say, magic man, I'm going to hesitate next time you offer me a drink."

When he was standing again, he saw that Vanessa remained seated. She caught his gaze as easily as she had the first time, but it was different. He sensed an aura of energy surrounding her. The eyes that had simply been beautiful, and compelling, glittered with an inner light he'd been unable to detect. When she moved, he felt the softest spider-silk touch of – something.

"Welcome back, Cletus," she said. "It has been some time since I've had such an effect on a man."

Cletus managed to grin. "Somehow, I have trouble believing that." He turned to Donovan. "How come you didn't keel over?"

"I was prepared," Donovan said. "And I was already a part of that bond. I should have known that it has grown stronger, that it would be more difficult for you. But you feel it, yes?"

Cletus nodded. "Everything feels and looks a little different. And when," he glanced at Vanessa, "when you move, or talk, it's like I sense it."

Amethyst frowned and glanced at Donovan, who shrugged.

"There is something different about you, Cletus Diggs," Vanessa said, rising. "Something old and powerful that I can't quite understand. I believe that our bond will be different. I look forward to seeing you again, should you survive what you are about to face."

"I guess you aren't coming with, then," Cletus said.

Vanessa smiled. "I am not. But I believe we have made a fair trade. My blood is very old. You will find it gives you... strength. There will be more, but it will take time to manifest. And I have a drop of yours to contemplate, and to study."

Cletus thought for just a second, and then said. "I give that gift freely."

Vanessa threw her head back and laughed. It was the most magical sound Cletus had ever heard. Then she rose and moved toward the door. "I will leave you to your plans," she said. "I will have eyes and ears where they need to be, watching."

Donovan nodded and gave a slight bow. Amethyst rose, crossed to Vanessa, and opened her arms. After only the slightest breath, Vanessa accepted the embrace. Then, so quickly it seemed she might have been a hallucination, she was gone. Only Dog and Cleo turned as she departed. Donovan reached up with one hand. It felt as if something had brushed his cheek.

"Well," Cletus said, "that happened. She *was* here, yeah?"

"She was," Donovan said. "And I can't put my finger on it, but there was some connection with you that she didn't fully explain. In any case, you and I have to get back to Old Mill. I think we're short on time."

"When aren't we?" Cletus said. He rubbed his head. It ached some, but his thoughts felt clearer than he could ever remember. He had flashes of images, and memories he didn't recognize, but that felt somehow familiar. "But hey," he added. "This whatever the hell it is going on in my head. Is it like, a drug? Tomorrow it fades and I have the headache of a lifetime and a story to tell over beers down at the Cotton Gin that no one will ever believe?"

"Yes, and no," Amethyst said, laying a hand on his shoulder. "Yes, it's like a drug, an amazing drug, but no, it won't be fading any time soon and you should be good on that hangover. You are just seeing

315

more of what has always been there. Ask him." She tilted her head toward Dog.

Cletus followed the motion. The connection he'd felt before had deepened. He sensed approval, and emotion. He knelt, and Dog came to him slowly. Cletus reached out and laid his hand on his friend's head, scratching behind the ears. The wash of emotion nearly dropped him, but he recovered. Then he turned to Donovan.

"Is it always like this for you? With Cleo, and Mo?"

"Sometimes," Donovan said. "Most of the time, we're companions. They are family. I don't fully understand it. They were never human, but they are old, and they always choose their companions. One day, maybe one of them will share with us as I shared with you tonight, and we'll know. For now, it's enough that they are with us."

Cletus nodded. He leaned down, pressed his forehead between Dog's ears, and closed his eyes. Then he stood and glanced longingly at the empty bottle.

"Reckon we'd best get to it then. Willow is back there, and Jasper. If whatever that thing in the swamp is gets out, no one is going to be safe."

Donovan nodded. "One more drink, then," he said. "Would you find something appropriate and pour, Amethyst? I have to gather some things we may need, and I think Cletus might need to sit for just a moment."

"I should be there with you," Amethyst said. "It's a stone, Earth magic."

"Not this Earth," Donovan said. He stepped close and hugged her tightly. "You have to stay behind, you and Cleo. Someone has to be ready, someone who knows what we know, and everyone who will be in Old Mill who might help will be in the line of fire. Whatever happens, it won't be long, and I'll be back."

"You'd better, magic man." She turned and left the room, and Cletus took a seat.

"This is, bar none, and I'm here to tell you that's a *very* high bar, the strangest double-D goddam day in my long, and very redneck life. I thought Nettie would be the thing I never understood, and then there was a dude with antlers on his head drowned in the swamp, albino

316

twins, and Bubba yackin' about aliens. Then there was that guy Whateley, and those damned potato farmers. Just a little weirder every time. That house… Dog," he glanced apologetically at his friend, then back to Donovan, "but this? I feel like someone gave me magic juice to drink and I stepped into a freakin' fantasy movie."

"Welcome to my world, old friend," Donovan said. "It's a one-way door."

Chapter Twelve

The old church in Eternity had become the center of a much larger monument. Trucks and trailers, small bulldozers and other farm equipment moved in and around the building. Stones, statues, equipment, and supplies rolled in, and out, and a steady stream of workers patched it into a cohesive, if bizarre whole. To either side of the front doors, damp stones had been pulled from the swamp and piled carefully. It should have been a slimy mess, but as the work progressed it became clear that, at some point in history, those stones had been shaped to fit together, and to hold the twin statues that rested just above the roof line.

At first glance they appeared to be massive frogs. From different angles, though, odd appendages rose from their shoulders. What should have been front feet ended in hands with elongated fingers and long, tapered nails. And the eyes. They were large, bulbous like an amphibian, but expressive, and hungry.

It didn't stop there. More and more stones were brought, and stacked, piled high around the walls and covering the windows. The Church of New Light and Starry Wisdom was being swallowed by a temple of mud and stone. No one supervised the work. The reverend appeared at times, walking out of the trees, or just standing in the shadows. He ran his hands over the smooth stone, and more than once he had been seen standing atop the roof in front of the steeple, now wound with heavy, rope-like vines that none of the faithful had ever seen in the swamp before. No one questioned it. In the darkness, the moon bright at his back, the man stood impossibly tall, one hand on each of the frog-creatures' shoulders, though they were clearly too far apart for a single person to touch.

At those times, a dim glow rose from within the church. It was deep green, flickering with gold highlights. There was sound, as well, almost a vibration. If you weren't paying attention, it found its way into your thoughts, a disturbing hum that could almost be a chant, if such sounds could represent words. They dug at the brains of those working nearby, leaving dull stares and slow, trudging steps in their wake.

It was spreading. Those closest to the building tended to remain there, working the walls, and the rings of men and women, children and even some animals stretched farther and farther from the new temple's center, toward the trees and the swamp. The cylinder of energy that Donovan and Asmodeus had experienced had expanded. To a point.

Standing once more atop what had been the church, the reverend stretched his senses, reaching for that barrier and pressing against it. There was a force beyond, one drawing power from the planet itself, pressing back. He had made progress, but it had slowed. He pressed harder, felt a slight tremble, and then, the wall actually inched closer to him. The difference was barely perceptible, but remarkable. He stared into the shadows, eyes dark and unblinking. He reached beyond that veil, just for an instant, seeking the source of that other power.

The attack was sudden and brutal. A flash of light that might have been lightning, had it originated in the clouds, drove through the tiny portal he'd created in his defenses and struck the wall of the church. He closed the gap, but the temple trembled. Great chunks of stone burst from the growing shell of stone and slime, and the reverend nearly lost his footing. He steadied himself, and pulled back, just slightly, from the barrier.

The temple wasn't ready. He held no personal fear of whatever lay outside his current sphere of influence, but he served other powers, and their will. The rituals would work, or they would not. He was a messenger, a conduit of power. He was also curious. Very seldom in the long span of his existence had he encountered anything resembling an actual threat. He'd failed many times to bring the will of his masters to fruition, but, in the vernacular of this time and place, they played a very long game. Those losses were mostly attributable to the failures of the newly 'faithful,' or the actions of unexpected human powers. His masters would barely be aware unless the portal opened. He, on the other hand, occasionally enjoyed the moment, and this felt like one of those times. A challenge on a more personal level. A break in the monotony of eternity.

He climbed down and examined the damage. It wasn't extensive, and he directed several of those nearby to begin restacking and packing the stones. They barely seemed aware of his presence, but they obeyed. This close to the temple, they had no choice. Soon, none of them would, and their influence would spread to others, draw them near, strengthen the voice beyond the veil and weaken the ancient bonds. They called it a temple, but it was a portal, and when it opened, all resistance and challenge would be inconsequential. There would be nothing left but to move on to the next realm and begin again.

As the work resumed, the reverend slipped in through the front door and disappeared into shadow.

Chapter Thirteen

Cletus, Donovan, Dog, and Mo sat on the porch of the old plantation house, staring across the fields toward the swamp. It was early afternoon, no shadows creeping from the tree line, but they were there, waiting, and Cletus sensed their hunger.

"We got to get to Nettie," he said. "Reckon we'd better grab us a bottle."

"I don't think that's going to be necessary," Donovan said, nodding toward the trees. Stepping into the field, Cletus saw Nettie, her hand on the shoulder of one of the biggest deer he'd ever seen. He knew the animal, if it was an animal, from previous meetings, but it never failed to bring a shiver.

"Don't that beat all," Cletus said. "Only seen that one other time."

"I remember," Donovan said. "That magnificent creature carried me out of that swamp, and without his help, I'd never have made it."

Cletus could only nod. Then he rose.

"We may not have gone to her shack," he said, "but I have some ideas about her whiskey, and sacrifices. I believe I'm going to find three glasses and a proper sacrifice."

Donovan's gaze never left the field, and when Nettie grew near, he rose and met her at the edge of the field, offering an arm. She took it with a grim smile, and they walked together to the long wooden porch where Cletus now waited.

"This place has changed," Nettie said. "It is here, but…"

"It's detached," Donovan said. "That's the best word I have for it. It's here, mostly, but it's not trapped in time, or place, in the normal sense."

"Like the tunnels," Nettie said, "only with doors."

"And a bar," Cletus cut in. He'd poured three even portions into crystal tumblers.

"And that," Donovan agreed.

They sat, raised their drinks, and sipped. Nettie closed her eyes and smiled. "You bring me the most *interesting* things," she said. She was looking at Cletus but glanced sideways at Donovan at the same time. "It does my heart good."

Cletus watched her, and thought, maybe, the lines in her face cleared just a little. He filed that away.

"I tested him," Nettie said without preamble. "I pushed at that wall, and I got through. I saw what he's doing, guessed more. He didn't expect that, and he pulled back."

"You scared him?" Cletus asked.

Nettie shook her head. "That one fears nothing. Not here. I learned two things. He serves greater forces faithfully, and he don't care a bit whether he succeeds. He's carrying out orders, building something – a doorway, I think. Like this place," she nodded at the house. "It's detached, but not between times and places in this world. It's a portal to something that would swallow us like a snake eating a frog and not even realize it happened."

"I believe I have an idea who he is," Donovan said. "Or at least, one of the names he's gone by. I brought some of the documents I obtained many years back. There is a being, possibly a god, who travels the realms. He is more easily amused than the more ancient powers that he serves, and he walks among men, and other beings, as if he belongs. It's a mask, a diversion from his truth, but in this world, men call him Nyarlathotep."

"Gnarly what now?" Cletus asked.

"It's not important. What is important is that we stop him. The powers he serves have been locked away from this world, and many others. If that portal gives them access, our swamp, family, friends, will simply cease to exist. They will swallow our world and use it as a passageway to others. They don't acknowledge our existence because we are simply too insignificant."

"So," Cletus said, "it's not personal…"

"We're going to need a plan," Donovan said. "What I've brought, what Cletus and I have brought, can control him. I don't know if it can control what he's bringing into being, and I don't know how we'll get close enough to put it to use. He has that entire temple, or portal, sealed, and all of us have felt his strength. You say you penetrated that?"

"I did," Nettie said, "and I damaged the temple, but not to any consequence. If he'd known it was coming, it might have ended differently. I'm not one to back down."

Cletus poured another round, took a sip, and looked over at Dog. Then he spoke, tentatively, like he wasn't sure he had anything of consequence to offer.

"We came at him from above. You," he nodded to Nettie, "from the side. I wonder, though, about beneath. I mean, that's your soil, your swamp. He knows you're here, but, like Donovan said, he doesn't really know this place. The connection between you and that swamp isn't airborne unless I'm misunderstanding it."

Donovan and Nettie stared at him, and then Nettie smiled.

"I'll be damned, Cletus, if you don't surprise me every time. I wonder if you understand how rare that is?"

"I don't think we dare test it, though," Donovan said. "I think we have to assume that is the vulnerability, and even so, how does it help?"

"What's your plan, Magic Man?" Nettie said. "You tell me that, I'll tell you how it helps."

"Two things," Donovan said. "I need him to let me walk in freely, and the key to that will need to be a distraction. I think I have the first worked out. When Mo and I are joined, I can let his thoughts obscure mine, leave mine with him. It's tricky, but it can be done. If that preacher, or whatever he is, can't sense my thoughts, that might buy us a few minutes. If he accepts a 'challenge' from one he has no reason to fear, and I can get inside with the stone, I think I can remove him from whatever comes after."

Cletus took another drink.

"That should be me. I ain't got enough in my head for him to even suspect, and I reckon you and Dog could teach me that trick."

Donovan started to reply, but Cletus held up a hand. "You said you need a distraction. I might be more than I was yesterday. Still not sure what all of it means, to be honest, but one thing I do know is that I'm no sort of distraction. There is nothing I could do that would catch his attention, but I'm from the swamp. I live here and I have history with that place. My going to him and trying to reason with him might make some weird sense. You going there is going to look like exactly what it is. He'll see you comin' from a country mile."

Donovan considered this, and then nodded. "We're all in this," he said. "And you're right. You can do it, but I'll warn you, even with the stone, he's not going to just stand down."

"Maybe you'd better give me more than one trick, then. I reckon I can keep his attention. If what you said about him is right, Nettie, and that temple falls, I don't think he'll have much interest in stayin' around."

"The swamp is old," Nettie said. "There are things there, sleeping, that ought never be woken. You met one not too long ago, but it wasn't old. Men put it there."

"That double-D goddam dinosaur," Cletus said.

Nettie nodded. "I knew it was here, but it wasn't mine. Just as happy to see it gone. It was lost in time. There are others, though. I can call, and they will answer. You get in there, and you keep that dark one quiet... I'll drop that temple back to the hell it rose from."

Donovan turned and winked at Asmodeus, who was watching them, head cocked, from the back of an empty chair. "Guess that leaves you and me to create a distraction," he said.

Mo let out a long caw and fluttered his wings. They all laughed.

"When it's time," Donovan said, "will you know?"

"Magic man," Nettie said, "There ain't nothin' in this swamp I don't know... or wasn't until this – thing – arrived. I'll be ready."

"Then I guess it's time for me to teach Cletus a couple of *tricks*. We have to act tonight. There's no telling how close they are to completion, and the risk is too great."

Nettie downed her whiskey and rose. The stag, who had stood a distance away during their conversation, trotted up to the steps and met her as she climbed down.

"Nettie," Cletus called after her. "How... how is that girl?"

Nettie turned and flashed a smile that dropped ages from her features. "She is well, and strong. And she is watching."

Cletus glanced at the trees, looking up and down for a slender figure with a bow and arrow. When he looked back, Nettie, and the stag, were simply gone.

Cletus shook his head. "*That* is a trick I would love to learn," he said.

"You and me both, my friend." Donovan replied. "Come inside, we need to talk, and I have to sort some things out. It's going to be a long night. We might want to make some coffee."

"All the same to you," Cletus said, "I'm sticking to the bourbon. If this ends up being my last night, the last way I want to spend it is sober."

Chapter Fourteen

Donovan stood among the trees. He sensed the nearness of the reverend's shield but held back. He needed Cletus to be in place first, and he needed to be certain he made no mistakes. He pulled a leather bag from a pocket in his jacket and poured a small pile of colored crystals into the palm of his hand. He closed his eyes and concentrated on a memory, a time when he and another had stood in the labyrinth, outside a strange portal, and these stones had held it open. The power opposing them had been insurmountable, but they'd held it. For a time. He was counting on the reverend being unfamiliar enough with this world that it would, at least for a moment, stop him as well. If the stone was discovered too soon, there would be no second chance.

There was a pattern necessary to use the stones. The crystals had to be placed in just the right order to create a doorway from one place to another. He wasn't certain where the doorway would lead because he wasn't going to be in the Labyrinth when it opened. It might open directly into the swamp, or to somewhere completely unexpected. The important thing was that it would form a breach large enough that the reverend couldn't ignore it.

In the labyrinth they'd been able to embed the stones in the wood of the door frame, but out here, where the wall was formed of energy, Donovan would have to control them and drive them into place with his mind. He would become that doorframe, and he would have to hold. Circling, but far enough back to remain clear, Asmodeus watched. Doorways like the one Donovan was about to create were something the old raven understood far better than his human companion; the intent was that he would be the anchor.

Donovan turned toward the south, where he knew Cletus was approaching Eternity via the only actual road. The last time Donovan had seen it, it had been overgrown and riddled with potholes, but now, with all the traffic in and out and the endless drudgery of the *faithful* it was cleared and worn smooth.

"Good luck, old friend," Donovan said softly. In the distance, he heard a dog howl.

There was something wrong with the light. Cletus couldn't quite put his finger on it, but it was closest to those few minutes just before a thunderstorm, when everything had that weird, ambient greenish glow, and ozone tingled through the air. Close, but wrong. Instead of a hint of storm on his skin, it was oily, like something huge and covered in slime was evaporating and misting the air. It stank too, and that was a problem, because Cletus' mind was far away, where Dog sat hunched and ready for whatever came next. Cletus was stuck with Dog's senses, his thoughts and reactions, and smart as that old canine might be, anything that smelled half-ass interesting drove him crazy.

He concentrated, stared straight ahead, and walked slowly forward. He knew better than to appear too naïve, so he carried a shotgun loosely. He didn't intend to use it. It was a good diversion, though, and it felt comfortable. He needed anything he could carry that would keep him calm.

"Cletus," he muttered, "you… are an idiot."

There was no way to tell, just by looking, where the barrier around Eternity began. He could see the piled stone and gargoyle-topped columns clearly. What had been the front doors was a gaping black hole from which no light emanated . He saw men, women, even some children moving slowly around what had once been the parking lot. Some carried small stones, others had buckets of some kind of mud, or concrete. He was too far away to tell for certain.

And he knew he was close. He sensed the wall of energy, and more powerfully, Dog sensed it. A tall, dark form peeled out of the shadows surrounding the temple. From where Cletus stood, it seemed as if the reverend's skin was carved from obsidian. Not African American, or any sort of complexion Cletus could recognize, but the same absolute lack of light he'd noticed in the temple's entrance.

There wasn't anything else to do but walk. It would be a mistake to show he knew he might run into something, that he might be kept out. He measured his steps, slow and steady, keeping his hand on the butt of the shotgun, but being careful not to let his finger stray too close to the trigger. He was there to talk. He was there to make sense of what was happening in the swamp. The gun was for protection.

Cletus concentrated on the past. He'd been down this road many times. Some of those times had been among the strangest of his long life, but they had been strange because of other men. Because of a secluded church, and crazy swamp people. He let that confusion wash through him. He forgot what he knew and at the same time, glanced from side to side, eyes darting at shadows as Dog's thoughts roared a mile a minute through his brain, preventing him from deeper concentration. When he passed through the barrier, he felt it, but he didn't let it show. He kept his eyes on the man ahead.

The reverend stood, waiting. There was a flash of white that must have been a smile, and that dark, mysterious head tilted to one side, like a curious bird. When he was about ten feet away, Cletus stopped. He knew he was cut off from the swamp, and the world. For whatever reason, the barrier hadn't stopped him, or the reverend had simply allowed him to pass. Not much chance he'd been given a round trip ticket.

"Howdy," he said. "Name's Cletus, Cletus Diggs. Been hearing rumors about some strange goings on out here, thought I'd drop by and see for myself. Can't say I like what you've done with the place."

The reverend threw back his head and laughed. The sound was human, and at the same time, shivered through Cletus like winding shards of ice.

"You are witnessing a great change," the reverend said. "There are powers you would not understand who have been denied their freedom. I could not explain to you in words how long that captivity has endured. I am merely following their commands. I am a messenger, and an observer."

"Funny, I thought you was a reverend. Can't say I care much for the idea of any sorta powers takin' root near Old Mill."

"Oh, you will not care for it, you can be certain of that. This world, your swamp, the cities beyond, all of it, will cease to exist. This world is a gateway."

Cletus raised the barrel of the shotgun slightly and slid his finger closer to the trigger guard. "Guess that wouldn't leave me much choice then. Seems to me if you was out of the picture, those men and women might remember they don't give a double-D goddam about frog statues and dig their church back out of that muck."

The reverend smiled. "You are more than welcome to try and stop me, but you should understand how futile that effort would be. The portal is nearly complete. It will be minutes, not hours."

Cletus raised the shotgun and aimed. The reverend flashed his smile again, but at that moment there was a screeching, tearing sound off to Cletus' left. The reverend turned, and Cletus, knowing it wasn't part of the plan but unable to shake off the sense of dread surrounding him, fired.

The shotgun was loaded with double-ought buck and should have ripped the man's head from his shoulders. Instead, the reverend staggered. His hat, and his dark coat, which now seemed part of the shadows surrounding him and not clothing at all, rippled and shimmered, then snapped back into shape. Cletus fired again, but his target was moving toward the sound, breaking into a trot.

Now or never, Cletus thought. He dropped the shotgun and dug the starstone out of his pocket. He started after the reverend, pulling one more thing from his pocket. It was like the bolos that hunters used in other lands, two dark crystals joined by a chain of iron.

"Magic Man," he whispered, "You'd better be right about this."

He stopped, drew his arm back, and threw the chained stones at the Reverend. At the same time, he cried out the single word he'd been taught.

"Estas atado!"

The chain sped, much faster than he could have sent it, and the reverend was forced to turn back. The chain caught his ankles solidly, and the stones whipped around so fast, and so tight it seemed the chain would sever his feet from his legs. He cried out briefly, then began to struggle, but in that moment, Cletus stepped near, and held up the stone. He had no idea how to use it, what it would do, but he held it high, and without knowing he was going to, he began to scream at the top of his lungs.

"Go! Get the hell out of my swamp you double-D goddam... thing"

The stone glowed, and the reverend's struggles slowed. His eyes widened, the first good glimpse that Cletus had gotten of them. It was as if shadows unraveled from a vaguely man-shaped form, struggling for its form, for consistency.

That was when the Earth began to shake, and the walls of the temple trembled. Cletus almost, not quite, but almost lost his nerve. The ground lurched again beneath his feet and there was a great grinding sound like nothing he'd ever heard, or, actually, very much like claws on stone, but so much louder, so much more powerful that within moments he couldn't hear his own screams.

"Oh hell," he said softly. He held the stone aloft, kept his feet planted as firmly as he could, but he turned toward the temple, eyes wide. He sensed Donovan, vaguely, and the struggling thing at his feet, but what overwhelmed him, what ate at his sanity, was a deeper voice. It was familiar but grown beyond sanity.

It was Nettie. Not all of it, but the force behind it. It was Nettie, and Cletus had never sensed such anger, such outrage. He nearly dropped to his knees, but felt Dog reaching out to him, lending strength. Then Donovan's voice cut through with a single word.

"Run!"

Cletus didn't hesitate. He turned tail and headed back the way he'd come, hoping against hope that the wall hadn't snapped shut, and that whatever he'd just done to the reverend had been enough. He glanced back once and saw the man had risen to his feet and turned, staring at the temple.

The ground shook so hard Cletus could barely keep his balance, and he stopped. He stood just shy of the first bend in the road and stared back into Eternity. The temple was rocking and swaying from side to side, and the grinding had become a scratching, scraping roar. The walls bowed outward, like something was pushing up into the interior of the building but was too large to be contained.

The reverend never moved. He stood very still, unhampered by the roiling ground beneath him. Cletus couldn't be certain, but it seemed as if the soil moved up and around and through the man's form. He wasn't interested in Cletus, just in the temple, and he didn't seem angry. If there was a single word Cletus would have chosen, it would have been "fascinated."

Then the world exploded. The temple, church, whatever it was, was driven up and out, stones and bits of statues flying up and out into the trees. Debris dropped all around him, but Cletus couldn't move, could only stare, as a giant head burst into sight, followed by two enormous, clawed feet. The thing's neck must have been thirty feet long and the huge, beaked jaws gnashed at the air. The creature let out a hissing roar, planted its feet, and dragged itself free of the ruined temple, turning toward the reverend, who still stood very still, just watching.

"I'll be double-D goddamned..." Cletus breathed.

The turtle was enormous, easily the size of a large elephant. Its jaws could have taken a chunk out of a semi-trailer, and its eyes were cold and dead. The gigantic claws dug into the earth, and it lurched toward the reverend. Those huge jaws opened and dove forward and down with incredible speed, but before they struck, the reverend was simply gone.

Cletus didn't wait to see if Nettie had control of the thing, or if it had noticed him. He turned, and he tore off around the bend and on down the road to where he'd left his truck.

Donovan stood transfixed. The crystals he'd held hung in the air, embedded in some force he barely understood, and it took all of his attention to hold them there. What wavered between was a window, but there was no glass, no barrier. He saw through to the other side, and this time, instead of opening a dimensional door, what had opened was a view of the temple.

But there was more. The temple didn't stand in Eternity. The landscape around and beyond it was desolate. There were flames in the distance, and nothing moved. There were no trees, no roads, simply dead, endless fields, and standing before that temple, turning toward him, was the reverend. He saw the breach, and he knew it for what it was. Whatever Donovan had created was a tiny version of the darkness in the temple. The temple was a gateway, but Donovan's window opened on the same world.

Then the sound began. The vision wavered. Donovan concentrated harder, forced his will into the pattern of crystals, and held the portal open. If something was breaking through into his world, he had to see it and know it.

331

The temple seemed to shimmer, lose focus, return to clarity, and then... after what seemed an eternity, crumbled. Something was destroying it, bursting up through the ground, and Donovan felt an unbelievable wave of strength course through him. He saw Cletus watching and sent a single thought, *run*, before returning his attention to the temple.

When the creature crawled out from beneath, it wavered between the image of a huge turtle, and a shapeless mass, covered in eyes, flowing and moving in every direction at once. It was difficult to tell if the motion was intentional or simply the work of gravity, drawing it down toward the reverend.

Donovan saw the man, creature, whatever he was turn toward the portal he held. He released his will, emptied himself of thought, and drained his energy from the crystals, but in the face of the preternatural speed of the reverend, he was too slow. The man hit the portal but did not come through. He snapped out of existence with a sizzle, and Donovan stood alone, staring at the trees blocking his view of Eternity, and listening to the crashing, impossible voice of the great turtle grinding its way from the town toward the swamp. He started to follow, but Nettie's voice whispered through his mind.

"Let him go. I will draw him back to the swamp."

Donovan shook his head, dropped to his knees in exhaustion and closed his eyes. He felt the breeze teasing at his hair, and the dampness of the swampy soil on the knees of his pants. Then he opened his eyes, threw his head back, and laughed.

Epilogue

Cletus, Donovan, and Nettie sat around the table on the porch of the plantation house sipping bourbon and sharing a deep silence. There was too much to say, and none of them felt the urge to provide the words. Asmodeus was perched on the porch rail, watching them, and Dog lay beside Cletus' chair. The sun was setting over the trees across what had once been cotton fields; crickets chirped and a soft breeze blew in from the swamp, carrying the loamy, dying and growing at the same time scent of nature.

Cletus finally drained his glass, poured another, and spoke.

"How long has that critter been down there? I know them snappers. One the size of a quarter can crack a pencil like it wasn't there. That thing must be a thousand years old..."

"Older," Nettie said. "I held him in my hand when he was young, showed him deeper, darker ways when I knew that if they found him, they would kill him and cut him open, study him like some sort of experiment. He's been hibernating for more than a century...I didn't want to wake him."

"Will he go back to sleep?" Donovan asked.

"If I am patient, and he is lucky," Nettie said, staring into her glass. "He's hungry. He'll have to feed, and a lot. If someone notices, or he strays too close to men..."

"I'll do what I can to steer folks away from the area," Cletus said. "Sheriff Bob'll help, though he likely won't believe me. I'll have to warn some others. John Tyler Gault and his friend live deep in there. Don't really think we need to worry about the reverend's flock. They'll clear out, or they'll be food. Can't say I'm really partial to either outcome."

"I can't help much inside the swamp," Donovan said, "but I think I can put a sort of haze over the area. All it will do is make people less willing to enter, maybe ruin a few fishing trips. Hopefully, it will all be enough. He saved us all."

"Funny," Cletus said. "I never spent any time playin' rednecks and dragons, or readin' fairy tales, but in the research I've done for the *Weekly Globe*, I've read some things. The Hindus believe a double-D goddam turtle holds the world on its back. Saw a show streaming on Willow's TV a while back where they said the turtle was on another turtle. It was turtles all the way down. I reckon we turned that on its ear. Damned turtle came all the way *up* and kicked Gnarly-whatsit's ass."

Donovan took a drink and laughed. "You have a way of getting right to the heart of things," he said. "That's about as accurate a description as I can imagine." He turned to Nettie. "We owe you, and your friend, a debt we can't repay," he said. "I know it was hard to make him a part of this. I will do anything in my power to see to it he returns to his rest."

"It's his world too, Magic Man," Nettie said. "We'll care for him. He's settled for the moment, and I've arranged to direct prey in his direction. I have seen powers come, and go, and sometimes there is a single purpose. This may, or may not, have been his. We will all face that moment one day."

"Here's to facin' it together," Cletus said.

Nettie smiled and finished her drink. "I'll see you again soon, Cletus," she said. "You need to spend some time with that girl, and Dog here can only teach you so much."

Cletus stared, blinked, closed his eyes, and downed his drink. When he opened them, Nettie was gone. He turned and saw the silhouettes of two women in the shadows by the trees.

"Maybe she could teach me that," he said, turning to Donovan. "Would come in right handy when Jasper starts yapping about NASCAR."

The two sat long into the night, letting the darkness fall around them, breathing the freshness of the air and the solid reality of the night. The level in the bottle followed the sunset into oblivion, and the swamp grew dark, and silent. Dog rose and laid his head on Cletus' lap, and Cletus closed his eyes.

"Savin' the world," he said softly, drifting off, "Is hard work."

He didn't hear Donovan's laugh. Exhaustion, and whiskey finally drew him into darkness. It was a good night to be alive.

The End

The Final Judgment

By C. T. Phipps

Nyarlathotep finished his last story and Apophis Zul found himself shaking off the visions he'd seen as if coming from a deep sleep. Nyarlathotep had been changed by the experience, his face no longer rotting but now looking like it was constructed from obsidian and the rest of his body as rigid as a sarcophagus' art. Yet, despite this impossibility, he moved as if a living man and Apophis Zul was briefly reminded of the time he could still believe in wonders.

It was a fleeting feeling, though, because such a time was long ago. He had seen magic that would make the sanest man go mad, climbed distant shores, and witnessed brutalities that would turn the so-called worst of mankind squeamish. His blackened heart had been opened to the mysteries of the universe long ago and instead of being frightened like a monkey fleeing a storm's thunder, he had craved more.

Seeing that Nyarlathotep awaited his reaction, Apophis Zul felt emboldened and stood up from the ground. If the Crawling Chaos desired to tell him so many stories, then surely, he was a man of importance and could risk trucking with the god as a peer if not an equal. He would not have wasted so much time on a being he viewed as without value, despite his words.

"Is that it?" Apophis Zul asked, waving his hand.

The stories themselves didn't impress him. If they were meant to horrify or amaze, then the Black Pharoah had severely underestimated his audience. Apophis Zul remembered when, centuries ago, he had been born to one of his father's many slave concubines. He'd strangled

336

his mother when he was twelve to eliminate the reminder of his cursed human heritage then poisoned all his father's true-born children with a Yig princess.

Apophis Zul remembered when he'd offered up his own lover's heart to the altar of Seth to prove his loyalty, and trapping the only one of his offspring that he'd ever cared for in a tomb with a host of jackals lest the man overthrow him. It would require a far more surreal group of stories than the ones presented here today to cause his knees to shake.

Apophis Zul had come here and offered up poor Narmer to be the host for the Many-Faced God in hopes of a genuinely impressive miracle. This seemed more like a collection of nomad campfire tales and the ramblings of old women to children. He wanted the secrets of how to destroy his enemies and rule the ashes as a proper god king. Nyarlathotep might allow himself to waste time playing with insects, but Apophis Zul was no scarab on the ground to be crushed underfoot but the greatest wizard of an age! Of any age! Men should worship him!

Nyarlathotep's expression, being literally made of stone or at least something stone-like, was unreadable.

"Is what it?"

"These stories," Apophis Zul said, risking a dismissive wave. "These children's tales. Old men and women fleeing from the sight of their own shadow. Fools thinking that they can stab a god and draw blood."

"It depends on the god, really," Nyarlathotep said. He rested his head on the palm of his hand, propping his arm up on the armrest by its elbow. It was such a human gesture that Apophis Zul briefly forgot he was not dealing with a mortal man. "In my mind's eye, I see the sons of Yog-Sothoth banished by a mortal scholar speaking words from the writing of a mad Arab who will not be born for millennia but is long dead by their time. I see in your past a lusty Cimmerian cutting through things your ancestors worshiped and his ancestor cutting through yours. I see in the far future, an Old Crow, Titus his name, riding around in a flying coffin as he unmakes the works of the Great Old Ones in a reality where they are as petty as men. I—"

337

"Enough *gibberish!*" Apophis Zul shouted before his heart seized up in absolute fear at what he'd just done. If he could have killed himself in that moment, he would have, for fear of what might have been done to him, but he was too paralyzed with terror to do so. Besides, if an afterlife existed outside of those dreams produced by mortals, he would not be able to escape his master's wrath.

"Am I boring you, Apophis?" Nyarlathotep asked.

"No, no, my master," Apophis said, almost choking on his words.

"Good," Nyarlathotep said, his voice even more amused and mocking than normal. "After all, we have a pact to consider."

In all the strange stories of distant worlds, times, and horrors, Apophis had almost forgotten the wish that his master had promised him if he could pass his test. Given it was the single most important thing in his long existence, Apophis could only blame the fact that Nyarlathotep's voice had been so mesmerizing that it had slipped his mind. Indeed, it had seemed he had been lost in the experience to the point that he did not entirely feel of this world during the tales. Apophis, even now, could not focus on anything but the Outer God himself.

"Yes, our pact," Apophis said. "You were going to test me."

"Yes," Nyarlathotep said, almost daring Apophis to back out but there was no power gained that did not require risk.

"Test away!" Apophis said, straightening himself. He felt stronger and more alive than he had in centuries with none of the decay even the Yithians started to feel after so many millennia of life. They were not immortal—contrary to their own claims—but merely ageless to the short-lived apes they shared some blood with.

True eternal life required draining the youth and vigor of their own kind, which had resulted in them dooming themselves to be outbred by the monkeys outside. A necessary sacrifice, though, to keep the sorcerer kings like him alive. Few of their bloodlines still lived, though, and it was for that reason in part that Stygia had to live. Without it, they would be a scattered race and become impure as more of their kind bred with humans instead of their own kind. Indeed, it had already happened if he was honest with himself.

"You have listened to my stories," Nyarlathotep said. "You have gained insight that few other beings have ever been blessed with. Heard my actions from my own mouth, or at least the slave's body I puppet, so I ask: what is my purpose?"

It was a trick question for who could know the mind of a god? Apophis knew that Nyarlathotep lowered himself to speak to beings of mortal flesh with minds of limited reasoning. Even the greatest of Earthly beings, Apophis judging himself to be among them, was still among the world's smartest locust compared to his glory. Yet, Nyarlathotep would not give him a question he could not answer. Apophis was certain. No, the God of Chaos was one who would not find that sporting.

Unfortunately, the usual answers that Apophis taught to his followers did not seem sufficient. Apophis had claimed to know the god's mind so many times that he, himself, had sometimes believed it. But that was a lie. Apophis had taught that Nyarlathotep was the herald of the Outer Gods, that he wished to awaken the Great Old Ones to destroy the world, that he wished to elevate other beings to enlightenment, as well as a hundred other reasons. All of them ascribed a personhood or humanity—if Apophis were to use such a vulgar word—to a being that transcended such description.

Yet the stories the Crawling Chaos had shared were empty of any insights. Indeed, they were aggressive in their pointlessness. Nyarlathotep appeared as whatever the tales required: a demon, a god, a friend, a teacher, or a monster with the only consistency being his complete lack of consistency. Even that he was mad or completely unpredictable did not fit into Apophis' image of the being before him. There was a purpose to the Dark One, but it was akin to a child overturning a turtle to simply watch it squirm.

Apophis could not imagine how long he stood there, pondering the mysteries of the unfathomable, before he simply spoke the thought that rang the truest. "Because it amuses you."

"Is that the mask you wish me to wear?" Nyarlathotep asked, surprising his audience. "The god who tortures and lords over other beings simply because it can? Because that is power to you?"

"It is the god I see," Apophis admitted. "It is what all men do once they have no limits upon them."

"And yet I am no man," Nyarlathotep said.

"No," Apophis said. "But that is what I see."

Nyarlathotep's face remained unchanged, its face frozen into the mask it wore. "It is an answer."

"But is it the right answer?" Apophis asked, his hands shaking. They felt strange, lightweight, and he was surprised at how dreamlike this all was. He wanted to turn away from the god on the throne but could not.

"Who knows?" Nyarlathotep said, straightening in his throne.

"You do!" Apophis said. "Please, grant me the power to save Stygia!"

"I think not," Nyarlathotep said. "Besides, it no longer matters."

"No longer…matters?" Apophis asked.

"If it ever did," Nyarlathotep said.

"What do you mean?" Apophis asked, feeling strangely sick. He had held his breath in for far longer than he should and yet felt no shortness of it.

"We have been talking for a while as you would reckon things," Nyarlathotep said. "Look around."

"I don't understand," Apophis said, suddenly freed from Nyarlathotep's gaze.

"Nor will you ever."

Much to Apophis' surprise, the chambers around him were different. Instead of the pristine inner chambers prepared only for the highest of the clergy, it was now decayed and ridden with dust as well as grime. The entrance was buried over with debris and rubble. The only light was provided by a strange aura about Nyarlathotep himself that glowed in a spectrum Apophis had never seen before.

It was not his surroundings that caught his attention most, though. Instead, Apophis' eyes drifted down to a pair of robes rotted to rags around a brittle skeleton. Apophis did not need to wield magic to know that it was his own corpse. He was a ghost now, or something similar, having become nothing more than a spirit serving as an audience.

Apophis had died of thirst, starvation, and exposure long before this day. Possibly he'd been stabbed to death by the followers of Re'Kithnid, the fanatics finding their archenemy kneeling like a slack jawed peasant before an empty throne room. Apophis dismissed that because he hoped they would at least carry his body away as a trophy, but it occurred to him that the zealots might not have even recognized him. After all, how were they to have known the High Priest of Stygia from any other without his accruements of state or guards? It was almost comical in its pointlessness and, of course, that was the point. That there was none.

"How long?" Apophis asked, his voice losing all of its usual arrogance. He had been tricked and, for once, had no reply or bluster to paper over his own failings. Humility had been taught and it was a bitter lesson indeed.

"Long enough for Stygia to have collapsed into dust, be consumed by the desert, and be built upon as many times as long dead Acheron," Nyarlathotep said.

"And I am dead?" Apophis asked, already knowing the answer.

"You speak of such limiting things," Nyarlathotep said. "I am still speaking to you, so you continue to exist."

"And when you withdraw your attention?" Apophis asked, now simply dreading the answer.

"You will cease to exist," Nyarlathotep said. "Not that you exist now."

"You promised me a wish," Apophis said, clenching teeth that did not have any more substance than thought.

"Did I?" Nyarlathotep said. "Do you think promises bind me any more than they did you while you lived?"

"I want to be a god," Apophis said, clenching his fists. "To live forever and be free of all mortal constraints! To be as the Great Old Ones! To be as you! Eternal! Immortal! Infinite!"

Nyarlathotep shrugged. "Alright."

Apophis almost laughed at his good fortune. It was a reversal of everything that had happened before. "Truly?"

"Such a pedestrian wish and yet you keep making it every time we speak, no matter the story." Nyarlathotep waved his hand and let forth his power to sculpt reality as thought.

"What?" Apophis spoke his last word and died as he lived: ignorant and full of unwarranted hopes.

Apophis Zul vanished. He became a dream that spread throughout time and buried itself in the minds of Stygians, Aegyptians, and other peoples. Immortalized as the giant serpent who opposed light and the sun. Nyarlathotep briefly pondered whether Apophis Zul had been named after the dream he'd been turned into or whether he'd even existed once he'd become nothing more than a flight of fancy that would last for an eternity in the Dreamlands.

Nyarlathotep left the statue he'd made of poor Narmer's body for future historians to pore over before speaking to himself for one last time as he abandoned this incarnation of Earth. The Old Ones would rise soon and make short work of its humanity. It mattered little. There were worlds to explore, mortals to play with, legends to inspire, and secrets to whisper.

An infinite number.

Just as there were an infinite number of faces for him to wear.

And all the time in forever.

The (True) End?

About the Authors

David Hambling lives in darkest Norwood, South London with his wife and cat. He is a journalist and his fiction, starting with the collection, *The Dulwich Horror & Others*, explores the Cthulhu mythos in his own locale. He continues the theme in a number of novels including the popular Harry Stubbs adventures, set in the 1920s, and the epic fantasy *War of the God Queen*, and has contributed to the anthologies *Black Wings V* and *VI* (PS publishing), *Tales of the Al-Azif* and *Time Loopers: Four Tales From a Time War*. Keep track of his fiction at the Shadows From Norwood page on Facebook: https://www.facebook.com/ ShadowsFromNorwood/

C. T. Phipps is a lifelong student of horror, science fiction, and fantasy. An avid tabletop gamer, he discovered this passion led him to write and turned him into a lifelong geek. He is the author of *Agent G*, the *Bright Falls Mysteries*, *Cthulhu Armageddon*, *Lucifer's Star*, *The Supervillainy Saga*, *Wraith Knight*, and others. His Twitter account is @CT_Phipps

Matthew Davenport hails from Des Moines, Iowa, where he lives with his wife, Ren, and daughter, Willow. When his scattered author brain isn't earning weird looks from the ladies of his life, he enjoys reading sci-fi and horror, tinkering with electronics, and doing escape rooms. Matt is the author of the *Andrew Doran* series, the *Broken Nights* series (along with his brother, Michael), *The Trials of Obed Marsh*, and *Satan's Salesman* among other titles.

He's also a self-styled student of the Cthulhu Mythos and exercises that influence in his stories and as an editor at the blog Shoggoth.net. You can keep track of Matthew through his twitter account: @spazenport.

Eric Malikyte is a neurodivergent author, illustrator, science communicator, and video editor. He has published works in various genres, including Lovecraftian horror, dark fantasy, and cyberpunk.

He has written for YouTube channels such as TopTenz, Geographics, and Biographics. He lives in Richmond, Virginia, with his wife and two cats, where he spends his spare time exploring used bookstores, Irish Pubs, and terrorizing the neighborhood children on Halloween.

Get a free copy of Eric's debut novel *Echoes of Olympus Mons* here: https://dl.bookfunnel.com/1cw07o2uyb

Andrea Pearson: Andrea Pearson, *USA Today* bestselling author of several series including the Kilenya, Mosaic, and Koven Chronicles, lives with her husband and children in a small valley framed with hills. She graduated from Brigham Young University with a Bachelor of Science degree in Communications Disorders. Her Mosaic Chronicles has been lauded as "a little bit Harry Potter, a little bit HP Lovecraft," and most of her books exemplify an appreciation of the works of Lovecraft and his peers.

Andrea spends as much time with her husband and kids as possible. Favorite activities include painting, watching movies, collecting and listening to music, and discussing books and authors.

David J. West, and his not-so-secret pen name of **James Alderdice**, writes dark fantasy and weird westerns because the voices in his head won't quiet until someone else can hear them. He is a great fan of sword & sorcery, ghosts, and lost ruins, so of course he lives in Utah with his wife and children.

David Niall Wilson is awesome. He has been known to edit, design, and write books simultaneously while carrying on Facebook chats with authors. He runs the publishing company, Crossroad Press, which will one day take over the world and believes that a time traveler named Frederick Douglass will be our salvation.

You can find him at http://www.davidniallwilson.com or on Facebook and Twitter.

Curious about other Crossroad Press books? Stop by our website:
http://crossroadpress.com
We offer quality writing
in digital, audio, and print formats.

Subscribe to our newsletter on the website homepage and receive a
free eBook.

www.ingramcontent.com/pod-product-compliance
Lightning Source LLC
Chambersburg PA
CBHW021440240626
47153CB00001B/220